Romantic Suspense

Danger. Passion. Drama.

Cavanaugh Justice:
Cold Case Squad
Marie Ferrarella

Texas Law: Lethal Encounter
Jennifer D. Bokal

MILLS & BOON

CAVANAUGH JUSTICE: COLD CASE SQUAD
© 2024 by Marie Rydzynski-Ferrarella
Philippine Copyright 2024
Australian Copyright 2024
New Zealand Copyright 2024

First Published 2024
First Australian Paperback Edition 2024
ISBN 978 1 867 29816 8

TEXAS LAW: LETHAL ENCOUNTER
© 2024 by Jennifer D. Bokal
Philippine Copyright 2024
Australian Copyright 2024
New Zealand Copyright 2024

First Published 2024
First Australian Paperback Edition 2024
ISBN 978 1 867 29816 8

MIX
Paper | Supporting
responsible forestry
FSC® C001695

Published by
Harlequin Mills & Boon
An imprint of Harlequin Enterprises (Australia) Pty Limited
(ABN 47 001 180 918), a subsidiary of HarperCollins
Publishers Australia Pty Limited
(ABN 36 009 913 517)
Level 19, 201 Elizabeth Street
SYDNEY NSW 2000 AUSTRALIA

Cover art used by arrangement with Harlequin Books S.A.. All rights reserved.

Printed and bound in Australia by McPherson's Printing Group

Cavanaugh Justice:
Cold Case Squad
Marie Ferrarella

MILLS & BOON

USA TODAY bestselling and RITA® Award–winning author **Marie Ferrarella** has written more than three hundred books for Harlequin, some under the name Marie Nicole. Her romances are beloved by fans worldwide. Visit her website, marieferrarella.com.

Dear Reader,

You are holding in your hands a book I wasn't at all sure I could do justice to. You have to understand that I have been writing and making up stories ever since I was eleven years old. This year, I fell victim to long COVID not once, not twice, but three times and suddenly, never mind the story, my mind had gone MIA. However, I refused to give up.

I don't know if I mentioned it previously (I probably did because I have a habit of repeating myself even when my mind is clear) but I am Polish. Polish women are exceedingly stubborn and we refuse to give up. EVER. I knew I had a serial killer story in me somewhere and although it took me longer to create and put down, I was positive that I could. Searching for it not only kept me sane, it also helped me recall all the fundamentals I always held near and dear to my heart (yes, writing about serial killers, doing love scenes and writing dialogue that I prayed would entertain my reader). If this story doesn't work for you, please don't let me know until I manage to write something you do enjoy reading.

Until then, I do thank you for reading and from the bottom of my heart, I wish you someone to love who loves you back. (Thank God I have someone like that. I don't know what I would have done without him.)

With love,

Marie Ferrarella

DEDICATION

THIS BOOK IS DEDICATED

TO

PATIENCE BLOOM

WITH A GREAT DEAL OF LOVE AND THANKS

FOR BEING SO KIND AND PATIENT

AND FOR MAKING ME FEEL

LIKE THE LUCKIEST WRITER

ON THE FACE OF THE EARTH

Prologue

You never thought that I would ever amount to anything, did you, Aunt Lily? the man asked sharply, his voice as taunting as he had once felt his aunt's had sounded. An ugly smile curved his mouth. *Well, I certainly fooled you, didn't I? The kid you always referred to as being such a big loser didn't turn out to be a loser after all, did he?*

Jon Murphy regarded the face of the woman in the picture on his desk.

He felt that the face was actually looking back at him. He could almost read her thoughts.

It was a big deal for him, keeping that framed photograph right there in front of him. There were times when he would have been a lot happier just hurling it, frame and all, across the room—if not into the garbage altogether.

But he knew that he needed the photograph. One, because he didn't want to answer a lot of questions about what had happened to it—people were incredibly nosy—and two, because it reminded him of his purpose and what he was doing here in the first place. Not in the classroom, but on earth.

His handsome face darkened as he thought about it. However, for once, he was at peace staring at the image of his late aunt.

For now.

For now because his appetite had been satisfied. But Jon Albert Murphy knew better than anyone that, at best, this was an extremely fleeting set of circumstances. His insatiable appetite to kill another woman would be back in full force before he could come to terms with it. It always ate away at him long before he was ready to eliminate the source of his anger.

A day lecturer, Murphy was sitting in his cubbyhole of an office—an insult to his honor as far as he was concerned—with the door closed. Even so, the lecturer was carrying on the discussion with the photograph entirely in his head. It wasn't the sort of "conversation" that he could risk having out loud, not when there was a chance that one of his students— or any student, really—could come walking into his office and overhear him.

For the most part, the students who attended Aurora Valley College were a rude bunch of wet-behind-the-ears kids, he thought angrily. Not at all like he had been at their age. He had learned early on, thanks to Aunt Lily, to keep to himself. And to never speak unless he was spoken to—and at times, not even then, because he might find himself the target of someone's unabashed wrath.

But then, the people who frequented the lecture hall where he spoke and the classroom where he taught hadn't been raised by his mother's aunt Lily. Aunt Lily who had used her razor-sharp tongue to create countless bleeding holes in his self-esteem from the very moment she had become his guardian.

Murphy remembered how stunned he had been when he discovered that his white trash mother had decided that she didn't want to be saddled with him any longer. That was when Aunt Lily had stepped up to take over.

At the time, he had been too naïve to understand why Aunt Lily had volunteered to do that. He had just thought that the woman was being kind to him. But he had learned all too quickly that that wasn't the case.

It had been his last innocent thought.

And then, for a moment, the lecturer smiled to himself. Murphy was more than willing to bet that, in the end, Aunt Lily wound up regretting the decision she had made to be his guardian. Things hadn't exactly turned out the way she had planned.

Murphy sighed, resigned, as he looked back at the paper he had half-heartedly been attempting to read.

These so-called "students" who attended Aurora Valley College, they were all a bunch of hopeless illiterates. Sometimes he couldn't help wondering why he bothered wasting his time with them.

But then, he thought, he knew exactly why he was doing this. Not to be dazzled by the magnitude of someone's brain. That was definitely not the reason why he had applied to Aurora Valley College for the position of lecturer in the English Department when it had come up.

He had come to the two-year college for an entirely different reason—a different agenda.

He had come here looking for another sort of gratification. One that Aurora Valley College had been able to provide him with.

Several times over, Murphy recalled with an eerie smile that would have unsettled anyone who looked at it.

Shifting, Murphy tried to make himself comfortable in the hand-me-down office chair he had inherited along with the desk. It was an impossible task as far as he was concerned. Another insult in his eyes.

The chair creaked as he leaned back in it and continued to read the incredibly dull paper. He could almost feel his eyes closing.

Talk about boring, he thought in disgust.

Murphy was surprised that he could read it and somehow still manage to remain awake. It was really a constant battle just to keep his eyes open.

Little by little, he forced himself to shift his mind

to the events he was anticipating happening later on this evening, after classes were over. Later this evening was when he was supposed to get together with Mrs. Lauren Dixon. The vivacious older blonde had asked him for help with her next paper. She had told him that she anticipated problems. Right.

As she made the request, the restaurant waitress had even blushed a little.

Like he didn't even know what was going on.

The corners of his mouth curved as he thought about meeting the woman in some little-frequented, off-campus location. Now all he had to do was decide if tonight was going to be the night when he made his move, or if he was going to put it off until some later date, anticipating the way it would feel.

Sometimes, he told himself, waiting for that final moment was half the fun.

Anticipation, Murphy thought as his pulse sped up and his smile widened, could be everything.

He finished reading the paper he was holding quickly, then decided to award it a giant C plus, far more than the execution was worth in his opinion. Who knew, he might want to cultivate some good-will with this student at a later date as well.

No stone unturned, he decided with a wicked smile.

Chapter 1

Detective Cheyenne Cavanaugh shifted uncomfortably at her desk and frowned. Up until this point, she had thought that her partner was only talking. Wade did have a tendency to do that. Realizing that he wasn't definitely put a damper on her newly appointed position of police detective. She didn't want to do this without him. It was like attempting to cross the high wire without a net.

"Are you sure about this—really sure?" she asked the man she had been partnered with since she had first walked into the Cold Case Department. Back then, she had not actually been Wade Jessup's partner—she had been more or less his underling. The one who had willingly run his errands in exchange for the privilege of learning from the old-time veteran.

Oh, granted, she could have just as easily learned from one of her siblings or her cousins, or even her uncles. Heaven knew there was no shortage of law enforcement agents milling around at any of the numerous family gatherings that she had attended over the years, or at the actual precinct. But Wade had provided a rather unique take on the job, and to her way of thinking, the more perspectives she was exposed to, the larger her field of learning became. She was like the proverbial thirsty sponge, soaking it all up as quickly as she was exposed to it.

The corners of Wade's mouth curved spasmodically as he looked at her.

"Yes, I'm sure," he answered in that raspy voice she had come to instantly recognize and gravitate toward. "I'm sorry, kid, but it's already a done deal," he told her. "The furniture is all in the moving van and I've packed all my bags. Actually," the man corrected himself, "Beth was the one who packed my bags." He laughed under his breath. "She said if she left it up to me to do, it would take another six months, if not longer, and she's just chomping at the bit to get going." Wade smiled kindly as he looked at his young partner. "Don't forget, Arkansas is home to her."

"But it's not home to you, Wade," Cheyenne insisted, pointing the fact out sullenly.

Wade's thin shoulders rose and then fell in a careless shrug. "So I'll adjust. Don't forget, I adjusted to you, didn't I, kid?" he asked her with a laugh, trying to bring her around as he made his point.

Her eyes met Wade's. "Hell, Wade, I was easy to adjust to," she told her partner defensively.

"Ha! You think so, huh?" Wade remarked with a laugh. And then his expression softened just a little as he looked at her. "Don't worry, kid. You'll adjust to your new partner, whoever he or she might be, in no time flat," Wade told her. "I guarantee it."

Cheyenne sighed, far from won over. "Damn it, Wade, I barely adjusted to you," she remembered aloud, recalling the early days of their partnership. And then she looked at him, attempting to appeal to the older man's sense of fair play. "Are you sure you can't talk your wife into staying?"

Wade eyed Cheyenne incredulously as he laughed at Cheyenne's suggestion under his breath. "Hell, kid, you've met Beth. Did she strike you as someone who could be talked into *anything* she didn't want to be talked into?" he asked the young woman he had referred to—more than once—as the best partner he had ever had.

Cheyenne did not answer his question, or at least she did not answer it directly. Instead, she made a request. "Let me have a crack at her, Wade."

"Not on your life," he told her with a laugh. "I know what you can be like and I want to go on living a little longer once I transfer to that precinct in Arkansas," he told Cheyenne. Slipping his arm around Cheyenne's shoulders, he gave her a quick, friendly hug. "It'll be all right," he promised her.

Cheyenne raised her chin as if she took his words

to be a challenge. "And if it's not?" she asked. "Then what?"

Wade laughed that raspy laugh of his that she was going to miss sorely. "You'll box their ears," he declared knowingly. "And don't worry, my money's on you, kid."

Cheyenne frowned. Deeply. Her slender eyebrows knitted together, forming a straight line. "I really wish that I had your confidence," she informed her about-to-be-former partner.

"That's because you're also not conceited, which is something you've always had to your credit," he pointed out confidently. And then he told her with a wide smile, "Anyone who gets partnered with you is going to be a damn lucky person, kid. Trust me on that."

"As I remember it, that wasn't the way you saw it when you initially found out that that the chief of d's was making me your new partner."

"Initially," Wade conceded with a nod of his head. "But what I was actually attempting to do was keep you on your toes." Wade's brown eyes met hers as he confided, "There's nothing more off-putting than working with someone who has a huge ego the size of a giant pizza."

"I didn't have a huge ego," Cheyenne protested.

A smile graced his lips as Wade shrugged his shoulders. "If you say so, kid," he told her cavalierly. And then his expression softened a little as he looked at her. "You're Cheyenne Cavanaugh," he reminded the young woman. "You can—and will—get through this."

"*Detective* Cheyenne Cavanaugh," she corrected him. The title still felt very new to her and she loved the sound of it and that the word *detective* rolled off her tongue as easily as it did. Lord knew it took a great deal of studying for her to earn the title.

"See?" Wade asked as he picked up the briefcase he had just finished stuffing with all his remaining miscellaneous papers. He smiled at Cheyenne. "It's just as I predicted. You're getting through it already."

She knew she could, but it would definitely take her a while. It was not about to happen in a blink of an eye. "I'd get through it better if you stayed," she said in all seriousness.

Wade patted his partner's shoulder. There was compassion in his eyes. He knew that change wasn't easy for some and Cheyenne numbered among those.

"I would if I could, Cheyenne, but I can't." He smiled at her. "You'll do fine, kid. My money's on you. It always has been," he told her with no shortage of confidence. And then he looked at his watch. It was time for him to wrap this all up or contrary to what he had said, he might never leave. "Well, I've got to go, Cheyenne. Beth's picking me up and she hates it when I'm late."

Cheyenne had a sudden thought. "Could Beth come up here to come get you? I'd like to say goodbye to her as well," Cheyenne told him, getting somewhat creative when it came to making excuses for him not to leave.

The expression on Wade's face told his former partner that he saw right through her. Not bothering with a somber expression, Wade laughed out loud at the suggestion that Cheyenne had just given him. The look he gave her all but asked if she actually thought that was going to work.

"Oh no, I'm not about to ask Beth to come up here. Senility has not set in yet," Wade told her. And then he paused beside her and like a doting uncle her gave her cheek a very quick kiss. "Take care of yourself, kid," he told her. His expression softened as he looked into her face. "You really were a great partner." He gave her arm a quick squeeze. "I'll send you my address and you can send me a line or two about how things are going whenever you have some free time and get the chance."

Her eyes narrowed a little as she pinned Wade with a look. "I can also send you the riot act as well."

Wade laughed as he gave her quick two-finger salute. His expression seemed to say, *Always the fighter.*

"I bet you can, too," the man acknowledged. And then he glanced at his watch again. "I've really got to get going," he told her. "Stay safe, kid," the man added as he began to take his leave.

"I'd stay safer if you continued being my partner," Cheyenne called after him in all seriousness.

For the most part, she was an independent person, but Wade had made an impression on her and she realized that, although it embarrassed her to admit it even to herself, she had grown attached to him.

Wade raised his hand above his head as he waved goodbye to her. Cutting the conversation short, he kept on walking. He was acutely aware of the fact that when it came to Cheyenne, one word would just continue to lead to another—and another. What he needed to do was stop talking and keep walking or he would never leave.

So he did.

Cheyenne pressed her lips together. She knew this was ridiculous, but she missed the man already. He had been a good, decent partner and he hadn't been out to get anything from her or from her connection to the rest of the Cavanaughs. He was just interested in being a good detective and turning her into one as well.

And for her part, Cheyenne had been determined to learn from him, not interested in taking advantage of the fact that when it came to the police department, she uniquely belonged to an almost dynasty-like group of people.

Cheyenne sighed as she looked at the file she was reviewing. That protracted goodbye with her former partner had happened almost four days ago.

Funny how that felt like an eternity.

She had technically been on her own for four days now. She was exceedingly aware of the fact that Brian Cavanaugh, the chief of detectives as well as her uncle, was actively looking to pair her with another partner. But for her part, she was in no hurry for that to happen. The other side of being paired off was preparing herself for the inevitable loss.

She had already gone through that. In the past six months, she had had the man she had assumed she would wind up marrying just abandon her because she wasn't willing to pull up her roots, leave her beloved extensive family and move to the East Coast. That was what Steve, her ex-fiancé, had wanted—and expected from a soon-to-be wife. And now her partner, a man who had trained her and carefully taught her how to be the kind of detective she felt she was meant to be, had left her as well.

She definitely wasn't looking to join forces with anyone else only to have that sort of thing happen to her again. Or at least certainly not any time soon.

So instead of ruminating over it, she threw herself headlong into her work with gusto.

There was no shortage of cold cases for her to dive into. She just needed to pick ones that sparked her sleuthing heart, cases that cried out for her special set of skills.

To remain on the safe side, Cheyenne didn't just pick one cold case—she picked several. She felt rather certain that if she applied herself to a number of cases, she was bound to be able to make some sort of headway on at least one of them, if not more.

The way she tackled her work was to come in early, stay late and work almost around the clock on the cases on her desk until she felt that she couldn't keep her eyes open for a second longer.

Cheyenne sighed and sat back in her chair. She closed her eyes for a moment in order to try to keep them from aching.

Taking another deep breath, she formed a pyramid with her fingertips directly above her nose.

Go home, Chey. You're not doing anyone any good this way. You can get a fresh start in the morning.

But her pep talk, as well intentioned as it was, did not help. She remained sitting at her desk, the file on Rita Connor's murder lying open in front of her. The words in the file were almost taunting her.

She stared at them, rereading the words until they all but swam in front of her. It didn't help. Enlightenment did not come. Her thoughts about the crime had no rhyme or reason to them. Cheyenne was aware of the fact that some murders occurred for no reason and those were much more difficult to solve.

It was almost as if the killer was standing somewhere hidden nearby taunting her.

She looked at the time of death marked in the file. There was actually a question mark in it. The killer could very well have committed the murder recently. The ME hadn't been able to pinpoint the time of death because the body had been discovered floating in an abandoned pool that in turn belonged to an abandoned house. It had been concluded that the victim, an older blonde who appeared to have been very mindful of keeping up on her looks, had died in the pool. A great deal of water was found in her lungs.

Due to the marks on her throat, it appeared as if the killer had strangled her and held her underwater until she had drowned.

Had the killer planned all this out carefully, or was this just a murder of opportunity?

"Why did you have to leave now, Wade? We could have solved this murder together and you could have gone out with a bang, " Cheyenne murmured under her breath.

She glanced at the phone on her desk, fighting the temptation to pick up the receiver and call her former partner. She knew that this was the sort of crime he loved poring over. Cheyenne debated using the number Wade had given her.

"And say what?" Cheyenne challenged herself, continuing to murmur under her breath. "That you can't solve the very first murder that comes across your desk now that your partner is gone? Since when have you become so helpless?" she asked herself in a wave of disgust.

She noticed one of the detectives, Abe Hamilton, looking her way and realized that she needed to keep her voice down—or better yet, not say anything out loud at all.

Cheyenne flashed a smile at Abe, then cleared her throat, as if something had impeded her breathing and she was most definitely not talking to herself.

"I'm fighting a cold," she told the detective, who was staring at her curiously.

After a beat Abe nodded as if what she had said made perfect sense to him. "So tell me, what are you taking for it?"

"I don't know, what will you give me for it?" Cheyenne asked before she could stop herself.

"Well, that cold of yours you're talking about has clearly gone to your head," her uncle Brian commented, amused as he walked into the room. "Would you like to go home?"

"No, sir. What I want to do is solve this crime—sooner rather than later," Cheyenne added with feeling.

Brian nodded, satisfied with her response and with the fact that she really didn't seem to be ill.

"Good answer," he told her. "By the way, there's someone here who I'd like you to meet, Cheyenne." The chief of d's turned toward the doorway, beckoning to the man who was standing off in the distance, talking to someone else.

Cheyenne's stomach sank even before she turned around. She had a feeling that the chief of d's was about to introduce her to her future partner.

And she really didn't want to meet him yet.

Chapter 2

Cheyenne knew it was a given rule that no one worked solo in the police force. At least not for long. Partnerships were encouraged.

There were of course unavoidable situations in the various departments where detectives went solo, but none of these situations lasted for more than a few days. So when she turned around to face whoever the chief of d's had brought with him, Cheyenne braced herself—at the same time mentally upbraiding Wade for having left Aurora and abandoning her.

Never mind that he had done it for the sake of his marriage and to ultimately please his wife. The bottom line was that Wade had left their day-to-day existence and a rather successful partnership. She was on her own.

Well, at least her uncle looked rather satisfied with the way things had turned out, and for the most part, Brian Cavanaugh was a decent man who always kept his eye on his people, determined to do his best for them and by them. He had not been wrong yet, Cheyenne thought, but then, there was always a first time.

Cheyenne had really no idea what to expect. But whatever it was, she was not expecting that her new partner was going to be an exceptionally good-looking man with dark hair and a smile that could melt the beholder from a distance of approximately fifty feet—if not a bit more.

She took in a deep breath after she realized that she had stopped breathing altogether.

This was not good.

Belatedly Cheyenne took in another breath as she waited for her pulse to slow down and her heart to resume beating normally. It took her longer than she was happy about. Having this sort of reaction was just not like her.

Rather than her uncle making the initial introduction to her new partner, Cheyenne heard a deep male voice say, "Hi, I'm Jefferson McDougall. You can call me Jeff or McDougall or 'hey you' or just about anything in between you feel comfortable with," the six-foot-two detective told her as he leaned forward and took her hand, shaking it.

It took Cheyenne a moment to respond. Caught somewhat off guard, she allowed the new man to continue holding her hand and shaking it. After another moment, she ended the connection.

"We'll work on it," Cheyenne responded noncommittally to her choice regarding what to call him. She took a step back.

Rather than take offense, or think she was being unfriendly, Jefferson smiled at her. "That sounds good to me."

The chief of d's was standing off to the side, watching the initial interaction between the two brand-new partners. Brian nodded to himself, satisfied. He had made a good call, he thought, pairing his niece with this Texas transplant.

"All right, McDougall, let me introduce you to your lieutenant. Earl Holloway," the chief of d's told Cheyenne's new partner.

Brian placed his hand on the new detective's shoulder as he turned the young man around. He directed him toward the back of the room and the glass-encased office that was located there.

The chief of d's looked over his shoulder at Cheyenne, who had remained where she was, rooted to the spot at her desk. His niece looked as if she didn't know whether or not she was supposed to tag along. Had this been Wade, there would have been no question in her mind.

Brian gave her a little verbal push. "Would you like to come with us, Detective, seeing as how you two are going to be a working duo for the foreseeable future?" the chief of d's asked his niece.

Cheyenne rose from her desk. "At least for the time being," she told her uncle, feeling it prudent to add in that particular proviso.

Brian didn't bother keeping his wide smile to himself. As a rule, he enjoyed his work and smiled easily, especially when things were going well. Solving crimes was in his blood. So was working with the people who solved them. And a good detective was a good detective. It made no difference to him if he was related to them or not.

"Oh, I think it'll be longer than that," he told his niece. He was aware that Cheyenne didn't like change and hadn't been happy when her partner had announced that he was leaving, but the chief of d's was fairly confident that this would turn out to be the right sort of change for the newly minted detective.

Cheyenne took a breath. She was doing her best to reassure herself that it was all going to turn out all right no matter what.

She could tell that her new partner was looking at her but at the same time she was managing to avoid making any actual eye contact as she secretly regarded him. She couldn't help wondering what she was ultimately going to wind up getting herself into by going along with this new partner being assigned to her.

She walked quickly, staying abreast of her uncle and deliberately stepping ahead of this new partner she had been paired up with.

For his part McDougall was happy to just hang

back, allowing Cheyenne to make her way ahead of him. It wasn't just chivalry that dictated his actions, although that was the largest part of it. It was also the view that being in this particular position afforded him. The woman had to have, he quickly concluded, pretty much the perfect figure.

Jefferson was not about to deny the fact that he liked the view he was looking at.

He liked it a great deal.

What still remained to be seen was if this new partner of his had a personality that matched her sterling figure. He hadn't asked around about Cheyenne Cavanaugh when he had found out that he was being partnered with the woman because, first of all, he doubted that he would get a totally honest answer since this woman belonged to the first family of law enforcement in the city of Aurora. And secondly, he liked forming his own opinion when it came to matters like this. He didn't particularly care to take anyone else's word for something—he needed to decide on his own.

Admittedly, the first thing that had struck him when he saw her siting here in the Cold Case Department was that the woman was incredibly easy on the eyes. That wasn't the most important thing and he knew that, but it certainly didn't hurt matters any. Not by a long shot.

Working with the woman on an everyday basis, Jefferson thought, should certainly prove to be exceedingly interesting.

Thinking about that, Jefferson was still smiling to himself as he crossed the threshold and walked into the lieutenant's office behind his new partner and the chief of d's.

Lieutenant Earl Holloway was a middle-aged man with a very full head of salt-and-pepper hair. Since even before he had joined the police force, Holloway had firmly believed in staying in fighting shape. Consequently the man looked younger than his actual age despite the fact that his hair had begun turning gray six months before he had turned thirty-five.

The lieutenant half rose in his chair now, greeting the three people who came into his office. The man gestured toward the three seats that had been arranged in front of his desk.

"Sit, please," Holloway requested, his deep brown eyes sweeping over the three individuals who had filed into his small office. Two, of course, he knew from frequently interacting with them. The third had come to his attention late last night when the Texas transplant had arrived in the Cold Case Department, saying that he had been sent here on the recommendation of Shane Cavanaugh, the head of the CSI Department. Oddly enough, Lieutenant Holloway had been told, the two had run into one another in Texas while McDougall was rethinking his choices and the direction that his career was taking.

"So, I hear that you went into law enforcement straight out of your stint with the Marines," the lieutenant said. Holloway smiled knowingly at Jefferson. "I guess that actually gives us something in common, Detective McDougall."

"How so, sir?" Jefferson asked politely, although he had a feeling that he already knew the answer to that. Still, he thought it only polite to ask the man.

The lieutenant smiled. There was nothing he enjoyed more than reliving his glory days as a Marine. He felt as if his years as a Marine testified to how courageous he had been as a young man—he had managed to fight overseas and return to the States without getting so much as a single scratch on his body.

"I was a Marine too," Lieutenant Holloway answered. And then he waved away his own words with his hand. "But this meeting isn't about me, McDougall. It's about you and, of course, your new partner, Detective Cheyenne Cavanaugh," he said. The lieutenant nodded his head toward Cheyenne. "Detective Cavanaugh here recently lost her partner."

Jefferson turned toward the two people sitting to his right. "I'm very sorry to hear that," he told his new partner with sincerity. "If you don't mind my asking, Detective, what happened?"

Cheyenne's expression hardened ever so slightly at the question. She didn't know if this new man was being sincere or just playing dumb. She decided to answer her new partner's question before her uncle had the chance to respond, thus clearing the matter up. "He moved to Arkansas so he and his wife could be near her family."

Jefferson was surprised at the answer. He had thought that this new partner's previous partner had either died or been seriously hurt. Embarrassed over his mistake, the man backtracked.

"That's a shame," Jefferson conceded. "I heard that he was a good man." That much was true. He noticed that his new partner's expression brightened ever so slightly. "But his loss is definitely my gain," Jefferson declared with a nod of his head.

Cheyenne's eyes narrowed just a little. He was playing her, she thought. Well, her guard was not about to go down. "Isn't your assessment of the situation just a little premature?" she asked the ex-Marine. "You don't even know me yet."

Rather than look embarrassed over her challenge, Jefferson smiled. "I guess you can call it a gut feeling."

A couple of her uncles as well as several of her cousins were quite big on trusting their gut feelings. She wasn't about to credit this newcomer with being correct in trusting his just yet. Not at this point.

"I'd say as far as you're concerned, it was more of a shot in the dark than anything else," Cheyenne informed her new partner coldly.

Jefferson did not seem to take any offense. "I guess we'll just have to see about that," her new partner told her cheerfully.

Blocking out the other two men seated in the small glass office, she fixed Jefferson with a penetrating look that was meant to pin him to his chair. "I guess we will," she answered the man stoically.

Looking to avoid any argument in the making, Holloway said to the newest detective joining his group, "The chief of d's gave me your file. At this point, I only gave it a cursory glance, but I did take note of the fact that you have a rather impressive record with the El Paso Police Department." Holloway flashed a wide smile at Jefferson. "Hope that comes with a boatload of patience as well because you're really going to need it when it comes to dealing with cold cases."

The lieutenant wasn't telling him anything new, McDougall thought. "In my experience, most crimes don't get solved in a hurry, sir," Jefferson replied.

The lieutenant nodded with a smile. "That's been my experience as well," Holloway agreed. "If you don't mind my asking, why did you leave the Marines?"

It wasn't the question that the detective had been expecting. He would have expected one along the lines of asking him about his police experience. "I just felt that my time was up, sir," the detective answered. "And that I could do more good as a police officer than as a Marine working my way up. I worked in the El Paso office to orient myself then decided I might be happier stationed in a California office. When I asked around, I heard nothing but very good things about the Aurora Police Department, so I thought that since I was packing up, I should make the most of it."

"And here you are," Holloway concluded with a smile.

"Lucky us," Cheyenne murmured under her breath.

She had yet to decide whether or not the new detective was on the level.

"Something you'd like to share, Detective?" Holloway asked, looking pointedly at Cheyenne.

"Not a thing, sir," Cheyenne answered without blinking an eye. The remark had just slipped out before she could stop it.

The lieutenant scanned the small room. "Anyone else have anything to say?" Holloway asked, then looked up at the chief of d's. "Chief?"

"Yes," Brian replied. He looked at the two detectives he had ushered into the lieutenant's office. "Let's get to work, shall we?"

Knowing that this signaled an end to the impromptu meeting, Cheyenne and her new partner rose to their feet almost in unison.

Jefferson took the lead and waved for her to walk out of the room first. Cheyenne said nothing as she moved out in front of the transplanted Texan.

Brian followed the new partners, closing the office door behind him.

There were only a few steps back into the main office and a few more to Cheyenne's desk.

Jefferson looked around the area, just slightly disoriented.

"Where would you like me to sit?" he asked, tossing the question out to both his new partner and the chief of d's.

Cheyenne bit back the urge to answer *Texas* in response to the man's question just as the chief of d's responded to her new partner by saying, "Right there looks about right."

"Right there" turned out to be a location that did not please Cheyenne. It was the desk positioned right next to hers.

"That's Wade's desk," she protested with a deep frown without thinking.

"That *was* Wade's desk," Brian corrected his niece. "From what I hear, unless you know something that I don't, he's not going to be using it anymore, which means that it's going to be empty and McDougall here will be free to use it. Right, Detective?" Brian asked, looking directly at her.

Cheyenne repressed a sigh and pressed her lips together to keep back any unwanted comments. "Right, Chief."

Brian smiled. "Glad you agree." He turned his attention toward the new man. "The detective here will show you how we do things around here, McDougall," he told the recently transferred detective. "And if you have any questions about anything—anything at all," Brian emphasized, "my door is always open."

And with that, Brian Cavanaugh patted the new man on the shoulder and then walked out of the Cold Case Department, leaving the new duo to begin fermenting their partnership.

Chapter 3

What Cheyenne really wanted to do was distance herself from this person who had unexpectedly invaded her life as her partner. Instead, she just decided to throw herself into going through the old case files the way she had been doing since she had first transferred into this department.

But she also knew that wouldn't be right, nor was it what the chief of d's or Lieutenant Holloway would expect her to do with this new person who had joined her work group.

They all worked as a team, not just here but in all the different departments that made up the entire police force. It was a given. Moreover, she was a Cavanaugh, which meant that she had a larger stake in the police force than the usual police officer or detective did. She had to work harder at the job and put in longer hours whenever necessary, and she had been raised to do so willingly.

It was actually this attachment to the police department that was the very reason why she hadn't agreed to transfer to the East Coast when her ex-fiancé had tried to convince her to move there with him.

What her mindset meant in this particular case was that she knew that it was up to her to take the initial steps to introduce her new partner to the other people who were working within the Cold Case Department.

Cheyenne didn't mind being friendly, but she wasn't thrilled about being forced into this position, either. Still, a responsibility was a responsibility. She had to face up to it and do whatever was required of her. She had never so much as been accused of being unfriendly before. But right now, missing Wade, her original partner, was getting in the way of living up to that.

Cheyenne raised her chin, silently telling herself that she couldn't allow that to ruin her reputation as a team player. She could focus on what she was feeling tonight, after she got back to her house. Right now, she needed to show Jefferson around and introduce the man to the people he would be working with.

"You need to meet some of the people in the office," she told Jefferson, stopping short of sitting down at her desk.

That, in turn, prevented the detective from taking his own seat.

Jefferson looked at his new partner in surprise. He had to admit that he hadn't expected her to go out of her way like this. That he would have expected this from the chief of d's, absolutely. Chief Brian Cavanaugh came across like the personification of friendliness. But as far as Cheyenne Cavanaugh went, although the woman was exceptionally attractive, she looked rather dour and not all that friendly when he observed her.

But then, maybe he had misjudged the woman, the detective thought. And this was unusual for him. He wasn't usually quick to jump to a conclusion.

He needed to rein himself in, he thought. That would be better for them both.

"Agreed," Jefferson replied amiably, curious to see just where this would wind up going.

"All right, so let's get to it," Cheyenne said.

She had almost slipped and said, *Let's get this over with*, but had managed to stop herself at the very last minute.

Instead, she moved away from her desk and made her way over to the two nearby detectives whose desks were butted up against one another.

"Guys, I'd like you to meet Detective Jefferson McDougall. He's freshly transplanted from the El Paso, Texas, police department. He's going to be taking Wade's place now that my former partner decided that he wanted to move to Arkansas." She tactfully did not add what she thought of that move.

Cheyenne only half turned toward her new partner as she waved a hand at first one detective and then the other as she made her introductions.

"This is Detective Jose Gonzales and Detective Jordan Nguyen," she told Jefferson, then smiled. "Between the two of them, Gonzales and Nguyen have twenty-eight and a half years' worth of knowledge and experience."

Jose was the first one on his feet, a heartbeat behind Jordan. Jose grinned broadly as he extended his wide, beefy hand toward Cheyenne's new partner. Grasping the man's hand, Jose shook it firmly.

"She likes to exaggerate whenever she can," the older man told Jefferson as he nodded toward Cheyenne.

"But not by much," Jordan added seriously, shaking the new detective's hand next. "If you've got any questions, feel free to ask them. If we can't answer them—"

"They'll make something up," Cheyenne couldn't resist telling her new partner.

Jose pretended to frown at Cheyenne's comment as he shook his head. "That's what's wrong with this younger generation," he told his partner, Jordan. "No respect for their elders."

Cheyenne fluttered her lashes at the slightly stocky older detective. "Respect has to be earned, Detective Gonzales," she told the man, doing her best to look serious as she said it.

Gonzales laughed shortly. "I don't envy you, McDougall, being paired up with this one." He jerked his thumb in Cheyenne's direction. "Listen, if it gets to be too much for you, I know a good bar that's located not too far from here. The place is run by former police officers and detectives. They'll make you feel right at home in minutes."

Cheyenne turned toward the older detective. "Are you saying I'm going to drive my new partner to drink?" she asked the man pointedly.

Gonzales held his hands up as if to protest his innocence. "That was never my intention," he told Cheyenne. "I'm sure he's perfectly capable of making up his own mind about what you have to offer. I just wanted him to know that there were a number of possible solutions available to him if it gets to be too much for him."

"Your partner's new," Nguyen explained his own partner's thinking to Cheyenne. "Right now, he doesn't know about our popular hangout."

Cheyenne had a hunch where this was going. "When the time comes, I'm sure that you'll take him there. All I ask is that you let McDougall get one sober day in under his belt before you introduce him to our friendly corner bar."

Nguyen nodded. "You survive one day with Cheyenne here and we will personally take you there to celebrate," he promised. "As for today, welcome to the Cold Case Department."

The corners of Jefferson's mouth curved as he nodded at the two detectives, returning their greetings. "Thanks, guys."

Cheyenne placed her hand squarely on her new partner's back, ushering the man over toward other detectives and officers who were in the room, men and women who he needed to get to know, at least in a cursory manner.

"You still have other people to meet," she told Jefferson. "You'll find that they each have their own special field of expertise and that their knowledge might come in handy when you least expect it. To solve these old crimes, we're going to need to cover a great deal more ground."

Jefferson eyed her thoughtfully. "Are you planning on making these introductions all in one day?" he asked.

"And if I am?" she asked him, giving him no indication which way she intended to lean. "Would you have a problem with that?"

Jefferson shook his head. "No, ma'am," he answered.

About to lead her new partner toward another area in the room, Cheyenne stopped short and held her hand up, calling for a halt.

She turned toward him, far from happy. "'Ma'am'?" she repeated, looking at him in disbelief. "Do I look like a 'ma'am' to you?" she asked him, stunned.

"I'm from Texas," Jefferson told the detective. "Addressing a woman as 'ma'am' is a sign of respect."

Cheyenne's eyes narrowed as she took exception to his explanation. "It's ageism," she informed the new detective. "I'm not your mother or your maiden aunt. I am your partner. You can call me 'Cavanaugh,' or 'Detective' or 'partner' or even, if we're working particularly late and you're punchy, 'Cheyenne.' But if you call me 'ma'am' again, I'll rip your tongue out and use it as a bookmark. Do I make myself clear, McDougall?" she asked her new partner.

"Perfectly," he answered without a moment's hesitation. In addition he had the good grace not to grin at her words.

Cheyenne inclined her head, nodding her approval. "Good. I have a few more people for you to meet," she told him, beckoning for the detective to follow her, which he did. Rather quickly at that.

The first of the people she brought her partner over to meet was Detective Barbara Baker, who had, according to Cheyenne, been part of the department ever since it had been first formed. Before then, Baker had been part of the Missing Persons Department Her crossover knowledge was rather extensive.

"She has an incredible amount of patience as well," Cheyenne told him, thinking that Baker might have actually been better suited to work with McDougall than she was. But that would mean that she might have to work with Baker's partner, Kevin Calhoun, and she had quickly learned that Detective Calhoun liked to take the easy way out whenever he could—which unfortunately for him was not as often as he would have liked. But that, Cheyenne reminded herself, was not her problem.

Bringing Jefferson over to the two desks, Cheyenne dutifully introduced her new partner to Baker and Calhoun. She noticed that McDougall seemed to take to this pair like he had to the first two detectives who she had introduced him to. The man was exceedingly friendly.

It seemed, Cheyenne thought as the introduction process continued throughout the day, that there wasn't anyone that her new partner didn't interact with well, and no one he seemed to have any difficulties with. The man could have gotten along with the devil himself, she concluded.

By the end of the day, Cheyenne had managed to introduce him to everyone she felt he might find helpful with any investigation he was involved in. Except for, of course, Valri, their resident computer wizard. But that, Cheyenne promised, would be an introduction for another time, when the need came up.

"Tomorrow," Cheyenne told her new partner at the end of the day, "the real work will begin. Slowly," she emphasized, hoping that the detective was as long on patience as she thought he was. "But it will begin."

"What are you working on?" Jefferson asked as they began packing up for the day. "I'm assuming that we're going to be working a case together." There was a hopeful note in the detective's voice.

Cheyenne had been working on several cases concurrently, looking for similarities between the cases or something that might wind up triggering something for her and tying the cold cases together. So far, though, she had come up empty. But she felt, that she might be missing something or overlooking it. Something of vital importance.

Maybe if she talked it out, it would become clearer to her in the morning. That was something to hope for, Cheyenne told herself.

"I'll lay it out for you in the morning," she promised, referring to what she was working on. "Right now, you have put in a full day of orientation and your brain probably needs a time-out to rest."

But her partner protested at being sent off like this. This was just the first day and he wanted to absorb as much as he could. "I'm used to long hours."

"And you'll get them, I promise," she told him, adding, "far more than you bargained for. But this is your first day here and the chief of d's doesn't want to have you run out screaming until you have at least a second day under your belt." She grinned at her new partner. "We try not to overwhelm you too fast."

"You're exaggerating," Jefferson laughed indulgently at his partner's words.

Cheyenne gave him a look that had been known stop other men dead in their tracks because they weren't sure just how to read it. "Am I?" she challenged.

"You know, it's going to take me some time, but I fully intend to figure out when you're kidding and when you're serious," he told her.

Cheyenne flashed a knowing look in her new partner's direction. She didn't intend to become anyone's flash card and she certainly wasn't about to become that easy to read. "Well, good luck with that," she told him.

"Are you daring me?" Jefferson asked, raising a quizzical eyebrow in her direction.

"No, just wishing you luck," she told him with an innocent expression.

"Don't torture him too much or he won't come back tomorrow, Cavanaugh," Gonzales told her as he took his jacket off the hook. The detective slipped it on, getting ready to leave the precinct.

"Oh, don't worry. He'll be back," Cheyenne said knowingly, her eyes meeting her partner's. "The man likes a challenge. Don't you, McDougall?"

"My dad told me that all of life is a challenge," Jefferson told her as they walked out of the office and to the elevator together.

Cheyenne's mouth quirked in a quick smile as she considered the relationship Jefferson might have shared with his father back in the day. As of yet, she really didn't know that much about her partner, or any of his family.

"Sounds like your dad's a smart man," she commented.

A distant, wistful look passed over Jefferson's face before he answered, "He was."

Cheyenne read between the lines. "Then he's gone?" she asked quietly, her heart going out to her partner.

Jefferson nodded. "Five years ago," he told her.

For a moment, pity came into Cheyenne's eyes. "I'm sorry to hear that."

Jefferson raised and lowered his shoulders, dismissing the element of sorrow that was ordinarily tied to death. He wasn't looking for pity, nor did he want any. "He died doing what he liked," Jefferson told her. "That's all any of us can ask for."

Cheyenne pressed her lips together. Well, this didn't happen often. Perhaps, on this rare occasion, she had made an initial wrong call. Could it be that she and her new partner were going to get along after all?

At least she could hope, Cheyenne thought.

When the elevator arrived, they got on and took it down to the ground floor. Within two minutes, it opened again and they got off.

"See you tomorrow," Jefferson told her, stepping back so that she could get off first.

"Tomorrow," Cheyenne echoed, then stopped short. Turning toward her partner, she surprised herself by asking, "Would you like to stop off at the local watering hole?"

Way to go, Chey. Talk about not keeping your distance.

Chapter 4

Taking a few quick steps, Jefferson caught up with his new partner.

"You mean with you?" he asked.

Cheyenne smirked at her partner as if he had just asked her a really dumb question. "No, with some homeless person looking for someone to buy him a drink. Yes, of course with me," she answered him, then decided that maybe she had spoken too hastily and, at least at this point of their association, she should really qualify the responses she gave the detective. "Unless you'd rather not share a drink with me. I don't want you to feel like I'm holding your back up against a wall and making you do this."

"No, you're not forcing me to do anything. I'd really like to have a drink with you. I'd think of it as toasting our new partnership. But I don't really know my way around Aurora yet," he confessed. "You're going to have to show me where this popular local hangout is located."

"No problem," Cheyenne assured him. "I can definitely lead the way for you to get over there. Just keep my vehicle in your sights and follow it there. Just promise me that once you get there and get a drink, you won't wind up overimbibing."

"On my first day?" he asked, looking at her incredulously. "No way I would ever do that. Actually, I wouldn't do that on my twentieth day—or twentieth year," he added. "As a law enforcement officer, I have a certain responsibility to remain on my best behavior. That means if I intend to overindulge, I don't go out. Or, at the very least, I don't drive anywhere and just hire a cab. That wouldn't be setting a good example for anyone, not the people I work with and not the townspeople I work for."

"'Townspeople'?" she questioned, doing her best to hide her amusement at his terminology.

Jefferson didn't see why the word he had used had tickled her to this extent. "Yes, townspeople," he repeated, then clarified, "The people who live in the town."

Cheyenne laughed softly under her breath. "I have a three-year-old nephew who would be pointing at you right now and saying 'he talks funny,'" she told Jefferson.

Her partner looked unfazed. "Townspeople," he repeated. "That's the way they talk where I come from."

She nodded, leading the way over to her vehicle. "I kind of figured that," she said. Pausing next to her car, Cheyenne dictated the address of the bar so he had some idea of where he was driving when he followed her. "It's not too far from here. And I'll be sure to drive slowly so I don't wind up losing you."

"You won't lose me," her partner told her with unshakeable confidence.

Cheyenne turned to look at McDougall and shook her head. "You know, you're really going to have to do something about that inferiority complex of yours," she told her partner.

The grin that Jefferson flashed her was wide and for a moment actually succeeded in pulling her in, before she was able to successfully block both the smile and the effect it was having on her. "I'm working on it," he told her.

Cheyenne raised a skeptical eyebrow as she looked at her partner. "Well, work harder," she said.

"It's at the top of my list of things to do," McDougall told her, opening his car door and getting in. The detective started up his vehicle, preparing to follow hers out of the parking lot.

As she drove, Cheyenne kept one eye on her rearview mirror, making sure that she didn't lose sight of her new partner's vehicle. The last thing she wanted to do was lose the man on the way to the bar.

Traffic at this hour was rather slow, but considering how close the establishment was to the police station, it hardly took any time at all to get there. In addition, for once she wasn't really in any hurry to get to the establishment where people from the police force gathered at the end of their workday. Cheyenne's primary goal in going to the bar was to be the first one to bring her new partner there and to introduce him around to the people from the force who frequented the place. She thought it might make him feel more welcomed to the force.

After she did her part, she would go, leaving the former Marine on his own. She had a feeling that the transplanted Texas detective would do rather well here. The bar was a friendly place and from what she had already assessed, McDougall was friendly as well. Friendly and outgoing. Those traits would do him very well in his choice of careers.

The small parking lot behind the short, squat building that housed the bar was almost full. She pulled up into one of the few spaces that were still available. The detective she had brought here took one of the others at the other end of the lot. Cheyenne got out of her vehicle and waited for her partner to join her.

"This isn't much of a parking lot," Jefferson commented as he crossed over to her. "Do they do much business here?" he asked.

"They do. You would be surprised at how much business transpires here. This place has three partners at this point. Latecomers usually wind up parking across the street, somewhere up or down the block. Farther if necessary," she added. "But proximity and walking distance aren't the main draw when it comes to the bar. Talking to your fellow law enforcement officers is." She paused for a moment, wanting to frame what she was about to say next. "Now, I really don't think you're going to need any help in this matter. All I'm going to do is provide initial introductions and I'm sure that you can take it from there."

They were now at the entrance of the bar, an unpretentious, welcoming little building. Jefferson opened the door and held it for his new partner. "You're being extremely helpful here, Cheyenne," he told her. "And I really appreciate it."

She walked into the bar ahead of him. "Hey, helpful is my middle name," she told him with a laugh. "Besides, it's up to me to provide you with the tools you're going to need to do this job right."

Jefferson raised a quizzical eyebrow. "You consider a mug of beer a tool?" he asked Cheyenne, intrigued with her reasoning.

Her mouth curved in amusement. "Sometimes."

Hearing that, the detective laughed to himself, getting a kick out of his partner's comment. "That's one I'm going to have to remember."

"Feel free to claim that as your own," she told him, and then she grew serious. "Like I told you earlier, we're a team here in the Cold Case Department. You never know when one tiny clue, one little tidbit, might wind up helping us solve the case."

The man behind the bar, Martin Colbert, a former

police detective who had been in several different departments during his career before he retired after putting in almost thirty years, looked Cheyenne's way and nodded a greeting at her.

Cheyenne waved at the heavyset man. "Hi, Marty, I brought my new partner in to meet you."

Setting aside the cloth he was using to clean the counter—which didn't look as if it needed any actual cleaning—the man put out his hand toward Jefferson. "Hello, New Partner." He cocked his head, looking at him with curiosity. "You got a name?"

Jefferson didn't hesitate in taking the extended hand. "As a matter of fact, I do. It's McDougall. Jefferson McDougall," he said, introducing himself formally.

"Nice to meet you, Jefferson McDougall." Marty released Jefferson's hand and cocked his head, listening more closely. "Is that a Texas twang I hear in your voice, son?"

"It is," Jefferson told Colbert with a proud smile.

"By way of El Paso if I don't miss my guess," the former detective said.

Jefferson didn't attempt to hide the fact that he was impressed. "Very good."

"Marty spends a lot of time here, talking to the police officers, police detectives and various people in between. He likes to pick everyone's brain, don't you, Marty?" Cheyenne asked. She thought that what he did, developing an ear for different dialects, was all to his credit.

"Hey, it's what makes life interesting," Marty freely admitted, then turned toward Jefferson and asked the man, "Am I right?"

"Absolutely," Jefferson agreed.

Marty smiled as he looked at Cheyenne. "I think I'm going to like this guy, Detective," he told her. "What are you drinking, son?" he asked the newcomer.

"Water," Jefferson replied in all innocence.

Marty frowned a little. "It's got to be something stronger than that," the man told Jefferson. "The first one's on the house and water doesn't count."

Jefferson paused, then gave Marty the name of a popular light beer.

Marty still looked somewhat disappointed. "Nothing stronger than that, son?"

Jefferson's eyes met the older man's. "No, sir. The light beer will be fine."

Marty raised and lowered his wide shoulders. "Have it your way," he said, resigned, then poured Jefferson a tall mug of light ale. Setting it on the counter in front of the new man, Marty said "Enjoy." And then he looked at Cheyenne. "And what can I get for you, Detective?"

"Nothing, Marty. I'm working tonight after I leave here," Cheyenne told the bartender she had known ever since she had graduated from the police academy and come to work in the Aurora Police Department.

But it was her new partner who was surprised by her statement. "You're working? I thought you were going to go home once you leave here."

She turned toward Jefferson. "I am."

He shook his head. "I don't understand," Jefferson admitted, confused.

"It's called taking your work home with you, Detective," Cheyenne told him. "I've got a couple of files I need to review. Don't bother yourself about that." She knew what he had to be thinking about the matter and she intended to work alone for now. "I brought you here to meet people and to get acclimated. Trust me, there's plenty of time for you to be studying the other side of the coin, McDougall." She turned toward the man behind the counter. "Do me a favor, Marty. Have one of your guys watch over his drink. I want to take him over to meet a couple of the guys," she told the bartender.

"Hey, I can carry my beer, walk and talk all at the same time," Jefferson protested.

"Looks like you've got yourself a regular functioning Ken doll, Cavanaugh," the bartender told her with a dry, amused laugh.

"What's my name, Marty?" she asked the bartender suspiciously, then turned toward her partner to explain why she had asked. "You see, there's a whole bunch of us crowded under the Cavanaugh banner, so if Marty here says 'Cavanaugh,' chances are that he's got a pretty good chance of being right."

Marty regarded the new man. "You'll find that your partner here is pretty damn suspicious about a lot of things most of the time. I don't envy you, boy. Where I come from, this whole ordeal would be known as trial by fire."

"Where do you come from?" Jefferson asked, curious. He wanted to learn as much as he could about the people he was interacting with, and that included the bartender. He prided himself on getting to know people within a short amount of time.

Cheyenne gave the bartender a look, then told her partner, "He's from East LA. Marty here figures that if he puts it that way, he makes it sound more mysterious than it really is."

The expression on Marty's face said that she had just made his point for him.

"I wish I could say you lucked out with this one, son. Tell you what, McDougall, your next drink will be on the house, too. If you ask me, you're going to need that second drink as well," Marty said, then chuckled at what he felt was his own display of wit.

"I think it's time for you to show me how well you can walk and talk and hold a drink at the same time," she told her partner, urging him to move to the rear side of the bar room.

"And the demands will only get more intense from here on in," Marty predicted, shouting after Jefferson's departing back.

"Ignore him," Cheyenne advised her partner.

"Ignore who?" Jefferson asked her innocently.

Cheyenne grinned, tickled. She had been right. She was going to get along just fine with the former Marine and Texas transplant.

Chapter 5

Cheyenne was intent on remaining at the bar for only a little while, then she wanted to go to her home to go over the files she had brought with her. However, she felt obligated to take her new partner around the familiar gathering place and introduce him to people who Jefferson hadn't met earlier in the day. Those were the people who weren't part of the Cold Case Department, but who did contribute to other departments within the precinct. People who were, in her opinion, important for him to know.

She had secretly hoped that she might cross paths with her cousin Valri so that she could introduce the computer wizard to her partner—everyone who worked at the precinct needed the woman's input every now and then for a number of reasons. But she was nowhere to be seen within the establishment.

Cheyenne was aware that the computer wizard kept really long hours at the precinct and then went straight home, but these days there was a reason for that. Being seven months pregnant had a way of taking it out of the poor woman, Cheyenne thought, hoping that one day, she would be able to find out firsthand what that was like.

You won't if you never find anyone, she reminded herself. And seeing as how she kept long hours working in the Cold Case Department, finding someone didn't look like very likely to her at the moment, Cheyenne thought.

Introducing her partner to a couple of old-time detectives, Cheyenne was just about to take her leave when she glanced toward the door. She saw Finley and Brodie, two of her brothers, walking into the establishment. Well, that put her leave-taking on hold, she thought. Cheyenne was well aware that she couldn't leave the place until she properly introduced her brothers to her new partner. It would be an oversight on her part and she knew that they would not allow her to live it down.

All of her siblings were like that, and she had eight of them. If they decided to gang up on her for some reason, she would be done for, Cheyenne thought, even though she could always hold her own. Everything would just grind to a halt.

"Well, I was about to leave you on your own here,

McDougall," she told her partner, turning toward the door, "but those two guys who just walked in happen to be two of my brothers and if I leave before introducing you to them and them to you, I will *never* hear the end of it."

Jefferson appeared surprised by her statement. "I wouldn't say anything about it," her partner assured her.

Cheyenne had her doubts about that. She felt that at bottom the man might just feel slighted by the omission. But it wasn't actually McDougall she was thinking of in this case.

"You might not, but I assure you that my brothers wouldn't let me ever forget it," she told him. Her mouth curved ever so slightly. "They act as if they've taken up permanent residence in my brain. And I have to admit that at times, it actually feels that way."

She beckoned for Jefferson to follow her over to the two men who had just entered the bar. When she made her way over to them, they didn't look surprised to see her. Burrowing between them, she reached up and placed a hand on each of their shoulders.

"Hi, guys, I'm assuming you're here to check out my new partner."

"We just wanted to meet the guy before he becomes history or takes to the hills," Finley told her. Putting his hand out to the new man, he said, "Hi, I'm Finley, one of Chey's older brothers."

"And I'm Brodie, one of her handsomer brothers,"

Brodie said, introducing himself and taking Jefferson's hand once Finley had released it.

Jefferson took each of their hands in turn, giving the brothers warm handshakes and an even warmer smile. "How many brothers do you have?" he asked his partner, curious.

He might have asked Cheyenne for the number, but it was her older brother who answered his question. "This lucky little lady has six brothers," Finley volunteered.

"And there are three sisters in the family," Brodie told him, rounding out the picture.

Finley smiled. "We outnumber our sisters six to three," he informed the new man.

"I take it that your family has some sort of a competition going among you?" Jefferson asked, attempting to gather as much information as possible about the dynamics of his partner's family.

"More or less," Brodie answered. He looked around the bar. "So where are you sitting?" he asked.

Jefferson indicated a table that had been pointed out by Marty when the bartender had served them.

"He was sitting," Cheyenne told her brothers, nodding at Jefferson. "I was in the process of leaving."

Brodie gave her a skeptical look. "You think that's wise?"

She knew exactly what her brother was saying. "If you wanted to, you two would find a way to poison McDougall's mind while I was standing guard right next to him so there's no point in my hovering around, keeping guard over the man now," she told her brothers.

Brodie and Finley exchanged looks.

"I think our sister's been around us too long. There's just no surprising her anymore," Finley said, pretending to sound disappointed about the situation.

Cheyenne gave her brothers a look. "You could act like decent human beings for a change. That would definitely surprise me."

Brodie shook his head, feigning disappointment. "The woman just has no respect for her elders," he said as an aside to Cheyenne's new partner. "I'd definitely watch my back if I were you, McDougall."

"Your back, your front and all the parts in between," Finley told the new man with emphasis, grinning at the image he had just painted.

"I'm not worried," Jefferson told the two brothers, sparing them a glance, then looking at Cheyenne. "I trust your sister."

"This is an even worse situation than I thought," Brodie said to his brother.

Cheyenne frowned dismissively at her brothers. "Very funny, guys."

"And very lucky for you," Finley told his sister, then looked over toward her new partner. "I wish you luck, McDougall. I really do."

"Yeah, me, too," Brodie said, adding his voice to that of his brother's. "You're going to need it. If you find that you need any help or advice," he began to tell her new partner,

"—Just call us, night or day, twenty-four hours a day."

"You two make me sound like some sort of a five-alarm fire that needs to be put out," Cheyenne complained.

"Oh, but you are, Cheyenne, you are," Brodie told his sister with a wide grin, then glanced at her new partner and further emphasized the point. "Trust me, she really is," he told Jefferson with a wide wink.

Cheyenne's partner appeared unconvinced. "If you don't mind, I'd like to judge that for myself," he told the two brothers in a friendly voice.

Brodie and Finley exchanged looks. Brodie laughed, amused by Cheyenne's partner's response.

"Looks like you've got yourself a live one, little sister," Finley said.

"And on that note," Cheyenne announced, looking around at the three men, "I will bid all of you a semi-fond adieu. See you tomorrow. Just make sure you don't damage him, boys. I need to put him to work first thing tomorrow morning."

"You know that you are a tough customer," Finley told his younger sister with a disparaging shake of his head.

"When you're one of nine, you pretty much have to be. It's called self-defense," Cheyenne concluded.

Her brothers regarded her partner with nothing short of heartfelt sympathy. "You know, McDougall, it's really not too early for you to put in a request to be switched to another department," Brodie told his sister's new partner.

Cheyenne shook her head. She knew them too well to take offense. "I'll see you guys around. Give your wives my love—and my complete sympathy."

And with that, Cheyenne made her way to the bar's front door.

She knew that what her brothers were saying was just their way of teasing her and of hazing the new man. She really hoped that they didn't wind up overwhelming McDougall. Piecing together the various clues she had gathered right now on the serial killer or killers was going to be hard enough on him.

When she made her way outside the bar, it was already growing dark. Cheyenne was really happy that her vehicle was not parked down the street or otherwise farther away than it was.

She hadn't realized how tired she was until just this moment. The walk to the car if it were down the block or farther would have taken a great deal out of her.

Great. She was tired and she still had all those files to review and organize. She didn't have all that much to go on. This was all one big hunch on her part.

But something in her gut told her that the three murders she was reviewing were somehow connected, although as of yet, she couldn't quite put her finger on exactly how.

Maybe some alone time in her house would help her sort things out and see her way clear to the answer, Cheyenne thought. Some alone time without a wall of noise throbbing around her. The Cold Case Department was not exactly the quietest place in the precinct. It certainly wasn't designed to foster any deep thoughts about related killings or killers.

Reaching her vehicle, Cheyenne unlocked the driver's-side door. After opening the door, she slid in behind the wheel, then closed and locked the door again. Aurora had a reputation for being an extremely safe city, one of the country's safest for its size for the last twenty years.

Cheyenne liked to think that her law enforcement family had something to do with that.

But despite its reputation, she wasn't one who believed in taking any needless chances. Things had a way of happening when a person least expected them no matter what the circumstances. That was why she was looking at files having to do with serial killers in what could be thought of as being an incredibly safe city.

Trusting to that sort of thing, she thought, starting up her car, was what got people to let their guards down—and that, she knew, backing out of her space, could be a fatal mistake.

The house that Cheyenne lived in was located not too far from the bar, which in turn was not too far from the police precinct.

Driving slowly, she was home in under ten minutes.

She parked her vehicle right at the curb rather

than inside her garage. Once out of her car, she hurried toward her quaint, two story house. She nodded at a neighbor who looked vaguely familiar. The man flashed a smile and then went back to his own thoughts. No words were exchanged and she for one was grateful. She didn't really feel up to having any sort of conversation. She had done enough talking at the bar as well as at the precinct today. She felt all talked out, Cheyenne thought, as she put her key into the lock and opened her door.

She had closed and locked her door when she remembered that she had forgotten to get her mail out of the mailbox down the block, but she was really too tired to backtrack.

Cheyenne shrugged dismissively. She wasn't expecting anything of importance anyway. Anything in her mailbox could wait until morning, she told herself.

At this point, she wasn't all that sure she was going to be able to keep her eyes open to review the files she had bought home. Luckily, she thought, she had remembered to bring those inside with her.

Stepping out of her high heels, Cheyenne moved them aside with her foot, then allowed herself to luxuriate for a moment in the feel of the thick carpet that was beneath her feet. A lot of people, including members of her own family, enjoyed walking on a bare floor. The idea of wood, marble or linoleum left her completely and utterly cold. Literally and otherwise.

Once in her bedroom, Cheyenne quickly changed

out of the formal clothes that she wore to work and into a pair of jeans and a pullover sweater.

Moving back into the living room, she eyed her oversize tan sofa longingly for a second.

But before Cheyenne allowed herself to drop down into the super comfortable cushion, she knew that she needed something that would keep her awake for longer than a few minutes.

Coffee, Cheyenne decided. She needed coffee. Coffee would do the trick and maybe, just maybe, keep her from falling asleep.

Black coffee.

Otherwise, she knew she would wind up getting herself comfortable on the sofa and her eyes would be shut in a matter of moments. And that would seriously hamper her ability to work.

She needed to review the files at least once in order to be prepared for tomorrow. She couldn't have her partner thinking she was a loser on the second day they were working together, she told herself as she went to prepare coffee.

Cheyenne just hoped she wouldn't wind up falling asleep standing next to the counter as she waited for the coffee to finish brewing.

It was a very distinct possibility at this point.

And it had happened to her once.

Chapter 6

Cheyenne wasn't sure if she had imagined it, dreamed it, or if she had had a moment of clarity just before she had wound up falling asleep, but a similarity between the three latest victims that had recently been dug up and subsequently made their way into Autopsy suddenly occurred to her.

Morning found her on the sofa, a couple of pages from the files she had been reading through stuck to her cheeks and a half-formed thought floating in her head.

Cheyenne stretched and yawned as she removed the pages from her skin and placed them back into the proper folders. It took her a few minutes to make sure she had the right papers in the right folders. She wasn't looking to accomplish much, just something to start her off and headed in the right direction.

All murders were unsettling, she thought, but there was something even more so about these bodies that had been dug up and were presently lying in the drawers within Autopsy.

Glancing at her watch, Cheyenne realized that she was running behind the schedule that she had set for herself. Breakfast would have to wait until later, she decided as she hurried to get ready for work. Maybe she could grab something from the cafeteria or from one of the vending machines in the building. But right now, what she needed to do was pack up her files and get going, Cheyenne told herself.

Cheyenne chewed on her lower lip, thinking as she got ready. Maybe she had just imagined those similarities between those murders that had been found once the bodies had been dug up.

Closer examination of the bodies needed to be done to unearth the actual similarities, she thought.

"To be continued," she announced to no one in particular as she dashed into the shower. She was out, dried and dressed within fifteen minutes. The desire to linger was put on hold. Maybe on the weekend.

Dashing out the door, she locked up. Being late to the office would not exactly be setting any sort of decent example for the new guy. There would be plenty of time to fall on her face when he got to know her.

Cheyenne told herself not to dwell on the three bodies that had been unearthed. That wouldn't do her any good in helping advance any theories at the moment. Right now, there were no identifying factors and the faces were not recognizable. The women's facial features had been all but methodically erased.

In her opinion, that alone testified to a great deal of rage and hatred on the part of the killer. Someone felt as if they had been greatly wronged by the persons who'd been killed. There could be no other reason why the killer had lashed out so savagely.

The victims' faces had been destroyed beyond recognition and the fingerprints had been completely removed. Somehow, without any clues to go on, her department would have to come up with the dead people's identities, Cheyenne thought, deeply frustrated.

She really needed some sort of a clue to point her in the right direction.

Cheyenne pulled her car up into its usual space in the police precinct's parking lot, turned off the engine and quickly got out. Taking out the files that she had brought home with her and had been studying, Cheyenne quickly locked up her car behind her, then dashed up the concrete stairs to the precinct's back entrance.

As she did so, she hurried past her cousin Shayla. It took a second for the woman's face to even register in her head, which was already racing a hundred miles an hour.

"In a hurry to get to work?" the blonde detective asked as Cheyenne sailed by her.

The latter came to a skidding halt. "Something like

that," Cheyenne answered, clutching her files against her chest as she flashed a quick smile at her cousin.

"Well, good luck!" Shayla called after her cousin's retreating back.

"Thanks," Cheyenne tossed over her shoulder, resuming her quick pace as she hurried toward the rear precinct door.

Making her way into the building, she decided not to take the elevator but to make her way up the stairwell. In reality, it would be faster.

Cheyenne moved quickly as she made it up to the Cold Case Division. When she reached it, she leaned against the door and paused to let out a rather deep sigh. Cheyenne took in a deep breath, then quickly entered the office.

She could feel her stomach hurting and twisting as it pulled into itself.

Breathing normally now, Cheyenne entered the Cold Case Department. She noted that most of the people who worked there, included Lieutenant Holloway, hadn't gotten in yet.

Releasing a sigh of relief that she had gotten here before her new partner—which was all she actually cared about—Cheyenne got to her desk and all but collapsed into her chair.

The next second, she heard someone entering the office almost right behind her. Cheyenne turned toward the sound. She was surprised to see that her new partner was walking in. The man was carrying two paper bags with him, one in each hand.

Was he that hungry that he was opting for two breakfasts, or was McDougall bringing a friend to the office with him? Thinking it might be the latter, Cheyenne scanned the immediate area, searching for someone she didn't recognize. But there wasn't anyone.

And her new partner was headed in her direction. "So, you came back," she concluded with a smile. "I see that my brothers didn't manage to scare you off," Cheyenne marveled.

"Hey, I always like to see how things wind up turning out," Jefferson told her. He placed one of the bags he had brought in with him on her desk in front of her.

Cheyenne regraded the bag with suspicion. She hadn't asked him to bring in anything in this morning.

"Hey, what's this?" she asked, nodding at the bag. For now, she left it unopened.

"Your brothers mentioned that you like your coffee inky black and that you like to have a toasted bagel for breakfast along with it," he told her.

She stared at Jefferson, attempting to absorb what he was telling her. This was highly unusual in her opinion. "You brought me coffee and a bagel?" she asked him incredulously.

He picked up on her tone and put his own interpretation to her words. "It's not a bribe. I just thought you might want to eat something for some extra energy," he told Cheyenne. "If I got it wrong, it's because I misunderstood what your brothers were telling me. There was a lot to take in and remember yesterday. If I did get it wrong, I can go down to the cafeteria and buy something else or make a quick stop to the local fast-food place and pick up something from there."

She put her hands on the bag to keep the man from taking it away. "No, no, this is fine. As a matter of fact, it's perfect," she amended. She looked at the bag again and said, "This was very thoughtful of you," then added, "I'm very grateful to you for going through all this trouble."

Jefferson shrugged and waved away her words of gratitude. "It's no big deal."

"Oh, but it is," Cheyenne said, contradicting him. "A good working relationship is always a big deal. And feeding me because you figured that I was going to be hungry and punchy at this hour of the morning is really very nice of you." Cheyenne took out her wallet that looked as if it had seen better days. "What do I owe you for this?"

Jefferson didn't hesitate in answering her. "Forgiveness the first time I mess up."

She had no problem with that. "Well, that goes without saying," she responded. "But I meant what do I owe you monetarily?"

Her partner waved his hand at her question. "Don't worry about it. What I paid for it isn't exactly going to break me." Making himself comfortable, he set down his own bag and sat at the desk that had been assigned to him. "As soon as I make short work of this, what do you say that I start working on whatever it is you're working on?" he suggested, then, pausing, thought to ask her, "Just what is it that you are working on?"

She turned toward him because she wanted to see his reaction. "Well, I think that we might have ourselves a genuine serial killer case."

Jefferson seemed instantly interested. "Oh? What makes you think that it's a serial killer who's making the rounds? Is it similar victims, or is he using the same kind of MO or—?"

Cheyenne spread out the three photographs she had managed to amass, the two bodies from the other day and also the most recent one that she had just discovered before she had fallen asleep last night. She decided this might just be a good way to test the new man.

"Tell you what," she said, indicating the photographs. "Why don't you tell me?"

Her partner had finished eating, except for the container of coffee, which he made certain had its lid securely put in place. He carefully studied the photographs that Cheyenne had spread out in front of him.

The women's facial features had all but been erased in the same brutal manner. He couldn't guess at what had been used in order to eradicate the women's features. A hammer? Brass knuckles? He didn't know. In addition, he couldn't even begin to hazard a guess as to what had been used to tie the victims down in each case.

"Well," he began thoughtfully, his face growing slightly pale, "it looks as if all three had been beaten without so much as even a trace of remorse evident. Their faces were heartlessly disfigured, almost erased, as if the killer enjoyed what he was doing. I don't know if whoever did this didn't want his victims recognized, or if he was really angry at his victims and was taking that anger out on them by disfiguring them."

She nodded. "That would have been my guess." And then she hit him with a question he wasn't prepared for. "What makes you think the killer is a male?"

At first her partner was surprised by the question. And then after he gave it some thought, Jeff answered, "I guess I'm guilty of typecasting," and then he picked up the photograph closest to him. "And looking at the photographs again, I don't think the average woman could beat her victim this way without a wave of fury urging her on." He studied the photograph, shaking his head. "You can see by the amount of damage done that the killer appears to be really unhinged."

Cheyenne nodded, glad that her partner saw things the way that she did. "I don't think anyone could possibly argue that serial killers are rational people capable of walking the straight and narrow. I doubt that they are capable of disguising their intentions from the average person for very long."

She sighed, sitting back. "The first thing we need

to do is see if we can identify these victims," Cheyenne said. "Any ideas?"

Jefferson frowned, studying the photographs. "Their faces were destroyed and all trace of fingerprints erased," he reiterated.

"Yes, we already know that," Cheyenne agreed, waiting for the detective to continue.

"Is there some sort of a database for teeth?" he asked her.

She shook her head. "No, no database."

He thought for a moment. "We can try circulating the X-rays of the teeth locally. We might get lucky," he said, watching her expression for a reaction to his suggestion.

She nodded. "Barring any pet theories that might send us looking in the right direction, that might be something for us to try. Good job," she commended her partner. "Why don't you jot down any ideas that you might have about working this case. Who knows, it might even help send us looking in the right direction."

"At the moment, I'm afraid that my brain feels empty," Jefferson confessed.

"Trust me, everyone faced with trying to make rhyme or reason out of the dealings of a serial killer feels like their brain is running on empty at one point or another," she guaranteed. "Sometimes, a lot more than that."

"You've felt that way?" he asked, unable to get himself to believe that, based on what her brothers had told him about Cheyenne. They all seemed pretty proud of her and her ability to deduce things.

"Of course me," she told him. "How do you think I would know that if I hadn't gone through that myself?"

"Because you're being kind?" he suggested.

She laughed out loud at his response. "Don't let any of my brothers hear you saying something like that," she told him. "They'd think I gave you something spiked to drink—or that you've been working too hard and are just hallucinating."

He wasn't buying that. "I got the distinct feeling that your brothers are all very proud of you. Don't forget, you left me alone with them when you went home. They did a lot of talking."

Her eyes narrowed as she looked at him. "I really doubt that they told you they were proud of me," she told her partner.

Her partner felt he had something to counter that opinion. "I don't know, they seemed pretty up on the fact that you are the youngest law enforcement officer in the family to make detective, and in the shortest amount of time."

Cheyenne blinked, surprised. He did sound pretty sincere. "They actually told you that?"

"Well, yeah," he assured her. "How else would I know a fact like that?"

Cheyenne shrugged. "You might have read about it in one of the precinct's newsletters."

"Before I came here, what reason would I have had to read the precinct's newsletters?" he asked.

She was slightly stymied for a moment, then gave in as she nodded her head. "Good point. I guess maybe my brothers are a tad proud of me—not that they would ever say something like that to my face."

"Brothers never do," Jefferson said knowingly. "Or so I'm told."

The admission surprised her. She remembered that she needed to read up on her partner. She still didn't know very much about him. "No siblings?"

The detective shook his head. "Nope."

"Well, I have more than enough to spare," she told him. "You help me solve this cold case and I'll give you one. Maybe even a couple."

His eyes met hers. "I'll hold you to that," he told her with a warm laugh.

She placed her hand in his and shook it. "Deal."

Jeff's eyes smiled at her as he echoed, "Deal."

Chapter 7

He was getting antsy.

He'd really thought he could keep this overwhelming desire that was eating away at him, bit by bit, under control.

But he'd been wrong. He couldn't.

Instead, he could feel that sensation inside him growing and expanding. It was feeding his hunger, making it become all but uncontrollable.

Making it huge.

As Murphy sat in the tiny cubbyhole of a classroom, its very existence an insult to him, he knew he was going to have to do something about this all-consuming hunger eating away at him.

And soon.

Murphy snapped the pencil he had in his hand without even realizing he had done it.

He was envisioning his next victim's neck.

A satisfied smile came over his lips, curving them.

Cheyenne stared at the notes she was rereading for the third time. Possibly even the fourth. It still wasn't making any real sense to her. How could anyone manage to all but erase a person's face the way that the serial killer obviously had?

And more importantly, *why* would the killer do that? To her it was more in keeping with a horror movie than anything real. In her experience, a lot of serial killers were egomaniacs who, while not wanting to get caught, did want the credit that went with the murders that they wound up pulling off. Part of that credit came with others discovering the identity of the people who had been murdered, and how they had been killed. Perhaps not immediately, but eventually.

The murders she had been studying didn't answer *any* questions—they just asked them. And once asked, those questions just continued to linger.

Was this the serial killer's way of taunting the police department, or was there something else going on behind the killer's actions that wasn't clear to her?

Cheyenne sighed. She really wished she knew and could make some sort of sense out of all this confusion.

The newest Cavanaugh detective frowned. This

was *really* frustrating. She honestly had no answers. For now, all she had were questions.

Lots and lots of overlapping questions.

Jefferson looked up, his attention drawn by the sound of her deep sigh.

"You know," her partner speculated, "if you sigh any harder, you're going to wind up blowing that bookshelf down." He jerked a thumb back toward the bookshelf standing behind her.

Cheyenne made a face. "As long as it winds up solving the mystery, I don't care how noisy it winds up being as it crashes," she told her partner honestly.

The detective wound up laughing to himself as he envisioned the bookshelf's fate. "Remind me never to go on a stakeout with you."

She gave her partner a long, penetrating look. "Consider yourself reminded." And then she drew closer to her desk, staring at the paperwork. "Have you managed to make heads or tails out of the killer's reasoning for killing his victims in this manner?" she asked her partner.

"Maybe he didn't have an actual reason," Jefferson guessed. "Maybe what he has is just this over-whelming hunger to kill."

But she shook her head. "Every serial killer has a reason. Doesn't have to make sense to the rest of us," she told the detective. "Just to him. But he still has to have a reason."

But her partner wasn't entirely sold on her reasoning. He eyed her skeptically. "Are you sure about that?"

"I am very sure," she said. And then she pushed herself back from her desk. "I am also getting pretty damn cross-eyed right about now. Do you want to break for lunch?" Time seemed to have gotten away from her.

He let the file folder he was looking at close. "That depends."

"Depends on what?"

"On what you're planning to get for lunch—and where," he told her simply.

She looked up at the detective in surprise. "Are you a fussy eater, McDougall?" She wouldn't have thought that of him, but she was still in the "getting to know you" stage.

Her partner smiled at her. "Let's just say I'm a discerning eater."

Cheyenne returned his smile for the qualification he had just used. "I've got news for you, McDougall. That's kind of the same thing."

For his part, McDougall seemed totally unfazed and unconvinced by her qualification. "If you say so," he told Cheyenne with a quick shrug.

"Tell you what," Cheyenne said, closing down her computer until they returned from lunch. "Why don't you pick the place? I'm assuming that you are familiar enough with the various fast-food places and eating establishments in the immediate vicinity to pick a place that serves food you find enjoyable." She fixed him with a curious look, "Or am I assuming wrong?"

"Well, I'm not exactly a big foodie," her partner began.

"You don't have to be very big on it, you just have to know what you like or what you find tastes good. Unless, of course, it doesn't matter to you what you like. Do you have any actual choices?" she asked, looking into McDougall's eyes.

He felt like he had been reviewing the three files all morning and part of the afternoon. Right now, he suddenly felt weary beyond words, though the words he had been reading and rereading were all dancing right before his eyes.

"I tell you what. Since you're the senior officer here, why don't you pick where we go?" he suggested. "At this point, I'm so hungry it's interfering with my ability to think," he admitted truthfully.

For the time being, Cheyenne put her folder to the side. She decided to try again. "All right, next question. What kind of food do you like? Plain food, Chinese food, pizza, hamburgers, or—" Her voice trailed off as she looked at her partner, waiting for the man to specify some kind of a choice.

Her partner grinned at the question. "I'm fine with 'or,'" he told her.

Cheyenne looked surprised and then laughed. "Well, I certainly can't say that you're a difficult man to please, McDougall." She glanced at her watch. They needed to get moving if they intended to get lunch before lunch wound up turning into dinner. "We've got a little more than forty-five minutes from right now." Patting her pocket to make sure she had her car keys—she did—she told her partner, "If it's all right with you, I'll drive."

"You're the one who knows where we're going," he pointed out. His tone told her that he was surrendering the idea of driving without bothering to contest it.

She flashed a quick smile at him. "In case you're wondering, we're going to this great Chinese restaurant that's been here for as long as the city has existed—maybe even longer."

He nodded as they went out to the elevator. "Sounds good to me. At this point, I'm hungry enough to probably be able to eat logs."

Her expression didn't change. "There's a forest not too far from the city. I could take you there, but you might have to share lunch with a beaver," she whimsically speculated.

Emulating her, Jefferson kept a straight face. "Chinese food will do fine."

Reaching her vehicle, Cheyenne opened all four of the doors simultaneously, then waited for her partner to get in on the passenger side. "Glad we could come to an agreement," she told Jefferson. In less than a minute, she started up her vehicle.

Like everything else, he had come to learn about the immediate area, the restaurant was located not too far from the precinct.

Because it was not the height of the lunch hour,

only a handful of people were waiting to get into the newly redecorated Chinese restaurant.

They were seated within minutes of arriving.

"It's in the back, by the aquarium," the young server apologized as he brought them to their table.

"I find watching fish soothing," Cheyenne told the server by way of letting him know that she was fine with his choice.

"Yeah, so do I," Jefferson said, although he doubted that the server was looking for his approval in this matter. The young guy seemed totally fixated on his partner, the detective noticed. Not that he could really blame the kid. Cheyenne was damn attractive to his way of thinking, Jefferson noted.

Having seated them at the table, the server handed each of them the menus he had brought with him. "I'll be back in a few minutes to take your orders," the boyish server promised, nodding at Cheyenne before he withdrew.

"I think you have a fan," Jefferson whispered to her with a warm smile as the server departed. "I don't think he even noticed that you were with anyone."

She laughed. "He's young," she told her partner magnanimously. "He's probably still trying to feel his way around."

Jefferson smiled broadly as he shrugged his shoulders. "If you ask me, he's got taste."

She wasn't sure how to take that. They had just begun working together and she wasn't able to read him yet. Was he complimenting her, or was there something more to her partner's words than that?

She decided to ask him outright. "Is that a compliment, McDougall?"

"It's an observation," he told her in an offhanded manner. "No more, no less."

She decided to let the matter drop for now. His intention would come to light soon enough and she could put him in his place if she needed to.

"You better get ready to make your choice quickly," Cheyenne told him. "If I remember correctly, they come back to take your order fast here. They like to stand by their service."

Jefferson opened his menu, glanced at it and then looked at her. "What's good here?" he asked.

She rattled off a number of selections, ending with, "Or you can have my favorite, Lobster Cantonese."

Her partner closed his menu and placed it on the table in front of him. "Sounds good to me."

"So, Lobster Cantonese?" she asked.

He partner nodded and smiled. "Yes."

She waited for a second. When he didn't say anything, she pressed, "And?"

"I need more?" he asked her, slightly confused.

She looked at him for a moment, then made a guess. "You don't eat Chinese food very often, do you?"

"I was born and raised eating Mexican food," her partner confessed. "I wouldn't know—Lobster Cantonese," he said, reading the choice from the menu, "from—Moo Goo Gai Pan," he said, reading another selection. "Whatever that is."

She laughed at him. "Trust me, taste-wise you'll like the first one a lot better." She thought for a moment. "I'll have the server throw in egg rolls, fortune cookies and a couple of other tidbits. We'll have you full in no time. Hopefully, we won't get too sleepy to concentrate on work when we finish eating," she told him.

Jefferson thought for a moment. "Okay," he announced, "I'm ready to order."

Cheyenne looked around for their server. The latter was approximately two tables over, bringing a fresh pot of hot tea to the occupants seated there. She waved toward him.

The server glanced over toward Cheyenne's table, nodded and promised, "I'll be right there."

She acknowledged his promise. "Thank you. We are in a little bit of a hurry," she told the server.

He was there to take their order within less than a minute, smiling broadly at Cheyenne. She barely noticed. Her mind was on Jefferson, thinking that their association looked as if it might turn out to be far more pleasant than she had anticipated,

"May I take you order?" the man asked.

She glanced at her partner, then told the server, "Absolutely."

Chapter 8

"**I** think I might have eaten too much," Jefferson said, groaning slightly as he debated loosening his belt. He decided to leave it alone, although it wasn't really easy.

Cheyenne's partner frowned. They were back in the office, pondering over the information found within the three folders and searching for some sort of a tangible connection between them. They had been working diligently on this cold case for several days now. Lunch today had been over an hour ago.

Cheyenne raised her eyes, looking at him across their desks. "It didn't look as if you had a lot to eat," she said honestly.

Her partner shrugged off her observation. "I guess I'm just not used to eating a lot." He glanced back at the files. At this point, he knew them all by heart. "It would have been nice if this homicidal monster had left us at least part of the faces to look at."

Cheyenne sighed as she stared at the disfigured face in the photograph she was holding. "Agreed, but we have to focus on working with what we do have, not what we *wished* we had."

"And what is it we have?" McDougall asked her pointedly. The way he looked at it, there really wasn't all that much.

She paused, choosing her words carefully. "Well, given the dead bodies' skeletal structures—predominantly their pelvises—I believe that all three of the disfigured victims were older women. None of them were heavyset and given the spread of their hips, the victims were all past the age of childbearing."

Jefferson seemed rather impressed at what Cheyenne had ascertained. "That's pretty astute," her partner told her.

"Not really," she contradicted. "We have a coroner in the family and I pay attention to the things she says, storing it away for use at some future date." Cheyenne looked through the file that was open on her desk for what had to be the umpteenth time and frowned. "I have to admit that right now, no matter how we slice it, we don't exactly have all that much to go on." Sighing, she closed the folder on her desk. "This is no longer the tiny little town that Aurora once was," she lamented, thinking back to the stories that her grandfather had told her when she was a kid. "Now the trail we might choose to follow can wind up leading us to any one of a number of places." Again, Cheyenne felt extremely frustrated.

Jefferson had a feeling that the cases on their desks were not isolated incidents. And he expected there would be more coming. Hopefully not a great many more.

"All these people couldn't have been living in vacuums all to themselves," her partner argued. "Maybe someone related to these women filed a missing persons report, trying to locate them or find out what happened to them."

Cheyenne's expression changed as she inclined her head. Turning the idea over in her mind, she nodded. "Sounds like that might have real possibilities," she agreed, thinking the matter over. "See if you can get hold of anyone in the Missing Persons Department and see if anyone came in recently to file a report on a missing older woman."

"Who do I ask for?" Jefferson asked. "Do you have a name? I'm assuming that there's someone in your family who works in that department." He looked at her from across his desk. "I always found it helps to have someone's name to start out with."

She nodded. "Good point," Cheyenne agreed, complimenting her partner. She thought for a moment. "You could try talking to Travis."

"Travis?" Jefferson repeated. There were a great many Cavanaughs working at the precinct that he didn't know by name yet.

Cheyenne nodded. "Travis," she repeated. "He's my baby brother." She made a note to herself regarding the file she was reviewing at the moment, not wanting to lose her place even though she had gone over it who knew how many times. And then she smiled at her own comment. "We all thought that the Missing Persons Department would be a good fit for him. Travis always had a penchant for being able to find things no matter how misplaced they might be.

"He might turn out to be a huge help to us in identifying these poor faceless victims," she told her partner.

Rolling the idea over in her head, she nodded to herself, picked up the receiver on the precinct's landline and dialed one of the extensions that she knew by heart.

The phone on the other end rang a number of times with no pickup. She was about to hang up and try again later when she heard the receiver on the other end finally being picked up.

"Missing Persons. This is Cavanaugh," a deep voice told her.

She recognized the speaker immediately. Settling back in her chair, she smiled to herself. "Travis? It's Cheyenne."

She heard her brother sigh. "I'll be there, I'll be there," he told her, anticipating her question.

He had caught her completely off guard and she had no idea what her younger brother was talking about. Did he think she was asking him to come to her office? She had no way of knowing what her brother was referring to. She just knew that it didn't make any sense to her.

"You'll be where?" she asked Travis.

"Aren't you calling to remind me to attend Uncle Andrew's birthday party?" he asked his sister.

She'd been so caught up in the serial killer case, Cheyenne had temporarily forgotten all about her uncle's birthday, she thought, stifling a sigh. "I've been so snowed under with this serial killer case and other details," she said, glancing over toward Jefferson, whom she considered to be one of those details, "I forgot all about the party," she confessed, embarrassed at her oversight.

"Oh." Her brother sounded embarrassed for jumping to his conclusion.

"Actually," Cheyenne continued, "that's the reason I'm calling you, Travis."

It was Travis's turn to be clueless as to what Cheyenne was getting at. "You're going to have to give me more of a hint than that, Cheyenne."

It killed her to admit this, but she was not about to beat around the bush regarding the reason for her call. "I need your help, Travis."

"I still need more words, Cheyenne," Travis told his sister.

"Okay, how are these for words?" she asked, getting down to business. "I have got three bodies in the morgue whose faces have been bashed in beyond recognition so we can't make any sort of identifications that would allow us to find out where these people had been and who might have hurt them in this horrible fashion," she said with emphasis.

"Have you tried tracking down their fingerprints through the various records that are available?" Travis asked.

She felt almost insulted that he would even ask her something like that. "Yes, I tried and I'm not exactly a newbie, Travis. And the dead bodies *have* no fingerprints. All of their fingerprints have been erased.

"All we know for sure is that all three victims were older women and they were found buried in various parks in Aurora. Whether the killer brought his victims there to get rid of them, or there was some sort of a message in burying them there,, I don't know. I admit that I am completely stumped over motive and frankly, I can use all the help I can get with these cases. Meaning you," she told her brother pointedly.

"That new partner you got to replace Wade, he isn't any help to you?" Travis asked his sister with a touch of sympathy. He knew that Cheyenne had been upset about her old partner leaving.

"Well, he wasn't trained in mind reading or séances so, so far, he hasn't been able to offer any real help," she said, lowering her voice so that Jeff couldn't overhear her.

He knew that his sister hadn't called him just to kill time. "What would you like me to do?" Travis asked.

"Well, I'm thinking that these faceless victims who had been discovered might turn out being the missing people who had been reported to your department. For now, just send over the names of the people who had been reported as missing and any useful information you might have come across searching for and researching these people."

"Sure thing," Travis agreed. "I'll email it to you. Who knows," he said with a laugh, "we might wind up solving each other's cases."

"We might be satisfied because we find the answers we're looking for," Cheyenne admitted, "but let's face it, we won't be able to tell the families anything positive or comforting about their missing daughters or wives," she concluded sadly, thinking of the possible consequences of this tradeoff.

It was obvious that Travis didn't share his sister's outlook. "Hey, an answer is an answer and we can move on and build from there," he told Cheyenne. "Me, I'll take whatever I can get."

"Well, it looks as if I will have to do the same. Send me the missing persons' names, any details you might have on them and any photos their family or friends gave to you," she told her brother.

"And Uncle Andrew's birthday party this Saturday?" Travis prodded Cheyenne.

"Goes without saying, I'll be there with bells on," she promised.

She heard her brother chuckle. "Nice working

with you, big sister. This is a first for us, isn't it?"
he asked as an afterthought.

"But not the last, I hope," she answered. "See you
Saturday," she told him just before she hung up the
landline receiver.

A couple minutes later, her computer made a
noise, announcing that it had received the photos
and information that Cheyenne had requested from
her brother.

"Hey, McDougall, want to see who we might be
looking for?" she asked, beckoning her partner over
to look at the photos that had been sent to her. Travis had sent her photos of five different women who
had recently been reported missing by their families
or friends.

Jefferson came over to stand behind his partner.
He studied the different images. "Did your brother
happen to send over the important details, like height,
weight and age?"

She nodded in response. "Travis is new to the
job, but not to the life." She saw that Jefferson was
looking at her curiously. "What I mean by 'the life'
is that Travis was practically born knowing the important points that go into conducting proper law
enforcement and solving crimes. He doesn't even
have to stop to think about it. It's just automatic."
She smiled at her partner as she pointed out the details on the screen that her partner had asked about.
"Here're the important points."

The five photos that had been included all contained descriptions of age, height and weight. Jefferson frowned as he reviewed each very carefully.

"This one sounds like practically a teenager," he said, pointing to the photograph. "I don't think she's one of our faceless victims."

"I agree, but what makes you think that?" Cheyenne wanted to know just how astute her partner could be.

"Because the coroner made that comment about the victims' hips being wide and them having been through childbirth. That means that our victims have families, or did at one point, depending on whether or not those children lived and if anything happened to them afterward."

Jefferson sighed, thinking over his assessment of the case. "There are a hell of a lot of variables to take into consideration."

She smiled as she nodded. "Welcome to the Cold Case Department, McDougall. There's a reason why they call it 'cold' case," she emphasized.

"And yet you're so chipper and upbeat," he couldn't help noting.

"I have to be," she said to her partner. "It's called being defensive. If I wasn't 'chipper' and 'upbeat,' I'd be sitting somewhere in the corner, curled up in a ball, sucking my thumb and trying desperately to find something to help cheer me up," Cheyenne told him.

Jefferson nodded and grinned. "I guess that this is the better alternative."

She looked at him for a moment, trying to make up

her mind, then made a decision. "By the way, are you busy this coming Saturday afternoon and evening?"

"Why? Are you asking me out on a date?" he asked with a grin as he returned to his seat.

"We're not dating, McDougall," she informed him firmly. "We're partners."

"I know that," he answered her dismissively. But then he couldn't make heads or tails out of the question she had just asked about Saturday. "But then why—?"

She came close to dropping the subject, but she knew that her uncle Andrew and her father, both of whom were going to be at the party, would be curious to meet her new partner. Everyone had known and liked her last one. Bringing him to Uncle Andrew's party would go a long way toward answering a lot of questions—and silencing other ones.

"Saturday is my uncle Andrew's birthday. He used to be the chief of police here. Moreover, he throws these incredible parties at the drop of a hat. This one is being thrown *for* him because it's his birthday and I know that my aunt Rose is going to be throwing him one. Would you like to come as my guest? You'll get to meet the rest of my family," she told him as if that would entice him to attend.

"Well, sure," Jefferson said agreeably, "but he doesn't know me."

"This way he will get to know you. And so will everyone else. You'll be more than welcome," she told her new partner.

He smiled broadly. "Then I will definitely come."

She nodded, pleased. "I'll give you the address. Or I can pick you up and take you there since you're new in the area."

"I'd actually appreciate that," he acknowledged. "What can I bring?"

"Just your sunny personality—and a birthday card if you see something that strikes your fancy," she told him.

"I can't go empty-handed," Jefferson protested. "What does your uncle like?"

"That's easy. A united front," she told him. "Okay," Cheyenne declared, picking up one of the folders on her desk. "Back to trying to solve this jigsaw puzzle."

Jefferson said nothing in response. He merely nodded, sighed deeply, then went back to doing as she had suggested.

Chapter 9

Cheyenne felt like she had been going over and over the files, looking for some sort of a hint, some sort of a clue to point her and her partner in the right direction for forever now.

These murders had to have a connection, something in common. Didn't they?

Coming up empty, she sighed for what was probably the dozenth time or so as she reviewed the files that were spread out before her on her desk.

She couldn't get away from the feeling that she was going around in circles and at this point, she almost felt as if she was getting dizzy.

She was missing something.

But what?

Jefferson looked up from the file he was reviewing. All three files had been duplicated so that he and Cheyenne were looking at the same documents, hoping something would strike them.

"You know, you sigh any louder," her partner commented, sparing her a look, "and you're liable to blow me away."

"I didn't know that you were prone to exaggerating," Cheyenne told the man.

Jeff paused to bend over and pick up a few pages that had managed to land on the floor. "I'm not," he said pointedly, taking the pages with him and placing them on her desk, then taking his seat again.

Cheyenne shrugged. Jeff was right. She was overreacting.

"It's just that I feel so frustrated," she complained. "Heaven knows I didn't expect the solution to be a simple one, but I didn't expect it to induce a really throbbing headache, either."

Her partner laughed shortly under his breath. "Tell me about it," he said. About to say something further, the transplanted Texan happened to look up toward the doorway. His attention was drawn to the police officer who was escorting a rather distraught-looking young woman into their office. "Don't look now, Cavanaugh," he said, lowering his voice, "but I think we've got company."

Cheyenne looked toward the doorway. "She might not be headed for us," she commented. "After all, there are other people working in this office."

"You really think that she's not being escorted in

our direction?" Jeff asked, his expression appearing rather skeptical.

"No. She's got that really distraught look on her face," Cheyenne pointed out, studying the woman.

The police officer, Joel Adams, brought the young woman over to Cheyenne's desk. "Detective Cavanaugh, this is Ms. Eve Richardson. I'll let her take it from here," the officer said. And with that, he politely withdrew.

The young woman appeared somewhat embarrassed as well as flustered and at a loss for words. "I'm not really sure if I should even be here," she apologized, looking from one detective to the other. She looked to be in her midthirties and more suited to be relaxing on a cruise ship than filing a report in a police station. The fair-haired woman shifted uncomfortably from side to side.

"Why don't you let us be the judge of that?" Jeff proposed, attempting to do what he could to put the woman who had just walked into their office at her ease. He gestured toward the chair that had been placed next to his partner's desk. "Please, have a seat and tell us exactly what brought you here to us."

Cheyenne was already on her feet, extending her hand to the woman. "Hello, Ms. Richardson. I'm Detective Cheyenne Cavanaugh and this is Detective Jefferson McDougall." She smiled as she said her partner's name. "And if you're wondering about his twang, it's because he's recently moved here from El Paso, Texas. But don't let the accent fool you. There's nothing laidback about him. Detective McDougall is as sharp as they come. Now," Cheyenne said, sitting back down in her chair, "how can we help you, Ms. Richardson?"

Nervous and uncomfortable, the woman was twisting the handkerchief she was holding in her hands, almost making it into a knot. She looked far from at ease with what she was about to say to the two detectives. In fact, she appeared to be at her wit's end.

"You'll probably think that I'm overreacting," the woman told the detectives, looking embarrassed.

"Why don't you tell us what has you so upset?" Cheyenne encouraged. "Then we can tell you if you're overreacting."

The woman took a deep breath, then dived right into the heart of her concern. "I don't know where my mother is."

"Is this something usual for her?" Cheyenne asked. "I mean, do you call each other regularly, or do days, or—"

"Or do weeks go by without any contact between the two of you?" Jeff interjected, doing what he could to attempt to nail the situation down.

The woman blew out a shaky breath. "It all depends. My mother and I—and my older sister—are kind of independent. Liz and I try not to make our mother feel as if we're hounding her every move. To be honest, we gave her a lot of grief about our own independence when we were growing up and in our teens and early twenties. Mom, to her credit, tried to do everything for us. She was like that with us, with our dad until he decided to take off and start a new life somewhere else. And she was definitely like that when it came to our grandmother until Grandma passed away. Mom was all things to all people," the woman told them, doing her best to draw as complete a picture of her mother as she could.

"Initially, after Dad took off, I thought that maybe Mom could use some alone time to just pull herself together. You know, catch up on her life," she said to the detectives, looking from one to the other. The woman smiled sadly. "Mom used the time to go back to school. She threw herself into that, working to support us and herself, until she got her high school diploma. With that under her belt, Mom decided to get her college degree as well."

"Where?" Jeff asked. He was taking notes to draw a fuller picture of the missing woman.

"Locally," she answered automatically.

"How local?" Cheyenne asked pointedly.

"Right here in Aurora College," the young woman was quick to reply. "To be very honest, I was rather pleased at how well things were working out for her and for me. With my mother busy with her job and getting her degree, I realized that I was long overdue for a vacation. So I decided to take one."

"Where did you go?" Cheyenne asked her.

For a moment, the woman's face softened as she thought about the vacation she had spent. "I spent two glorious weeks on a cruise ship. I sent my mother a couple of postcards, asking her how things were going back home, you know, things like that."

"And did she answer you, or acknowledge the postcards?" Jeff asked, trying to get a handle on when communication broke down.

"She didn't say anything specific, but yes, she did say she got the postcards—and that she was happy I was able to get some time away," Eve Richardson said.

Cheyenne studied her expression. "You don't sound entirely sure," the detective commented.

The woman looked disturbed. "Right now, I'm not sure of anything." There were furrows on her forehead. "And there's been all this talk about a serial killer…" Her voice trailed off as she looked at the two detectives for some sort of comfort and reassurance.

"There's no need to let your imagination run away with you," Jefferson said. "Most likely, your mother's just having a good time, or remembering what it was like to be young and carefree, without responsibilities."

"I don't think she was ever young and carefree," the young woman commented. "And definitely not without responsibilities."

Cheyenne felt sorry for the woman. "Parents have a way of surprising us," she told her. "Why don't you give us all the information about your mother that you can—where she worked, what she did, the classes she took at Aurora Valley, things like that. Plus any pictures of your mother you can spare. The more of a complete picture we can put together of your mother, the more of a chance we have of being able to track her down and find her."

Eve Richardson began to look hopeful for the first time since she had walked into the office. "Do you really think that we can?" she asked.

"Thinking negatively won't help," Jefferson told the woman.

"I know," the distraught young woman answered. "It's just that I feel so terribly guilty that I let so much time pass without going to the police about this," Eve Richardson told the detectives.

"Why—specifically?" Cheyenne asked. "You have to have a reason why you feel so guilty about all this," she insisted. Was there something the woman wasn't telling them, or was this just a general wave of guilt she was experiencing?

The woman blew out a shaky breath. "I couldn't wait to go on vacation," she explained.

"There's nothing wrong with that," Cheyenne insisted, waiting to hear the actual reason the woman was so upset.

"And when I came back, I got so busy at work that I didn't touch base with my mother for several weeks. When I finally did," the young woman said. "Mom just wasn't there."

"By 'wasn't there,'" Jeff prompted, "do you mean that she was missing or just going out late at night, or...?" His voice trailed off as he looked at her, waiting for the woman to fill them in on the missing details.

Eve Richardson stared down at her nails, tears forming in her eyes and threatening to fall. "I'm really embarrassed that I can't be more specific than that. I was trying to give my mother her space because I felt that she sacrificed so much for Liz and for me that the best thing I could do was not haunt her every waking moment." The tears that had gathered in her eyes were beginning to fall.

Seeing them, Cheyenne pulled a tissue out of a box on her desk and offered it to the woman.

The distraught woman took it and used the tissue to wipe her eyes. Stifling a sob, she said, "At least, that's what I told myself."

Cheyenne offered her a sympathetic look. "And how's that going for you?" she asked, curious.

Eve Richardson shook her head as she pressed her lips together. "Not well," the woman admitted. There was a hitch in her voice. "Not well at all."

"Well, don't give up yet," Cheyenne encouraged the woman. "Sometimes things have a way of working out when you least expect them to. Trust me, I know."

"I really hope so," Eve Richardson sniffled. She was sounding more and more despondent.

"Okay, let's get practical," Cheyenne told her. "We need the name of the place where your mother worked. Was it a full-time job, or part-time?"

"Part-time ever since she began going back to school. Mom was really intent on getting her degree. She decided that it was high time that she became something," the woman told them. Eve's mouth curved. "Like she needed a degree for that." Amid the hopelessness was a touch of pride as well.

Cheyenne turned a pad over to the woman. "Write down everything you can think of," she urged Eve. "No matter how minor it might seem. Sometimes the smallest detail might wind up being the thing that could very well break the case."

For the first time, she saw real hope entering the woman's eyes.

"Really?" Eve asked the detectives.

"Really," Jeff assured the woman. He took out a card and handed it to the missing woman's daughter. "If you think of anything at all—*anything*," Cheyenne's partner underscored with feeling, "don't hesitate to give me a call. Day or night."

For her part, Cheyenne took out a business card of her own and pressed it into the woman's hand. "The same goes for me," she told Lauren Dixon's distraught daughter.

"And you'll call me? Day or night, you'll call me?" the young woman pressed. "No matter what?"

"No matter what," the detectives said, their voices blending almost in unison.

Finished for the time being with their interview, the two detectives walked the woman back to the officer who had escorted her into the office. He in turn brought her back to the elevator and then downstairs.

With that done, Jefferson went back with Cheyenne to their office. Once there, Cheyenne looked at her partner. They both knew what their next step was going to be—interviewing the people that the missing woman worked with and went to school with.

"Okay," she said, glancing at the list of names that the woman's daughter had handed them, "let's get to this."

"You took the words right out of my mouth," Jefferson told his partner as they got their things and walked into the hallway to the elevator.

Chapter 10

"So do you want to ask the questions or do you want me to?" Jefferson asked his partner.

Cheyenne was surprised by her partner's question. "Why don't we take turns as the questions occur to us?" she suggested after a beat. That seemed to be the better way to go in her opinion.

They had left the precinct and Cheyenne was now driving them to the missing woman's place of work that her daughter had told them about. A Taste of Heaven was a catering restaurant where Lauren Dixon had been working part-time to help her pay for her college education ever since she had gotten her high school degree. According to her daughter, the woman had worked there until she had inexplicably disappeared.

Jefferson nodded. "That sounds good to me," he told Cheyenne. Wanting to make sure that they were on the same page, Jeff asked his partner, "Exactly what information are we going to go with on this missing woman?"

Cheyenne thought for a moment, reviewing what had been said. She didn't want them to get ahead of themselves or say too much to begin with. "Well, according to her daughter, Lauren Dixon is almost sixty-one years young and she's eager to start, as Eve Richardson put it, the second half of her life." She found that a very admirable sentiment.

"The second half of her life," McDougall repeated, amused. "Does that mean that the woman is planning on living until she's one hundred and twenty-eight years old?"

Cheyenne shrugged. All things considered in this day and age, that was not a total impossibility.

"Who knows? Science and medicine are making tremendous strides these days. Anything could be possible." She could almost feel the detective staring at her profile. She spared him a quick glance. "What?"

Jefferson laughed. "You really are an optimist, aren't you?"

She was obviously amusing him, Cheyenne thought. But that wasn't exactly her goal.

"I don't see a point in wallowing in dark thoughts," she told him. "Dark thoughts will find you soon enough if that's the intention."

Cheyenne's new partner nodded. "Can't argue with that, I guess."

Sure he could, she thought. Out loud she declared, "Good," tossing the comment in her partner's general direction.

A Taste of Heaven was located in a small, neat-looking little shopping center that was located in the southern section of Aurora. Since it was a weekday, there was plenty of available parking at this time of day.

Pulling up into the first available space she found, Cheyenne set the hand brake and turned off the engine, then got out of her vehicle.

Jefferson was right there next to her.

"Looks like a nice place to work," he commented, looking up at the freshly painted single-story restaurant.

"Looks can be deceiving," she told him. "But offhand, I'd have to agree that you're right."

Cheyenne led the way into the restaurant. As she pushed open the door, an old-fashioned bell hanging overhead made a tinkling sound, announcing their entrance. She caught herself thinking that it really did seem like a rather charming place.

"I'll be right with you," a heavyset woman called out, writing something down on an electronic pad she was holding.

Jefferson looked around the restaurant, trying to visualize it through the missing woman's eyes. "It really does look like a nice place to work," he reiterated to Cheyenne.

She really wasn't all that willing to agree with him yet. She had a very healthy sense of skepticism. "That all depends on the pace they expect you to keep up," she told her partner. "Some places appear welcoming on the outside but are conducted like sweatshops from within."

The other detective shrugged, thinking the judgment to be a bit harsh. "I'll take your word for it."

At that point, the woman with the electronic pad approached them. There was a broad pasted-on smile on her lips. "Now then, what can I get for you folks?" she wanted to know, her sweeping glance taking them both in.

"We're here to ask you a few questions about one of the people who works at your restaurant," Cheyenne told the woman as she flashed her police credentials. Jefferson had taken out his silently. "A Lauren Dixon."

The woman's smile faded and she shook her head. "I'm afraid Lauren doesn't work here anymore. It's a shame," she commented, "because she was a really good worker. She was here full-time for years, then went part-time," the woman, whose name according to the name tag she wore was Cecilia, told them.

"Did you fire her?" Cheyenne asked the woman bluntly. She felt that was the quickest way to get the woman's story out of her.

"In theory I guess you could say that," Cecelia answered.

"Would you care to explain that?" Cheyenne asked.

The other woman just shrugged almost helplessly in response. "She just stopped showing up one day. It was kind of ironic, really," she told the two detectives, "because I was about to give her a raise. But like I said, Lauren just stopped showing up. One of the other women who work here speculated that she probably got caught up in going for her college degree. Undoubtedly she had bigger things in mind than just working in a restaurant." The woman, who Cheyenne assumed was the manager, frowned. "I have to admit that I'm ticked off with her for just walking away like that without giving me any notice, but ultimately I do wish her luck."

"Even though she just walked out on you like that?" Jefferson asked, trying to reconcile the two stories.

"What can I tell you? From the very first day she started working here, Lauren always inspired nothing but feelings of goodwill and loyalty. Until she inexplicably decided to play hooky, she was always the most dependable, the most loyal person I ever encountered." Cecilia sighed. "I just know that I'm never going to find anyone else like her," the manager lamented.

"Do you have any idea why she would just take off the way she did? Maybe she had an argument with one of the people she worked with or…?" Cheyenne's voice trailed off, leaving a space for the manager to fill in a reason if she was able to do that.

The restaurant manager shook her head, appearing at a total loss.

"Believe me, I did ask around. If there was some sort of an argument that caused Lauren to just walk out, no one here knows anything about it, or at least they aren't admitting to it. Besides, in my opinion, that sort of thing just wasn't her style. I think I knew her well enough to say that if there was a problem, she would have dealt with it, not just walked out without so much as a backward glance." The restaurant manager just sighed. "If you ask me, this is a really big mystery," she admitted.

"Do you think that something could have happened to her?" Cheyenne asked the woman.

"Like what? A car accident?" the manager asked. "I think I would have heard about it," she told them. "Or one of the other girls would have read or heard about it and told me."

"Maybe someone took her prisoner or did something to her," Jefferson quietly suggested, watching the woman's face to see what her reaction to that would be.

It was clear that the very idea horrified the restaurant manager. Her eyes widened. "You don't really think that happened, do you?"

"We're not about to rule anything out for certain until we check out every possibility," Jefferson told the restaurant manager.

"If you hear anything or think of anything," Cheyenne told the woman, taking out her business card and putting it into her hand, "please don't hesitate to call us—day or night," she emphasized.

The woman stared at the cárd in her hand, as if committing what was written on it to memory. "I will," she whispered, more to herself than to the police detectives standing before her.

Satisfied that the manager was taking the instruction to heart, Cheyenne continued. "If you don't mind, we'd also like to talk to the other people that Lauren knew and worked with."

"Of course, of course," the restaurant manager agreed wholeheartedly, bringing them over to the women who were working the counter and the register. The two women had been covertly watching them since they had begun talking to the manager.

"We'll keep it brief," Jefferson promised, thinking that the mere idea of questioning these women might wind up scaring them off.

An hour and a half later, Cheyenne and her partner were no closer to discovering just what had happened to Lauren Dixon, what had caused her to disappear off the face of the earth, than they had been when they'd first walked in. No one Lauren had worked with had any sort of clue as to what had happened to her.

"You want to go to the junior college and question the people there? Maybe they have an idea about what happened to Lauren Dixon," Jefferson suggested to his partner.

Cheyenne unlocked her car and waited for him to get in on his side. "Well, we do have a few hours of daylight left, we might as well use it," she speculated. Heaven knew that this mystery was not about to solve itself, she thought.

"Do you know what class or classes Lauren was taking at the college?" Jeff asked as he got into Cheyenne's car. "In other words, where do we start?"

"We start at the registrar's office," she told her partner. "With any luck, Lauren Dixon won't have been enrolled in too many classes. That'll keep the number of people we need to talk to and interview hopefully down to a manageable minimum." Cheyenne crossed her fingers for a second, holding her hand up in the air, before starting her vehicle and taking the wheel.

Aurora Valley College was located along Aurora's old main thoroughfare. Initially it had been an incredibly small college. It had grown over the last twenty-five years, almost doubling in size as the years went on.

Fortunately, the registrar's office had remained in the exact same location it'd been since the school was erected.

Cheyenne didn't hesitate when it came to parking her vehicle. She pulled the car up into an area meant just for visitors rather than students or instructors.

Turning off her engine, she told her partner, "We'll

start here. Hopefully, we'll have better luck than we had with Lauren Dixon's place of work."

"You know there is a possibility that Lauren Dixon might have just gotten fed up with her life and decided to take off," Jefferson said.

"From everything her daughter told us, that woman was not the type to just take off on a whim. Lauren sounded extremely dependable. That meant she would have told one of her daughters or one of her friends what she was planning on doing. Given the personality Eve said her mother had, she was not the type to disregard people's feelings and just do whatever she wanted to on a whim."

Jefferson followed his partner as she led the way to the registrar's building. "Do you think Lauren Dixon is one of the women lying in our morgue?"

"I sincerely hope not," Cheyenne answered her partner with feeling. "But right now we honestly have no way of knowing." Pausing, she stopped outside the door and read the words written on it that declared it was the main registrar office. "Looks like this must be the place," she said to her partner just before she opened the door.

A harried-looking woman looked up as Cheyenne and Jefferson walked in. She made no effort to disguise the sigh that escaped her lips.

"May I help you?" the woman asked in voice that indicated she was clearly stressed out.

Cheyenne and Jefferson took out their credentials almost simultaneously and held them up for the woman's viewing.

"Detectives Cavanaugh and McDougall," Cheyenne told the woman. "We're with the Aurora police's Cold Case Department. We would like to speak to someone about one of the students who was enrolled at Aurora Valley College."

"Which student?" the woman asked, addressing her question to Jefferson.

"Her name is Lauren Dixon," Cheyenne said, answering the woman behind the counter, who stopped what she was doing and went to a computer located on the other side of the room.

"What was that name again?" the woman asked.

"Lauren Dixon," Jefferson repeated. "We were told that she was enrolled here this semester."

"We don't have semesters, we have quarters," the woman corrected with a flicker of a smile as she pulled up the current registration lists and looked up the missing student's name. "Lauren Dixon. Is that the traditional spelling?" she asked. This time she addressed her question to both of them. "These days, everything is subject to some fancy change or other," the woman explained.

"Traditional spelling," Cheyenne answered. Then, as she spelled the missing woman's name for the clerk's benefit, she also held up the photograph the woman's daughter had given them so that the clerk had a visual aid. "This is what she looks like, in case she might have had a reason to come in recently."

Cheyenne hoped that the photo might jar the clerk's memory if that were the case.

There was no sign of recognition in the woman's eyes as she looked at the picture. She shook her head.

"Sorry. This office sees a lot of foot traffic during each quarter. When was she supposed to have been registered here?" she asked.

"This quarter," Jefferson said, going by their most recent information, then added, "Last quarter for sure."

The woman smiled at him before going through the listings. "Lauren Dixon, you said?"

"Yes," Jefferson answered the woman, watching her face.

After a few moments, the woman located the name. "She signed up for two classes this quarter, both given in the evening."

"Could you give us the names of the courses and the instructors who are teaching them?" Cheyenne requested. She was still hoping they might be able to jar someone's memory.

"I'll be happy to, but Professor Jon Murphy isn't in today. His class is in the lecture hall. Dr. Joanna Barnes, the other instructor, is in, though. One out of two isn't bad," the woman told Jefferson, flashing a smile at him.

"When is Professor Murphy in?" Cheyenne asked.

"He might be in tomorrow. He'll definitely be in on Monday. But like I said, Dr. Barnes is in tonight. She's teaching," the woman said.

"If you give us her room number, we'll be out of your hair," Jefferson promised.

The woman wrote down the class and room number and then handed the sheet of paper to Jefferson. "You can be in my hair anytime," she told him with a wide, inviting smile.

Avoiding the woman's eyes, Jeff folded the paper and then handed it to Cheyenne. "Thank you," he told the woman, then followed his partner out of the building.

Chapter 11

"I think that woman in the registrar's office would have been more than happy to take you over to the professor's lecture hall," Cheyenne observed.

"Well, to be honest, I got the feeling she was more than happy to be rid of us," Jefferson emphasized, calling an end to the conversation.

Cheyenne had left her vehicle parked right outside the office. He stopped right next to it. "Do you want to drive over there, or should we just walk?"

Glancing at the paper the woman in the registrar's officer had given them, Cheyenne shook her head. "This is close enough for us to walk to. Class starts on the hour. With luck, we can catch Professor Barnes just as she arrives and before she starts to teach her class. That way we'll be able to ask her a few questions about Lauren Dixon."

"You've got this all worked out, don't you?" her partner asked. There was a note of admiration evident in his voice.

"I used to attend this college," she told him, then amended, "at least, Aurora Valley was my starting point."

"Your starting point," he repeated as they continued to walk. "What happened?"

That was easy enough to explain. "The second I got my grades up, I transferred to the University of Aurora." The latter had a lot more to offer. She saw the question in Jefferson's eyes and quickly explained the difference to him. "Aurora Valley is a two-year college. The University of Aurora is a four-year college and rather well regarded."

Her partner nodded. The names of the universities were all new to him. "Consider me educated," he told her. He looked at her profile and asked, "Did you like going to Aurora Valley?"

She shrugged slightly. "It had a nice, homey feel. It was a good place to get your feet wet starting a college education," she told him. "It was definitely not too overwhelming or intimidating a place to start out."

The words *to start out* stuck in his head. "But you didn't stay the full two years."

Cheyenne shrugged again, then grinned. "I suppose that I wasn't overwhelmed or intimidated for very long."

Jefferson nodded. "I wouldn't think that you would be. You don't strike me as the type to be intimidated." He saw his partner stopping before a large round building. This had to be the lecture hall, he thought, but just to be on the safe side, he asked, "Is this where Professor Barnes is teaching?"

Cheyenne smiled at him in response. Some of the landscaping had changed at Aurora Valley, but not this area. "Yes, this is it," she confirmed. "We've got a little less than fifteen minutes before class starts."

He opened the door for her, but before she walked in, he told her, "I think that you should do all the talking."

His statement took her by surprise. "Any particular reason why?"

"Yeah," he confirmed with a smile. "You can talk a lot faster than I can, which means you can get a lot more words out," Jeff told her.

She gazed at him a little uncertainly. "You know, I don't know if I should be flattered or insulted by that comment."

"It's just a given," he told her. "But if you're torn and waffling between leaning in one direction or the other, I'd say you should go with being flattered. I didn't mean it as an insult."

"Flattered it is," Cheyenne told him with an amused, agreeable smile as she walked into the hall ahead of her partner.

The thing that first struck Cheyenne was how dimly lit the lecture hall was. She paused, as did her partner, then took baby steps into the hall, making sure that she didn't trip.

None of the students appeared to be there yet and the lighting took some getting used to. Adjusting to it definitely took at least a couple of minutes.

Cheyenne remained standing at one spot for a couple of seconds before she finally took a tentative step forward. She could feel her partner doing the same thing. He was following her lead. For a moment, she thought he would take her arm to help keep her steady and she had to admit, she rather liked the idea, although she wasn't about to say it out loud.

The dark-haired woman sitting at the desk on the raised platform looked up even though the people who had walked in had made absolutely no noise to alert her.

"Dr. Barnes?" Cheyenne asked, moving forward. Her partner didn't miss a step and was right there behind her.

Curiosity entered the professor's brown eyes as they swept over the strangers who had just walked in. "Yes?"

Cheyenne took out her wallet and flashed her identification for the woman to see. "We're detectives Cavanaugh and McDougall with the Aurora PD," she said, nodding at her partner, "and we're looking into the possible disappearance of one of your students."

The professor rose and came around her desk in order to look at the credentials. Verifying their authenticity, the professor nodded.

"You're talking about Lauren Dixon, aren't you?" she asked. A slight frown graced her lips.

That struck Cheyenne as a really good guess on the professor's part. In a class of this size, the instructor wouldn't have been aware of a missing student unless there was a good reason for it. This Lauren Dixon had to have made an impression on the lecturer and possibly the rest of her class.

"As a matter of fact, we are." The professor tilted her head, looking at the detectives quizzically. "How did you know that?" Cheyenne asked.

"I've had other students drop out or stop showing up to class during the school year, of course, but Lauren always struck me as being very conscientious about attending classes. When she stopped showing up to class, I actually got her home number from the registrar's office and called her to see what had happened and why she'd stopped coming."

"And what did you find out?" Jefferson asked, urging the instructor to get on with her story.

Professor Barnes shook her head. "Nothing. I didn't find out anything. Lauren never answered. I called her a couple of times and then I just gave up. I decided that if taking my class was important enough to her, she would eventually turn up." She looked at the two detectives. "Wouldn't she?" the instructor asked them, clearly wanting the detectives to agree with her.

"If she could," Cheyenne answered the professor guardedly.

The professor's brow furrowed as she looked from one detective to another. "Meaning that she can't?" Barnes questioned, looking somewhat unnerved.

"That's what we're trying to ascertain," Cheyenne told the instructor honestly.

"Did she just take off?" Barnes asked, attempting to get a handle on the situation.

"That would be the simplest explanation," Jefferson said. "If you don't mind, Professor, when your students file in, would you possibly be able to point out the ones who you knew were friendly with Mrs. Dixon? Maybe they can tell us something that might be able to help our search."

The professor nodded. She looked more than willing to help find the missing woman. "When they come in, I can ask the class if any of them were friendly with Ms. Dixon. To be honest, I really don't know who she socialized with and who she didn't, but I can certainly ask. Maybe someone in the class can give us some insight into the situation." The professor was obviously curious and appeared as if she felt she was facing an honest-to-goodness mystery.

"Any help you can provide us with will be more than gratefully appreciated," Jefferson told the professor.

The woman seemed to brighten up right before their very eyes in response to Jefferson's statement. "I am more than happy to do my part in finding Mrs. Dixon. It's really hard to believe that in this day and age someone can just disappear off the face of the earth this way," the professor lamented. "We have to be able to find her."

Just then the instructor was interrupted by the sound of raised voices as students began walking into the lecture hall.

Most of the students looked to be in their early- to midtwenties, Cheyenne judged, watching them filing in. Those students, she thought, would have little to nothing in common with the missing woman. But she noticed a few students, women for the most part, were the missing Lauren Dixon's age, or close to it. With any luck, Lauren had shared confidences with these people. If she and Jefferson talked to the students, they might be able to find out something pertinent that would help them discover what might have happened to Lauren Dixon.

As the ninety-five or so students filed into the auditorium and took seats that could be described as being around the lecturer, many of them threw curious glances in the strangers' direction.

The professor waited for her students to be seated before she addressed them.

"Ladies and gentlemen, you might have noticed that we have visitors in our lecture hall." She looked around the room, making eye contact with a great many of her students. "They are investigating what happened to one of your fellow students. According to her family, Lauren Dixon, the lady who always sat up front and to the left side—" the professor pointed the area out "—has been missing from her home. They are hoping that one of you might be able to provide a clue as to where she might have gone. Do any one of you have any idea as to what might have happened to Lauren Dixon or where she might have gone?"

There was a low murmuring of voices as this was discussed among several of the older students.

"Can any of you provide us with any insight into Ms. Dixon's dealings?" the professor asked.

There were more voices murmuring, but no one seemed as if they had any information to volunteer. Nor did they appear to be holding back a secret.

It was a case of no one knowing anything, Cheyenne thought.

Cheyenne decided to try to appeal to the students' sense of sympathy.

"Professor Barnes has our cards and can get in contact with us, If anyone knows anything at all, no matter how small it might seem, we would really appreciate you letting us know. Put yourselves in the family's position," she said to the students in the lecture hall. "What if this was one of you and your family was going through hell, wondering what had happened to you and why no one had any insight into what might have happened to their loved one? The slightest hint you can provide us with will be greatly appreciated," Cheyenne said, scanning the faces of the students sitting in the lecture hall.

"She kept to herself, but I know she liked the material we were assigned to read," one older student volunteered, speaking up.

Cheyenne did her best not to show her disappointment over this lack of insight. Instead, she nodded and thanked the person who had volunteered this meager piece of information. "Thank you."

"Does anyone have anything else to add?" Jefferson asked. He scanned the faces that appeared to be focused on him and his partner, but no one seemed to have anything more to add.

And then one of the older students raised her hand. When Cheyenne called on her, the woman added, "I know she liked this class more than she liked going to her other class, even though she liked that reading material, too."

"What class was that?" Jefferson asked before his partner had the chance. He wanted to be sure they were on the same page and that the student was talking about the same class.

"Professor Murphy's class," the woman told them, confirming the impression.

"Professor Murphy's class?" Cheyenne asked. She was vaguely familiar with the name, but she didn't really know the instructor. She told herself that she really needed to get her hands on the present class schedule. "Murphy" was a common enough name. Maybe the college had more than one Professor Murphy.

"He lectures on he development of murder mysteries throughout the ages," another one of the students answered, raising her voice. "I take that class, too. Professor Murphy makes it sound so realistic, I have to admit that he gives me the creeps," the woman confided. She shivered to emphasize her point.

"Why is that?" Jefferson asked.

The woman sighed, then said, "He takes such relish in going over all the fine points of murdering a victim," the woman emphasized. "I swear his eyes light up."

Cheyenne exchanged glances with her partner. "We need to talk to the professor as soon as we can. Where can we find him?" she asked Professor Barnes, hoping to get a different answer than the one provided by the woman in the registrar's office.

"He's got a class on Monday," the professor told them, repeating what they're already gleaned from her colleague.

That wasn't good enough, Cheyenne thought. She was experiencing one of those famous Cavanaugh gut feelings several of her uncles and cousins liked to talk about. They needed to pin this man down. "We need to speak to Professor Murphy before Monday. Which means that we're going to have to go back to the registrar's office so we can get the man's home address," she told Professor Barnes as well as her partner. She turned toward Professor Barnes. "Unless, of course, you have it."

But the instructor adamantly shook her head. "Sorry. Professor Murphy and I don't socialize off-campus. We hardly socialize *on* the campus," she emphasized.

"Any particular reason for that?" Cheyenne asked the woman.

The professor turned her back toward her students in order not to be overheard. "Between you and me, the man has a way of looking at you that seems to go straight through you. He makes me shiver," she confided to the two detectives. "I know I'm not being very fair, but very frankly, I am much too busy to care about that. I have too many students to juggle, too many papers to grade."

"We understand," Jefferson told her. "Thank you for your help and for allowing us to invade your lecture hall, Dr. Barnes. But right now, if we want to catch the woman in the registrar's office before she leaves for the night, I'm afraid we really need to get going."

"Of course, of course." The professor walked out with Cheyenne and her partner. "If you think of anything else that you might need, don't hesitate to let me know," she said, and to the professor's credit, she addressed her words to both of the police detectives, not just to Jefferson.

Cheyenne nodded her head. "We'll be sure to do that," she promised the professor, then turned toward her partner. "Okay, McDougall, let's get going," she urged the man.

She noticed that her partner nodded at the instructor as they left. Several of the students noticed as well—and sighed as their thoughts appeared to take off, creating potentially interesting scenarios.

Chapter 12

When they approached the registrar's office, Wanda, the woman who ran it, was just in the process of locking up and going home. Jeff quickened his pace, managing to get in the woman's way before she was able to leave.

"We need a word—Wanda," he called out, belatedly remembering the woman's name.

Startled, the woman turned around. When she saw who was calling to her, she smiled and waited for the detectives to approach her.

"I'm in a hurry. It's my night to make dinner," she explained, appearing to be rather antsy about what she was telling them. Smiling, she told Jefferson, "You're going to have to talk fast."

Jeff grinned. "Fast talking is my partner's specialty," he told the woman as he looked at Cheyenne.

The woman raised one eyebrow as she looked in Cheyenne's direction. "Okay, so talk," she urged.

"We need you to give us Professor Murphy's home address," Cheyenne told the woman.

Looking extremely apologetic, Wanda shook her head. "I'm afraid that the college isn't at liberty to release that kind of information."

"You said that Professor Murphy wouldn't be back at the college until Monday," Cheyenne reminded the woman.

"He won't be—" Wanda began.

"I'm afraid we can't wait until Monday," Cheyenne told the woman. "We need to question Professor Murphy as soon as possible." She paused, then added, "The matter might involve a murder victim—"

Wanda held up her hand to stop the flow of conversation before it could get too far. "The professor isn't home," she told them.

"Why? Where is he?" Jeff asked, putting the question to her.

Wanda shook her head. "All I know is that this is the anniversary of his aunt's death and he said something about planning on visiting her grave."

"Which is where?" Cheyenne prodded. Wherever it was, she and Jeff could stake out the area and wait for the professor to show up. Who knew? It might even wind up providing them with an important clue. At least she could hope.

But Wanda shook her head. "I honestly haven't a clue," the woman confessed. "He never told anyone where it was."

"Who would have that information?" Cheyenne asked the woman.

She shrugged her shoulders, at a loss. "I really don't know. Professor Murphy doesn't talk to anyone that I know of. To be honest, the professor gets here just before his class starts and then he teaches his students." The wind was picking up and Wanda drew her collar up and pulled her coat closer around her to shut out the cold. "Sometimes, if the students have any questions for him, Murphy does stay after hours. But that really doesn't happen all that often.

"Most of the time, from what I hear, the students are in a rush to leave and go home themselves. The professor's class is the last one of the evening. It is pretty late right now. And since there's no class tonight—" the woman gestured around the area "—there isn't anyone around for you to ask."

"And you really don't have his address on file?" Cheyenne pressed.

"We do," Wanda admitted, "but like I said, it is a privacy issue and I am not able to release it. Besides, even if I did, most likely the professor is not going to be there anyway."

Jefferson's eyes met the woman's. "Even so, keeping that in mind, could you give us the address anyway?" he asked.

"I would really like to," Wanda told him in all

sincerity. "But I can't give it to you without risking losing my job," she said honestly.

"We wouldn't tell anyone," Cheyenne promised, although she had a feeling that really wouldn't do the trick and change the woman's mind.

"Well, maybe you wouldn't, but if the professor somehow got wind of his address getting out, like I said, I would lose my job." She lowered her voice as she shared how she felt about the situation. "Professor Murphy is *not* the forgiving type and I really need my job. I am the only source of income for my widowed mother as well as for myself." She attempted to shift the detectives' focus away from the topic. "Professor Murphy said he would be in early on Monday. Well, early for him," she clarified.

"And that would be—?" Cheyenne prodded, wanting the woman to pinpoint a time.

Wanda thought for a moment, wanting to be as accurate as possible. "On Mondays Professor Murphy is in at four," the woman told the two detectives.

Cheyenne exchanged glances with her partner. "I guess we'll be here on Monday right before four o'clock," she told Jefferson.

"I wouldn't suggest getting here too much before four," Wanda cautioned, then said, "I've never known the professor to come in early."

Jefferson laughed drily under his breath. "I think I'm in the wrong line of work."

Cheyenne made no comment until they left the building. "Do you get a sense of satisfaction when you solve a crime?" she asked her partner as they walked out and headed back to her car.

"Well, yeah," her partner said, wondering what she was getting at. "I wouldn't be here if I didn't."

"Then I'd say you're in exactly the right line of work," she told him. "There's no satisfaction in shirking your responsibility—if you did that sort of thing."

Jefferson thought for a moment. "I guess you're right."

She grinned at him. "Thanks. I generally am. Okay," Cheyenne declared. "Let's call it a night. I'll bring you back to your vehicle in the precinct parking lot. Tomorrow we can look into seeing if either of the other two faceless women has an identity we can actually attempt to pin down. Maybe we'll get lucky," she told him. "In any case, we have my uncle's party to go to on the following day."

Jefferson had almost forgotten all about the party she had invited him to. "Oh, about that," her partner began.

Cheyenne glanced in his direction. "No," she told him flatly.

"No?" Jefferson asked.

"No," Cheyenne repeated, then explained, "The time to wiggle out of having to attend my uncle's birthday party has come and gone, Jefferson. My uncle Andrew wants to meet you and this birthday party for him is going to be the easiest way to accomplish that. Actually," she amended, "my whole family is looking forward to meeting you."

"I've already met some of them," Jefferson reminded her. For some people, he thought, that would have been enough.

"You met *a couple* of them," Cheyenne pointed out. "But definitely not anywhere near all of them. You have to remember that the Aurora police force is actually more like the family business than anything else. So no more arguing, McDougall. You're coming, no ifs, ands, or buts," his partner told him forcefully. Her eyes all but pinned him in place. "Have I made myself clear, McDougall?"

He laughed as he absorbed his partner's words. "Crystal," he told her, then asked, "Has anyone ever told you that you're really bossy?"

"You want that answer alphabetically or chronologically?" she asked her partner.

"Then I take it that the answer to that is yes, huh?" he asked her.

"Well, except for a few cousins in that group, the answer is that it's mostly my brothers saying so," Cheyenne answered, lifting her shoulders, then letting them drop in a casual shrug. "Sorry. I'm afraid that you're not being very original."

"I wasn't trying for originality," her partner admitted. "I was just trying to make a point." And they both knew what that was, he thought.

"Consider it made," she answered with a small, soft smile. "Look, for this partnership to work, McDougall, we always have to be honest with one another. No tiptoeing around important points, and just practicing basic honesty," she emphasized. And then she raised her eyebrows. "Have I made myself clear?"

"Well, if you want honesty..." her partner began, doing his best to try to get his point across.

"I do, but we're moving away from that subject now," she told him. "Besides, you wouldn't want to insult the rest of my family. As a rule, they're not a vindictive bunch of people, but they don't take well to having their own insulted and the first thing that would come to mind for them is that you're my partner and you're shining me—and them—on by not attending the birthday party if you choose to skip it."

Jefferson nodded. "Well, I certainly wouldn't want to do that," he assured Cheyenne. And then he smiled at her. Cheyenne caught herself thinking that the man really did have a very nice smile. "To be honest," her partner told her, "I really wouldn't mind meeting your family all at once. I just wanted to see what you'd say if I told you I wasn't going to show up."

They got to her car and got in. "Well, for one thing, I wouldn't recommend you flashing that sense of humor around them. It might not be taken well," she warned him.

"Duly noted," he told her.

It took only a few more minutes for Cheyenne to arrive at the precinct parking lot. Because of the time of day, the lot was for the most part empty.

Entering it via the back way, she was able to pull up next to her partner's car before stopping her vehicle.

"Tomorrow, I'll give you my uncle's home address, but that'll be strictly for your own information. I've decided to pick you up at the apartment you're renting and take you to my uncle's house myself. It'll be easier for you that way."

"You don't have to do that. I can get myself there," Jefferson promised her.

"I know that," she answered. "But this way, you can enjoy a few drinks without worrying about driving with a higher alcohol content than you should have."

"Don't worry, the new guy has no intention of getting drunk," he assured her.

But Cheyenne wanted to cover all the bases, just in case. "Well, this way the 'new guy' won't have to worry if he decides to have one too many—or more."

He didn't want her getting the wrong idea about him. "I appreciate that, but—"

Cheyenne pulled her lips back into a wide smile. "No 'buts,' partner," she told him, then glanced at her watch. "Time for me to get going, but for that to happen, you need to get out of my car." She looked pointedly at the passenger door.

Jefferson nodded. "And that would be my cue," he declared, his hand on the door latch. He pushed it open. "See you tomorrow, partner."

Cheyenne nodded. "Same time, same place," she said, her eyes sparkling.

And with that, Cheyenne took off feeling rather accomplished.

She needed to get her sleep. Tomorrow already looked as if it had all the makings of another very long day. She intended to check out the address that was on file for Jon Murphy to see if the professor actually was gone for the weekend, or if he was just sending up a smoke screen to hide where he really was.

There were also those two other faceless bodies lying in their morgue whose identities were still a complete mystery. She didn't think that she and her partner would be able to find out who they were, but who knew? Maybe they would get lucky.

Negative thinking never solved anything.

It was a short drive from the precinct to her home. Cheyenne pulled up in front of her garage in a few minutes and decided to park her vehicle at the curb. She was too tired to maneuver her car into the garage, certainly not without nicking it. Besides, this way she could just hop into her car in the morning and take off.

Granted it only shaved a couple of minutes off her departure time, but in her opinion, every little bit helped. Besides, she silently argued with herself, she did have a new partner to set an example for and from what she had gathered, he seemed to like coming in early. It wouldn't do to be shown up by the detective she was in the process of training, she thought, despite the fact that she had gotten him in a completely pretrained mode.

Getting out of her car, Cheyenne hit the button

that locked all four doors simultaneously, then made her way to the front door. She opened it and caught herself wishing that she had a pet dog or cat waiting to greet her.

It wasn't the first time she had entertained this thought. Most of her family had either pets or children, not to mention significant others waiting for them to come home to.

For some reason, the house felt lonelier to her tonight. It undoubtedly had to be all this talk about her uncle's party being thrown Saturday and her family showing up.

She should have gotten more involved in the planning stages, Cheyenne thought. Being busy planning a family get-together would have probably taken the edge off this odd loneliness that seemed to insist on nibbling away at her.

Cheyenne turned on the light as she entered the two-story house. Maybe she needed to get one of those devices that turned the lights on after a certain time, she thought. It wouldn't feel as empty—or as lonely—walking into the house after sundown—and she always came in after sundown, she thought.

Tomorrow, she promised herself as she stepped out of her shoes. She'd think about all this tomorrow. If she didn't get to bed right now, she wasn't going to be good for anything come tomorrow.

With that, Cheyenne stripped off her clothes one piece at a time as she quickly made her way into her bedroom. Tomorrow, if there was any extra time, she was going to look into getting a pet, she promised herself.

Anything except a goldfish.

Cheyenne smiled to herself. After all, she thought, she couldn't very well hug a goldfish.

Chapter 13

Cheyenne got into the office the next morning barely ahead of her partner, which meant that she had gotten in extremely early.

Consequently, the day wound up feeling as if it was at least thirty-six hours long—maybe even longer.

After spending an hour attempting to do further research to ascertain if the woman they were looking into was indeed the mother that Eve Richardson had asked them to find, they decided to temporarily suspend that search until they were able to talk to Professor Murphy face-to-face.

Closing her folder, Cheyenne looked up at her partner.

"Let's see if the bodies in the morgue wind up triggering anything for us or not," Cheyenne told him after an hour of futile searching had gone by.

"Well, you sold me. Doing that is better than going around in circles, getting cross-eyed looking through the files," Jeff agreed.

Cheyenne took her time getting up. As she rose to her feet, she looked at her partner. "I get the feeling that whoever did this is one and the same person." She paused for a second as she searched his face. "How about you?"

Jeff reviewed the points that they had discovered that the victims had in common. "Their fingerprints were rubbed off. The same could be said for the women's facial features. Not exactly something that's usually done in a run-of-the-mill murder. So yes, I think that the same person could very well be behind these slayings."

Though she didn't know him all that well yet, her gut told her that Jefferson wouldn't be saying that if he didn't believe it.

"Nice to know that we're on the same page, Jefferson," she said to her partner.

He nodded. "Still remains to be seen if that page is empty or not," he told Cheyenne.

"You really are a happy-go-lucky person, aren't you?" she asked the man with a touch of sarcasm.

He didn't take offense at her words. Instead, he shrugged and told her, "I have been known to be, at times. It depends on the crime and on what was going down at the time. This crime, however, does not fall in the simple range." He knew she knew that, but he reviewed the reasons he thought that way. "Think of the time it must have taken to rub off not just the fingerprints, but the victim's facial features as well."

"The time and the stomach," Cheyenne pointed out, doing her best not to envision the crime or allow it to get to her. "My guess is that it takes a strong kind of stomach to be able to look at a person and then eliminate every single one of their facial features."

She couldn't help shivering as she considered someone doing that sort of thing.

"If you want my thinking on it," her partner said, "My guess is that sort of gruesome undertaking probably gave the person a great deal of satisfaction. Possibly he felt like he was doling out overdue justice."

"To the person he was killing?" Cheyenne asked, trying to ascertain exactly what her partner was thinking.

"Or to the person who that victim represented," her partner suggested.

"So you think the killer felt he was meting out justice?" Cheyenne asked, intrigued and trying to get to the bottom of what her partner was thinking.

"Did you ever see a little kid getting angry at a toy and beat it up? You know that the toy is an inanimate object that couldn't have done anything to the kid to merit that sort of reaction, but he still beats up on it for some imagined slight or wrongdoing. Well, in a way this is kind of the same thing. The killer feels he's correcting some sort of wrongdoing that he suffered at the hands of the person that the victim obviously represents."

"Which means that we're dealing with a real psychopath," she pointed out.

"Terrific," Jeff murmured with a shake of his head. "If that's the case, we really need to put an end to him."

"If we're right," Cheyenne qualified, "that isn't going to be as easy as you might think," she told him as they got into the elevator. She pressed for the basement, which was where the morgue was located. "First we're going to need to find the person who is killing these women, and in effect, attempting to wipe them off the face of the earth. For that to happen, we're going to need to take baby steps, McDougall. Baby steps," she emphasized as they got out of the elevator.

The medical examiner looked up from what he was doing when the two detectives walked into the man's autopsy room. He was one of several MEs who were on call to perform the autopsies. No one wanted to wear these medical professionals out. It was a rather gruesome business.

"Detective Cavanaugh," the medical examiner said, nodding at her. "And I take it that this is your new partner." He allowed his voice to trail off, waiting for the name to be filled in.

Cheyenne smiled. "Right as usual, Dr. Barlow. This is Detective Jefferson McDougall, fresh from a precinct in Texas," she told the ME. "Jeff, this is one of our medical examiners, Dr. Adrian Barlow."

Barlow, who was shorter than Cheyenne's new partner, nodded as he put his hand out to the new man. "Welcome to Autopsy, Detective McDougall." And then he looked at Cheyenne. "So, how's he working out? Is he filling your old partner's slot?" he asked genially.

"Well, I definitely miss Wade, but yes, he actually is. Rather admirably, I'm happy to report," she told the medical examiner.

Barlow nodded. "Good to hear. So, what can I do for you?" he asked, looking from Cheyenne's partner to the woman herself.

"Have you gotten any closer to finding out any of these women's identities?" Detective Cavanaugh asked the medical examiner.

The ME appeared far from happy. "I wish I could say yes and see that beautiful smile of yours, Detective Cavanaugh, but no, I am no closer to identifying these women now than I was when they were first brought in."

"Why don't we do what we did to try to narrow down that first woman who was brought in? Go through the photos of the women who were reported missing in the last six to nine months and try to match them as best we can to these bodies?" Jefferson suggested.

"The woman's daughter came in to tell us she was missing," Cheyenne reminded him. "We're still not a hundred percent positive that we have the right person. But it is beginning to look that way." She was going to hate having to notify that woman about her mother, if it came to that.

"No reason one of these other women couldn't belong to a relative who's trying to locate them," Jefferson brought up.

The medical examiner nodded in agreement. "I'm no detective, but that suggestion gets my vote," Barlow told Cheyenne.

Cheyenne sighed. "Well, we've got a full day ahead of us and we have to do something. That's as good a way to proceed as any, I suppose." Sometimes she really wished her job was a little easier. "Who knows? We might just get lucky."

Jefferson looked at his partner. "You know, I don't hear any enthusiasm in your voice."

"The enthusiasm materializes when we discover that we're actually on the right path," she answered Jeff. "Dr. Barlow, send me all the photographs that you've taken of these two women, along with any other information you might have, including their height and weight, so we have at least *something* to go on."

"Why don't I take care of making those copies?" Jefferson told his partner. He glanced toward Barlow. "The good doctor here already has his hands full."

Barlow smiled broadly at the suggestion. "I'd say that this new partner of yours is a definite step up from the last partner you had. If you ask me, Wade tended to be on the grumpy-old-man side of things," the medical examiner confided to Jeff. The doctor's words were accompanied with a rather broad wink.

"This will be my pleasure, Doctor," Jefferson told the ME. "If you could give me the photos and point me toward your copy machine," Cheyenne's partner requested, "I will be out of your hair as soon as possible."

The medical examiner reached for the files on a nearby table, turned and handed them to Jefferson. "There you go. I do need these back," the doctor emphasized.

"Don't worry, I just need to make copies. There's not much need for them on the open market, Doc," Jefferson told the older man.

Barlow chuckled. "If there was, I can tell you one thing. I'd be a rich man," the medical examiner quipped.

Jefferson smiled. "We're all shooting for that," Cheyenne's partner told the medical examiner.

"Then I hate to tell you this, but I'm afraid that you are definitely in the wrong profession, McDougall," Cheyenne informed her partner.

Jefferson laughed under his breath as he glanced at her. "You think?"

"Oh, I know," Cheyenne emphasized. "Believe me, I definitely *should* know. All my relatives are in law enforcement or at least in some form of law enforcement. There's not a rich person among us— unless you happen to count being rich in accomplishments."

"I don't know. You can't really buy anything with

accomplishments," Cheyenne's partner told her. "It's not exactly currency."

"No, not outright," Cheyenne agreed. "But you can certainly buy a great deal of goodwill with it."

"I'll keep that in mind if I'm ever in the market for goodwill," Jefferson told her. He saw the smile spreading over Cheyenne's lips and that did manage to get his curiosity up. "What?"

"You'd be surprised," she prophesized. "Stoking goodwill though actions happens more often than you might think."

He shrugged. "If you say so," he said. It was obvious to her that her partner didn't think so.

She grinned at him. "I do—and so will you. Your time to be convinced will come," she told him. "Most likely when you least expect it. Okay," she declared, looking at the collection of papers that he had made copies of after returning the originals to the ME. "Let's see if we can find a match to one of these in our recent photos of missing women."

Holding the photos and copies of the files in his hands, Jefferson gestured toward the exit. "Lead the way, O Fearless Leader," her partner said.

"I'm not fearless," Cheyenne denied. "I just happen to be a wee bit pushy."

Both men smiled at one another over that. But when she looked their way, she saw them holding up their hands in abject denial of what she could see they were actually thinking.

"I wouldn't have said that," the medical examiner protested.

"I certainly wouldn't have," her partner quickly assured her.

"Uh-huh," Cheyenne answered. "You're just worried that I'd sic my brothers on you. Well, you don't have to worry about that," she told them, raising her chin. "I fight my own battles if they're there to be fought," she assured the two men. Having said that, she turned her attention toward her partner. "Shall we go?" Cheyenne asked Jefferson.

He nodded. "Yes, ma'am."

Her eyes narrowed, making him think of a pending storm. "Don't 'ma'am' me, Jefferson. It makes me feel like I'm a hundred years old."

Jefferson collected the photos and the folders concerning the two bodies currently residing in the morgue that he had copied so that he and Cheyenne could pore over them and review.

"Well, you certainly don't look anywhere near that," he told her with a smile. "As a matter of fact, if you don't mind me saying it, you look damn good for someone not even a quarter of that age. Sexy, even," he told her with a wide smile.

"Now you have me thinking that I should be sending you over to the eye doctor," Cheyenne told him.

He shook his head as they left the autopsy area. "No, what you should do is just learn to take a compliment, partner."

"If I felt it was merited, I would," she began.

Jefferson held up his hand, stopping her before she could continue.

"Trust me, Cavanaugh, it is definitely merited. I figure that you've got to own at least one mirror. Otherwise you wouldn't be able to style your hair as well as you do. Am I right?" he asked her, his eyes meeting hers.

She felt a warm shiver going up and down her spine. "Just get on the elevator," she told him, gesturing toward it as she pressed the up arrow.

He smiled at her widely as he inclined his head, lessening the space between them. "With pleasure."

Cheyenne murmured something under her breath, but he figured he was better off not asking her to repeat it.

Chapter 14

Cheyenne didn't see it coming until just before it was time to call it a day and finally go home. Even then, she had almost missed it.

"McDougall, come look at this," Cheyenne called to her partner.

Jefferson got up and made his way around her desk and over to her. When he was standing behind her, Cheyenne pointed to a photograph of one of the recently dug-up victims who was presently lying in Autopsy. Cheyenne had the photograph on her desk.

"What does this look like to you?" she asked her partner.

About to go home, Jefferson came up behind her and looked at the area on the photograph she was pointing to. The photograph was of one of the two women who had been discovered buried in the forest and brought in a couple of weeks ago.

"Like something my mother would have definitely punished me for having in my possession as a kid," Jefferson admitted honestly.

Cheyenne nodded. "Good woman, your mother," she commented. "No little boy should be looking at pictures like that. But I'm talking about the victim's left wrist, not the rest of her." She tapped the specific area that she was referring to.

The detective leaned in closer to get a better look at the area being discussed. "Looks to me like some small animal decided to snack on the victim."

"Not entirely. The hungry little critter didn't get it all," she told her partner. "Look closer," she instructed Jefferson. "What do you see?"

Cheyenne caught a little whiff of her partner's aftershave lotion as he bent in over the photograph. It was a slightly heady scent.

The man did smell good, Cheyenne couldn't help thinking. For just a second, she felt aroused, then quickly locked away that feeling. This was neither the time nor the place for that sort of indulgence, she told herself.

He turned toward Cheyenne. Their faces were rather close to one another, Jefferson couldn't help thinking. He looked at the victim's left wrist again. "Is that part of a rose tattoo?" he asked his partner.

"That's what I saw, too," she told him. "Now we have at least part of a description to feed into the computer and look for." And *at least part* was better than nothing, she thought. "People have been caught from far less to go on," she told Jefferson.

"*If* that *is* part of a rose tattoo," Jeff said, squinting as he attempted to study the lower part of the dead woman's left wrist.

"My suggestion is that we make another copy of the photograph. We can each carry a copy with us. That way we can sleep on it and take another look at the tattoo in the morning."

"You mean at your uncle's party?" Jefferson asked, slightly bewildered.

"You know, ordinarily I'd say that isn't such a bad idea," she told her partner as they walked out of the room and into the elevator. "My family members tend to solve crimes together if something really stumps one of us," she told her partner. "But this *is* Uncle Andrew's birthday party and I don't want anything taking away from that, even though I know that Uncle Andrew really wouldn't mind. I know for a fact that he misses being mentally challenged by cases, but I don't think Aunt Rose would take kindly to us bringing 'work' to the party." Cheyenne smiled at the thought. "As it is, she's going to have all she can handle just keeping Uncle Andrew out of the kitchen and not attempting to cook anything."

"Cooking?" Jefferson questioned. Cooking for him meant putting a frozen meal into the microwave, pushing a few buttons and waiting for the prepackaged meal to be done.

Cheyenne nodded as she began to pack up her things for the day. "Yes. Uncle Andrew loves to cook. Cooking at a local restaurant was how Uncle Andrew put himself through school back in the day. And when circumstances necessitated his retiring early as the police chief from the force in order to take care of his five kids when his wife disappeared, he supported his family by going back to cooking."

"His wife disappeared," Jefferson repeated, somewhat bewildered. "Then your aunt Rose wasn't his first wife?" he asked, doing his best to understand and keep the family dynamics straight in his mind.

"Oh, she was. And is," Cheyenne told her partner as they walked out to the elevator.

He looked at her, really confused now. "Let me get this straight. She was lost, causing him to retire. And then she just suddenly turned up? Now I'm really lost."

"The answer is rather simple. Uncle Andrew and Aunt Rose never argued, but they did that night. Aunt Rose drove off in order to cool off. The area was having one of its really rare rainstorms and Aunt Rose wound up driving off the road and into the lake. Her car was found there the next morning, floating in the water. Empty.

"Uncle Andrew hired all sorts of people to search for her, but they didn't find anything. However, he never gave up," Cheyenne told her partner.

"Thirteen years later, while following a lead on a case upstate, Uncle Andrew's youngest daughter, Rayne, ran into a waitress at a diner that she thought looked a great deal like a photograph of Aunt Rose that she carried around in her wallet." Cheyenne pressed the down button to the elevator. "When Rayne went home, she immediately told her father about the waitress. Uncle Andrew lost no time in driving up to the diner to see for himself and check the woman out.

"Long story short—" Cheyenne said.

"Too late," Jefferson told her as they got off the elevator. "But please, continue."

Cheyenne gave her partner a look, then told him, "The waitress turned out to be Aunt Rose. The experience of plunging into the lake in her car was such a shock, it caused her to get amnesia. Uncle Andrew turning up at the diner, telling her the story about how they wound up being separated and then taking her back home with him eventually wound up jarring Aunt Rose's memory.

"I'm told," Cheyenne concluded, "that Aunt Rose hasn't taken a moment for granted since she came back to the land of the living when the whole story that Uncle Andrew told her finally sank in."

Standing at the outer door, ready to leave, Jefferson looked at his partner and whistled softly under his breath. "Wow."

"I guess that sums it up rather nicely," Cheyenne admitted with a wide smile.

"Makes my life seem really dull and boring in comparison," Jefferson answered.

"I certainly wouldn't call it dull and boring. You were in the Marines and when you completed your tour of duty, you joined the police department in El Paso, Texas. That hardly seems dull and boring to me," she pointed out to her partner.

"It all depends on where your focus is. Searching for a missing wife for thirteen years certainly requires a great deal of dedication and patience," he said with conviction.

"Tell you what," Cheyenne said brightly, one hand on the door, about to push it open. "This will definitely give you something to talk about with my aunt and uncle tomorrow."

Her comment caught him off guard. "Is that still on?" he asked.

"Why shouldn't it be?" she questioned. "Uncle Andrew's birthday hasn't changed dates and my aunt Rose is still throwing him the biggest party she can. Everyone is planning on coming—and 'everyone' includes you. Remember, Uncle Andrew is looking forward to meeting you, both as my uncle and as the former chief of the Aurora Police Department," Cheyenne said.

"What if I don't measure up in your uncle's opinion?" Jefferson asked Cheyenne.

"Only way that could possibly happen is if you turn out to be the serial killer we're looking for," she told the man. "You're not, are you?" she asked, tongue-in-cheek.

"Nope," he answered, shaking his head from side to side in denial.

"So you're fine," Cheyenne assured him. "I will be around to either pick you up at one o'clock, or have you follow me in your car to my uncle's house around that time. Your choice."

"You don't have to do that," he told her.

"I didn't say I *had* to," she pointed out. "I thought I made it clear that I *wanted* to. So, is one o'clock all right with you, or do you want to go earlier?"

"One o'clock is fine. I know I asked before, but I don't remember what you answered. Should I bring anything?" Jefferson asked her.

"And I told you just bring yourself and that'll be more than enough. If you really want to bring something…" Cheyenne began.

"Yes?" he asked, prodding eagerly.

"Bring a card," she told him.

He looked at her in disappointment and all but rolled his eyes. "That hardly seems like anything."

"A *nice* card," she underscored.

Jefferson sighed. Cheyenne was definitely not helping. "What's your uncle's favorite wine or alcoholic beverage?"

"Oh no, don't go that route. My other uncles and cousins will definitely inundate Uncle Andrew with enough alcohol to practically drown the man," she assured her partner. "It's very hard shopping for someone who says he doesn't want anything except for his family to be happy and well fed."

"I can see how that might be frustrating," Jefferson agreed.

"Just come and have a good time. That's guaranteed to make the man happy. Trust me," Cheyenne told her partner.

"You really are a selfless bunch of people, aren't you?" Jefferson asked, shaking his head in disbelief.

"That's what I've been trying to tell you," Cheyenne said. "Okay, I'll be by your apartment in the morning."

"I thought you said you'd be there at one," he said.

"What I meant is that we'll be at Uncle Andrew's at one, and since I never learned Dorothy's trick of clicking my heels together to instantly be transported to my destination, I'm going to have to be at your place before one o'clock."

"Dorothy?" he questioned, confused.

She looked at him to see if he was on the level. "Dorothy Gale. The heroine in *The Wizard of Oz*," she prompted, then said in disbelief, "You're kidding, right? Didn't you ever watch it on TV?"

"Sorry, I didn't have a traditional childhood. My mother didn't believe in wasting time with cartoons."

"*The Wizard of Oz* wasn't a cartoon, at least not in the beginning. It was a classic story written for children. I can see that there are a lot of gaps in your education. It'll give us something to talk about during those long stakeouts," she told him. "But right now, we need to hit the road in order to get some sleep. Okay, let's get going, partner."

"Right behind you," Jefferson told her as they walked toward the parking lot.

Cheyenne caught herself smiling. She found that she was enjoying being with Jefferson more and more with each passing day. The situation was becoming promising.

Chapter 15

It was a shame that she couldn't sleep in, given that this wasn't a workday and that for once, there weren't any emergency calls from the precinct sending her to the scene of some crime or other, or even anything remotely close to that. In all honesty, Cheyenne sincerely doubted that there would be, given that everyone knew that this was the former chief of police's birthday and close family members were all planning on being at the gathering, celebrating the occasion.

Of course there were patrolmen and women on duty, but in addition to that Aurora had never been exactly known for being the hub of any real ongoing crime wave, or anything even remotely like that.

But the moment she opened her eyes, Cheyenne

threw off her covers and was on her feet, making her way into the bathroom for a quick, bracing shower.

She was in and out, showered and dried in less than ten minutes.

Not exactly her personal best, she thought, but it would definitely do. Cheyenne wanted to get going as soon as humanly possible.

She dried her long blond hair and carefully put it up in the style she knew her uncle favored seeing on her. Finished arranging her hair, Cheyenne slipped into a soft, silky aqua dress that flirted with the tops of her knees and lovingly hugged her curves. After dealing with the ugliness she sometimes came in contact with on the job, Cheyenne savored the gentler, nicer moments that came her way. Her uncle's birthday definitely fell under that heading.

Once she finished putting on her makeup, Cheyenne critically surveyed the results from all angles. With a nod of her head, she decided that for once, she was satisfied.

She slipped on her high heels, grabbed her purse from the side table where she had dropped it the night before, and checked to make sure she had her car keys with her. She picked up the beautiful card she had chosen expressly for her uncle and then made her way to her front door.

Cheyenne caught her reflection in the mirror by the door and looked herself over one last time.

"Look out, Detective Jefferson McDougall—prepare to have your socks melted right off your feet," she murmured to the man who wasn't there.

With that, Cheyenne made her way out the front door, then paused to lock it. She tried the lock to make sure that it took and couldn't accidentally be opened.

This was a safe house within a very safe neighborhood that was domiciled in a very safe city, she thought, but she had learned that it never paid to be cocky when it came to personal safety. Taking the extra precaution was always a good thing because fate was always waiting to prove you wrong and cause things to wind up caving in on themselves.

She had learned a long time ago that if anything could go wrong, it definitely would.

It was a jaded way to approach things, but she knew that it was far from wrong.

Once in her car, it took her a moment to recall the address where her new partner was staying. When she did, she turned the ignition on, moved her foot off the brake and took off.

Jefferson lived less than fifteen minutes away from her own home, which in turn wasn't all that far away from where the police precinct was located. She liked that, liked being that close to work. From her point of view, it made things a great deal simpler.

It was an exceptionally nice neighborhood, she thought, taking the area in as she drove through it. She was familiar with every inch of Aurora in one form or another. The city itself had been built up in stages. This particular part of the development had been erected at a later time, after the university and hospital had been built.

Initially, there were only a handful of schools and shopping centers put into the area. Eventually things developed further and yet, remarkably, Aurora never had that crowded, overdone look to it, she marveled. From a very young age, when things like this began to sink in, Cheyenne found herself never wanting to live anywhere else but right here in Aurora.

She couldn't help wondering what her partner thought of it, coming from Texas the way he had.

That was why she had joined the rest of her family in law enforcement. She wanted to keep her city peaceful and orderly, free of any wrongdoers—like the serial killer she suspected was currently haunting Aurora's streets. She was itching to bring that man's reign of terror to an end, and quickly.

"No, no shop talk," she told herself out loud. "Today is all about Uncle Andrew. Time enough to find and end this hateful man tomorrow."

She turned down a side street, following it to the next light, then into a residential development that was across from an area that contained four movie theaters.

Cheyenne thought that she hadn't been in one of those for a long time. There never seemed to be enough time for that, she realized. Any free time she actually managed to find she used to just kick back and relax—or at least tried to, she thought.

After parking her vehicle down the block, she got

out and made her way to the address she had input into her cell phone.

"124 Hamilton Street," she murmured to herself as she read it out loud. "This must be the place," she said in a comedic voice. Bracing herself, Cheyenne rang the doorbell. Within seconds, the front door swung open.

Jefferson was in the doorway, about to say something, but then the words seemed to just dry up on his lips, never managing to emerge as his mouth dropped open.

"Something wrong?" she asked him, not sure just how to interpret the look on her partner's face.

His eyes washed over her. It was obvious that he was enjoying what he was seeing. "No, not a thing," he told her with simple honesty.

"You're staring," she pointed out.

The look in his eyes was smiling at her. "I know," Jefferson acknowledged. "You clean up really well, Cavanaugh," he told her with a broad smile.

"Thank you. I wasn't aware that I needed cleaning up," she told him drolly.

"You don't, which is what makes looking at you this way such a fantastic pleasure," he informed his partner.

"I had no idea that you could lay it on so thickly," she said.

He merely grinned at her, his eyes washing over her again. "I guess there are a lot of things about me that you don't know yet," he said.

"I guess not. That's what working together is for, I

suppose. So we can learn about one another," Cheyenne told the man. "Not that you having that look on your face doesn't do a lot for my ego, but if you don't want one of my brothers taking you aside for 'a talk,' maybe you should find a way to table that expression for a while."

"I wasn't aware that I was looking at you in any particular way," Jefferson told her, doing his best to disguise the look on his face.

"You were," she said, reaching her vehicle as she smiled at him. "And if you really weren't aware of it, then maybe you're not as good a detective as I thought you were."

The detective's smile only broadened. "There's a reason behind everything. I'd hold off making a judgment if I were you."

She nodded. "No problem." She paused to look at him. "Now, do you want to follow me to the party, or would you prefer that I do the driving to my uncle's place?"

Jeff laughed under his breath. "I know my father would have hated to hear me saying this, but since you're familiar with wherever it is that we're going, why don't you just do the driving to the chief's house?" her partner suggested to her.

"You don't strike me as the type to raise your hands and just back away from something like driving a vehicle. You mind if I ask you why?" Cheyenne asked.

"It's very simple. I don't want to risk arriving at your uncle's place uptight," he said honestly. "Facing your entire family is enough of an uptight situation. Not to mention that the chief of detectives and the head of CSI are going to be there as well. That, in my opinion, is definitely facing a full plate. Actually, more than a full plate."

Cheyenne inclined her head and then nodded in response. "I can definitely accept that," Cheyenne told her partner.

He smiled at her. "Glad we're in agreement."

She started her car and put it in gear. "Ready?" she asked him whimsically as she pulled her car away from the curb.

Her question amused him. "If I said 'no,' would you pull over?"

"No," she answered, on the road. "I would however ask you why you suddenly changed your mind."

"I suppose that the best answer to that is that I'm a little worried about putting my best foot forward," he admitted.

"Don't be," she told him. "You got along well with the brothers you did meet at the bar that first day. The same goes for the cousins you met there." She glanced in his direction. "Maybe I shouldn't say this, but in my opinion, you seem to get along very well with just about anyone you meet or interact with," Cheyenne told him.

"Thank you. But why shouldn't you say it?" he asked. "It's not like I'm about to get a swelled head or lord it over anyone."

She spared him a quick look from the corner of her

eye. "No, I don't believe that you would. And you'll find that my entire family is incredibly easy to get along with."

Jefferson nodded his head. He was allowing this to mean too much to him, he thought. "Okay," her partner said, squaring his shoulders, "I'm ready to meet them."

"Good," she responded, adding, "because we're almost there."

She turned down the next street, then drove about half a block farther. That took her past a local inner park. By the time she reached the end of that, she stopped at a large two-story house that seemed to go on forever in both directions.

"Okay, Jefferson, we're here," Cheyenne finally announced.

Jeff's eyes grew huge as he looked at the house. "This? This is your uncle Andrew's house?"

"This is Uncle Andrew's house," Cheyenne acknowledged.

"It's huge," his partner declared as she drove past the building.

"Aren't we going in?" Jeff asked. "You just went by it."

"I know. Parking is going to be really tricky. I'm going to leave this car on the other side of the park," she explained. "There are a lot of people who're going to be coming to Uncle Andrew's house. We have to leave some space for them."

He thought that was being exceedingly thoughtful

of her, but he was beginning to see that that was her way. "This is some house," he commented, turning in his seat to get a better look at it.

"Uncle Andrew bought this house almost forty-five years ago," she told her partner. "Houses in Aurora were going for a song back then. Now it's a song, a dance and a lot of other things thrown in as well," she told him, her mouth curving. "Those early houses were a real bargain back then."

Cheyenne stopped her car and then pulled up the handbrake. "Ready?" she asked with a smile.

"Lead the way," her partner told her, gesturing beyond her vehicle.

She got out, rounded the hood and then waited for Jefferson to join her. When he did, they walked back to the house together.

"Remember," she coached, "My uncle is a very kind man. They are all very kind men—and women," she emphasized, watching her partner's expression. "And you are going to look back on today as the beginning of a brand-new life," she promised.

Jefferson had his doubts about that, but he wasn't about to argue with her, definitely not right before they walked into the house.

Later would take care of itself, he thought as he watched her open the front door and walk in.

Squaring his shoulders, Jefferson followed his partner inside.

Chapter 16

Andrew Cavanaugh did not look overly happy when Cheyenne and her new partner walked into the former chief of police's house. But it had nothing to do with them, or with the other dozen or so people who had arrived early to pay honor to the much-loved patriarch.

"She's banning me from my own kitchen," Cheyenne's uncle Andrew complained with feeling as he waved his hand in his wife's general direction. He couldn't remember a time when he had not been allowed into his own kitchen—*ever*.

Rose overheard him and raised her voice. "You are not supposed to be cooking for yourself, not to mention for a whole bunch of other people who are going to be here on your own birthday, Andrew,"

Rose told her husband. She turned toward Cheyenne. "Tell him he can't, please, Cheyenne."

There was sympathy in the young woman's eyes for both her uncle and her aunt. She sided with both of them for different reasons.

"He knows that, Aunt Rose." Cheyenne turned toward her uncle. "It's just that his cooking is really quite exceptional."

Feeling vindicated, Andrew smiled his thanks at his niece. But that thanks turned out to be short-lived.

"Even so," Cheyenne continued pointedly, "you have to allow people to do things for you, Uncle Andrew. Look at it this way, it makes them feel as good to do that as you feel when you're cooking for them."

Andrew raised his eyebrow. "She has the makings of a real negotiator, this one," the chief commented to Jefferson, nodding at Cheyenne. And then he looked more closely at the young detective. "I take it that you're the new partner I've heard so much about."

Jeff instantly put out his hand to her uncle Andrew, happy to officially meet the man. "Yes, sir. I'm Jefferson McDougall," he said, introducing himself.

Andrew inclined his head, making it seem that he was listening closely to the young man. "You're the one who came here from Texas, am I right?"

"Yes, sir. By way of the El Paso Police Department," Jeff said, quickly elaborating.

"McDougall was a Marine before he joined the

police department," Cheyenne told her uncle. She knew her uncle would be interested in that as well.

Andrew nodded. "All very good character-building experiences," the former police chief declared with approval. After a beat, the chief realized that he was hogging the spotlight. That just wasn't his way. "Well, come in, come in. Join the party," he urged, gesturing toward the large living room that was already beginning to become rather crowded. "Cheyenne can do the honors when it comes to the introductions."

"You can come join us," Cheyenne told her uncle, adding, "since you're not cooking or baking anything for once."

Andrew glanced over his shoulder in his wife's direction, a touch of concern etched into his face. "I think that I should hang around, staying close by," he explained to the two detectives who had just arrived. "You know, just in case Rose decides that maybe she actually *does* need me."

"I heard that," Rose said, raising her voice so that she could to be heard across the kitchen. She crossed over to where her husband and they others were standing. "Don't get me wrong, Andrew. I worship the ground you walk on, I always have. But I really *can* handle this."

"No one is saying that you can't handle it, dear," Andrew told his wife. "I just want to hang around so I can pretend to feel useful. You wouldn't want to deny me that on my birthday, would you?"

Rose laughed as she shook her head, then looked in Cheyenne and her partner's direction. "Who would have ever thought that my husband could actually be such a manipulator?"

Rather than be offended, Andrew laughed as he wrapped one arm around his wife's shoulders and hugged her to him. "You flatter me."

Rose laughed. "Hardly." She turned toward Cheyenne and the young detective with her. "Go. Mingle. Introduce this nice young man around. I promise I will call for help if it turns out that I need you."

The latter bent forward and brushed her lips against her uncle Andrew's cheek. "Remember to behave," Cheyenne teased him.

Turning toward her partner, she hooked her arm through Jeff's, drawing him into the large living room. "In case you missed it, that's our cue to go and mingle."

Beginning to leave the entrance, Jeff regarded his hostess and asked, "Do you need any help? I'm not much of a cook, but if you need anything else done, like potatoes peeled, glasses put out, beverages poured…" The detective's voice trailed off, letting the woman fill in the blank spaces the way she saw fit.

"Well, aren't you sweet?" Aunt Rose enthused. "But no," she replied, waving the duo on their way into the living room. "Everything is under control. You two just go on out and mingle. Introduce your partner to anyone who might not have met him yet,

Cheyenne, you can guess how confusing it is when you're the new kid on the block."

Cheyenne nodded.

"I can vividly sympathize with that feeling," she replied even though she had never experienced it herself. She looked at Jeff. "C'mon, 'new kid,' let's start getting you circulated."

Jeff allowed himself to be led off to join the cluster of family members gathered in the next room.

"Your aunt seems really nice," Jefferson told Cheyenne.

"I'd say that all my relatives are," Cheyenne said to her partner. "I told you that when you said yes to my invitation."

"Yes, you did," Jeff agreed. "But I didn't think you really meant it. That's something almost everyone says about their family to a stranger who they are inviting over for the first time."

Cheyenne fixed him with a look that was meant to put him in his place. She didn't like being lumped in with other people in this sort of fashion.

"I never say anything that I don't mean," she informed her partner.

"That would make you a very unique woman," he informed Cheyenne.

"What's that supposed to mean?" she asked him. "Are you trying to say that all women lie?"

"No, I didn't mean that they did it outright," he told her quickly, then added, "They just bend the truth once in a while."

"Well, I don't," she informed her skeptical partner sharply. "I'm a firm believer in either telling the truth, or saying nothing at all. Now, can we table this please, until we're not surrounded by members of my family?"

He was more than willing to leave the subject. "Sure, we can get back to this at a later date," Jeff told his partner genially. "Any time that you want to."

"Good," Cheyenne responded with a nod of her head. "Now, put your happy face on. I've got a whole bunch of cousins to introduce you to."

Jefferson glanced in her direction. "Is there going to be some sort of a quiz at the end of the evening?"

It wasn't easy, but Cheyenne found that she managed to maintain a straight face as she answered, "Yes," in confirmation. "You won't be able to leave my uncle's house and go home unless you are able to score at least eighty out of a hundred."

Jeff suddenly stopped moving and just stared at her. "You're kidding."

Cheyenne had a hard time answering his question without laughing out loud. "Yes, I'm kidding. Did your sense of humor get completely erased when you walked into my uncle's house?"

Her partner frowned. "No. It's just that you seem to be able to deadpan incredibly well."

"Next time I'll try to remember to snicker in between statements," Cheyenne promised, her mouth curving.

It was Jeff's turn to maintain a straight face while

answering. "Yes, I can see how that might be help-ful."

"So, you do have a sense of humor," she said as if that was some sort of a huge revelation in itself. The corners of her mouth curved as her eyes sparkled.

"Yeah, every once in a while, if I dig deep enough, I can actually find it," Jefferson told said.

Cheyenne nodded her head in approval. "Well, I suggest that you keep on digging. It definitely helps move the situation along," she told him with a warm smile. "Since the line of work we're involved in can be extremely grim, it really helps to have a sense of humor within reach. Otherwise what we do for a living and the people we come in contact with can wind up sucking every bit of joy right out of you and just leave you completely dry and empty on the inside."

Replaying her own words in her head, Cheyenne blew out a breath. "You know, I think that Uncle Andrew's birthday arrived just in time to make me feel better. Nothing like mingling with people you love to keep your mind moving on the straight and narrow."

"What if you didn't have any people you love?" Jefferson asked her.

She had a feeling that her partner was talking about himself. She could feel her heart going out to him. "Tell you what, I'll lend you some of mine," she told him, flashing a warm smile in her partner's direction. "No charge. As a matter of fact, I can start right now. Come meet my cousins, Dugan, Morgan and Sully," Cheyenne told him as she drew her partner over to the three men she had mentioned. All three looked very similar to each other.

But then, truthfully, Jeff had begun to feel that all the Cavanaughs, at least those who were related to one another by blood, seemed to have exceedingly similar features.

Cheyenne could almost tell what her partner was thinking. "They're my uncle Angus's sons," she said.

Jeff was beginning to feel rather lost as more and more names came flying in his direction. Nodding and smiling at the three men she had just introduced to him, he felt honor-bound to admit his confusion.

"Which is which?" he asked and then went on to say, "You know, this whole thing might be easier if you just wore name badges at this gathering. At least in the beginning when you have someone new attending," he told the group of cousins she had just brought him over to.

"There's no penalty for getting anyone's name wrong," Dugan, the tallest of the threesome, told Jefferson. "We know this has to be pretty confusing to someone new to the group."

"See, I told you they were nice," Cheyenne told her partner. "Besides, there's only one of you they have to meet, while you have a huge slew of relatives to attempt to keep straight. It definitely does get easier over time, but it's definitely not an immediate process."

"I guess I can live with that," Jeff murmured more to himself than to Cheyenne.

"That's the spirit," another cousin said, catching Jefferson's statement as he joined the group. He clapped Cheyenne's partner on the back. "Hi, I'm Murdoch," he told Jeff, shaking his hand.

"Murdoch," Jeff repeated. He caught himself thinking that it wasn't exactly a common name, at least to the best of his knowledge. "Hello," he said, doing his best to commit the man's face and name to memory.

Murdoch turned toward Cheyenne, taking her in as well. "I hear you two might have a cold case involving a serial killer on your hands," he said to his cousin. He looked extremely interested.

"Word does seem to get around," was Cheyenne's only comment on Murdoch's words.

But Murdoch was not about to drop the subject just yet. "How's that coming along?" he asked.

"Slowly," Cheyenne answered honestly. "Very slowly." She definitely was not happy about the pace. "Why do you ask? Surely you've got enough cases of your own to keep you busy," she told her cousin.

"Oh, I do, I do," he assured his cousin and her partner. "Except that now I think I might have a case on my hands that just might tie in with yours. Or at least might be connected to your killer."

Jeff's ears instantly perked up at that. "Send the evidence over on Monday morning," he told the other man. "But as intriguing as all this sounds, I think your aunt Rose might be upset if she finds us talking about serial killers—or police business in general—here today."

Dugan nodded, placing an arm around both Cheyenne's and Jeff's shoulders. "The new guy is right, little cousin. As interesting as this case might be, we don't want Aunt Rose getting wind of this."

"I don't find it interesting," Cheyenne informed Dugan. "I just want to stop this horrid person cold in his tracks."

"So do we," Dugan agreed. "But Uncle Andrew only has one birthday to celebrate. So let's celebrate it."

"Amen to that. So any of you catch that new mystery series that was on last night?" Morgan asked, deftly switching subjects.

He slowly looked at the faces of his brothers and cousins who were currently gathered together in a corner of the room. In his opinion, the program was basically a safe enough topic for him to be able to broach and talk about at the moment.

Chapter 17

His face turned ugly as he glared at the woman lying in a heap on the forest ground. "You shouldn't have scratched me, you bitch," he growled, running his hand over the fresh marks on his face.

Glancing down at his hand, he saw that there was blood on it.

That bitch had drawn blood! He fairly fumed.

The anger he felt increased tenfold. He could all but feel it flaring in his veins. If he hadn't already killed the woman, he would have done it right this minute. She certainly deserved it.

No loss, the instructor told himself. Lauren Dixon had thought of herself as a scholar.

A *scholar* of all things, he sneered.

The pathetic old woman should have been exceedingly grateful that he'd even allowed her to sit in on his lectures, much less looked at and graded the paper she'd handed in.

In his opinion, he had been generous, giving her a Sixty-five. If he had been honest, it would have been less than that. Much less than that. And then she had had the unmitigated gall to actually argue with him about it, telling him he wasn't being fair. That she deserved a better grade than that.

Deserved, of all things, he thought bitterly. He'd show her *deserved*, Murphy thought as he dragged the woman's freshly wrapped and covered body through the woods.

Because the old bat reminded him of his aunt Lily, he thought it only fitting that he bury her in the same area where he had once disposed of his aunt—though there wasn't a drop of oxygen left in Lauren Dixon's lungs the way there had been in Aunt Lily's when he'd buried her.

Oh well, Murphy thought philosophically, he supposed he couldn't have everything.

But he could still hope, he told himself.

Hope.

The hallmark of little men and women. His mother had taught him that just before she had finally taken off, he recalled. It was a lesson that had stuck with him over the years.

The expression on his face turned even uglier than it already had been. Memories of his aunt always did that to him, he thought. The hunger for revenge had been growing and eating away at him for several days now, but he really had had no intention of killing this old grandmother to alleviate the pain.

Old grandmother, he mocked to himself. The old crone had made sure everyone knew that about her, like it was some sort of a badge of honor. Like every stray dog or cat couldn't have a litter at the drop of a hat.

The true accomplishment was to make the litter feel as if they were wanted.

Fresh anger creased Murphy's brow as he threw dirt on top of the wrapped body, intending to bury it from view. He needed to get a grip on himself. As good as it felt, choking the life out of these old biddies, he couldn't allow himself to get carried away like that.

Suspicions would be aroused and he could certainly do without that.

Murphy moved a little faster. He needed to bury the old crow's body before the sun began coming up.

He blamed the old bat for the growing ache in his shoulders.

She had forced him to do this, he thought angrily, damning her in his heart.

"It's really getting late," Jefferson noted, glancing at the watch on his left wrist.

He and Cheyenne were still at the former chief of police's house. Only a little less than half the guests had left the party so far. It was very obvious that no one really wanted to leave. They were having much too good a time.

"I never took you for Cinderella," Cheyenne commented, looking at her partner. "Is this really too late for you?"

She had gotten the distinct impression that he was the type who could stay up, partying all night long when the whim hit him.

"No, I just thought that a lot of these people probably have to be on call tomorrow," her partner said, sipping from his glass as he surveyed all the faces that were surrounding them.

"Trust me, if they have to be on call and alert, they will be," she assured him. "This bunch doesn't let work slide. Neither would they let a good time slide if that came up," she added, telling him, "You'll find that out after being in Aurora for a while."

Her partner shrugged in response to her comment. "Uh-huh."

"This was a really wonderful dinner, Aunt Rose," Cheyenne told her aunt almost an hour later, adding her voice to those of many of the people who were preparing to leave the party.

Rose flashed a smile at her niece, obviously grateful for the kind words. "Granted it wasn't as good as it could have been if Andrew had done the cooking, but at least I had the satisfaction of seeing my husband sit back and allow himself to be served." She leaned into Andrew, stood on her toes and affectionately ruffled his full head of gray-streaked hair.

"It wasn't that bad, being served, right, honey?" she asked pointedly.

Andrew sighed deeply at her question. "Whatever you say, darling," he answered her. He looked around at the guests who were closest to him. "What do you say? Are you guys about ready for another round of drinks?"

"Much as we'd love to toast you again," Brian told his older brother, "I think if we indulged in another round—or twelve as is your habit—you and Seamus are going to have to wind up pouring us and the rest of this crowd into our cars," the chief of d's said.

"Well, you're all welcome to sleep here if you need to," Rose said warmly to the family members who had not cleared out of the big house yet.

"I know it's a big house," Brian told his sister-in-law, "but having the rest of us stay here is really asking for trouble, even if you could actually stuff the rest of us all in here."

And he should know, Brian thought. He had watched as his family members had grown in number over the years, from a small cluster of people until the resulting mass of members seemed to become almost insurmountable. Incalculable.

"Well then," Rose asked whimsically, looking around at her guests, "do you want me to start singing 'The Party's Over' as I hold the front door open for you?"

Andrew laughed as he hugged his wife to him. "Nothing subtle about my little wife here," he couldn't help commenting with a chuckle. "Seriously, maybe you all should start heading home before you run the risk of falling asleep behind the wheel. I don't want any of you to risk getting into an accident on my account—or even not on my account."

Brian laughed as he shook his head. "That's my big brother for you, always thinking about making sure that we're all safe."

"Well, it's a lot better than thinking about work. We all deserve to take a break from that once in a while," Sean said, adding his voice to that of his brothers.

"Amen to that," Seamus said, agreeing wholeheartedly with his sons' sentiments. Even at his age, he definitely enjoyed partying with his family.

It had been years since Seamus Cavanaugh had been an active member of law enforcement, but that didn't mean that he had lost all interest in the matter. The cases that the law enforcement officers—even those who were not part of his family—were involved in still really managed to pique his interest and he followed them whenever he could.

"All right, so if you're not staying here," Andrew told his guests and relatives, "like I said, it's time for all of you to hit the road and go home—slowly," the former chief of police told his family and guests. "And I want to thank you all for coming," he said in all sincerity.

A lot of voices chimed in, echoing what a great time they'd all had and how much they were looking forward to the next gathering Andrew was going to have. Everyone knew that it would be soon.

Family and friends left the former chief of police's home. Every one of them was beaming.

People were funneling out through the front door, looking somewhat sleepy but extremely satisfied with what had gone down.

Jeff was directly beside Cheyenne. A misstep had her suddenly slipping and stumbling.

Instantly alert, her partner made a grab for her arm, wrapping his own arm around her to steady her before she wound up falling.

It was hard to say which of them was more surprised, Cheyenne or Jefferson. Jeff was afraid that she might wind up being resentful over his reaction, but instead, Cheyenne beamed at him and wound up squeezing his hand.

"Thank you," she told him as they made their way to the curb. They were going toward where she had parked her car hours earlier. The area didn't appear to be nearly as crowded as it had been when they had arrived and most likely not nearly as crowded as it had become when the cars were parked here for the height of the event.

"Well, at least I won't have to fight traffic in order to get out of the area," she told Jeff as they came up to her vehicle.

Pointing her keys at her car, Cheyenne hit the single button on her key fob. That caused all four of the locks on her car to pop open simultaneously, sounding not unlike soldiers standing at attention and shooting their guns at the same time.

Glancing over the roof of her vehicle, she told Jeff, "Go on, get in."

He frowned slightly. "You know, it just doesn't seem right, you driving me home. I should be the one driving you."

"That's okay. Next time, I'll let you drive me home," Cheyenne told him. "That's what working at the precinct in Aurora is all about, Jeff. People looking out for one another. Being nice to one another."

He heard what wasn't being said. "So there's going to be a next time?"

"Of course there will be a next time." How could he even doubt that? "Now that you've gotten your feet wet, gatherings at Uncle Andrew's are going to be a recurring part of life for you."

Jefferson had to admit that he was surprised. At his last job, at the precinct in El Paso, the people he worked with would always go home at the end of the day and, other than getting together for the occasional drink at the local bar, they wouldn't see one another until the following morning.

"Seeing each other at work isn't enough?" Jefferson questioned Cheyenne.

She laughed. She supposed her partner had a point, but it definitely was not *her* point. "Seeing each other at work is only the beginning."

They made their way down the quiet, darkened streets, heading toward the apartment that Jeff was renting. "So," Cheyenne asked him pointedly, "what do you think?"

Jefferson wasn't quite sure exactly what she was asking him. "You're going to have to be a little clearer than that with your question, Cavanaugh. What do I think about what?" he asked. "Are you asking about the food, the company, the…" His voice trailed off, letting Cheyenne fill in the blank any way that she saw fit.

"That's easy," she answered him. "I'm asking about all of it. Knowing you, I expect you probably have an opinion about everything." She saw his building directly up ahead. "You strike me as someone who forms opinions on a great many subjects as he goes along."

Finally reaching the apartment building, Cheyenne pulled up in front of it. Turning off the engine, she pivoted toward Jefferson and waited for him to answer her question.

"Well, you were right," her partner admitted. "I did have a really great time. Even better than I actually thought I would. Your uncles and aunts and all the rest of your family and friends went out of their way to make not just me comfortable, but everyone else who was there as well," he told his partner. "I honestly didn't think that could happen, given that I didn't actually know any of them before this party. But I really have to give them credit—all of them," he emphasized, smiling at Cheyenne. "By the middle of the evening, I felt as if I had known them not just for a few hours, or even that whole day, but really for a very long time. I think that's a gift," he admitted. And then his eyes washed over her. "The same sort of gift that you have." Jeff smiled to himself. "I think that I did a really good thing, coming out here to Aurora."

"Why did you come out here?" she asked, curious as to what his motivation had been.

"Someone actually told me about Aurora in passing," he admitted. "My dad had died. I didn't have any real family ties to where I was living, so I thought I'd give Aurora it a shot."

The story moved her. Turning toward him, Cheyenne smiled into her partner's eyes. "Well, I for one am glad that you did."

If asked, Cheyenne wouldn't have been able to say which of them actually made the first move toward the other, or how she went from sitting there, talking to her partner, to tilting her head toward him and giving in to the wave of overwhelming curiosity that came over her.

Without a hint of a prelude, she found herself kissing her partner.

And enjoying the hell out of it.

At bottom, she knew it wasn't something she should have done, not here, not now. But she definitely was not sorry about it.

Chapter 18

When Jefferson drew his head back and looked at the woman before him, he wasn't sure if he had just wistfully imagined the whole thing, or if it had really happened.

The way his blood was pounding in his veins told him that he hadn't imagined it. He desperately found himself wanting to take what he was feeling to its logical conclusion. But he didn't want to insult his partner and make her think that he was some sort of predator, because he wasn't. Jeff was a man who believed in maintaining a good working relationship and held women in high regard. That being said, he was also extremely attracted to the woman he was working with.

Things had been a great deal simpler in his dad's

day, Jeff thought. His dad had told him, more than once, about how he had courted his mom. There had been flowers and quiet, romantic dinners at a little out-of-the-way restaurant located on the outskirts of El Paso.

He wasn't sure how Cheyenne would react to any of that, Jefferson mused. She might think that he was trying to talk her into something.

The only way to find out was to go ahead and do it. At least she hadn't read him the riot act for what had already just transpired between them. That fact at least gave him a little bit of hope.

"Would you like to come upstairs for a drink?" he asked, watching her face carefully for a reaction to his question.

"Yes," Cheyenne answered honestly. "But if I did, I'd have to hang around for a while. It wouldn't exactly be very responsible of me to drive home with a high level of alcoholic content in my blood."

He certainly didn't see anything wrong with that. "You could stay for as long as you felt was necessary for you to stabilize. Or," he said, offering his partner an alternative solution, "I could just make you some tea."

Tea, right, she thought. She couldn't see him having any tea on hand for any reason. "You're just fishing for a way to get me upstairs," Cheyenne told him with an amused smile.

Jeff shrugged noncommittedly in response to her comment. "I could always bring the tea downstairs to you," her partner told her. "No harm in that."

"No, upstairs to your apartment will be just fine," she told him. "Besides, it's getting rather chilly out here. Your apartment will be a lot warmer."

She was right. The wind was seeping into the car, Jeff realized, bringing a chill with it. Getting out, he closed the door behind him.

"Upstairs it is," he agreed, rounding the hood of her vehicle. Her partner offered her his arm. After a beat, she took it. "By the way, this is not a comment on my thinking you're being a little unstable. It's just my way of trying to display a little gallantry on my part."

She laughed softly under her breath. "I wasn't taking it as an insult."

They entered the building and the difference between outside and inside was rather amazing, she thought. She stopped shivering the moment she crossed the ground floor and approached the elevator.

"How do you like living here?" she asked her partner, indicating the immediate area.

He assumed she was referring to the living quarters. "It's a lot neater than the place where I used to live when I came home from serving in the Marines. That place was practically just a small cabin and in fact the place was close to being over eighty years old." He shook his head as he remembered the space. "As a matter of fact, it looked every inch of that."

Reaching the second floor, Jefferson got out of the elevator and led the way to his apartment. Unlocking the door, he stepped back to allow her to enter first.

"Go ahead," he told her, bracing himself.

"Go ahead what?" Cheyenne asked, assuming that he wasn't just telling her to walk in, that there was something more involved in viewing the apartment.

"Tell me what's wrong with it," he said.

She looked at him in surprise. "There's nothing wrong with it," she told him. "Oh, it could probably stand a little dusting here and there, but other than that, it looks fine. Tell you this much, you're a lot better at housekeeping than any of my brothers were before they got married."

Her partner smiled at her as he closed the door behind them and flipped the lock. "That's gratifying to hear," Jeff told her.

"Glad I could gratify you," she teased, then she looked slowly around the kitchen. "Where do you keep your coffee?"

He appeared rather surprised at her question. "You're passing on the tea?"

It was her turn to be surprised. "You were serious about the tea?"

"Yes, I was serious," her partner told her. "I offered it to you, didn't I?"

"Well, yes, you did, but to be very honest and even a little sexist, I never knew any man who actually chose to *drink* tea. Coffee or even a trendy latte or two, yes. But tea?" Cheyenne shook her head. "Never."

Jefferson decided that perhaps an explanation might be in order. "When I was a kid, I had a really bad case of the stomach flu. I couldn't keep anything down and I mean *anything*. I just kept throwing up absolutely everything I put in my mouth and tried to swallow. My mother was desperate to help me and as a last resort, she brewed a pot of tea for me to drink.

"I wound up practically living on the stuff," he told his partner. "Eventually, it managed to settle my stomach enough that I was able to keep some food down. Very slowly, I became human again and I gained new respect for the brew."

"What did you wind up having, illness-wise?" she asked her partner, curious.

He could only shrug. "Who knows? We couldn't afford a doctor back then. My mother fell back on using old remedies that she was raised with. Luckily for me, they worked. Because they did, I've had a fondness for tea ever since."

Cheyenne could readily understand that. "Then I'll let you do the honors," she told him, raising her hands in surrender as she backed away from the stove to give him complete access to it.

"All right, then, let me get to it," he told Cheyenne, moving past her to get to the stove. Taking the kettle, he poured water into it, deposited the proper amount of tea leaves into it and started to prepare the beverage for steaming.

"Is there anything you want me to do?" she asked he partner. It wasn't in Cheyenne to just stand around doing nothing. She was used to being perpetually busy. Besides, if she kept busy, she wouldn't feel tempted by her partner, which at the moment, she was. There was just something about the man that seemed to tempt her—especially now.

Jefferson spared her a glance. "Why don't you just make yourself comfortable?"

She knew he'd say that. "Besides that," she responded.

Jefferson's smile widened as his eyes washed over her. "Nothing that can bear repeating in mixed company." And then he caught himself. "I shouldn't have even said that."

In this day and age, every remark made could be held suspect.

Cheyenne appreciated her partner's thoughtfulness. "Don't worry, I won't hold it against you."

The remark tempted him. Jeff found he just couldn't resist asking her, "So what will you hold against me?"

Heaven help her but her heart began to pound really hard in her chest, anticipation managing to send it into double time. Her breathing grew a good deal harder to regulate.

"What do you want me to hold against you?" she asked him, her voice no louder than a whisper. She caught herself shivering as she felt his breath go up and down her spine.

His eyes were already making love to her.

"Guess," he said to her as he turned away from the stove, the water that was about to boil temporarily forgotten about.

With that, he took her into his arms and, ever so slowly, he brought his lips down to hers. The growing hunger within him seemed to just explode in his veins, all but consuming every last bit of him.

Jefferson kissed her over and over again, each time with even more passion than the last. Rather than satiate him, it just made the hunger within him grow to larger and larger proportions.

Her partner found that his head was spinning wildly, making him almost unbelievably dizzy. He didn't remember moving, didn't remember picking her up in his arms and beginning to walk with her toward his bedroom until the teakettle on the stovetop suddenly began whistling to the point that it all but made his teeth rattle. That definitely caught his attention.

When that happened, he stopped kissing her and drew his head away. Her partner smiled into her eyes.

"What?" she asked.

"I think that's nature's way of calling a time-out," Jeff told her.

"Or just telling us to take a breath," she said, amused, "so we don't wind up suffocating."

A thrill danced up and down her spine, making her shiver in anticipation. "Well, if you ask me, I can't think of a better way to go," he told her.

She all but laughed as she shook her head, causing him to ask her in confusion, "What?"

"I just would have never pegged you as being a romantic," she said.

"Funny, neither would I," he admitted, then added, "until just now. Look, I don't want you thinking that I'm pushing things, or rushing them."

Before he could say anything further, Cheyenne placed her finger against his lips, silencing them. When he raised his eyebrows in quizzical surprise, she told him, "I'm not thinking anything at all—except that maybe you talk a little too much."

Jeff took a deep breath. He needed to get this out before he wasn't able to talk. In his opinion, Cheyenne needed to know this. "The way things are in this day and age, I just want you to know—"

Her eyes met his. She could almost read his mind. "I know," she told him quietly in all sincerity. "Trust me, I know."

With that, her partner pulled her into his arms and kissed her, putting his entire heart and soul into that kiss. The next moment, hoping that she understood what he was trying to get across to her, Jefferson picked her up into his arms and carried Cheyenne into his bedroom.

Her heart was pounding hard as Jefferson deposited her onto his bed, placing her as carefully as if he was laying down an angel.

During all this time, his lips hardly left hers.

They were sealed against her in such a way that he wound up lying down against her, absorbing all of her into his very system.

The time for words, Jefferson thought, had passed.

Jefferson ran his hands along every part of her body, memorizing every dip, every warm curve he touched. Taking it all in until it felt as if it became an absolute part of him as well.

When Cheyenne began to unbutton his shirt, pulling the shirttails out of the waistband of his pants, the hunger he was attempting to contain just got completely out of hand. It exploded in his veins, consuming him, feeding the fire that was blazing within him.

Jefferson returned the compliment and she struggled hard not to cry out as mounting desire seemed to shoot throughout her entire body. Especially when he started to undress her, replacing the material that left her body with long, languid, hot kisses that strategically covered her from top to bottom.

He was nibbling on and branding areas that were all but throbbing with each pass of his hot lips along her aching, wanting skin.

Cheyenne twisted and turned beneath him, glorying in the heat his mouth generated along her.

She wanted to retaliate, to repay him, but she could barely move, barely draw in even so much as a lungful of air to help keep her mind from spinning off into oblivion.

"Stop," she begged. "Stop."

He pulled back, concerned. "Am I hurting you?" he asked, afraid he had somehow managed to go too far.

"No," she told him hoarsely.

He didn't understand. "When why—"

"Because I didn't want this to be just one-sided," she answered. And with that, Cheyenne proceeded to lay siege to Jefferson's body, teasing him and branding him to create just a little of the impression that he had managed to leave along her body.

They went on like that for a couple of go-rounds, making each other crazy until they were all but weak with desire, until their bodies were completely throbbing and aching.

And then, finally, unable to resist the final step, Cheyenne turned into her partner, opening herself up to him as her mouth was sealed against his.

She felt Jefferson part her legs beneath him and she caught her breath as he slipped into her.

With her heart pounding, they became engaged in the timeless dance that had seized couples since the very beginning of time.

Their hips began to move faster and faster in time to a song that their bodies had been dancing to since this had begun between them.

Desire exploded within them, absorbing them and eventually leaving them smiling, satisfied and incredibly grateful that this had happened between them.

Without realizing it, they fell asleep in each other's arms, happy and deeply contented. The sound of their breathing mingled until it grew fainter and fainter. Finally the sound faded away as it wound up generating a heart-softening warmth around them.

Chapter 19

The ringing noise penetrated the fog that had descended around Cheyenne's and Jeff's brains. The fog had locked them into a state of sleep that eventually broke apart, thanks to the noise.

They opened their eyes almost simultaneously and looked at one another, trying to orient themselves as well as identifying the source of the ringing.

Rubbing the sleep from her eyes, Cheyenne looked at the man beside her. He was awake, she realized.

Stifling a yawn, she asked her partner, "Is that yours or mine?" Her voice was still somewhat thick with sleep.

"Both, I think," he answered, stifling a yawn of his own.

The ringing noise helped to guide them to where

their phones were lying. Jeff's was on the nightstand next to the lamp while Cheyenne's cell phone was on the floor, just beneath the bed.

Jefferson leaned over her to reach his phone while Cheyenne reached down beneath the bed in order to retrieve hers.

They answered their phones within moments of one another.

Cheyenne was first. When he spoke, she instantly recognized her uncle's voice. Brian Cavanaugh, the chief of d's, was on the other end of the line.

Sitting back up on the bed, she leaned her head against the headboard and pulled her legs in under her. Because of the hour—5:00 a.m.—she abandoned all pretext of formality. Also because of the hour, her mind went instantly to a bad place. Cheyenne's fingertips were cold and she stiffened as she held the phone against her ear.

"Uncle Brian, what's wrong?" she asked nervously.

But when her uncle answered her, it wasn't what she had expected him to say.

"That damn serial killer struck again, Cheyenne," he told her. The chief of d's wasted no time filling her in on the details. "Some hiker making his way through the woods late last night stumbled across a fresh grave. This time the victim's face was just bashed in, not really erased, like the others had been. But there's no doubt in anyone's mind that it's the work of the same man."

Although it made her feel guilty, Cheyenne couldn't

deny that she was relieved to hear that the reason for the call had nothing to do with an emergency involving her uncle or any of the other older members of her family. Dealing with the uglier side of life had her worrying about things closer to home more than she usually did.

"Where?" she asked a bit breathlessly.

From the look on Jefferson's face when she glanced in his direction, he was apparently on the receiving end of a similar call. The Aurora precinct was on the alert.

So much for being able to go back to sleep, Cheyenne thought, resigning herself to the fact that this was the beginning of her day.

As Cheyenne listened, her uncle Brian rattled off the specifics of the crime. She was wide awake now.

"I just sent the medical examiner to the scene where the body was discovered. He's going to collect it and bring the murdered woman back to Autopsy. But he won't do anything until you and your team get there since this has become your case," Brian told her.

She nodded even though she knew that he couldn't see her. "I'll get the others together and we'll be there as soon as we possibly can," Cheyenne promised her uncle.

"I know you will." She heard him let out a long sigh. "Hell of a way to end the evening, isn't it?" the chief of detectives asked her.

"You certainly said a mouthful, Chief," she told

the man as she ended the call. The next moment, she was throwing off the blanket she'd had wrapped around her torso and turning toward the man sitting up beside her. "Looks like duty calls," she said.

"Maybe after we take care of what needs to be done and collect all the necessary information, we might be able to pick up where we left off?" Jeff suggested, raising his brow, a touch of hope in his eyes.

That took her by surprise. Despite the nature of the situation, she could feel a smile forming within her. "Is that what you want to do?" she asked him in complete innocence. After all, there had been no words exchanged between them, no hint of any sort of commitment beyond the moment and the evening.

Jefferson had never been someone who believed in playing any sort of games. Honesty had always been his hallmark and he had always believed in shooting straight from the hip.

It was no different now and he answered her in all honesty.

"Hell, yes." And then he decided to temper his response. After all, he didn't want to scare her away. "Unless you think I'm being too pushy and you just want to take a raincheck on anything else that might be in the offing when we get back from whatever it is that the rest of today might hold for us."

Cheyenne paused for a moment, as if attempting to unscramble what her partner had just said to her. It wasn't in her to jump to conclusions, no matter how much she might be tempted to do just that.

"We'll talk when we get back," she told him. "And for the record," Cheyenne decided to add for good measure, "neither one of us is being too pushy. And I think that if this serial killer had just taught us anything, it's that life should be grabbed and held on to with both hands whenever possible."

With that, Cheyenne rose from his bed, wrapping the blanket around herself. "Now, would you mind if I showered first?" she asked him, making her way toward the bathroom. "I want to get ready and I guarantee that I am really fast."

Jeff grinned at her. The woman really amused him. One way or the other, he intended to let his partner go first. "What kind of a gentleman would I be if I said no?" he asked her with an innocent shrug.

"A cleaner one," Cheyenne commented with a laugh. "Okay, I'll be right out," she promised. She grabbed the rest of her clothes and a towel and made her way into the bathroom to grab a quick shower.

True to her promise, Cheyenne was in and out of the shower—and the bathroom—in what seemed to Jefferson to be lightning speed.

She saw that her partner had just finished brewing their coffee and had just put in four slices of bread into the toaster.

"Your turn," Cheyenne declared as she finished toweling her hair dry.

She had managed to catch Jefferson totally by surprise. "You sure the water even hit you?" he marveled.

Cheyenne laughed. "Yes, I'm very sure. Go take your shower," she urged. Gesturing around the kitchen, she told him, "I'll finish making breakfast."

"Will do," he told her, putting down his knife. "And you don't have to bother making my breakfast," he told her on his way out. "We can pick up something at the diner on the way to the crime scene."

She waved her partner on his way. "Just go take your shower."

Something in her voice caught his attention. "You're not planning on timing me, are you?" he asked, even though he knew there was no way he could possibly compete with her. Her speed had managed to take his breath away.

A smile played on Cheyenne's lips. "Only if you take too long," she answered.

Jefferson paused for a second in the doorway leading into the bathroom. He turned around to look at her. "Then what?" he asked. "You'll come in to drag me out?"

Humor gleamed in her eyes. "I might," she said, her expression remaining unchanged.

Her partner grinned at her, apparently rolling the matter over in his mind. "It might be worth it," he responded with relish.

Cheyenne waved her partner on his way. "Go, shower, get ready. I still have to stop at my place to change my clothes. It might look really suspicious if I turn up at the crime scene wearing the same outfit that I wore to the party yesterday."

"Not suspicious," her partner contradicted. "They'll just think that I was one really lucky son of a gun."

"Go!" Cheyenne ordered, pointing to the bathroom door just behind him.

"Gone," her partner told her, holding his hands up to indicate his surrender as he went into the bathroom to take his shower.

Jefferson walked out of the bathroom some twenty minutes later to the warm, tempting scent of brewed coffee, toast and eggs.

"That smells really good," Jefferson enthused as he closed the door behind him and walked into the kitchen.

"Thank you." She deposited the plate of eggs, bacon and toast in front of him. "Eat fast. I told my uncle we'd be there as soon as possible and I still have to grab a change of clothes at my place."

"We?" he questioned.

"My team," she clarified. "We're all being summoned to the scene and I called them while you were in the shower. They weren't overly happy about the wake-up call."

"I know how they feel," he told her, sitting down at the table. "Aren't you having any?" he asked, noticing that there was no plate in front of her.

"I already ate," she told him.

Jefferson looked at her in total disbelief. "You cooked, notified the rest of the team and ate breakfast all in an incredibly short amount of time." He glanced over his shoulder toward the sink. "And I notice that you washed and dried the frying pan and put it away as well. Wow. I had no idea that you had these superpowers."

"Not superpowers," she corrected. "I can move really fast. I always have been able to. It comes in handy when you're one of nine siblings. Otherwise, you run the risk of going hungry and getting left behind while the others wind up cleaning everything out."

"I never thought of it that way," he admitted with a shrug of his shoulders. "That kind of thing doesn't come up when you're an only child."

"Everything has its advantages and disadvantages," she told her partner. "I guess it all depends on how you look at things." Finished drinking her coffee, Cheyenne rose to her feet, pushing her chair back. "Ready to go?" she asked him as she rinsed out her cup.

He laughed. "I guess I can digest my breakfast on the way there."

Cheyenne smiled at him. "You read my mind."

"Not hardly, but I can definitely make a calculated guess." Her partner looked over toward the counter. "I'm assuming you found my coffee thermos."

Beaming, she placed the full thermos on the table as she whisked away Jefferson's breakfast dish and deposited it into the sink.

"There you go," she told him, nodded at the thermos as she quickly cleaned and rinsed his plate and coffee cup. She had always hated having dishes pile up in the sink.

Jefferson could only shake his head. "I am really impressed."

"Save that," Cheyenne told her partner, "for when we finally find the serial killer and have irrefutable proof that he's our man."

Something about her wording caught his attention. "You're that sure that the killer is a male?" Jefferson asked her.

"Let's just say I'm ninety-nine percent sure," she told him. "Statistics show that most serial killers are males and white, which is why both males of color and females usually slip under the radar and elude capture for a long time if they have the misfortune of actually being guilty. And sometimes," she added unhappily, "they even manage to get away with the crime."

There was admiration in his eyes as he looked at his partner. "Working with you is proving to be a real education," Jefferson told her, then confessed, "I never counted on that when I came here."

Cheyenne beamed at her partner. "I do my best," she replied. "All right, follow me in your car. That way we can tell my uncle and the others that I swung around to bring you to the scene of the murder since you still don't know your way around the area. It'll explain why we arrived more or less at the same time. Don't worry, I'll change my clothes really fast."

At this point, he had no reason to doubt her. "You

really do seem to have everything covered," Jeff marveled.

She smiled at him as she got into her vehicle. "This is not my first rodeo," she told her partner.

"I wouldn't have thought that it was," he told her, then asked, "How long did you say you've been on the police force?"

"I've been on the force for five years," she told him. "However, I've been a Cavanaugh all my life. You learn things by observing. Being a Cavanaugh family member is an education all on its own." Taking out her key, Cheyenne pointed it toward the car. All four locks sprang open. "Ready?"

Her partner quickly followed suit, opening his own car door. "Ready," he declared.

"Then let's go," she told him.

With that, Cheyenne got in behind the wheel of her vehicle. In less than a moment, she was ready to lead the way to her place.

Chapter 20

The edge of the forest where the latest victim had been found was swimming with police personnel moving in all directions. Along with officers, a medical examiner and his assistant as well as several other people who worked for the police department, a number of detectives who had been attached to the serial killer cold case, appeared on the scene.

After they reached the area, Cheyenne and her partner had parked their cars and made their way to the center of the group.

Cheyenne went to the first person she knew was working the case. "What do we have, Dr. Barlow?" Cheyenne asked the medical examiner.

"Offhand I'd say that it looks like our guy didn't

get a chance to savor his handiwork," the medical examiner said answering her question.

The man was standing over the body that had just been placed on the gurney, looking rather pensive.

"What makes you say that?" Jefferson asked. He glanced in his partner's direction, a silent apology on his face for usurping her by asking the question first. But he was really curious.

"All the other dead women who we found had their clothing carefully removed as well as their facial features all but erased and bashed in. I think in this case, the serial killer was surprised in the middle of what he was doing and was forced to do a hasty cover-up. Her grave was an extremely shallow one. It turned out to be hardly deep enough to even cover her," the doctor said. There was pity in his voice as he shook his head, gazing down at the victim.

"Do we have any idea who the victim was yet?" Cheyenne asked. How could anyone do such an awful thing once, much less several times? She just couldn't bring herself to understand it.

"Not yet, but like I said, I think our killer got sloppy this time around because he was in a hurry. Her fingerprints weren't all rubbed away and as for her facial features, he didn't eliminate them in his customary manner by bashing her face in. My guess is that the serial killer feels cheated and deprived and unless I really miss my guess, he's undoubtedly going to strike again in order to try to satisfy his hunger," the medical examiner pointed out.

If the killer had gotten sloppy, maybe that meant there were clues that were left behind. "Did the killer leave behind any telltale evidence we might be able to use?" Cheyenne asked.

"Nothing that I can see, but your team and the people assisting them haven't finished going through all the evidence that was left behind. Granted this was still a terrible crime, but maybe we'll get lucky this time," the medical examiner said hopefully.

Cheyenne frowned. "'Getting lucky' in my book would mean that there would be no killers, serial or otherwise," Cheyenne told the older man.

The medical examiner paused as he started to pack up his medical bag, preparing to go back to Autopsy with the body. He looked at Cheyenne intently. A hint of a smile played on his lips.

"They told me that you were an optimist. I guess they were right beyond their wildest dreams," Dr. Barlow speculated.

"Looking for the good in people is hardly being optimistic. It's just being hopeful." Cheyenne could feel her partner as well as the medical examiner looking at her. She, meanwhile, was looking down at the draped body lying on the gurney. "Poor woman, the killer not only stripped her of her clothes, but of her dignity as well." Anger creased her features. "If I could get my hands on the scum, it would be really hard not to give in to the temptation to choke the life out of this heartless creep," she told the medical examiner as well as her partner.

Jefferson laughed warily. "Remind me never to get on the wrong side of you," he told his partner.

Cheyenne gave him a spasmodic smile that he had absolutely no idea how to read. "Don't do anything wrong and there won't be a problem," she told her partner.

A warm feeling came over him as he thought of last night and making love with her. Despite the nature of the crime they were dealing with, thoughts of last night had left him in an excellent place mentally. "That's easier said than done," he told her.

They remained in the immediate area, working the crime scene and dealing with the evidence for a good long while, until everything had been packed up and as accounted for as humanly possible.

By day's end it was easy to see that everyone felt weary from the inside out. "That makes at least four victims that we know of," Cheyenne told her partner. "And who knows how many others have been killed that we haven't been able to find—or how many this killer has eliminated and disposed of that we haven't found yet." She shivered as she turned the matter over in her mind. "For all we know, this serial killer hasn't contained his killing spree to just one area. Who knows how far his reach has extended?"

"You know what I said about you being an optimist?" her partner asked her.

She watched as her team packed up and withdrew from the scene, more than ready to call it a day. "Yes?"

A hint of a smile teased his lips. "I think I've changed my mind about that," Jefferson told her.

Cheyenne laughed softly. "I guess that you're entitled," she told him.

"Are you hungry?" her partner asked Cheyenne. "I don't think we've eaten since you made breakfast early this morning," he pointed out.

She thought for a moment. "You know, I think you're right. I just got so caught up in this awful crime, I guess I wound up losing my appetite."

"Well, the way I see it," her partner said, "you need to keep up your strength or we won't be able to bring this creep down. Say, why don't I buy you dinner tonight? You name the place."

She wasn't trying to be coy, Cheyenne thought. Her appetite really did feel as if it was missing in action.

At this point, they were walking to their vehicles. Instead of answering her partner, Cheyenne thought for a moment, mentally taking inventory of the contents of her refrigerator. And then she looked at him as a solution hit her.

"I've got a couple of steaks in my refrigerator. Why don't I make them and we can have that? After spending all day around a bunch of people on this new case, I really don't feel up to going out to a restaurant and listening to people talk and exchange pleasantries with one another around us."

"Aren't you the one who said we shouldn't allow this to get to us?" her partner reminded her.

Cheyenne pressed her lips together, doing her best to try to raise her spirits. "You're right," she told Jefferson. "If I let this get to me, I'm not going to be of any good to anyone." And that, she silently added, wouldn't be very responsible of her, nor would it help the victims or their families. She was a Cavanaugh and had a reputation to maintain.

Because there was no one around them and they were basically alone inside her vehicle, Cheyenne leaned over to brush her lips against his cheek. The move on her part managed to take him completely by surprise.

Jefferson ran his fingertips against his cheek, tracing the outline of her kiss and almost pressing it into his skin. "Well, I wouldn't exactly say that you wouldn't be any good to anyone," he responded, then dropped his hand from his face. "Does this mean that we're going steady?"

She laughed out loud at his reference. "I don't think I've heard that line being used in a very long time."

He blew out a breath as Cheyenne stepped on the gas and they took off, driving to her house.

"Maybe if we attempted to go back to the way things once were in the past, things might actually get better," Jefferson told her.

She spared him a look. "I totally agree, but right now, we need to focus on the immediate case and get this sick individual off our streets," she said with feeling. This killer was making her sick to her stomach.

"Amen to that," her partner responded. He decided to give it one last try. "Are you sure you don't want me to buy dinner for us?"

"I'm sure. Besides, cooking always manages to relax me," she added by way of an explanation.

The remark had her partner laughing in response.

She looked at him, confused and somewhat mystified as to what struck him as being so funny. "What's so funny?" Cheyenne asked.

"I was just thinking about my late mother's reaction to cooking. She used to complain whenever she had to even boil water." Jefferson smiled to himself. "My mother was a really warm, loving person but cooking definitely was not her forte."

"Well, cooking as a passion runs in my family," Cheyenne reminded her partner. "You met my uncle Andrew. He acted like he was being punished when he had to keep out of the kitchen," she pointed out to Jefferson.

Her partner nodded in response. "You Cavanaughs definitely are a very unique breed of people."

She smiled as she drove the rest of the way to her house. "I won't argue with that."

Reaching her destination, Cheyenne pulled up and left her vehicle parked in front of her house.

Getting out, Jefferson looked at her. "You don't park your car in the garage?" he asked, curious. If he had a garage, he would have parked his vehicle in it all the time.

"This makes jumping into my car and taking off a lot easier," she told him.

He frowned, trying to make sense out of what she was telling him. "Is that a regular thing? Jumping into your car and having to take off?"

"Once or twice," she allowed, then added, "I just like being prepared for all contingencies."

"I don't think I've ever met anyone quite like you," her partner told Cheyenne.

"Is that a good thing or a bad thing?" she asked.

His eyes smiled at her as he put his arm around her shoulders to usher her into her house. "At the risk of possibly scaring you off, I'd say that it's definitely a very good thing."

She nodded in response. "Make yourself comfortable. The steaks should be ready in fifteen minutes—or less," Cheyenne hedged.

"Sounds good," he told her. "Anything you'd like me to do?"

"Just sit there and look pretty," she told him with an inviting smile. His stomach growled rather loudly just then. Her smile grew into a grin. "And try to be patient," she added, glancing down at his stomach.

"I'll do my best," Jefferson promised. "Do you have anything to drink?"

Cheyenne got busy preparing the steaks. She enumerated what she knew was currently in her refrigerator. "I have ginger ale, orange juice, the ever-present water and there's half a bottle of red wine on the back shelf from about six months ago."

"I take it that you took the instruction to 'sip slowly' to heart," he told her with a laugh.

"Let's put it this way. If I'm going to drink something alcoholic, it would be something tastier, like along the lines of a sloe gin fizz or something with an equally cute name," she said. "I don't drink alone and usually when I come home, I'm too tired to do anything but fall asleep," she told him as she continued to go through the steps of preparing the steak. "How do you like your steak?"

"Barely dead," he told her honestly.

Her brow furrowed. "Do you want me to take that literally?" Cheyenne asked him.

"Absolutely," he answered. "I've always had a weakness for rare meat."

"Barely dead it is," she told him, turning up the flame beneath the frying pan.

"Shouldn't it be lower?" he asked her, nodding at the stove top.

"It'll be done faster this way," she told him.

He looked at the flame beneath the frying pan. "As long as you don't burn down the house along the way."

"Hasn't happened yet," she told him with satisfaction. "Relax and let me do my thing."

Jeff inclined his head and saluted her. "You got it."

Her eyes crinkled as she beamed at him. "Good answer."

Chapter 21

After spending the night together—something that was becoming a habit although Cheyenne didn't intend to raise that point if Jefferson did not—she and her partner went to the precinct to do some further research on the case, the same thing that they did the following day. And the day after that.

Cheyenne was determined to use every single resource available to them, hoping that somehow, by using what was available, they could find and identify the serial killer in order to stop the man in his tracks. They needed to find a way to keep the man from killing more defenseless older women. She was positive that the killer was attempting to fill some sort of imaginary quota he had come up with for himself. Where had it come from?

"Not that it actually matters whether these women are older or younger," Cheyenne muttered. "This animal has absolutely no business killing anyone. What kind of scum thinks he has the right to deprive someone of their life, no matter how he tries to justify what he's doing?"

Jeff looked up at the woman from where he was sitting at his desk. He thought that the question she was asking was a rhetorical one.

"If we could answer that, we could very well wind up unscrambling the mystery of the universe," her partner told her. "Or at least come damn close to actually solving that mystery."

Cheyenne leaned back in her chair as she momentarily closed her eyes. "I cannot tell you how frustrating all this is, going around in circles and, for the moment, feeling as if I'm getting absolutely nowhere."

Jeff laughed shortly. "You don't have to tell me," her partner said. "I'm right there right next to you, remember?"

Opening her eyes again, Cheyenne nodded as her eyes met his. She hadn't meant to sound disparaging or depressed, although having this killer out there was getting to her. She needed to shut her mind to that part of this ordeal.

"Sorry. Sometimes it just helps to say things out loud," she told her partner, trying to explain her way of thinking.

The next moment, her eyes were drawn toward the department doorway. There was a police officer escorting a woman into their department. It was the same woman who had come to them the other day, asking them to find the whereabouts of her missing mother. Cheyenne exchanged glances with her partner, bracing herself for the same questions. Namely, did they have any word about the woman's missing mother? So far, they didn't.

In Cheyenne's opinion there were two terrible things about this job that she was so dedicated to working. The first, of course, was having to inform a person that their loved one was never going to be coming home again. That was akin to taking a knife and carving up their insides. The second was telling a person that they had no new news to tell them about any sort of development in a missing persons case. The hopeless look in their eyes always got to her, Cheyenne thought.

The case she and Jeff were working was still in the latter realm.

To her relief, Jeff greeted the woman before she came over to her desk to ask her that awful question.

"No, I'm sorry, Ms. Richardson, there's been no new news about your mother's whereabouts as of yet, but we still haven't given up," Jefferson told her.

The woman looked at the two detectives, appearing rather nervous about what she was about to impart. "I might be able to help with that," she finally told them.

Cheyenne exchanged looks with her partner. She

knew better than to allow herself to get carried away or become unrealistically hopeful.

"Please, have a seat, Ms. Richardson," Cheyenne urged, gesturing the woman over toward a nearby free chair. When the woman sat down, Cheyenne asked, "What is it that you have for us?"

The missing woman's daughter appeared to be even more nervous. "I'm almost embarrassed to tell you this."

"Please, Ms. Richardson, we are way past the point of embarrassment here," Jefferson assured the woman. "The only important thing here is for us to be able to find your mother."

Cheyenne noted that, mercifully, he did not say anything about finding out what *happened* to her mother, but simply said that they needed to find the woman—which she thought sounded a great deal more encouraging and comforting.

Meanwhile, the woman in question's daughter nodded in response. "The reason I'm here was that I was trying to comfort myself by going through my mother's things. I was looking through them in order to reacquaint myself with the kind of person my mother was." She sighed. "As it turns out, there are things about my mother I never knew."

Cheyenne's interest was instantly piqued. "Such as?" she asked, waiting to be enlightened.

"Such as I never knew that my mother enlisted in the Army straight out of high school. Something must have happened that she wasn't happy about or proud of because she never said anything about that to either my sister or to me. Not only that, but she did it under another name. The only way I knew it was her was because she used an old photograph that I recognized."

She frowned sadly. "I always thought my mother was the most honest person on the face of the earth. From what I can tell, it looks like I was wrong about that," she told the detectives, embarrassed.

"You don't know that for a fact yet," Jeff told the woman. "There could be a lot of reasons that explain your mother keeping this information to herself and from you."

"According to what I could piece together from her various entries, she left the service because my father, who she wound up marrying at the time, didn't want her to serve in the army. I only found this out by reading entries in a diary she kept—a diary I didn't even know she had." She stopped to look from one detective to the other. She was quite distraught. "Apparently," she said unhappily, "there were a great many things about my mother that I didn't know. She was a totally different person from the one who I thought I knew."

"Don't feel too badly," Jeff told the woman in a sympathetic voice. "Everybody has their secrets."

"The important thing," Cheyenne was quick to point out, "is that as a former soldier, her DNA is registered in a database. We can use that information to identify your mother no matter what name she was using."

"You're talking about one of the people you have lying in your morgue," the woman guessed unhappily.

"Not necessarily," Jeff stressed.

That response caused the woman to brighten more than a little bit, looking really hopeful for the first time since she had walked into their department.

"Really?" Richardson asked. "You can actually do that?"

"Absolutely." Cheyenne's eyes met the woman's. "We can bring this information—the DNA—to the woman who runs our computer lab," she said, thinking of her cousin Valri, who everyone in the precinct regarded as being a complete computer wizard. "Her hobby is working miracles on the side."

The woman's face practically lit up. "If this woman has an answer, you'll call me?" the woman all but begged. "Night or day, I don't care what time it is, or if the news turns out to be good or bad, promise that you'll call me." Her eyes went from one detective to the other, begging them to say yes.

Despite all his lectures to the contrary, he was allowing this case to get to him, Jefferson thought. But he really couldn't pretend otherwise. He knew what the woman was experiencing and what she had to be going through during this trying time. "We will call you," Jeff promised.

The corners of the woman's mouth curved as a

second wave of relief washed over her, all but stealing her breath. "I'll be waiting for your call."

"As soon as we know something—anything at all," Cheyenne underscored, "we will call." She knew the kind of hell that the uncertainty had to be generating within her.

With that, Jeff escorted the woman to the door, turning her over to the police officer who had brought her up to the department today in the first place.

Cheyenne was smiling at her partner when he turned around to face her. "What?" he asked uncertainly, immediately noticing her expression.

"Nothing. It's just that you turned out to be a real softie," she told him. "I wasn't prepared for that," she admitted.

Jefferson didn't look happy about the description. "I resent that," he told her.

"Resent it all you want. It doesn't change a thing. It's still true," she told him with a smile totally softening her features. She saw a protest forming on her partner's lips and quickly said, "You're turning out to be a much better guy than I thought you would."

"You didn't think I'd be a good partner?" he asked her, somewhat surprised by her admission.

"Well, you did seem a little cocky when you first came in," she reminded him even though it wasn't all that long ago.

"Cocky?" Jeff echoed, putting a hand to his chest and feigning overwhelming surprise. "Me?"

"I know, I know, what was I thinking?" she responded with an amused laugh. "All right," she said, moving on, "let's see if we can find that woman's DNA and then turn that over to Valri to see if she can find a match to a female soldier. That match just might pair up with one of the bodies that're lying in Autopsy. Or," she went on, thinking best-case scenario, "we find out that her DNA *doesn't* match one of the bodies in Autopsy and that woman's mother is actually alive somewhere."

Listening, Jeff shook his head as the magnitude of the investigation hit him. "This case is getting really complex," he said with a deep sigh.

"No, on the contrary, at last it's finally pointing to some sort of a resolution. Maybe with this new input, we now stand a decent chance of getting this creature off the streets and behind bars—preferably in solitary confinement," Cheyenne added, frowning as she thought about the serial killer who was haunting their streets. "And maybe, just maybe, reuniting a mother and daughter in a positive way."

Jeff nodded. "All right, let's see if we can finally start the process of putting this guy's heinous killing spree to an end."

"I'm on board for that," Cheyenne said, leading her partner down toward the computer lab.

Valri Cavanaugh Brody was in the process of attempting to resolve several of the problems that had been dropped on her desk during the course of the last twenty-four hours. When she heard someone entering her lab, she reluctantly glanced up, sensing yet another problem coming her way and being dropped in her lap.

"Oh Lord, I know that look," she groaned when she saw who it was. "It's a 'put me at the head of the line because I'm a Cavanaugh' look," Valri lamented.

"Actually, it's an 'I've got a simple problem' look," Cheyenne explained to her cousin.

Valri looked past Cheyenne toward the man who had come in with her.

"Hi, I'm Valri," she said, introducing herself to the man she hadn't met as of yet. "And you are…?"

"Cheyenne's new partner, Jefferson McDougall," Jefferson said, stepping forward to shake Valri's hand. He remembered seeing her at Andrew Cavanaugh's birthday party, but only at a distance.

Valri smiled at the man. "Well, you seem to be holding up well. What can I do for you?" she asked, directing her question toward the new partner as a courtesy.

"We need you to access some old military records so that you can tell us what this former soldier's name is," Cheyenne said, cutting in. "We have her DNA, thanks to her daughter."

"Am I allowed to ask why?" Valri asked, glancing at the name, which struck her as being rather generic.

"We think that it might help us identify the body that's lying in the morgue," Jeff told her.

"Or let us know that it's *not* that person," Cheyenne told her cousin.

"Does it have anything to do with the current serial killer case?" Valri asked.

"It has *everything* to do with the serial killer case," Cheyenne told her cousin.

Valri put her hand out for the information. "By all means, bring it on. Anything to capture this hateful killer."

"My sentiments exactly." Cheyenne handed over the folder with the information she had just printed up. "I figured that you could give us the most amount of information in the fastest amount of time."

Valri opened up the folder. Looking at what was inside, she said, "That would be a very pleasant change." She quickly looked at the name that had been supplied, then keyed it into the appropriate area on her screen to see what she could find.

Ten minutes later, using the information that had been supplied, Valri had managed to locate the person that Cheyenne and her partner had been looking for.

"The former soldier's name is Lauren Master. Her DNA is AB negative." She looked up at her cousin. "AB negative is pretty rare."

"That makes it easier to identify the victim, right?" Jeff asked the woman.

"As long as you can match it to one of the victims tucked away in the autopsy drawer," she told the duo. The printer next to her computer came to life, printing out the information she had just accessed and had now keyed into the screen. Once it was printed, Valri handed the single sheet that had emerged out of her printer to Cheyenne. "There you go," she declared. "And please keep me apprised of how this case goes. I want to see this guy be put away."

Cheyenne looked at her cousin in amazement. "I've never seen you get caught up in a case before," she told her cousin.

"I have to restrain myself," Valri told her in all honesty. "Otherwise, I'd never be able to fall asleep. These kind of things will just prey on my mind and never leave me alone."

"Well, good luck," she added, calling after the detectives as they left her lab.

"That went well," Jeff said to his partner as they went down the hallway to the stairs.

"Hold off on that until the medical examiner tells us we have a match," she cautioned Jefferson.

Jefferson saluted his partner. "Will do," he told Cheyenne.

Chapter 22

"Kristin?" Cheyenne said in surprise as she and her partner Jefferson walked into the room where the autopsies were performed.

Cheyenne looked around the imposing area, looking for the man she thought of as a slightly oversized gremlin. Adrian Barlow, the medical examiner, was nowhere to be seen.

"Where's Dr. Barlow?" Cheyenne asked the young woman at the desk who had been busy writing notes for a file when they had walked in.

"Not here," her cousin-in-law told the detectives. "He had a family emergency. So I'm afraid that you're stuck with me," the attractive young woman wearing hospital fatigues told the two detectives.

"I wouldn't exactly call getting the best medical examiner in the county, maybe the state, 'being stuck,'" Cheyenne said to Dr. Kristin Alberghetti Cavanaugh. "Truth be told, you are definitely my favorite medical examiner by far." She turned toward her partner and said, "She's extremely competent, very easy to talk to and on top of that, she married Malloy, one of my former playboy cousins, domesticating him. That brought a huge sense of relief to my uncle."

Kristin grinned at the narrative. "Occasionally, when the spirit moves me, I walk on water as well," the medical examiner teased. She put a hand out toward Cheyenne's partner. "Hi, you must be Cheyenne's new partner. I believe I saw you at Uncle Andrew's party the other night."

"Probably," Jeff agreed. "There were an awful lot of faces swimming around in front of me. It was hard to keep everyone straight," he said by way of an apology.

Cheyenne flashed a wide smile at the medical examiner. "He flunked the quiz at the end of the evening, but I decided to give him another chance." She became serious. "We're actually here to possibly help you identify one of the serial killer victims who might be lying here."

Rising, Kristin led the way over to the drawers that were against the wall. "Bring it on, I'm all ears," she said, looking at the duo. "What have you got for me and how did you come by the information?"

"It's actually a rather unusual story," Cheyenne admitted. "The young woman who initially came to us about her missing mother said she was going through her mother's things the other evening when she discovered that the woman who had raised her, who she thought she knew like the back of her hand, was once enlisted in the army."

Kristin's eyes immediately lit up at the information. "The military. That means that her DNA has to be filed somewhere in some database," she declared with no small degree of excitement.

Cheyenne grinned back at the woman. "Exactly. Even though there are no fingerprints or identifying facial features, you can't just eliminate DNA out of the victim's system at will."

"And you do have the woman's DNA?" Kristin asked, not about to assume anything.

Cheyenne unfolded the note she had, which contained the woman's military name, her record as well as her DNA on it. "Everything is right here," she said, placing the paper on the table right in front of the medical examiner.

Kristin picked up the paper, looking at it. "AB negative," she read, then murmured, "That's rare." She looked up at the two people in the room with her. "It's going to take me a little while to run the test to determine her DNA," she told them. When the detectives made no move to leave, Kristin found herself telling her cousin-in-law and the woman's partner, "I work better without having my every move scrutinized closely."

"I think that's our cue to leave," Jefferson said,

not overly happy about the fact. "So when would you want us to come back?"

"It takes from two to five days to run the test," Kristin informed the duo. "Sometimes longer." She heard her cousin as well as Jefferson groan at the news. "But I have a friend who knows someone who might be able to speed things up. I will let you know how things go. I just want you to know that I don't need to stand over the lab slide waiting for the results to materialize. I can do other things in the lab while the results are fermenting—so to speak."

"So close and yet so far," Cheyenne murmured with a deep sigh.

Amused, Kristin laughed. "Welcome to my world," she told the two detectives. "Now shoo." She waved Cheyenne and her cousin-in-law's partner on their way. "Let me get started on this."

"Be sure to call me if you need anything, Kristin. Anything at all," Cheyenne emphasized pointedly.

"Oh, don't worry, I will," Kristin told her cousin-in-law in all seriousness.

"I'm beginning to understand the meaning of the phrase 'hurry up and wait,'" Jefferson told his partner as they walked out of Autopsy and headed into the hallway. He clearly looked rather disappointed. "I thought that being as connected as you are, the process to get answers would go a lot faster."

"Maybe faster," she allowed, "but it's still a process. There's only so much that can be done to make the process move along."

"Okay," her partner agreed, resigned. For now it was obvious that there was nothing more that could be done. "So what is our next step?"

She smiled at Jefferson. The man obviously did not like remaining idle any more than she did. She liked that about him. They really were going to get along, she decided, which was a good thing.

Cheyenne thought for a moment and came up with a solution as to how to handle their inertia. "We could return to Aurora Valley to see if we can catch that lecturer we weren't able to corner on Friday. Maybe this time we'll be able to talk to him about that student of his who seems to have gone AWOL, find out if he knows anything about it or has an opinion on the subject."

"Even if we do manage to catch him in, this so-called 'professor' might not want to talk to us," Jefferson pointed out. It was a gut feeling he had, but he didn't want to call it that, given what she had said about some of her family's feelings about the subject.

Cheyenne's eyes narrowed as she thought of the lecturer possibly attempting to avoid her questions if it came down to that. Her eyebrows almost touched, forming an angry vee.

"Oh, he'll talk to us," she told her partner pointedly. "I guarantee he'll talk."

To her surprise, her partner laughed at her tone. "You certainly are a tough little cookie, aren't you?"

Cheyenne thought of all the years that she had competed against her older brothers, going up against them in all sorts of different scenario. She had to admit that it had wound up hardening her and making her that much more determined to win.

"Oh, you don't even know the half of it," she told him with no small amount of conviction.

Something in his partner's voice caught Jeff's attention, causing him to have questions about the woman next to him. "Maybe," he granted, "but I do know that I'd certainly like to find out more."

His words and the expression on his face sent a warm shiver all through her.

Her eyes met his as she smiled. "We can talk about that once we get back tonight."

Back tonight. That definitely sounded promising, her partner thought. Jefferson flashed a smile at her. "Sounds good to me," he told her.

They drove to the college using Cheyenne's vehicle. The campus seemed to be in the middle of shifting from the students who frequented the college in a full-time capacity in the daytime to the students who could only attend classes on a part-time, after-hours basis because they needed to be employed in order to pay for the classes they were taking.

Siting in the passenger seat, Jeff was able to look around the campus and take in the surrounding area. It made more of an impression on him now than it had the first time they had come to check the campus out.

Cheyenne got the impression that there was something on his mind. "What?" she asked him as she guided her car farther into the campus.

"If you ask me, this looks like the perfect area for a crime," Jefferson told her with feeling.

"That's only because you know what might have gone down here," Cheyenne said as she guided her vehicle into an available parking space. "We don't really have any proof to substantiate that," she pointed out.

"Granted that does help add to the aura," Jeff agreed, getting out of Cheyenne's car.

"And seeing how deserted this particular part of the campus is right now just adds to the sense that something less than uplifting could have gone down here," Cheyenne said to him. She turned toward her partner. "Am I right?"

"You, Cheyenne, are always right," he told her.

She looked at him, curiosity etched into her features. "When did I go from 'Cavanaugh' to 'Cheyenne'?"

He smiled broadly at her. "I'd say sometime during our second night together." His eyes were shining at the memory of that night.

"Well, that certainly wasn't coy," she concluded, looking at him.

"I wasn't aware that you were looking for me to be coy," he told Cheyenne.

She drew her shoulders back, bracing herself as they approached the building where they knew their possible suspect was supposed to be teaching in a few hours.

"Right now, what I want," she told her partner, "is to find our possible suspect where he's supposed to be and get him to answer a few questions that we're going to ask him."

"I just want to get him to confess his part in all this if he's actually guilty," her partner said.

"Yes, there's that, too," Cheyenne responded, pushing the door open.

As she did so, Jefferson put his hand up against it and held it for her so she could walk through the entrance and into the ground-floor lobby.

"I guess they don't believe in putting up the heat," he observed, noticing how chilly it felt inside the building. It didn't feel all that different than it did outside.

"Why should they do that?" she asked, pretending to sound surprised. "These are the evening and part-time students who are coming in. They're used to having to put up with hardships," Cheyenne pointed out. "By and large, they are a hardier breed than the ones who attend the school during the day."

Jefferson had trouble containing his laughter. "A little prejudiced are we?"

"I'm not prejudiced," she told him with indignation. "I've just had some experience dealing with privileged kids—the ones who never had to work for anything that they got. I have to admit that I don't exactly think very kindly of them."

"I've had to deal with those types as well," her partner admitted. "But you can't let those types get to you or it'll wind up eating your insides."

She glanced at her partner, clearly impressed with his attitude. "You're more intuitive than I thought you were."

Having him assigned as her new partner had obviously been a good development, Cheyenne thought. She really needed to tell her uncle Brian that she was grateful to him for his forethought and insight.

As they approached Professor Murphy's classroom, they saw movement inside the room via the dark-inted window. There appeared to be only one person visible through the opaque window. The professor? Or was it someone else?

"Looks like we're on," Cheyenne told her partner in a lowered tone of voice.

Jefferson didn't answer. A look came over his face. A cold look that told Cheyenne she wouldn't have wanted to run into the man in the middle of a battlefield when he had been a Marine.

"Looks like," her partner said under his breath.

Cheyenne glanced at her watch. "Class hasn't started yet. This is the perfect time. Let's go," she urged.

They didn't bother knocking on the classroom door—they just walked in.

As if sensing that something was off, the evening lecturer's eyes immediately looked toward the door.

His expression hardened as he seemed to all but shut down right in front of them.

Murphy didn't really look at the man who had crossed the threshold and entered his domain. But the woman was another matter entirely.

He recognized her from a news story he had caught on TV the other day. She was the one that certain sources speculated was trying to find information on a serial killer that people feared was haunting the area and might even be attempting to kill older victims specifically.

The speculation almost made him smile.

Almost.

It looked as if they might be onto him after all this time. Ah well, Murphy always knew that it couldn't last forever, but he had no intention of going quietly, he thought, his face darkening again.

"You're not in my class," he said. He made it sound like an accusation.

"No, we're not," Cheyenne said, taking out her ID and holding it up for his benefit. Jefferson followed suit with his ID. "My partner and I are detectives with the Aurora Police Department and we have a few questions to ask you."

Rage clawed at his throat, all but choking him, although the lecturer's expression didn't change.

The witch who had just sauntered into his classroom had a tone that reminded him of the way his aunt Lily used to sound when she spoke. Like she was in charge of the situation, pretending to be all-knowing.

And that, he thought, struggling to blanket his fury, was going to be this woman's downfall, just the way it had been with his aunt.

A downfall, the lecturer promised himself, he intended to enjoy immensely as he brought it about.

Apparently, Christmas was coming early this year.

Murphy caught himself smiling as he stifled a chuckle.

Chapter 23

Jon Murphy gestured toward the empty seats in the row that was right in front of him. Cheyenne noticed that those seats were lower than the one that the lecturer was sitting in. Most likely to give him a feeling of superiority, she guessed.

"Sit," the lecturer said in a less-than-inviting tone of voice. "What questions would you like me to answer for you?"

Jefferson sensed that the lecturer would respond more to him than he would to Cheyenne. Hoping that his partner wouldn't feel that he was attempting to usurp her, he forged ahead and asked the professor, "We understand that you had a Lauren Dixon in your class until recently."

"I did," the lecturer answered. He waited to see

who or what the two people would bring up next, if anything. Confident in himself, he felt as if he was prepared to tackle anything.

Jefferson wanted to be sure that he had gotten the matter straight. "But she's not in your class anymore?" Cheyenne's partner questioned.

"No, she's not," the lecturer answered the detective, his voice echoing with finality. Mentally, he dared the two detectives to attempt to trip him up.

"Did she decide to take a leave of absence or just drop out of your class or...?" Cheyenne let her voice just drift away, deciding that she had said enough. She was curious to discover just what Murphy would answer.

"Since I have no idea why she is no longer attending my class, I suppose that the best answer to that would be 'or,'" Murphy told the detectives questioning him. For good measure, he decided to add, "It's a shame, really, because she struck me as having the makings of a good student whenever she did speak up in class. And the one paper she handed in was very well written. It did show me that she was able to think on her feet when the occasion called for it."

Cheyenne glanced at her partner. The professor was being rather generous in his praise. That did surprise her. Had they made a mistake suspecting the man? she wondered.

Or was he just trying to hide his true feelings toward the older woman?

"Would you happen to have that paper of hers on file?" Cheyenne asked the lecturer, curious.

Murphy shook his head. "I'm afraid not. I handed back all the papers after I graded and recorded them. I was certain that reviewing her own work would definitely encourage Ms. Dixon," he told the detectives. "Obviously not. Years on the job and I'm still being educated."

Something just didn't ring right to Cheyenne although she couldn't quite put her finger on exactly what was wrong. Maybe, she told herself, she was just being prejudiced against the man. It was as if she was so intent on finding the serial killer who was out there, her mind had been made up even before she ever met the lecturer, although she wasn't usually so dead set against a possible murder suspect. Maybe she had become jaded.

Or maybe she was right.

As if reading his partner's mind, Jeff asked the lecturer point-blank, "Did Ms. Dixon seem to be a little off or preoccupied to you?"

Murphy began to respond and it seemed as if he was about to agree with the assessment the male detective had made, but then apparently he changed his mind about the answer he was about to give.

"I'd like to say yes, but you have to understand that I have a lot of students attending my classes and unless one of them does something noteworthy or outstanding, I'm afraid they just fall through the cracks for me or meld with the other students," Murphy told the two detectives.

The lecturer made a show of glancing at his watch. It was almost time to begin the class. "Looks like your time's up," he told the duo. He almost regretted that. He did enjoy baiting and matching wits with the police, especially when one of them was a woman. The female detective definitely deserved to be put in her place. "Tell you what, why don't you give me your cards," he suggested, "and if I think of anything, anything at all, I'll give one of you a call."

Jefferson was quick to produce his card. Maybe he was being overly protective of his partner, but he didn't want her having to deal with the lecturer. Quite honestly, the man just gave him the creeps. There just seemed to be something off about Jon Murphy and despite the little time he and Cheyenne had had together, he could sense that she saw the man as being a challenge.

To his consternation, he saw Cheyenne produce a card a beat ahead of him. He held it out to the lecturer. Murphy took her card first, although the lecturer did take Jeff's card as well.

The man tucked both cards into his pocket.

"If anything occurs to me, I'll be sure to call," Murphy promised again, a sick, oily smile gracing his lips. The words made Jefferson sick to his stomach.

Jefferson noticed that the lecturer was looking at Cheyenne as he made the promise about calling. It left Jefferson with an admittedly uneasy feeling, not to mention a rather sour taste in his mouth.

"Then it's settled. We'll be waiting to hear from you," Jefferson told the lecturer with finality. And with that, he placed his hand against the small of Cheyenne's back, ushering his partner out of the lecture room and out into the hallway.

"I remember where the hall is, Jefferson. I don't need to be guided like some lost child," Cheyenne told her partner. It was all she could do not to swing around and face him as she made her annoyed accusation.

"Nobody said that you did," Jeff told her. He pressed his lips together, making an effort to choose his words carefully. He didn't want to get into an argument with the woman.

Finally, he decided to just say what was on his mind. "Did you get the same uncomfortable feeling about that guy as I just did?"

Cheyenne chewed on her lower lip, thinking. "I don't want to be responsible for influencing the way that you're regarding this case," she told her partner.

"Too late," Jefferson said honestly. "I think we view this guy in the same exact light. There's just something there, something beneath the surface," he admitted as they walked from the building to her car in the parking lot. "The guy just gives me the creeps—and you have nothing to do with that."

Cheyenne eyed him doubtfully. "You would have thought of that on your own?"

Jefferson knew she didn't mean that the way that it sounded. He did his best not to take offense. "I'm a former Marine and a trained investigator. So yes. I most definitely would have thought of this on my own, even without your help, although it's nice to have you agree with me."

The lecture hall was filling up quickly around him, but Murphy was preoccupied, hardy noticing the students who were filing in. His mind was elsewhere, engaged in planning his next move—and the way he would savor the results.

That witch had it coming to her, he told himself, even more than the others he had eliminated over the last year and a half or so. He couldn't recall feeling this degree of excitement since he had managed to drain the last breath of air out of his aunt Lily's body. But that, she decided, was actually a good thing, because if this feeling had been a regular occurrence, then it definitely wouldn't have felt as special as it did—and he needed that feeling. It was feeding his soul.

The phrase made him laugh to himself.

Waiting to do this ate away at his patience, but it also felt exceedingly rewarding at the same time, the lecturer thought.

His eyes scanned the rows before him. Wouldn't his students be surprised at the double life he led.?

Murphy fingered the business cards tucked away in his pocket. His mouth curved ever so slightly as he smiled to himself. Fulfillment was a mere heart-beat away.

Or it would be very soon.

The overhead bell went off, signaling the beginning of the hour as well as class. Murphy pulled his shoulders back.

Time to perform again, the lecturer told himself.

"Settle down, people," he told them in a harsh, authoritarian voice.

And because the students mostly belonged to an older generation and actually rejoiced over the opportunity to be able to wedge their studies into what could be perceived as the little free time that they had, even at this late date in their lives, they complied.

Murphy scanned the area, taking everyone he saw into view. Ordinarily, he would have been looking for his next victim. There were a lot of candidates for him to choose from, he would have ordinarily thought. However, after meeting that police detective, the search had suddenly been abandoned. At least for the time being.

The policewoman would be the perfect candidate, he told himself. The fact actually put him in a rare good mood.

He could even feel his mouth curving.

"All right, who can tell me the significance of the passage that I assigned to you the last time we were together?"

A sea of hands shot up, eagerly seeking his attention, which to Murphy meant that his students were looking for his approval.

It made him smile.

It was a chilling smile to the students in the first few rows.

"Do you feel like having a drink?" Cheyenne asked Jefferson as they pulled up into her driveway a few minutes after they had left the scene of Aurora Valley College.

"I wouldn't mind. But I'm surprised that you're the one who's suggesting it," her partner told her. "He get to you that much?"

Cheyenne wanted to deny it, but in all honesty, she knew she really couldn't. Because the truth of it was, the lecturer actually *had* gotten to her. There was something completely unnerving about the man. It wasn't anything she could even put into words—it was just a feeling that was eating away at her.

A gut feeling so to speak, Cheyenne thought. She was convinced that the lecturer had something to do with his student's disappearance. There was just something in his eyes. Something cold and unnerving. It wasn't anything that she could even cite, or have been able to bring up in court.

It was something that just *was*.

Jeff got out of the car. He appeared to be choosing his words with care, aware that if he said the wrong thing, it would wind up setting Cheyenne off, and he definitely didn't want to do that. He just wanted

Cheyenne to understand that he was concerned about her. They were in the business of capturing "the bad guys" and he knew that.

He definitely didn't want "the bad guy" capturing her.

And since he had found himself falling for his partner, he was doubly wary about her safety and he *knew* that saying anything to that effect could very well set the woman off. He knew that he needed to tread very lightly here.

"Personally, I think that having a drink might not be such a bad idea," he told Cheyenne, watching her face.

"Just to be clear, I don't want you to think I'm looking to drink myself numb or senseless," she told him.

He raised his hands as if he was attesting to his innocence in the matter. "Never even crossed my mind."

She nodded. "Okay, just so we're clear. But you do agree with me, right? There is something about that man that just makes your flesh all but curl up and want to creep away."

Jefferson nodded his agreement at her words. "Oh, absolutely—in double time," her partner told her, stifling a shiver.

"But we can't drink on an empty stomach," Cheyenne pointed out. "Tell you what, I'll make dinner for us and then we can decide whether or not we want to cap off the evening with a drink."

Jefferson's eyes crinkled as he smiled at her.

"That's not exactly the way I was thinking of capping off the evening."

Cheyenne smiled, her eyes crinkling. "We'll talk about that, too," she told him. "But first we eat."

Jefferson inclined his head, then gave his partner a smart salute. He refrained from hugging her, although he really wanted to.

"Fine with me," he told her as they walked into the kitchen, "but I have to admit that I do feel guilty, making you do all this work. I can still order something in for us," he told her.

Cheyenne put her hands on her hips. "Do you hear me complaining?"

"Well, no, I don't. But—" he started to tell her only to have Cheyenne cut into his words to put a stop to his protest before it could get underway.

"No, no buts, Jefferson," Cheyenne informed her partner. "All I want from you is to have you just sit and wait—and eat your dinner once it's ready for you," she ordered her partner.

And then with that, she turned her attention to preparing dinner.

Chapter 24

Cheyenne couldn't shake the feeling that she was being watched. It had been going on for several days now. Evenings, actually.

Admittedly, it was nothing she could really put her finger on, but the feeling just seemed to cling to her nonetheless. It had nothing to do with the way that Jeff was looking at her. They had been sharing dinners now whenever they could—and breakfasts as well.

Tonight, after dinner was over—and surprisingly he had volunteered to help her with the dishes—they had gone into her bedroom to enjoy some much-deserved "alone" time—together.

But although she responded to him more and more, Cheyenne couldn't sufficiently relax enough to enjoy herself with him this time, not the way she had previous times.

Holding her in his arms, Jeff sensed that something was off this time. He drew back and looked at the woman he had come to not only have a great deal of respect for, but growing affection toward as well.

As a matter of fact, he felt as if he was in love with her. He just didn't want to admit it to her as of yet because he was afraid that he would wind up scaring her off. He had been taught to tread lightly in everything he did, which was what he intended on doing until he felt he could safely proceed and take the next step.

She felt almost as stiff as a board in his arms. "What's the matter?" Jefferson finally asked her.

His question took her by surprise. She had been trying so hard to act as if everything was all right. Cheyenne glanced at him quizzically. "What makes you think that there's something the matter?" she asked Jefferson, doing her best to feign innocence.

Jefferson frowned ever so slightly. "Because I'm not an idiot. Because I've gotten to know you quite well in a short amount of time and because I can just feel it in my gut. And yes, you aren't the only one with gut feelings. Now, talk to me, Cheyenne," her partner urged. "What has you looking as if you're anticipating having something explode on you? What's wrong?"

Cheyenne raised her chin a little. "Nothing's wrong," she insisted flatly.

Jefferson blew out a breath as he leaned back against the headboard, looking at her. "You know, I think we should mark this date down on the calendar. This is the first time that you've lied to me. Unless, of course, I was so enamored with you that I was totally blind to the first time that you lied to me."

Cheyenne sighed, tucking herself into the space that was created against Jefferson's body by his arm. "No, there was no 'first time' before this one," she admitted honestly. With a soulful sigh, she turned her entire body into Jefferson's and looked up at his face. "I'm sorry. It's just that I can't seem to get away from the feeling that I'm being watched."

Jeff honestly wasn't expecting that and thought maybe he had misunderstood what she was saying. "Do you mean that *we're* being watched?"

Cheyenne shook her head with feeling. "No, just me," she told him. Sitting up in bed, she pulled her knees up against her and leaned her chin on them. "I know that I'm being foolish and most likely I'm just imagining things, but I still can't seem to shake the feeling that there's someone watching me. That feeling is holding me pretty tightly in its grip." She sighed, looking at the man next to her. "You probably think I'm crazy or, best-case scenario, just imagining things."

"Are you kidding? I've got a great deal of respect for the legendry Cavanaugh 'gut.' If you feel like you're being watched, then that feeling deserves to be explored," Jefferson said in all seriousness.

Cheyenne regarded him with abject wonder, as well as with huge secret relief. "You're serious," she cried in astonishment.

"Of course I'm serious," he told her. "Why wouldn't I be?" her partner asked. And then he added, "We've already slept together a number of times—all glorious, I might add. And I'm not attempting to convince you to do anything or to weaponize anything to use to my advantage. In case you haven't figured it out yet, I'm not that kind of guy. For what's going on between us to really progress, it needs to progress with honesty."

Cheyenne nodded at him, her manner turning exceedingly friendly. The man was being honest, she thought as joy slithered though her. Very honest. "You know, that realization is beginning to dawn on me."

"Well, I'm very glad to hear that," Jeff told her. His mind cast about for ways to get her to unwind and relax. "How would you feel about watching some TV, or doing something else to relax? Or, if you're really being haunted by that feeling that there's someone watching us, I could just stand guard, keeping an eye out on you and you could get some much-needed rest," he suggested.

Cheyenne looked at him in complete speechless wonder. "You'd do that for me?" she questioned her partner.

Jefferson's smile was compelling. "Of course I'd do that."

"You wouldn't report me to some authority on the

premises, or tell some higher-up that I was asking for preferential treatment?" she asked.

He laughed at the suggestion. "You're a Cavanaugh. Who am I going to report you to? And for that matter, who would believe me?"

She smiled at him. "I'm not about to abuse my so-called 'power,'" she informed him with a touch of indignity.

Her partner chuckled. "Good to know," he told her. With that, he took Cheyenne back into his arms.

She savored the warmth of his body penetrating hers and for a moment said nothing. And then she looked up at him. "Jeff?"

"Yes?" he asked, glancing down into her face as he held her close against him.

"Could I change my answer?" she asked him.

He wasn't following her. "Your answer about what?"

"My answer about making love with you right now," she explained.

Jeff grinned broadly into her face, a face he was finding himself falling for extremely quickly and extremely harder every passing day. "If you're up for a do-over, so am I—as long as you don't worry that that whoever is watching you is about to get one hell of an eyeful."

She laughed, tickled as she waved the thought away. And, with any luck, waved it totally out of existence.

"That is the creep's problem, not mine," Cheyenne informed her partner, making a nebulous reference to whoever might be watching the two of them. She turned her body into his.

Cheyenne found that she really appreciated her partner being this thoughtful toward her. Appreciated the fact that he wasn't telling her that she was imagining things, or that all of this existed just in her head. Those sort of assertions would have just made her furious.

It would have also made her feel abandoned. Jeff cutting her this slack just made her unsettled feelings that much easier for her to cope with and she was really grateful to him for that.

"Come here," she coaxed. "The embers under my fire just might wind up going out if you don't make up your mind to feed them in the next few minutes," Cheyenne warned her partner with a broad wink.

"We wouldn't want that," Jeff told her, bringing his mouth down to hers.

Within moments, Cheyenne's partner was getting lost in her lips.

Murphy's breathing grew labored as he watched the two performers going through their motions. He had his binoculars trained on the pair and had, patiently, for a while now.

He was positioned in a hiding place in a house across the street. The people whose house this was were on vacation, so for all intents and purposes, the house he was using was abandoned.

Anger creased his features. The witch was doing

this just to control the detective, the lecturer thought. The bitch had no shame to her. There was certainly nothing straightforward or even a drop of innocence about her, Murphy thought angrily.

He could feel tension sharply lancing through his body. He savored the anticipation of being able to bring her down—and it would be soon, he promised himself.

Very, very soon.

The first time he could get these two so-called detectives to separate so that he could make his move, he would, the man promised himself. And it was going to be a good one. That detective would pay for that high-and-mighty attitude she was projecting and for parading around controlling the men surrounding her.

Just like Aunt Lily had done, he thought bitterly, remembering the taste of death as life flowed away through his hands and out of his victim's body.

The very thought made his nostrils flare. He savored the anticipation of what was to come. Savored the thought of making it happen.

Soon.

Very, very soon, the college lecturer promised himself.

Despite her very strong common sense, Cheyenne had to admit that she couldn't completely eliminate that uneasy feeling that seemed to be haunting her every move. It haunted her even during their lovemaking and the time that came after that.

It was there, in the background, during every waking minute she was aware of.

In the morning, after Cheyenne had made them both breakfast, she had decided that for a change of pace, her partner needed to go to his place to get a change of clothing. They agreed that they would go into the precinct separately.

"Most likely, if they're paying any attention, the members of our team are undoubtedly talking about us being an item," she told Jefferson. "But there's no reason for us to hurry that along more than we need to at the moment."

"Cheyenne, these are trained investigators," he pointed out to her as he made his way to the door. "If they're really speculating about the situation between us, how long do you think that we can actually fool them?"

"At least for a little while," she said. "Longer if they're being polite. Tell you what, let's just take this one step at a time."

Jeff paused to take her into his arms and kiss her goodbye. "One step at a time it is," he promised, repeating what she had said to him earlier. "I'll see you in the office in a little while."

Cheyenne nodded. "You've got it, stranger," she told him with a laugh. "I've got a few things to clean up here and then I plan on heading out to the precinct."

He nodded as he walked out of her house. "Sounds

like a plan to me," Jefferson said just before he closed the front door behind him.

The man really brought a smile to her face, Cheyenne couldn't help thinking, a warm feeling stirring all through her.

"C'mon, Chey, get a move on," she instructed herself. "You haven't done a single thing around this place for days now. For all you know, you might not get another chance to do anything for another few days more. There's dust around here celebrating an anniversary."

Saying that, Cheyenne grabbed a dust rag and got busy, starting to move it around the area that was all but begging for a cleanup—or at least seemed to be begging for one in her eyes.

Because she had to get to her place of work, she moved quickly, running the vacuum cleaner with one hand and moving the dust rag with the other. Cheyenne was so busy, trying to get the job done as quickly as possible, that she wound up being oblivious to everything else.

Speed to her was of the essence. She had to get to the precinct as quickly as she possibly could. She had the feeling that she and Jefferson were onto something. They suspected that smug lecturer no matter what he'd said to try to dissuade them from doing so. She wanted to dig into the man's records as well as into his students' records. Something might just lead them in the right direction.

While she knew that coincidences did happen,

something in her gut made her feel that this was way too much of one. Jon Murphy had had at least three of the missing older women attending his classes. That just didn't seem possible.

Granted it could have just "happened" that way, but why would it? she couldn't help wondering. This was not a tiny college. Could the missing women have more in common than just being missing? And if so, what was it?

There was no time like the present to find out, she told herself. As soon as she and Jeff got in, she wanted to check a few things out and then she and her partner were going to make their way to the college to talk to administrators who knew the lecturer.

Maybe she and Jefferson were barking up the wrong tree, as it were.

Shutting off the vacuum cleaner, Cheyenne turned around to lean it against the wall.

Startled, she wound up dropping the appliance on the floor.

Murphy was standing in her living room.

Cheyenne's eyebrows immediately drew together in anger. She knew instinctively that she couldn't display even a hint of fear to this man despite the fact that her heart was slamming against her chest so hard right now, it was all but creating a hole where it hit.

She immediately thought of her weapon. It had been locked up last night and was still locked away. She needed to get her hands on it, if only to make him back away—although she sensed that the man was a great deal more dangerous than he had initially been given credit for.

"What are you doing here, Professor Murphy?" Cheyenne asked, the sheer anger in her eyes holding him back.

The smile on his lips was cold and absolutely bone-chilling. "What do you think I'm doing here?"

"Invading my space without an invitation," Cheyenne snapped at him. "I'll thank you to get out of here."

"I will, when I've done what I've come here to do," he told her, taking measured steps toward her.

"No," she told him firmly. "You will go *now*," Cheyenne ordered him.

The eerie smile on Murphy's face continued as he took another step toward her. "You sound pretty brave for a woman with only a few more minutes to live," he informed her icily.

Chapter 25

Cheyenne knew she had to keep the man who had broken into her house talking until she could figure out a way to get her hands on her weapon and make him back away. The really odd thing was that she was about to actually go get her weapon when her attention had been diverted to vacuuming her floors and rugs instead. Had she put that off, even for a short while, she would have already been armed when the lecturer had broken into her house the way he had.

"How did you know where I lived?" Cheyenne demanded, hostility echoing in her voice as she tried to divert his attention.

The expression on the lecturer's face was filled with sheer anger and hostility. "Oh come on, give me some credit, Detective Cavanaugh." Murphy smirked as he talked down to her. "You're not the only one who knows how to track a person down."

Murphy took another step toward her, managing to crowd her into a small space against the wall. "This is the part where I tell you that if you don't fight this too hard, it won't hurt you as much." His mouth curved as an ugly expression took over his face. "But we both know that isn't true. Personally, I hope you *do* fight this. You know, seeing you struggle with fear radiating from your eyes would be a great deal more rewarding for me than having you crumble in front of me and just give up." He leered at her in anticipation. "That part will come later."

What Cheyenne heard in his voice made her blood run cold. Cheyenne grabbed a small metal statue of an eagle that was in the middle of the end table closest to her. With a bloodcurdling scream, she threw the statue, pitching it right at Murphy. She managed to hit the man square in the face.

The lecturer shrieked in pain. Running a hand over his face, he looked down at it and saw that there was blood on his palm and fingers.

Fury entered his eyes.

"Oh, you're going to pay for that, you bitch," he promised, savoring every syllable that he uttered. "Pay big-time!"

Cheyenne did what she could to project complete and nonchalant defiance.

"Big-time?" she repeated with a sneer. "You mean even more than just being killed?" she asked, showing Murphy how patently absurd that claim of his had sounded to her.

Jon Murphy's expression turned menacing and looked even uglier than it already had. He wanted to see even more fear evident in her face, but all he could see was defiance there—and that fact completely enraged him.

"I am going to kill you by inches, bitch!" Murphy promised viciously, shouting the words almost into her face. "You hear me? Bloody inches!"

"You know, I think that it's safe to say that the neighbors heard you," Cheyenne told him, doing what she could to bait the man.

Cutting the distance between them short, Murphy made a dive for her. At the last minute, Cheyenne managed to kick the lecturer, delivering the blow dead center to his stomach, then another to his genitals. She knocked the air right out of him.

The killer tried to catch her and made a grab for her throat, but Cheyenne managed to twist out of his reach at the very last moment.

She had the presence of mind to make her way over to the cabinet where she always kept her weapon locked up. She knew that she somehow needed to get the cabinet open in order to get at her handgun.

Murphy made another grab for her, trying to get hold of her waist. Again, Cheyenne succeeded in eluding the serial killer's grasp, just managing to duck out of his reach.

Her heart slammed against her chest. It almost

hurt in its intensity this time. She knew that if Murphy—or whatever his actual name was—managed to get his hands on her, that very well might spell the end of her. He had a look in his eyes that was absolutely frightening. Hardened killers had that sort of look about them.

Murphy managed to twist around again, reaching for her as he cursed her viciously.

Damn but she really wished she hadn't been so conscientious about locking up her weapon. After all, she mocked herself, who was going to break into her house just to get their hands on her gun? Right now, she was the one who needed to get her hands on her gun, not some theoretical stranger, Cheyenne thought in frustration.

Eluding the maniacal lecturer's grasping hands, Cheyenne twisted and turned, managing to continue getting away from Murphy as he continued to keep trying to grab her.

She could see that she was making the lecturer furious.

"You're just fighting the inevitable, you stupid bitch," he said, taunting her. "The more you fight, the more I'm going to really enjoy squeezing the very life out of you," he promised her nastily. "Bit by bit. Just like with Aunt Lily."

She wanted to ask him who this "Aunt Lily" person was, but this was not the time to get that information out of him. She could do that once he was handcuffed in front of her.

Just then, as Murphy was about to make another grab for her, uttering yet another bloodcurdling yell, Cheyenne's front door suddenly flew open. The impact made it bang loudly against the back wall. The doorknob left a slight hole in the wall where it had made contact.

Caught completely by surprise, the lecturer swung around and stared at this newest development.

His mouth dropped open.

Murphy continued to watch the person who had just come rushing in.

"You!" he spat when he realized that it was the police detective's partner who had just rushed into the house. "So now it's officially a party," Murphy declared with a nasty, laugh.

Murphy saw the gun that was in the police detective's hand. His scowling face darkened even more.

"You can't shoot me," the lecturer sneered at McDougall's face. "I'm unarmed," he pointed out, reveling in the fact that he was correct.

It was just the minor distraction that she needed, Cheyenne thought. Propelling herself forward, she made a grab for Murphy's arm. She twisted it as hard as she could, moving it behind the lecturer's back.

Murphy screamed in pain.

"You certainly look unarmed, but that still won't save you," Cheyenne told him, thoroughly enjoying being able to strike at least a little fear into the man's heart.

In her view, it was nothing short of payback. As

a matter of fact, she had to exercise extreme control to keep from breaking Murphy's arm. In her heart, she felt that she would have been completely justified if she had. But she also knew that that wasn't what she and the other agents of law enforcement were all about.

There was the slightest bit of hesitation on Cheyenne's part and Murphy instantly attempted to use that to his advantage. Lunging, he grabbed the gun that her partner had drawn when he'd entered Cheyenne's house and taken in what was going on.

The lecturer tried to shoot at Jefferson but wound up missing the man because Cheyenne's partner had ducked.

For her part, Cheyenne made a grab for the same eagle statue she had previously thrown at the lecturer. Holding on to it by its base, she swung the statue at the lecturer as hard as she could and managed to hit Murphy in the back of his head.

She'd brought the lecturer down before he could do any harm to her partner or to her.

Dusting herself off, Cheyenne looked down at the unconscious man. A feeling of triumph washed over her. She couldn't help smiling.

Breathing hard, she told her partner with satisfaction, "I believe that this is what is referred to as 'checkmate.'"

She allowed herself one precious moment, after looking over to assure herself that the lecturer was indeed really out, to throw herself into her partner's arms. And then she hugged him for all she was worth.

"What made you come back?" she asked her partner, amazed at how close she had come to actually meeting her end. The same, she knew, could be said for Jefferson.

She had naturally assumed that her partner had left for the apartment where he was staying so he could get a change of clothes. That would have taken him some time and she could have been dead before he'd finished.

"The answer to that is really funny. I realized that I had walked off with your keys instead of taking mine," he told her, holding up the keys for her benefit. "When I tried putting the key into the ignition, the key actually fit, which was the strange part, but then it refused to turn. After two attempts, when I couldn't get the car to start up, I realized that I had picked up your keys instead of mine by accident. What threw me," he continued, "was that the key did fit into the ignition, which was highly unusual."

Cheyenne's eyes fluttered shut for a second as she thought of how close she had come to her own demise. And then they flew open again. She was sincerely grateful that there had been such a mix-up.

"Thank God for mistakes," she said to her partner in all sincerity. "I honestly believe that this guy would have just as happily killed me as looked at me."

Jeff had learned something that he hadn't had a

chance to share with his partner as of yet. "This scum and his sickening killings have been making the rounds on all the podcast shows recently," he told Cheyenne. "Seems that this serial killer took a great deal of joy in killing strong-willed women, and 'strong-willed woman' definitely describes you to a tee," Jefferson pointed out.

Just then, the lecturer moaned. He was regaining consciousness. When he turned his eyes toward Cheyenne, there was nothing short of sheer contempt and hatred in them. When he spoke, he sounded almost maniacal.

"You haven't escaped me, Aunt Lily," he told her angrily. "You're going to die. If it's the last thing I do, I'm going to kill you. You're going to pay for what you did to me. Pay dearly, do you hear?"

Cheyenne eyed her partner. "Well, that solves that mystery," she told Jeff with finality. "I guess the other victims reminded Murphy of his aunt Lily, too."

"Don't talk about her!" Murphy shrieked at the woman he had taken a vehement dislike to. And then he spat, "You're not fit to even say her name."

Cheyenne exchanged looks with her partner. "He definitely has a problem, and we," she went on with a satisfied, relieved smile, "definitely have the serial killer we were looking for."

"Nothing! You have nothing!" Murphy fairly shrieked at Cheyenne, his expression looking as if he wanted to vivisect her. The next second, he managed to knock her out of the way and hurdled himself at Jefferson. Grabbing his throat, he knocked Cheyenne's partner's head against the floor.

For a second, Jefferson looked as if he had passed out. Frightened, Cheyenne clawed the lecturer away, digging her nails into Murphy's face. She was determined to separate the man from her partner in any way that she possibly could.

The man was going to hurt Jefferson over her dead body, Cheyenne promised herself.

The lecturer tried to fight her off, but a surge of almost superhuman strength surged through Cheyenne, helping her keep the man at bay.

She knew it wouldn't last.

Just in time, Jefferson came to. He wrestled the lecturer away from Cheyenne and bent the man's arms behind his back really hard.

"Cuff him, Cheyenne," Jeff ordered his partner at the exact same time that Murphy shrieked in pain.

Cheyenne managed to straighten up just as her partner dragged Murphy to his feet. He decided to put the cuffs on the serial killer himself.

"Call backup," Jefferson instructed Cheyenne, referring to the precinct. "This guy isn't going to let up until he winds up killing one of us, if not both. We need to get backup here."

Breathing hard, Cheyenne started to place the call to the precinct. With a guttural yell, Murphy threw himself at her partner, pointing his gun at Jefferson.

It all happened so fast, it seemed like one huge blur. Murphy began to aim his gun at her partner and Cheyenne swung up her hand, shooting the lecturer. Murphy went down in a bloody heap, screaming in pain.

He was dead as he hit the floor.

Cheyenne fell back, exhausted and breathless, never taking her eyes off the man. She couldn't believe he was dead.

But the lecturer's eyes remained lifeless as they stared upward. His face was pale.

Relieved, Cheyenne all but collapsed into her partner's arms. "I think we're finally safe," she cried.

"If we're not, then this creep belongs to the breed of the undead," her partner told her. Holding Cheyenne to him with one arm while watching the prone man on the floor, Jeff placed a call to the nearby EMT.

Giving the driver directions on how to get there, he continued looking at Cheyenne. When he ended the call, he told his partner that the driver would be there to pick up the serial killer's body very soon.

The nightmare, at least for now, was finally over.

"If anything ever called for a celebration, it's this," Andrew Cavanaugh declared the following afternoon as paperwork was being filed and all the i's were dotted and the t's were crossed. The former chief of police looked around at the members of the department who were surrounding him as the announcement was made that the serial killer who had been plaguing the city was finally dead. "I know what you're thinking," Andrew said. "We just had one.

But our newest detective from Texas, working with his partner, my very stubborn niece, just managed to take a serial killer out of circulation and that deserves acknowledgment. Big-time. Besides, this'll give me a chance to cook," he said with a wink. "I like evening the score."

"After all these years, it's a competition?" Brian asked his brother in surprise.

"It's always been a competition," Andrew said with another wink.

Cheyenne turned toward her partner. "Welcome to the family," she told him with an amused laugh. She was unbelievably grateful that this was finally over and that it had ended the way that it had.

Standing amid the others, Jefferson looked at her in surprise. And then, as her words sank in, his expression changed, warming. "You mean that?"

She detected an undercurrent in his words. Well, she had come this far, she might as well say the rest of it. "I do if you want me to," she told him.

Brian walked up between them, putting one hand on each of their shoulders. "Say yes," he encouraged Jefferson, adding, "Cheyenne probably doesn't want this to be public knowledge but she was engaged to a guy who wanted her to move to the East Coast with him. When she refused to go because it would mean leaving everything she knew behind, he broke off the engagement and just walked out on her. This—" he gestured toward Cheyenne "—is the happiest the family has seen Cheyenne in six months."

"Uncle Brian," Cheyenne protested with a warning note in her voice.

Brian shrugged. "Well, it's true," he said pointedly. "Go home," he ordered the detectives who were in his office, then added, "Rest up for the next case." And then the chief of detectives smiled broadly. "We get our rest whenever we can get it," he reminded the others.

"Sounds like a good suggestion to me," Cheyenne told her partner.

"And I know just the way I'd like to relax," Jefferson said, his eyes meeting hers.

She leaned her head in toward his, whispering, "Your place or mine?"

"Doesn't matter as long as we're together," Jefferson told her in all honesty as they and the others all filed out of the chief of d's office.

"You're serious?" she asked, looking up at her partner.

"I've learned never to lie to my partner," he told her as he grinned. "You taught me that."

Her eyes were smiling at him. "You're a good learner," she told him.

"I'd like to think so," Jefferson answered.

"So, we'll be getting together this weekend in order to celebrate getting this guy off the streets and ultimately into a coffin?" Andrew asked as he followed his niece and her partner out. He had been invited to the precinct expressly for this announcement.

"All right then, we will be there with bells on," Cheyenne promised.

"With something else on as well, I hope," one of her brothers, walking out behind them, said with a laugh.

Jefferson gave his partner's brother a censoring look. "I'd say speak for yourself, but it would probably get me in trouble," he laughed, avoiding her brother's smirking look.

With one arm tucked around Cheyenne's waist, he ushered his partner toward the elevator. The best, he knew, was yet to come.

Because tonight, Jefferson promised himself, he was planning to set the stage to ask Cheyenne to marry him. Their life together would truly begin from that point on and he, for one, could hardly wait for that to happen.

Epilogue

Andrew didn't usually scan the internet news sources on his computer for his daily information. But he was short on time today, so he had decided to indulge his curiosity this one time, especially since it would be a quick perusal just to get the highlights.

The internet had just been coming into fruition when he had wound up resigning his position as the chief of police in Aurora in order to take care of his children.

He definitely hadn't expected to stumble across anything of interest. And yet, he did.

The headline caught his attention immediately.

His mouth fell open as he read. As did the sick feeling in the pit of his stomach.

Is there another serial killer lurking in Aurora's shadows?

Have we really seen the last of the serial killer who had been terrorizing the good people of Aurora? We were told that he was dead, but maybe we have all been lied to. Or worse yet, maybe the serial killer has come back from the dead to avenge himself on the unsuspecting citizens of this fair city. A body mutilated in the exact same manner as with the first wave of executions was found just on the edge of the Santa Ana Freeway in the center of Aurora.

I would seriously advise the people of Aurora to exercise extreme caution and be very, very careful when they venture out of their homes.

Andrew frowned, curling his hands against his thighs in frustration—another thing about reading stories on the internet that he found extremely annoying. Had he been reading this article in a local newspaper, he would have now had the satisfying pleasure of tearing the pages out of the newspaper and then shredding those same pages into teeny-tiny unreadable confetti.

He couldn't do that with what he read on the screen. Not unless he printed the pages first and then tore them up. It seemed to him like a colossal waste of ink and paper, doing that.

"What mindless nonsense," Andrew grumbled. As far as he was concerned, this article was just a piece of sensationalism. It was merely meant to drum fear into the local citizens' hearts. There was no other reason for this article to exist. "They should be ashamed of themselves," he declared angrily.

"Who are you talking to, dear?" Rose asked her husband as she walked into the room. "Who should be ashamed of themselves?" she asked. And then her eyes narrowed as she saw that the usually dormant laptop was on and open to a news site.

This was a highly unusual situation, Rose thought, given that there wasn't a recipe being highlighted on the screen. She frowned, drawing closer and reading. Her eyes weren't what they used to be.

Andrew was not given to using the internet for random searches. If he wanted to find out something about someone, he would call them or get in contact with that person the tradition way—by driving over and dropping by.

"Andrew, what's going on?" she asked her husband, concerned. "Is there something wrong?"

He wasn't about to lie to Rose, even to spare his wife the worry and concern that mentioning something like this—the appearance of another serial killer—would wind up generating. If he made something up, it just wouldn't work.

Ever since they had first gotten married, Rose could always see right through him if he wasn't being completely truthful with her.

"Possibly," he said, answering her question regarding something being wrong.

Rose blew out a breath as she shook her head. "English, Andrew. Speak English," his wife told him.

"I can't help you if I don't have a clue what you're saying."

Andrew sighed. He *really* didn't want to pull her into this. Waving his hand at his words, he told her, "Forget I said anything."

But his wife shook her head rather emphatically. "I'm afraid that it's too late for that, Andrew. All right, my love. Time to come clean."

Andrew sighed. He was beginning to believe that years of living a rather laidback, sedate life, helping him prepare the complex menus he had become known for had gotten to his wife. Rather than Rose getting a hobby for herself or something along those lines, his quiet, reasonable, loving wife had suddenly taken a second look at the sort of life her husband had led before he had resigned his position and found herself longing for a more exciting life than the one she was now leading.

Andrew slanted a look in Rose's direction. She appeared intensely focused on what he was about to say. He knew in his heart that she would give him no peace until he answered her question.

Truthfully.

"It looks as if that serial killer that Cheyenne and Jefferson took down either had a groupie bent on following in his footsteps, or some other twisted human being was hoping to drum up the sort of 'hero worship' the original killer had generated.

"In other words, according to this article I found on the internet, someone is attempting to emulate that sick serial killer and has left a body, killed in the same fashion, on the edge of the freeway." Andrew gestured toward the yellow pad next to the computer that he had been writing on. "I wrote down the location where the body was found and I intend to give it to Brian so he can send out some of his people to check it out."

He sighed, looking at the pad. "This could all be a tempest in a teapot, or it could very possibly be round two of the worst serial killer the city of Aurora has ever seen." Andrew raised his eyebrows as he pinned down his wife. "Satisfied?"

Rose shook her head. "No, I'm not—and I won't be until this so-called serial killer wannabe is behind bars—or made to pay the ultimate price for what he has done and for what he intends to do."

"Much as I would like to, sweetheart, we can't get ahead of ourselves and arrest this slime for his future crimes," Andrew told his wife. "But arresting this mad dog will stop him from committing those future murders."

Rose nodded. "I'll buy that. Have you told the family that you suspect that there's a serial killer wannabe roaming around our city?"

Andrew shook his head. "No, not yet. I just stumbled across this article on the internet—just before you walked in on me."

Rose pressed her lips together thoughtfully. "Well, dear, I think I have the theme for your next party— or at least the excuse for it," she said with a smile, winking at Andrew.

"A supposed serial killer lurking in the shadows isn't exactly something to celebrate, Rose," the former chief of police told his wife.

"No, it isn't," Rose agreed. "But getting him off the streets and behind bars certainly is," his wife told him. She paused to kiss Andrew's lips with feeling.

Andrew chuckled. "Well, I certainly can't argue with that," he agreed.

He felt as if he was finally able to release the monster that was living and growing inside of him—and it was really such a huge relief to do that. He had been living with these fantasies for so long.

And then, when he had read about that college lecturer, the one the article had said was killing women who resembled and reminded him of his aunt, something within him had just snapped. He had no aunt that had made his life miserable, no aunt that he wanted to destroy, over and over again. No aunt at all, or family for that matter, really.

Ever since he could remember, he had been making his way from foster home to cold, lonely foster home, all the while picking up basic survival tactics.

Because he had a slight build until he reached the age of seventeen, he had been picked on and belittled over and over again, dreaming of the day he would be able to get his revenge on his tormentors.

And then, miraculously, he'd had a growth spurt—a really *big* growth spurt—and the kids weren't picking on him anymore. What they did do was avoid making any eye contact with him at all, hoping that he would forget that they had tormented him.

But he didn't forget.

He didn't forget one single moment of their ridicule. Not one single display of cruelty that they had sent his way.

He had patience.

He could wait to get his revenge.

Waiting just made it that much sweeter when the moment of revenge finally materialized.

And then, when he had read that article about the serial killer that had lived right here, lived among them completely undetected, something inside him had suddenly blossomed. It felt as if his way had just been highlighted for him and he knew just what he needed to do to achieve his ultimate revenge for all those years he had suffered.

He would get his revenge and strike fear into all those worthless hearts that had made his life so miserable for so long.

He would show them, he promised himself. He would show them all.

He savored the thought.

And he had already started his journey, he thought with glee. His jaw hardened, remembering.

Make fun of him, would they?

Belittle him, would they?

Well, he'd show them. He'd show them all, he silently promised himself.

All he needed was a coherent plan to kill all the

people he had been forced to cohabitate with when he had been a young boy in the foster system.

He closed his eyes, envisioning it all. A wave of glee mixed with anticipation washed over him, sending shivers all up and down his spine.

His hands grew damp as he envisioned how he planned to get even. And the marks he planned to leave in their flesh.

He couldn't wait until he was able to put his plan in motion.

Opening his laptop, he typed in the name of the man he wanted to be his second victim.

In order for that to come about, he needed to find Glen Shaffer's address.

Locating the man was a lot simpler than he would have thought. He congratulated himself as he stared at the address.

"I hope you have your affairs in order, Glen," he told the name on the screen, laughing in anticipation. "Because you don't have much time left to do that, you worthless waste of human flesh. When I'm finished with you, you'll wish that you had never been born. Just the way you made me feel," he said angrily between teeth that were clenched so hard, they threatened to break if he exerted any more pressure on them.

And then, suddenly, he smiled in anticipation.

* * * * *

Texas Law: Lethal Encounter
Jennifer D. Bokal

MILLS & BOON

Jennifer D. Bokal is the author of several books, including the Harlequin Romantic Suspense series Rocky Mountain Justice, Wyoming Nights, Texas Law and several books that are part of the Colton continuity.

Happily married to her own alpha male for more than twenty-five years, she enjoys writing stories that explore the wonders of love. Jen and her manly husband have three beautiful grown daughters, two very spoiled dogs and a cat who runs the house.

Visit the Author Profile page at millsandboon.com.au for more titles.

Dear Reader,

For me, every book is unique. While I love them all equally, it's for different reasons. Sometimes, I find it a challenge to explain what makes a certain book special. But that is not the case with *Texas Law: Lethal Encounter*.

I love the characters.

The heroine, Kathryn Glass, is the undersheriff in her small Texas town. She's good at her job and has the confidence of her department. She's a smart, strong woman who loves her family and her community. A widow for over six years, she's ready to put parts of the past behind her and see what the future holds. And that's when she finds Ryan Steele trespassing in her backyard...

Ryan has made some bad choices in his life. But now, he's ready to make up for his misdeeds. There's just one problem—he's not sure how a *good person* should act. What's more, he's attracted to beautiful Kathryn. The one thing he knows is that a woman like her will never want to be with a guy like him.

But when the neighbouring towns of Mercy and Encantador are thrown into deadly chaos by the return of serial killer Decker Newcombe, Kathryn and Ryan have to work together.

This time, Decker's come back with a plan—and help.

No spoilers from me, but the outcome is unpredictable.

There is one other thing I love about this book and it's you, Dear Reader. Thank you for taking this journey with me and I hope you come to love these characters as much as I do!

All the best,
Jennifer D. Bokal

DEDICATION

To John: My love, my life, my everything.

Chapter 1

The song of insects filtered through the open windows. Ryan Steele sat in the cab of his truck and stared into the night. A bead of sweat rolled down the side of his face, and he wiped it away with his shoulder. Old Blue, his dog, sat in the passenger seat and panted.

"Hell of a night," he said to the dog. "It's…" He glanced at his phone. It was 8:32 p.m. and it was still 81 degrees. "Well, it's too late to be this hot."

After slipping his phone into the cup holder, he shifted in his seat. Ryan didn't mind spending the night in the cab of his truck. In fact, he'd slept in worse places. Jail. A bare mattress on the floor of a house that smelled like stale beer, body odor, and worse. For most of his thirty-eight years, he'd wandered—avoiding anything that would tie him to one place for too long. Not for the first time, he contemplated how things would've been different if Decker Newcombe hadn't been a part of his life.

Decker had been born bad—plain and simple.

And Ryan? Well, his misdeeds were more of a choice.

He remembered how they'd started in elementary school. Both boys lived in the same neighborhood outside of Dallas. It began with a few sodas swiped from the convenience store next to their trailer park. Kid stuff, right? Then, by middle school, they were breaking into trailers. They kept some of their loot but quickly learned how to sell the stolen property for cash. The summer before high school, Decker was paid to beat up a classmate who'd flirted with the wrong girl.

To be honest, he imagined that his old compatriot would have done the crimes for free. But Ryan saw them mainly as a way to make bank. Money was the only way to escape the crappy life he'd been given.

For decades, he'd managed the business end while Decker committed offenses for hire—assault, robbery, arson, even assassinations Then they took a job that ended with a Wyoming DA dead, and both Decker and Ryan were wanted for the murder. Sure, Decker was the killer, but Ryan had accepted payment for the hit. That was enough to be considered an accessory to the murder.

Decker disappeared.

Ryan was arrested.

Corny as it sounded, even in his own mind, that was when he got a chance to start over. It all began when Isaac Patton visited him in jail. Ryan was waiting for trial— held without being given bail. Isaac had just opened a private security firm—Texas Law—and he had a plan to catch Decker. It was as simple as it was audacious.

In exchange for being used as bait to draw Decker out of hiding, Ryan would have his criminal record expunged.

It had taken nearly a year of watching and waiting for the killer to emerge. During that time, Ryan had been set up with several businesses to run in the town of Mercy, Texas—not far from where he now sat. For the first time in his life, he'd been legit. During the months he worked, his businesses made a profit. He took care of his employees. He was part of a community. Life wasn't perfect, especially since he was living a lie. But he'd been happy.

What's more, it gave him a glimpse of how things could be different.

As they all hoped, Decker had contacted Ryan. From there, things had gotten seriously messed up. Decker had gone on a killing spree—leaving four people dead and several more seriously wounded.

After a shootout, the killer had escaped into the desert. More than a year later, and Decker was still at large.

Since Ryan had kept up his end of the bargain with Isaac and his federal partners, his criminal record had been cleared.But even life without a criminal record hadn't been easy. Without his felonious history, he had no history at all. It turned him into a ghost, walking among the living but never really being seen or heard. Legit employers were leery of hiring him because they all knew he had a tale—and the ending wasn't happy. He'd thought about selling his story for profit. After all, he was one of the people who'd known Decker best. But if he was going to cash in on his former association, his past would follow him like a shadow forever.

Luckily, he'd found a general contractor who needed help and didn't ask too many questions. Ryan worked hard and got paid for his time. Now he had enough money in his pocket for a down payment on a small house. Or maybe there was a business for sale that he could turn over.

Anyway, after 15 months, he was back—and this time, he planned to stay.

Too bad there were no vacancies at the motel, in Encantador. It forced Ryan to find an out-of-the-way place to park his truck where he could spend the night. The vehicle sat at the edge of a gravel lot. It was bordered on one side by a canal. On the other side, there was a county route and endless Texas desert. In the distance sat a housing development that was filled with small homes.

Old Blue looked at him and whined. After turning in several circles on the passenger seat, he dropped into a ball. With a sigh, he placed his head on his paws.

"I know how you feel." Reaching over the center console, he scratched the top of the dog's head. "I didn't want to spend the night in the truck, either. Sorry, boy."

The heat leeched his energy, and he was ready for a rest. After folding his arms across his chest, he let his eyes drift closed. Old Blue sat up. The sound drew Ryan from the edge of sleep. He glanced at his canine companion. The dog's spine was ramrod straight. His ears were back. Peering into the darkness, Old Blue growled.

Something—or someone—was out there. Ryan was awake now. "What is it, boy?"

The dog growled louder. He followed Old Blue's gaze. A figure emerged from the canal's bank. The hair at the dog's nape stood on end. The person looked male, and they wore dark clothes. They crept along the trail, keeping to the shadows. After a moment, he lost sight of them in the darkness. But a moment was all he needed.

Ryan was sure he'd just caught a glimpse of Decker Newcombe.

For a moment, he tried to think rationally. He'd seen someone, sure. But it wasn't Decker. After all, he'd just been thinking about the killer, who was still at large. So of course, he imagined seeing him emerge from the shadows. But the killer was presumed to be dead, for Christ's sake.

Ryan settled back in the seat, his hand drifting to his side. The scar ran right under his ribs, still a raised weal. It was a reminder of the last time he'd seen Decker and the killer had stabbed him in the gut. Again, he looked out of the windshield. The man—whoever he was—was gone.

An upstanding citizen would call 911. Leaning forward, Ryan reached for his cell. The sheriff's personal information was still in his contacts. He placed the call.

Before it even rang on his end, voicemail answered. "You've reached Sheriff Parsons…"

He didn't want to leave a message, he wanted to talk to the man. With a curse, Ryan ended the call and threw the phone back in the cupholder.

"What do I do now?" he asked, although he knew the answer. He still had to call 911.

The dog glanced over his shoulder. Looking back to the open window, Old Blue sprang out of the truck.

"Boy." Ryan leaned across the center console and yelled through the window. "Get back here."

The dog paid no attention. Old Blue sprinted toward the trail until the only thing Ryan could see was the white tip of his tail. Soon, even that was gone.

He opened the door of his truck and stepped into the night. Somehow, it was hotter outside than in the cab. "Blue." He patted his thigh as he called out. "Get back here, boy." He held his breath and waited. The dog did not return. "Blue," he called again. "Come here."

Ryan wanted to curse. Instead, he jogged into the darkness, following the dog's path.

The housing development was less than five hundred yards from where he'd left his truck. The narrow dirt trail was bordered on one side by a tall, wooden fence that ran along the back side of the neighborhood. On the other side was a canal with concrete banks. A trickle of water ran down the center. Scraggly trees and bushes clung to life next to the waterway.

"Blue," he called out. "Where are you, boy?"

Ryan's chest was tight. Sweat dripped from his hairline. It soaked the collar of his T-shirt and burned his eyes. Earlier in the day, he'd tied a flannel shirt around his waist. Now, he used the hem to dry his face. He peered into the darkness and looked for any sign of the dog. The glint of his collar in the night. The rustle of bushes a moment before the dog emerged. The sound of a happy bark.

There was nothing.

Heart still pounding, he slowed his gait to a walk. The dog couldn't have gone far, right? Although, he knew that was wrong. If Old Blue started running, Ryan would never see him again. He'd gotten used to the canine's company. Was he on his own once again? A sour taste filled his mouth.

A bridge had been built across the canal, and the path rose to the berm. He climbed the hill and he sagged with relief. Sitting next to the fence was Old Blue. The dog looked up. His tail started to wag.

"You scared me, running off like that." He moved to the dog's side and rubbed behind his ears. *Damn.* He hadn't thought to grab the dog's leash from the truck. Now, he just had to hope that Old Blue would follow. "C'mon, let's go."

Old Blue whined and looked toward the fence.

Ryan gripped the dog's collar and tugged. Old Blue didn't budge.

"What's the matter?"

The dog sat next to a gap in the fencing. Between the slats, Ryan could see a flat backyard with a large tree. A concrete patio sat off the back door of a single-level home. There was a grill and patio furniture. It was all covered by a striped awning.

Then he saw it. Movement in the shadows next to the house. It was a person. A man. Holding his breath, he stood still and watched. The way the man moved—his posture, the tilt of his head—was familiar.

Ryan knew that it might not be Decker. But what if it was?

Over the years, he'd gotten used to minding his own business. He was good at looking the other way when trouble was near. But he also knew that if he wanted a different life, he had to be a different person.

It meant he had to warn someone.

Besides, he had a score to settle with Decker.

Slipping a hand into his pocket, he reached for his phone. *Damn it*. He'd left it in his vehicle. Still, he had to know if he'd really seen Decker.

Looking through the gap in the fence, he scanned the yard. The back of the house was visible, but the man was gone. Despite the heat, a chill ran down his spine.

"Where'd you go, you son of a bitch?" he asked, though nobody was around to hear his question.

Old Blue nudged his side. He looked down at the dog, who regarded him with brown eyes.

"Should we find out if Decker's in the neighborhood?"

Old Blue stood and stared into the yard.

Well, he supposed it was settled.

Ryan was a big guy, over six foot two. What's more, his broad shoulders had gotten more muscular from months of working construction. A few slats in the fence were missing, but the opening was narrow. Turning sideways, he slipped between the boards.

Old Blue followed.

With the dog at his side, he crept across the yard. Light spilled from a window where the curtains had yet to be drawn. Decker could've snuck into the house already. The family who lived there might not even know that their lives were in danger.

Ryan hadn't always done the right thing. But he had to stop his old associate—no matter the personal costs.

Undersheriff Kathryn Glass stood in her bedroom. It had been an especially long day. The sheriff, Mooky Parsons, was on vacation in Cancun for two weeks to celebrate his wedding anniversary. His absence left

Kathryn in charge. She didn't mind the responsibility that came with being the acting sheriff. But the Encantador Sheriff's Department was small to begin with. A missing set of hands made everyone's workload heavier.

It was almost 8:45 p.m. on a Saturday evening and Kathryn was still in her sweaty uniform. But she had been at a back-to-school fair hosted by the elementary school's parent–teacher group and had spent the evening talking about internet safety.

Her mind wandered, as it did often now, to her eldest child. Morgan was just beginning her senior year of high school. The past few years had been rough on her daughter. She'd experimented with drinking and some drugs and boys. Kathryn always struggled to find the right parental balance between discipline and understanding. Especially since she suspected that much of her daughter's behavior was a way of dealing with the death of her father and Kathryn's husband two years earlier.

Her son, Brock, a sophomore, was completely opposite to his sister. He was class treasurer and had recently made the varsity football team.

Working her wedding band up and down her finger, she wondered what her husband might think if he were still alive. But she knew. He'd be like Kathryn and love their kids so much that it hurt.

Staring at the golden band on her finger, her chest ached with loneliness. There were still times she picked up the phone, ready to call Edward. But now, those moments no longer ended with her in tears. A few months back, she'd even managed a wistful smile as she recalled how he'd greet everyone with a cheery "Yello!"

His own little joke, he used to say when she or the kids teased him.

She missed Edward, truly she did. Yet, recently, Kathryn wasn't so focused on the past. She was looking forward to the future—like Morgan's pending college applications and Brock's talent on the gridiron. She glanced at her ring once more, but movement behind her caught her eye.

Looking up, she scanned her room through a mirror atop her dresser.

Nothing was out of place.

The bed was made. A pile of clean clothes—folded, but yet to be put away—sat on a chair. A book lay on a nightstand.

She turned.

A face peered through the window.

Her blood turned cold as her heart started to race. Then her training kicked in. Kathryn's pulse thundered in her ears as she ran from her bedroom. She sprinted down the short hallway and dashed through the kitchen. Thank goodness both of her kids were out with their friends.

Kathryn fumbled with the handle on the kitchen door as she unlatched the locks. She jerked the door open. It hit the wall with a crack. She ran into the night, just in time to see the man as he sprinted around the side of her house.

"Stop!" she yelled as she ran after him. "Encantador Sheriff."

She skidded around the corner. The man was already running down the sidewalk. A large, brown dog loped at his side.

"Hold your hands up," she called again, "and turn to face me."

The man didn't stop.

Neither did Kathryn.

As she ran, porch lights turned on. Opening their curtains and front doors, her neighbors looked into the street, eager to see who or what the undersheriff was chasing.

The man veered to the left, sprinting across another lawn. He was headed toward the canal.

Kathryn had lived in the area her whole life. She knew the town better than she knew herself. If the man made it to the path and the canal, he could get away.

Unless…

She cut through a neighbor's yard. The grass was baked, brittle and brown, by the long Texas summer, and the blades crunched underfoot. Running through the backyard, she reached for the top of the fence and scaled the boards with her feet. Sweat trickled down her back and dampened her shirt. She had a clear view of the canal path and waited for the man to appear. He still ran at a full sprint, and his speed only gave her seconds to react. She came down, landing hard. The impact sent a shock wave through her knees. She turned, just as she and the man collided. He slammed into her, knocking her down. Lying on the ground. she had a sense of having been hit by a brick wall, and white dots floated in her vision.

Rolling to her hands and knees, she watched the man as he sprinted away. The dog sniffed her as he passed. Once again, she was driven more by instinct than thought. Reaching for the dog, her fingers looped through the collar. She pulled him to a stop.

The canine yelped. The sound was one part terror, one part fury. He bared his teeth at Kathryn. She quickly rose to her feet and straddled the dog near his front legs. She wasn't exactly sure what she'd do with the mutt. Hopefully, the pet had a rabies tag that linked him to his owner.

"You're coming with me," she said to the canine. Her breath came in short gasps. "Let's go."

She tugged on the dog. He snarled, lunging at her. She jerked her hand back, barely avoiding the sharp teeth.

"Old Blue," a male voice called from the darkness. "It's okay. It'll be okay."

She looked up. The man was standing on the trail, less than ten yards from where Kathryn held his dog. From where she stood, she could see that he was tall. He had dark hair. A five-o'clock shadow covered his cheeks and chin.

It occurred to her that the guy could've gotten away. Instead, he'd come back for his companion. She admired that kind of loyalty—even in a person who looked through windows.

"You stay where you are," Kathryn ordered the man.

Holding up his hands in surrender, he said, "I won't move, so long as you let go of my dog."

Old Blue whimpered and wagged his tail.

"I don't think so," said Kathryn. With the dog calm, she commanded, "Sit."

The canine dropped to his haunches. Still holding his collar, she scratched the back of his neck.

"Traitor," the guy muttered.

She refused to smile. "You want your dog back? Come to my office and answer some questions."

"I really don't think that's necessary, do you?"

This time, she gave a quick laugh. "Buddy, I caught you looking through my bedroom window. You want your dog, you come to my office." Did she feel bad using the dog as a bargaining chip? Maybe a little.

Still, she had a job to do. She needed to find out if the guy had any outstanding arrest warrants. She might have to charge him with trespassing or stalking. Mostly, she wanted him out of her town—because Kathryn knew one thing. "You aren't from these parts, are you?"

"Well…" he scratched his chin "…not exactly."

Not exactly? "What's that supposed to mean?"

"I lived in Mercy for a year a while back."

She recognized the voice. Kathryn's heartbeat raced. She swallowed. "Take a few steps closer. Let me get a look at you."

The man took three steps in her direction. He cut the distance between them by half.

"That's enough. Keep your hands up." She rested a palm on the gun at her hip, a not-too-subtle warning.

With her eyes adjusted to the darkness and the man standing closer, she saw him clearly. The last time she'd seen him, his hair had been shorter. He'd been stockier but was now all muscle. But still, it was him.

"Talk about a bad penny turning up again. Ryan Steele. What in the hell are you doing?" She paused a beat. The dog, whose collar she held, must've been the canine who survived the Decker Newcombe massacre. She'd heard that Ryan had adopted the mutt. "Why were you in my backyard?"

"I didn't realize it was your yard, Undersheriff. Honest," he said.

"What were you doing in someone's backyard at all? Trespassing is a crime." She'd also heard that for helping the feds, Ryan's criminal history had been erased. That didn't save him from being charged with something now.

"I thought I saw something. Someone." His voice was barely above a whisper. She had to strain to hear what was said. "They were in your backyard. I was worried."

Despite the heat, gooseflesh covered her arms.

"Then why were you running from me?"

He lifted one large shoulder and let it drop. "Old habits, I guess."

She didn't really like his answer, which brought up more questions. "Who did you see?"

He shook his head.

The law-enforcement officer inside her had to consider that Ryan was lying. He hadn't seen anyone lurking in the shadows. The only reason he'd been in her yard—or anyone else's—was to find an easy house to rob.

Yet, there was another part that believed Ryan had seen someone else. But why? Maybe it was because he'd come back to save his dog. Or maybe there was something sincere in his tone of voice.

She tried once more. "You aren't giving me much to go on, Ryan. Who was it that you saw?"

He stared at her. Their gazes met and held. "I saw…" he swallowed "…I thought I saw him."

Him. A hard knot formed in her gut. She could already guess the answer. Yet, she had to ask, "Him who?"

"Decker Newcombe," he said, his voice still a whisper. "He's back."

Chapter 2

"You saw who?" Kathryn choked on the last word. Decker Newcombe was worse than the boogeyman to those who lived in Encantador and the neighboring town of Mercy.

Her hearing was fine. But Ryan's words were unbelievable.

"Decker," he said again. This time his voice was louder. "I only caught a glimpse of the guy, but the way he moved was just the same." With an exhale, he continued, "Anyway, I saw someone. I followed him—whoever it was—into your backyard."

Kathryn had been first on the scene when one of Decker's victims had been found. The one-time assassin—killing only for money—had switched his modus operandi to become a serial killer. The image of the woman—bloody and bruised—still haunted her dreams. Past trauma aside, she had to think. She was the undersheriff, after all. While running her fingers through the dog's fur, she said, "Your story doesn't make sense." She paused a beat to let him comment. He didn't. "If you thought you saw a serial killer, you should've called 9-1-1. Why go after him yourself?"

"It wasn't exactly my plan." He nodded toward the dog that sat at her feet. "Old Blue jumped out of my truck window."

He answered some of her questions and created others. "Your truck?"

"I was parked at the end of this trail." He hooked his finger over his shoulder.

Parking in the middle of nowhere was suspicious. "Why?"

"Just getting some rest."

"In your truck?"

Even in the dark, she could see Ryan stiffen. "That's not against the law. What do you call camping?"

"Camping usually includes someplace nicer than the end of the canal trail." She nodded toward the dog. "You got a leash for him?"

"In the truck," said Ryan.

"Not a problem." Still holding the dog's collar, Kathryn used her other hand to loosen the belt that was around her waist. After pulling it free of the loops on her uniform pants, she secured the end to the dog's collar. It wasn't a long lead, but at least Old Blue could be walked.

Then to Ryan, she said, "Step toward me. Spread your feet and put your arms out at your side." He followed her order. "You got any weapons? Anything I should know about?"

He gave a quick shake of his head. "Nothing."

She patted him down quickly. His pockets were empty and there was nothing hidden in his clothes. "Let's go," she said.

"You talking to me or the dog?" Ryan asked.

"Both. You've got some questions to answer. And you're going to do that in my office. If I buy what you have to say, I'll give you a ride back to your truck." She didn't want to get ambushed from behind and gestured for him to pass. "You go first." Ryan walked by, and Kathryn followed.

Tongue lolling from his mouth, Old Blue seemed content to go on a walk.

As they walked, Kathryn couldn't help but ask, "You saw someone in the dark and you thought it might be Decker. Why's that?"

Raising his large shoulders, he let them drop with a sigh. "Like I said, it was just the way he moved, I guess. I tried to call Mooky but he didn't answer. Before I had the chance to call 9-1-1, Old Blue took off. I went after him, and we ended up in your yard." He paused. "Maybe we should call the sheriff now. He could meet us at your office."

She shouldn't be surprised that Ryan wanted to speak to her boss. The two men had worked together to find the killer months before. Yet, his suggestion stung, like a slap to the cheek. "He's on vacation, so you're stuck dealing with me." She tried to keep the snark out of her voice, but it was a losing battle.

Ten years earlier, Kathryn had been hired as a sheriff's deputy. It didn't take long for her to be promoted to undersheriff. Since Mooky had a decade's more experience in law enforcement, she'd never get the top job. What's more, he was a popular figure in the community. But she worked hard every day, too. So, it always left a bad taste in her mouth when she was overlooked by those who only wanted the sheriff. Right now, with Mooky out of the country, Kathryn was the first line of defense in protecting her town.

"There's a gap in the fencing, just ahead." A storm had pulled slats off her fence months earlier, and Kathryn had yet to repair all the damage. Until she did, it provided a passage from her yard to the canal trail.

After ducking and turning sideways, Ryan barely squeezed through the narrow opening. It made it impossible for her to miss his toned physique. His T-shirt hugged the muscles in his pecs. The cuff on his short sleeve was snug around his biceps. She really shouldn't be noticing the handsome ex-con—especially since she didn't trust him at all.

Drawing in a shaky breath, Kathryn shoved aside all thoughts of hard arms and tight abs. She followed Ryan. The dog was the last to squeeze through the gap. Using her free hand, she pointed to the side of her house. "My cruiser is parked at the curb."

"Your place looks nice," said Ryan, while walking through her backyard.

On the back patio, she'd created an outdoor-living space. "Thanks," she mumbled.

"You eat out here often?" he asked.

She understood that Ryan was just making small talk. But the patio had been a year-long project for her, the first after Edward's death. It was a place that brought a sense of accomplishment and peace. What's more, she served dinner alfresco whenever she could. Not that her kids were around much for meals. It meant she ate alone most nights. Still, she said, "Actually, we use the patio a lot."

"I don't blame you."

"Go around the house to the right. You can't miss my car."

She followed Ryan. Old Blue, still on his makeshift leash, trotted happily at her side. Kathryn's house was like many in South Texas. Sitting on a square foundation, the one-story residence had adobe walls and a tile roof. Everything was built to keep out the heat. From her front yard, she could see several open doors along her street. People stood on stoops and watched the road.

When she stepped onto the curb, the elderly woman who lived across the road called out. "What's happening, Undersheriff? We all saw you chasing that man. What'd he do?"

She hadn't expected to be questioned by her neighbors. Working her jaw back and forth, she thought through her answer before speaking. "I've got it under control, Gladys. You can go back into your house."

Gladys wasn't ready to give up. "Who is he?"

"I can't comment on anything right now," she said, trying to strike a balance between in-control and amiable. "Y'all go back inside."

Another neighbor called out, "Is that the guy who used to own the bar in Mercy?"

And another, "Where'd you get the dog?"

Another neighbor, named Joe, said, "I thought I saw someone slinking through my backyard."

The last comment caught her attention. Ryan had certainly been in her yard. It didn't matter that he swore that he was following a man he thought could be Decker. From the beginning, she suspected that he was lying to her. Was this witness going to give her proof?

She stopped and turned to the man who'd spoken. Joe was in his late fifties and had two grown children. "Was this the man you saw?" She pointed at Ryan with her free hand.

Joe stood on the sidewalk, next to his driveway. He slowly shook his head. "I don't think so. The guy I saw was shorter. Thinner. He was dressed in all-black—like a ninja with a hoodie."

If Ryan had been telling Kathryn the truth, then someone else was roaming through her neighborhood. Someone who had an uncanny resemblance to Decker Newcombe.

Was the killer back?

The metallic taste of panic coated her tongue. She inhaled. Exhaled. "Y'all get back inside. Lock your doors. There's nothing to see here. But if anything turns up on a doorbell camera, text me the footage right away." Her car keys were still in the pocket of her uniform pants. Using the fob, she unlocked the doors. She opened the back door for Ryan. The man got into her cruiser. Old Blue pulled on his lead. She let the dog follow his owner. After shutting the back door, she rounded to the driver's side and slipped behind the steering wheel. The air in the car was hot and stale. She turned on the engine and set the air-conditioning on high.

A wall of mesh wire separated the backseat from the front. "Let me know if you get enough cool air back there," she said.

Old Blue sat next to Ryan and panted. For his part, Ryan scratched the back of the dog's shoulders and stared out the side window. "We're good."

"Can you hand me my belt?" She didn't exactly need the belt to hold up her pants, but she didn't want to give Ryan anything that he could turn into a weapon, either. He'd been compliant so far. But she'd be naive to think that his mood was guaranteed to stay so friendly.

He passed the leather belt through the wall of wire that separated the back seat from the front. "Here you go."

She took the strap and shoved it into the console. "Thanks." The car's interior was starting to cool. After pulling the door closed, she placed the gearshift into Drive and eased away from the curb.

"What now?" Ryan raised his voice to be heard over the engine.

Kathryn had to focus on the facts as she knew them. Right now, she didn't know a lot. If Ryan was right, then a dangerous and deranged man was in her town once again. And it was her job to bring the elusive serial killer to justice.

Ryan sat in the back seat of the cruiser. It wasn't the first time he'd been in the back of a police car. Still, he had hoped that those days were behind him. Scratching Old Blue's ears, he watched the undersheriff.

At least his situation had improved in one way. Kathryn Glass was better-looking than any other cop he'd met over his lifetime. Hell, she was an attractive woman. Full stop. She wore her long brown hair in a ponytail that skimmed the back of her neck. Her skin was tanned by the Texas sun. Her eyes were the same blue as the sky on a summer's day.

Blue as the sky?

When did he get so poetic?

Still, there was more about Kathryn to admire beyond her looks. He'd heard her life's story more than once, though she was never the one to tell him. A widow with two kids, she worked hard to keep her family together. She was smart, good at her job, and dedicated to her community. In short, she was the ideal partner for any guy with half a brain.

Despite his lack of formal education, Ryan wasn't stupid.

He knew that the beautiful undersheriff would never want a guy with a past like his.

She glanced at him through the rearview mirror. "Come on. You don't expect me to believe that you saw Decker tonight."

He'd spent a lifetime of lying, so telling the truth never came easy. Yet, he was determined to be candid with the cop. "It was dark. I can't be sure," he said. "But it surely resembled him."

Kathryn said nothing. After a moment, she reached for a mic on a radio that was set into her console. Pressing down on the talk button, she said, "Todd, you there?"

A moment later a male voice came from the radio. "I'm here. What do you need?"

"I want you to increase patrols tonight," she said, speaking into the mic. "Someone's sneaking around the neighborhood by the canal trail. From the description I've gotten, it's a male. Not too tall. Dressed in dark clothes."

There was a burst of static. It was followed by the deputy's voice. "That doesn't give me a lot to work with."

"You see anyone out of place, stop them. Check their ID," said Kathryn.

"Will do," Todd replied.

She set the mic back in its cradle.

Old Blue laid his head on Ryan's lap. "So you believe me?"

"I didn't say that, either. There are several possibilities." She held up a single finger. "One. You weren't out chasing some shadowy figure, like you said. Rather you and the other guy are working together. Since you got picked up, you needed an excuse. Telling me you saw Decker Newcombe is just a way to redirect my attention."

He sighed. If he were a cop, he'd probably have the same suspicions. "It's not a lie. I'm not working with anyone to break into houses. I'm not stupid enough to do anything like that, anyway." He paused a beat. "Not anymore, at least."

Looking out the window, he knew there was nothing more he could say. He'd been a criminal his entire life. No cop would trust him.

"What are you doing back in town?" Her question drew him from his reverie.

Ryan didn't know how to answer her. How was he supposed to tell her that Mercy had been the closest thing to a home he'd ever had in his life? This was the first place he'd felt a sense of community. But his belonging had been a result of the cover story. The words didn't come to him, so he remained silent.

"You awake back there?" Kathryn glanced in the rearview mirror once again. She waited a moment for him to answer. Ryan remained mute, not sure what to say next. "Everything okay?"

"I'm fine," he said with a sigh.

"But you didn't answer my question," the undersheriff pressed.

He looked back out the window. They were in downtown Encantador. There was the grocery store. The small hospital. Phil's, the barbecue restaurant, was permanently closed. Then again, who'd want to eat in a place where Decker had killed one person and seriously wounded another—even if it was more than a year past?

She continued, "Why did you come back? What is it that you want?"

Ryan wasn't ready to tell anyone what he wanted—not yet at least. But he'd gain nothing from lying to Undersheriff Glass.

"Well," he said, turning to her with a grin that he hoped covered the loneliness beneath, "I guess I'm looking for a place to call home."

Tessa Wray stood on her front lawn. Less than five minutes had passed since the undersheriff had driven away. Kathryn had told everyone to go inside and lock their doors, but hardly anyone had listened. The neighbors, gathered into a tight knot on the sidewalk, were discussing the recent events.

Joe, at fiftysomething, was the eldest of the group. Plus, he'd lived in the development the longest. He had lots to say. "People walk up and down the canal trail all the time."

Tessa jogged the mile-long trail every morning. She gave a slow nod. "That's true. We all use it."

Joe continued, "Since that big storm a few months ago, I've noticed that people use the undersheriff's yard to pass through to the development. If she wanted to keep strange people out of the neighborhood, she'd fix her fence."

"Yeah," said Tessa. "But she's really busy. She's got a full-time job and two kids."

Tessa was the branch manager for one of the local banks. Her work hours were set. Monday through Friday, 8:30 a.m. to 5:30 p.m. Even with her evenings free, she didn't have all the time needed for the upkeep her home required. What's more, she saw how often the undersheriff came and went. It surprised Tessa that Kathryn had any time for property maintenance at all.

"Her kids are older," snapped Joe. "She could get them working on the fence. Look at me. I got kids and a job. My fence is fine."

Joe also had a wife who worked from home and children who were grown and gone from the area. Yet, Tessa knew enough not to argue. Joe did his banking at Tessa's branch for both his personal account and the engineering firm where he worked as the accountant.

"All's I'm saying," Joe continued, "is that I expected more concern for security from the second-in-command of local our law-enforcement."

"Anyone know when Mooky's getting back?" another neighbor asked.

Joe sniffed, as if he could catch the sheriff's scent

on the air. "Can't be too soon." He paused a moment. "Who was that guy she arrested? He looked familiar."

"I know who he is," another neighbor offered. "Ryan Steele. He's the fella who owned House of Steele. The bar in Mercy."

"Of course, you'd know all about that bar in Mercy," Joe said with a laugh. Then again, everyone knew about the bar—even if they never frequented the establishment. House of Steele had been shown on the TV news constantly for weeks. And not just regional stations, either. The national and cable-news networks had covered the story of Decker Newcombe. "But I wonder why Ryan's back in town."

Tessa hadn't lived in Encantador when Decker Newcombe had terrorized this community. At the time, she'd been an assistant branch manager at a bank in the Panhandle. But she'd heard about the killer. Shoot, everyone in the country had heard about Decker Newcombe. It was said that he was a descendant of Jack the Ripper—the infamous Victorian era killer.

Was he back?

The possibility left her light-headed.

"You saw the prowler," said Tessa to Joe. "Was it Decker Newcombe?"

"Don't think so."

"Are you sure?" she pressed.

Joe exhaled loudly. "I've seen pictures of that bastard."

Tessa breathed deeply. Humid air filled her lungs, and she felt like she was drowning. For an instant, her body sizzled with alarm. But it wasn't just the suffocating air that filled her with panic. It was this place. She hadn't wanted the job here—which was part of the problem. Nobody had wanted the position because of what happened with Decker. But Tessa had been offered a promotion into the corporate level, so long as she stayed in Encantador for a few years. At least her neighbors were nice—or nice enough. She exhaled and turned to Joe. "So long as you're sure."

Gladys shuffled out onto her porch. "Y'all heard what the undersheriff said. Get back inside. Go to bed. It's late."

It wasn't too late—only 9:54 p.m. Still, Tessa wanted to watch an episode of her latest bingeworthy show before going to bed. "Well," she said, thankful that Gladys had shooed everyone back to their own homes, "good night."

Joe said, "Good night, y'all. Holler if you see anything."

Tessa strode up her walkway and opened her front door. After pulling it closed, she engaged the lock. Pressing her forehead into the jamb, she had to admit one thing. She didn't like the idea of a night spent alone.

While standing on the street, she'd felt exposed. But here, in her own house, she was truly isolated. Maybe she should go and visit Gladys. Or she could stop by and chat with Joe and his wife.

No. She refused to be afraid of her own shadow.

Tessa was a grown woman. She could take care of herself. Yet, she'd sleep better knowing all her doors and windows were locked. Moving through her living room, she turned on the hallway light. There were four doors off the corridor. Three bedrooms and a bathroom. All the doors stood ajar, and each room beyond was black as pitch.

A killer could be hiding in one of those rooms.

The thought came to her, unbidden. Pushing the notion away, she reminded herself that nobody had seen Decker Newcombe in months. The arrival of Ryan Steele meant nothing. As much as she tried to convince herself there was nothing to fear, her body betrayed her brain. Her stomach started to churn. After wiping her damp palms on the seat of her shorts, she pushed the door open with her toe.

A wedge of light stretched across the floor. There wasn't much furniture in her home office. A desk with a chair. Two metal filing cabinets and a bookshelf filled with manuals from work.

From where she stood, the room looked empty. But the corners were lost in the gloom. Inching her hand along the wall, her fingertips brushed the cool plastic of the switch plate. Her finger darted to the switch, turning on the light.

With the room fully illuminated, it was easy to tell nobody was hidden in the corner. She laughed. *Way to freak yourself out.* Crossing the room, she tugged on the window. It was also locked.

She turned to the closed closet door. Her mouth went dry. It had been decades since she'd feared monsters in the wardrobe. Standing alone, she knew even the worst things were possible. Still, she had to check.

Jerking the door open, she stepped back. Several coats that she'd never need this far south hung on a metal bar. Other than that, the closet was empty.

Tessa spent the next few minutes searching the rooms

along the hallway. With each empty room, her anxiety evaporated like a puddle in the sun.

At the end of the hall, she walked through her living room and turned to the left. The kitchen was dark, but Tessa could see well enough. This time, she didn't bother turning on the overhead light. There was a window over the sink and a back door, which she headed for, and her flip-flops slapped the linoleum floor with each step.

Reaching for the handle, she twisted. The door opened. *Strange.*

She didn't recall having left the back door unlocked. She closed it and engaged the dead bolt. "There," she said out loud. Talking to herself was a habit born of years of living alone. "Safe and sound."

There was a soft click a moment before a bright light shone on her from behind. Her heart ceased to beat. She spun around quickly, blinded by the glare. An illuminated ring light stood atop a tripod. A phone—it was hers—was secured in the holder.

Tessa felt as if the floor was tilting and she was sliding into a void. Nothing made sense. But then, she saw him. Standing in the corner, near the refrigerator, was the shadowy outline of a man. She gasped, and her heart began to race. Tessa tried to think, but her mind went blank. Her hands and feet felt like lead—cold, hard, and too heavy to move.

"I doubt that," the man said, taking a step toward her. He held a knife. The blade glinted in the brightness of the ring light. He moved to the phone and turned on the camera. Her own terrified face filled the screen.

Now that he was closer, she could see his features.

His long hair. His thin face. His silver-blue eyes, icy and cold. A chill shot through her body as recognition hit her hard.

Swallowing, she found her voice. "You doubt what?"

"I heard what you just said, 'safe and sound.' You might be sound," said Decker, his voice low, "but you definitely aren't safe."

Chapter 3

Kathryn flipped on the blinker a moment before letting her foot off the gas. Her exterior control covered up her runaway pulse and racing mind. She couldn't tell if Ryan's story was legit or not. Obviously, her life would be so much easier if the guy she had in the back of her cruiser was working with another crook to break into houses.

A little grand larceny she could handle. But a serial killer? Well, that was a whole different level of dangerous.

True, she was dedicated to her job. But she was a mother first and worried about her kids. Kathryn made a mental note to text Morgan and Brock as soon as she could.

Guiding her cruiser into the parking lot, she pulled into a spot at the back of the sheriff's office. Turning in her seat, she faced Ryan. He regarded her with his bright blue eyes.

Damn. He was too good looking for his own good. Just the sight of him left her with a thirst. She turned off her libido before images began to fill her mind.

Fighting to keep her gaze locked with his, she said, "I'm going to open your door. Don't run." She wasn't sure if he had committed any crimes, but she still had to be prudent.

"I wasn't going to run."

Old Blue sat up. His tail thumped against the back seat, the sound like a bass drum. Kathryn wondered if he understood the word *run*.

She couldn't help but smile. After putting the gear-shift into Park, she turned off the ignition. After opening her door and exiting the car, she opened the back door for Ryan.

Holding onto Old Blue's collar, Ryan led the dog from the vehicle as he got out himself. Standing on the pavement, he waited as she closed and locked the car doors. She scratched Old Blue behind the ear. "Good boy," she said.

"Thanks," said Ryan. "I'm trying to behave."

Despite herself, she gave a quiet chuckle. "Come with me."

The sheriff's office was a one-story building made of red brick. Kathryn climbed the four steps leading to the back door. There, she entered a passcode into an electronic keypad. A light on the side of the device turned from red to green as the lock disengaged. After turning the handle, she opened the door.

Kathryn let Ryan and his dog pass. An automatic

light in the ceiling turned on, illuminating a long hallway. Doors lined each side of the corridor.

As undersheriff, Kathryn had an office of her own. "Second door on the left," she said. While walking, she sent a quick text to the family group chat she shared with her kids.

Checking in to see how you're both doing.

Brock replied immediately.

Still at Lazaro's. He has a new game and his parents ordered pizza.

She smiled. At least her son was having a nice evening. She sent another message.

I'd like both of you to stay in tonight. No going to parties, even if your friends' parents say it's okay.

Brock sent a thumbs-up emoji.

Morgan had yet to reply.

Kathryn tamped down her emotions, a mixture of annoyance and anxiety, and slipped her phone into her pocket.

Ryan stopped next to her office and waited. She used a key to unlock the door. Another automatic light turned on. Her windowless office was as large as Mooky's. Against one wall sat a sofa, covered in blue fabric. Next to the couch was an oval-shaped coffee table. A single-serve coffeemaker sat atop a three-drawer filing cabinet in the corner. On her walls were framed pictures of her kids alongside Kathryn's work commendations and awards.

A leather chair had been pushed under her desk. She pulled it free before taking a seat. Gesturing to the sofa, she said, "Make yourself comfortable."

Ryan sat. Old Blue lay on the floor, next to his owner's feet, and panted.

"Can I get you anything? Coffee? Tea?"

"Is there any way my dog could get some water? I don't want him to get dehydrated."

It didn't matter that Ryan's record had been cleared; to her he'd always be a criminal. Still, he was good to his dog. Without comment, she swiveled in her chair. Behind her desk was a coffee station. Packets of sugar and creamer sat in a ceramic bowl. After dumping the packets onto her desk, she wiped out the bowl with a paper towel. Using the reservoir from her coffeemaker, she poured water into the dish. Rising from her seat, she set the bowl on the floor next to Old Blue. "How's that, boy?"

The dog rose to his feet and lapped at the water. Within a minute, he'd licked the dish dry.

"Looks like he was thirsty." She bent to the floor, reaching for the bowl.

At the same moment, Ryan reached for the bowl as well.

Her fingers grazed the back of his hand. An electric current ran up her arm. Her heart skipped a beat. It'd been more than six years since a man's touch had done much of anything for her. Ryan raised his eyes. Their gazes met, and her palms turned damp. The pulse at the base of his neck thrummed.

So he'd felt the connection, too?

Kathryn licked her lips. She wondered what it would feel like to kiss him—but she knew that there'd be hell to pay if she ever found out. Lifting the bowl from the floor, she stood. "I'll get Old Blue more water. You want some, too?"

He shrugged. "Sure."

She walked across the room. Wrapped in plastic, a case of water bottles sat in the corner. She peeled two away from the pack and set both on the coffee table, not sure what would happen if they accidentally touched again.

"Thank you very much," he said.

She nodded and returned to her desk. Jiggling the mouse for the computer, she woke her desktop. The monitor winked to life. The screen was filled with the seal of the sheriff's office, along with two fields. One was for Kathryn's username and the other was for her password. She entered both. Next, she opened a search engine for outstanding warrants. After typing in Ryan's name, she glanced up at him.

"Birthdate? Social Security number?"

He gave her both, and she entered them into the search engine as well. A colorful ball twirled in the middle of her screen. "This might take a minute," she commented.

The phone in her pocket shimmied. She pulled it out and read the caller ID.

It was Morgan.

Without a thought, Kathryn swiped the call open.

"Hey, sweetheart. What's up?"

"Don't give me that *sweetheart* crap—especially since you are literally trying to ruin my life."

Oh Lord, save her from the disrespect. "Do not take that tone with me," she began.

She bit the inside of her cheek, keenly aware that Ryan could hear every word she said. Hell, her office was so small, he could probably hear Morgan, too. It brought up an interesting question. What did she do with him? She couldn't leave him in her office while she stepped into the hallway to take the call. Nor could she ask him to be the one to wait in the hallway. There was no guarantee that he'd be there when she hung up. Calling Morgan back later was out of the question.

Turning in her seat, she kept Ryan in her periphery. It wasn't much. Still, it gave the illusion of privacy. "Do not take that tone with me," she hissed again. "I am your mother."

"Then, as my *mother*—" the last word was filled with a heavy amount of sass "—you should know how important tonight is to me."

Kathryn didn't know what made tonight more special than any other. Had she missed something big? She knew that it wasn't Homecoming.

"Omigod," Morgan whined. "It's Elliot's eighteenth birthday. He's having a midnight party at his house. He has a pool. Everyone in the senior class will be there. If you make me stay home, then I'll be a worse freak than I already am."

"You aren't a freak," Kathryn said, aiming to soothe.

"Who else, aside from Brock the Perfect, has a dead dad and a mom who's a cop?"

A hard kernel stuck in her throat. She did recall agreeing to let Morgan go to an all-night party a few weeks back. Could she really go back on her word? "Which one is Elliot?" she asked. "Is he the kid who constantly smells like marijuana?"

"I told you, Mom. A family of skunks live under his back deck. It's not weed."

"Is this back deck with all the skunks near the pool? Are you sure you want to go?"

Morgan huffed. "I called you instead of texting because I'm trying to work this out with you like an adult. Ashley's going to the party whether I go or not. So if I can't go anywhere, then I'll have to come home."

Kathryn wasn't sure how late she'd be working. If there was a stalker in their neighborhood, then her daughter was safer at a large party than home and alone. "Fine," she sighed. "You can go. I expect you home early tomorrow, though."

"Thanks, Mom." Morgan's tone was suddenly sunny. "Love you."

"Love you, too."

The call ended, and she exhaled. *Now, what was she doing?* Oh yeah. Swiveling her chair to face the front, she glanced at her computer. The report had been run. *No warrants found. No prior arrests.*

She turned her gaze to Ryan. Certainly, he'd heard every word of her exchange. At least he had the good manners to pretend he hadn't been interested in what was said. Currently, he watched his dog, who remained on the floor.

"Looks like you're good," she said.

"You know," he said, raising his gaze to meet hers, "my record was cleared after I left Mercy."

"I didn't expect to see anything from years ago," she said. "Who knows what you've been up to since you left the area?" She sat back in her chair and flicked her fingers at the screen. "But you aren't wanted for anything right now."

"Am I free to go?" he asked.

"Not yet," she said. "I really need to know what—and who—you saw tonight. If Decker's come back to town, that's a problem. A big problem." *What an understatement.* The specter of Decker Newcombe haunted every person in Encantador and Mercy both. "So let's go over this one more time—"

Her words were cut off by the ping of an incoming text. Her phone sat on her desk. She glanced at the screen. It was from one of her neighbors, Stan Vargasky.

A short video clip and a picture were attached to a two-word message.

Mystery solved.

The video was taken from a home-security camera. It was ten seconds of a male, clad in black, approaching the back of a house. A photo had been taken from the video and enlarged to show his face. She recognized him at once. He was a classmate of her son's.

Kathryn opened the video and rose from her desk. Handing the phone to Ryan, she asked, "Is this who you saw?"

Looking at her phone, he drew his eyebrows together. "Could be," he said, sounding uncertain. "I mean, I only saw a guy dressed in black." He paused a beat. "Who is he?"

"That's Romeo Rogers. He's a sophomore and plays football with my son. He's a charming kid who has probably dated half the girls at the high school." She rolled her eyes. "His parents must've known something about him at birth to give him a name like Romeo." Ryan held out her phone. She grabbed it with the tips of her fingers, careful not to touch him again. "My guess is that Romeo was stopping by the Vargasky house to see one of their daughters. They have twins in ninth grade, and the older girl is in eleventh."

She typed out a text to Stan.

Where's Romeo now?

He replied, My wife invited him in for cake. He'd inserted a face-palm emoji.

Emelia was planning on sneaking out with him, I'm sure. She's still dressed and has on enough perfume to choke a horse.

She read his text out loud.

Ryan shook his head. "The would-be lovers sound sweet but stupid."

"That's a pretty apt description," she admitted.

Kathryn typed out a reply.

Good luck with your kids. Let me know if you need anything else, and thanks for sending the video.

She hit Send.

Stan replied with a thumbs-up emoji.

Kathryn slipped her phone into her pocket. "I'll admit, I'm glad that this story had a happy ending."

"Happy for everyone but Emelia and Romeo." Ryan rose to his feet. "I guess we really are done. Can I get a ride back to my truck?"

There was no reason—legal or otherwise—to keep him. "Give me a minute to close down my computer."

Standing at her desk, she clicked the cursor on the X to exit the database. Then, she signed out of her account. "Let's roll."

They walked out of her office, Ryan first, then Old Blue, Kathryn at the rear. She pulled the door to her office closed and turned the handle, making sure the automatic lock was engaged. She retraced her steps to the back door. When Ryan opened the door at the end of the corridor, heat rolled down the hallway like a tidal wave. Even before she stepped outside, she started to sweat.

"Wonder if this heat will ever break," he said.

Kathryn wasn't much for chitchat. She saw all the meaningless conversation as little more than noise. Still, she felt as if there was something she should say to Ryan. The weather was always a safe topic. "It won't," she said with a snort. "This is West Texas. It's always hot. Some days the temperature is less brutal."

He nodded slowly.

Using the fob, she unlocked the doors to her police cruiser. "Tonight's one of those brutal nights," she continued. "You can sit up front and get more cool air."

"That's kind of you."

There was more to her offer than simple kindness. When she'd asked him why he'd returned to Encantador, he told her that he was looking for a place to settle. She had a duty to protect her community. She intended to do her job, and that meant having a serious talk with Ryan.

After opening the passenger door, he snapped his fingers. Old Blue jumped onto the seat, and Ryan followed. She rounded past the front fender as dog and master got settled. Opening her own door, she slid behind the steering wheel and started the engine.

While backing out of the space, Kathryn pressed her lips together. She needed to talk with Ryan, but the words had to be just right. "I've lived in this area my whole life," she began. "The people are kind. They work hard. For the most part, everyone gets along."

"Until now, I never really cared about where I lived. To me, one bed was the same as any other. When I found out that I had to live in Mercy…" he shook his head "…well, I wasn't exactly happy to run a bar in the middle of nowhere. In the end, I liked it more than I imagined."

He watched her as she drove. She swore that she wouldn't look at Ryan, focusing instead on the road and the flying insects that were in the beams of her headlights. But she felt drawn to his gaze. She let her eyes meet his. God, he really was handsome. More than handsome—if that was even possible. It made what she had to say more difficult. Then again, he had given her the perfect segue. "You know, this isn't really in the middle of nowhere. Sure, we have a lot of land, but plenty of people call Encantador and Mercy home."

"I didn't mean to come off that way," he began.

She ignored his comment and continued. "Decker killing all those people has affected everyone. And not in a good way, either," she added. "I've seen it on the job. People are more mistrustful. They're quicker to quarrel with their neighbors. Decker Newcombe stole our sense of security." His gaze turned hard. She looked back at the road.

"Just say what you want to say." Ryan's tone was filled with flint.

For a minute, she drove. The businesses on Main Street were closed. The windows were dark. Streetlamps cast pools of yellow light onto the sidewalk.

"There are two things I value most," she said, her eyes still on the road. "My home and my family. Because of that, I don't blame you for wanting to put down roots and grow your own life, so to speak. This is not the place for you, though. For a year, you lied to us about why you came here. What's more, a killer came to town looking for you." Sure, her words sounded cruel. But Ryan Steele living in Encantador would cause more problems than he'd ever solve. "You might want a home, but it's not going to be here."

She glanced in his direction. He stared out the passenger window. Old Blue sat at his side. Tongue hanging out of his mouth, the dog smiled at Kathryn.

God, she felt like a heel. What else was she supposed to do? "Is there anything you want to say?"

He glanced at her. "Is there anything I could say that would make a difference?"

"Not really. But you know I'm right." She decided to give him some unsolicited advice. "There are lots of small towns like ours. Find a new one. Make it your own."

He made a sound. She couldn't tell if it was a snort, a grunt, or a guttural laugh. Then again, it didn't matter. She imagined they all meant the same thing. Ryan didn't care for her less-than-warm welcome.

Drawing in a sharp breath, he braced his hands on the dashboard. "Goddamn it!"

Instinctively, she dropped her foot on the break. Her heart slammed against her chest.

"You okay?" Obviously, he wasn't. "What's wrong?"

He turned to her. His eyes were wide. His pallor was ghostly. "On the sidewalk," he said, swallowing. "There's a body."

Her head snapped around. Ryan was right. A figure was sprawled across the concrete and covered in blood. Slamming the gearshift into Park, she sprinted from the car.

She recognized the victim. There was a tangle of blond hair. A pool of blood surrounded the lifeless form. The clothes were torn and stained red with gore.

Dropping to her knees, she lifted Tessa's arm. The flesh was cool, but still Kathryn pressed her fingers into the wrist, feeling for a pulse. There was none.

A flashlight was attached to her utility belt—Kathryn shone it up and down the street. There was no perp hiding in the shadows. No obvious clues, either. Using the mic attached to her shoulder, she sent out a call. "Todd, I need backup." She gave him the address while rising to her feet. "Contact Doctor Garcia." She was the medical examiner.

"What's going on?" the deputy asked.

How was she supposed to describe the scene? Kathryn didn't have the words. "Just get here as quick as you can and tell Doctor Garcia to hurry, too."

He exhaled. "I'll be there in a few minutes."

Ryan stood right behind Kathryn, and his breath washed over the back of her neck. Old Blue was still in the car. The engine was running, and the air-conditioning was on. The dog would be fine for a few minutes. "Tessa, what happened to you?" she asked, the last word morphed into a groan.

"You know this woman?" Ryan asked.

She nodded. "She is—was—Tessa Wray. She's the new bank manager and lives a few houses up from me."

While standing next to the body, she compartmentalized her feelings. There was no other way for her to do her job—especially since she'd known the victim. Tessa's throat had been sliced open. A ghoulish smile ran across her neck. Her torso had been cut open, too. "I haven't seen anything this bad since we found Trinity Jackson's body." Trinity was Decker's first victim who had lived in Mercy, less than twenty miles from Encantador.

"You know what this means?" he asked.

She didn't bother to look up. "What does this mean?"

"It means that Romeo Rogers wasn't the only person sneaking through backyards tonight."

She stood and faced Ryan. "You still think it was him, don't you?"

"Think?" He shook his head. "I know it. This was done by Decker Newcombe. The killer's back."

Like she'd been plunged into ice water, Kathryn went numb. Her hands shook. Folding her arms across her chest, she drew in a long breath. "You don't know anything," she challenged. Speaking as a law-enforcement officer, she was right. There was evidence that needed to be collected. So far, they had a murder victim—which was bad enough—but nothing connected Newcombe to the crime. "We're going to conduct this investigation professionally. We won't jump to conclusions—even though the injuries sustained by this victim look like the other woman's."

"We?"

"I," she corrected. She needed to remember certain facts. "I'm in charge of the investigation."

She returned to her car and opened the passenger door. Old Blue had been lying on the seat. He sat up, and she scratched him behind the ears. The interior of the car was cool. "You'll be okay in here for a bit." She opened her glove box and removed two pairs of latex gloves from a bag.

Returning to the body, she handed one set to Ryan.

"Put these on," she ordered, while slipping on her own. "I don't want any fingerprints to accidentally end up on the corpse."

She knelt next to the body again. Ryan knelt next to her.

The wounds were as gruesome as before. A long and bloody cut ran up the middle of Tessa's torso. Kathryn needed to wait for the autopsy, but she imagined that several of the victim's internal organs had been removed—just like last time. Decker might not be the killer, but whoever had done this was a definite copycat.

"If Decker's back," said Ryan, "he isn't done yet. More people will die."

"That is only—" she could hear the conviction in her own voice "—if we don't find him first."

Chapter 4

By Kathryn's accounting, the body of Tessa Wray had been discovered at 9:21 p.m. Slipping her phone from her pocket, she checked the time again: 10:57 p.m.

After replacing the phone, she rubbed her gritty eyes. Since finding the corpse, Kathryn had done several things. First, she'd ordered barricades on the road, set up two blocks apart. Tessa's body was in the middle of the cordoned off area. Even though the street was closed to the public, the road was filled with first responders. She'd also completed the heartbreaking task of notifying Tessa's family that their daughter was dead. Her parents were on their way from Oklahoma. It would take them a full night of driving to get to Encantador.

She'd sent her deputies to the victim's home to look for evidence. From what they reported, the murder most likely had taken place at the house. Until the body was taken away by the ME, she wanted to stay with Tessa out of respect. She'd also contacted her kids and made sure they were okay. Both were safely back at their respective parties. With a sigh, she slipped the phone back into her pocket.

"Rough night," said Ryan at her side.

She wasn't sure if it was a question or a statement. Still, there was no way to answer other than by saying, "Sure is." She exhaled. "When we first found Trinity Jackson, Mooky didn't want any outside help. He thought he could solve the murder all on his own." She shook her head, knowing she'd come dangerously close to criticizing her boss. "Sorry. I shouldn't have said anything. Mooky's a good sheriff."

"But he didn't realize who he was dealing with in Decker," he said. "He didn't ask for help right away but should have."

It was as if Ryan had read her mind. She looked at the street. A yellow tent had been erected over the victim's body. Lights atop emergency vehicles strobed blue and red. The voices of more than a dozen first responders filled the night. With the garish yellow tent, the whole scene resembled a sideshow more than a crime scene. "I had to call in help," she said, not sure if she'd made the right choice. With all the other agencies involved, Kathryn had little to do.

"You did," he agreed.

She glanced at Ryan and smiled. "Thanks for hanging around."

"Where else am I supposed to go? Besides, I'm not leaving without Old Blue."

After finding the body, Kathryn had ordered a deputy to take the dog to her office. The mutt had been given water, food, and a walk. So even if he wasn't happy to be separated from his master, he was at least safe.

A black SUV maneuvered through the crowd and pulled up behind her car. The back doors opened. Two men exited the vehicle. She recognized both of them.

Ryan smiled and stepped forward with his hand outstretched. "Jason Jones. Isaac Patton. It's great to see you two."

He shook hands with Special Agent Jason Jones, the Supervisory Special Agent from the San Antonio field office. Then, he shook hands with Isaac Patton, who was the owner of a private security firm, Texas Law. It was Isaac who Ryan worked with when they were trying to find Decker. She'd heard that the relationship between the men had been complicated—starting with enmity and ending with something close to friendship. "How goes it?" Ryan asked.

Isaac was almost as tall as Ryan and wore a black T-shirt and jeans. He pounded on Ryan's back. "Good to see you. Weird to be back here, though."

Agent Jones stepped toward Kathryn with his hand extended. He was six feet tall with blond hair, kept short. It was the middle of the night, but he was still dressed in a white shirt, dark suit, and no tie. He had a firm handshake. She respected anyone who knew how to shake hands properly. Gripping his palm she said, "Thanks for coming on such short notice. I know it's quite a drive from San Antonio."

Jason withdrew his hand and waved away her comment. "I wanted to come here personally, especially after I heard that you'd found another body."

Isaac stepped forward. "Nice to see you again." He offered his hand to shake. She slipped her palm into his. "Wish it was under different circumstances. I heard that Mooky was out of town. Is that right?"

Letting her hand slip from his grip, she gave a terse nod. "He's on an anniversary trip to Mexico for two weeks."

"Have you briefed the sheriff?" Jason asked.

Kathryn had expected the question. Still, a spark of annoyance burned at her chest. "Until I know what we're dealing with, I don't want to waste his time. Besides, what's he going to do from the beach other than worry and ruin his wife's vacation?" What she said was true. But she was also determined to do a good job on her own.

"What is it that you have?" Isaac asked.

"We found the body of a thirty-two-year-old female. Her throat's been cut. Her body cavity's been sliced open as well." She placed two fingers on her own abdomen. One just under the rib cage, and the other above the pelvis. "The gash is about this long." She tilted her head toward the tent that covered the body. "Sheila Garcia and Michael O'Brien are with the body now."

"Can we get a look?" Jason asked.

Kathryn had seen Tessa's corpse and Trinity Jackson's during Decker's last killing spree. Both murders had been brutal, and bloody. Still, she said, "Come with me."

She walked the short distance to the tent and pulled back the flap. A single spotlight on a stand stood in the corner. The beam was directed at the body. The bright light turned Tessa's skin to pure white. The blood was bright red—and black, where it was dry. The contrast between colors was stark. Kathryn missed a step as she crossed the threshold.

"Stop right there," Dr. Garcia warned. She wore a lab coat and surgical gloves. Her dark hair was wound into a bun atop her head. "You can't come in here without PPE."

One of the several CSI techs handed Kathryn a pair of blue gloves and paper booties. "Here you go," the man said. "To keep you from contaminating the evidence."

He handed the same gloves and booties to Isaac, Jason, and Ryan. It took them all only a moment to don their protective gear.

Forensic pathologist Michael O'Brien was already on the scene. Where Ryan was muscular, Michael O'Brien was tall and lanky. Stepping away from the body, he asked, "How's everyone holding up?"

"Okay, I guess," Isaac said with a smile. "But we gotta stop meeting like this."

"Are we done with the jokes?" Dr. Garcia snapped. "Because if we are, then there are some things I'd like to show you."

Ryan gave Kathryn a side-eye. She could imagine what he must be thinking about the doctor. *Was this woman for real?*

Sheila and Kathryn had been classmates beginning in elementary school. More than being in the same grade, they were friends. The thing was, Sheila didn't mean to be rude. It's just that she could get so focused on her task that she didn't care about being polite. She'd always been that way, even as a little kid.

Clearing her throat, Kathryn asked, "What do you have for us?"

"Michael and I agree these wounds look like the ones inflicted on Trinity Jackson."

Jason asked, "Can you say conclusively that Decker murdered this woman? Are you sure it's not a copycat killer?"

Sheila glanced at Michael. He shook his head. "We can't say conclusively that Decker killed Tessa Wray. But…"

Isaac said, "For now, it's safe to assume that he's the killer."

"Assume," Kathryn echoed. A knot of disbelief was stuck in her throat. She choked on the single word. One of the first tenets of law enforcement was never to assume anything. Assumptions tainted investigations. "We aren't going to assume anything. What I need are facts." She paused. "Do you know what kind of uproar it's going to cause if we tell folks that we assume—" she made air quotes "—Decker's back? Tessa being filleted like a fish is bad enough. We can't cause mass hysteria without proof." She drew in a breath, slowing her racing heart.

The tent was silent.

The FBI agent was the first to speak. "Even if this isn't Decker, people should be alerted. Another young woman's been murdered. Besides, we were briefed that Decker might've been sighted near the victim's home earlier this evening."

"I'm not going to cause a panic until I know who

actually committed this murder." Kathryn realized she was being stubborn. She might not have a fancy college degree or expensive gadgets, but she did know her community, and the FBI agent had been right. People needed to be informed. She could release a carefully worded statement to the press.

Before she got a chance to acquiesce, Isaac spoke. "You know," he said, his voice icy, "you're being unreasonable, Kathryn."

Oh hell no. She wasn't going to be bullied by the feds or some high-priced security operative, like Isaac Patton. "You know that you've been invited to my town by me. This is my investigation. I'm the one who makes the final decisions. Got it?"

Michael raised his palms and stepped between Isaac and Kathryn. "I have another solution. We've taken several samples of hair and fibers from the victim's clothing." A small table stood in the corner of the tent. Several clear plastic bags lay on the tabletop. To Kathryn, they looked empty. But she knew better: each bag contained evidence taken from the victim, and that evidence might be as small as a single hair. Michael continued. "My lab is in Mercy. I can run these samples overnight. By morning, we'll have an analysis. If the killer left behind DNA, we'll get an ID."

"Fair enough." She drew in a calming breath. "And speaking of DNA, the body was dumped here. We believe that the killing actually took place at her home." To Sheila, she said, "How much longer will you be here?"

"We're done," said the doctor. "I'm going to get the body to the morgue. The autopsy will be in the morning."

Since the body was being taken from the crime

scene, Kathryn had done her due diligence. Now she could move on to other parts of the investigation. She spoke to both Jason and Isaac. "We can head over to the victim's house now."

"Lead the way," said Jason.

Kathryn exited the tent. She pulled off the booties first and then the gloves. Standing on the sidewalk, she shook out her hands and took deep breaths.

"You okay?" Ryan asked.

"Yeah, I..." She looked back at the tent. Jason, Michael, and Isaac stood in a knot next to the flap and spoke to each other in hushed tones. Were those men discussing her case and how to keep her from being involved in the investigation? "Maybe Mooky was right to try and handle Decker in-house." Although, it was worse for her than it had been for him. At least he was actually the sheriff. She was just a stand-in.

He followed her gaze. "Everyone here wants the same thing. To discover the truth and to stop the killer."

"You're right," she said with a sigh.

"It sounds like you don't believe me."

How was she supposed to describe the feeling of living in her own skin? That the desire to please was more of a need than a want. The fact that she relied on Mooky's as a taskmaster first. Then, her own judgment. Despite her uncertainty, she knew that failure wasn't an option. She stood taller. "You're right. We're all on the same team."

She watched as the conversation ended. Jason pointed to the black SUV, and Michael nodded. The trio began to walk toward the vehicle.

"We'll follow you to the victim's house," Isaac said,

his voice raised to be heard from a distance. "Ryan, you want to ride with us?"

"Nah, man. I'm good. I'll go with the undersheriff." He turned to look at her quickly. "Hope that's okay with you?"

When had Ryan become her ally? Then again, it didn't matter. She needed someone on her team. A spark of gratitude glowed in her chest. Pulling the car keys from her pocket, she said, "That sounds good." She unlocked the doors. Then to Jason, Isaac, and Michael, she said, "Follow me."

Kathryn opened her door and slid behind the wheel. Ryan slipped into the passenger seat. She started the engine, and the air-conditioning began to blow. Holding her fingers in front of the vent, she let the stream of air swirl around her hand.

Placing the gearshift into Drive, she pulled away from the curb. The street was filled with emergency workers. She flipped a toggle switch on her console, and the siren gave a single whoop. People stepped aside to let her pass. In the rearview mirror, she could see the SUV following her car like a shadow.

At the end of the block, a deputy stood next to a pair of yellow sawhorses that blocked off the street. He saw her coming and pulled one aside.

A group of twenty people had gathered on the opposite side of the barricade. She recognized Alicia Sanchez, the editor and lead writer of the town's weekly newspaper. Prior to becoming the editor, Alicia had worked for a major media outlet in Dallas. She'd only come back to Encantador to care for her aging mother.

Since her arrival, Alicia had improved the paper with her writing, editing skills, and dogged reporting.

Stepping toward the car, the editor waved. "Kathryn." She raised her voice to be heard over the engine. "You got a minute?"

As the undersheriff, she often acted as the de facto media specialist for the department. Mooky always said that she was good with the press. It was true that she and Alicia got on well enough.

Easing her foot onto the brake, she lowered the window. "What can I do for you?"

"Mind telling me what's going on?" Alicia asked. Despite the fact that it was the middle of the night and still hot, she wore a button-up blouse and a pair of slacks. Neither were creased or stained with sweat.

Kathryn glanced down at her own wrinkled uniform. She looked back at the other woman. "I can't comment right now. There's an open investigation."

"Does it have anything to do with the bank's manager, Tessa Wray?" Alicia paused. "There's a CSI team at her home now." She held up her phone. The screen was filled with a social-media post. It was a picture of Tessa's house with crime-scene tape across the door, along with the caption *What happened this time? #toomuchcrimeinEncantador.*

Her shoulders pinched together with tension. Rubbing the back of her neck, she sighed. "I can't comment on anything right now."

"You'll want to get ahead of this story." Alicia tucked a lock of dark hair streaked with gray behind an ear.

She imagined that the reporter was right. She also knew that Alicia's advice wasn't exactly altruistic. The reporter was looking for something to put in the online edition of the paper.

"When there's something to say," she said, "you'll be the first person I call."

Alicia leaned her elbow on the windowsill. "Can I ask you another question?" She didn't give Kathryn a chance to answer. "What's Ryan Steele doing in your car? I heard you were chasing him down the street earlier this evening. Why? Does he have anything to do with this street being blocked off and a CSI team being at Ms. Wray's house?"

Wow. That was a lot more than one question.

She replied, "I can't comment on an open investigation. In fact, I can't even comment enough to say if there is an investigation." Easing her foot off the brake, she let the car roll forward. Alicia stood up and stepped back. "I have to get back to work."

Using the lever, she raised the window. The knot of onlookers stared at her car as she drove slowly past. They said nothing, but she could feel the tension in their gaze. Keeping her eyes on the beams of her headlights, she focused on driving. As she passed the corner, she dropped her foot onto the accelerator and exhaled loudly.

"That was uncomfortable," said Ryan.

"Hella awkward." Her shoulders sagged, weighed down by exhaustion and the gravity of the situation. "Here's what I hope." She glanced in the rearview mirror to make sure that the black SUV was still following her car. It was. "I hope that there are no more surprises, like Alicia Sanchez, or the gawkers on the corner. I'd like to get a look at the crime scene quietly and without a lot of fuss."

"Well, I hope you get your wish," he said.

She glanced at Ryan. He smiled.

She couldn't help herself and smiled back.

As she drove, she knew two things for certain. First, Ryan's insights might help her to find Decker Newcombe. After all, nobody knew the killer better. And second, if she was going to be working with him, then she was going to have a hell of a time keeping her libido in check. But if she wanted to find and capture the elusive killer, she needed to do both.

She flipped the switch for a left turn more than a hundred yards from the road that led to her housing development. The blinker ticked, like a clockwork heart. While turning onto the road, she'd almost convinced herself that she'd get what she wanted. The neighborhood would be quiet. Then, she'd have plenty of uninterrupted time to examine the crime scene. But as she drove up the road leading to her house, she knew her wish for a discreet investigation wasn't going to come true.

Every house was filled with light. Her neighbors stood on the sidewalk in groups. The energy of a hundred frightened and furious people filled the night, like a lightning strike. A TV news van was also parked at the curb.

People stopped talking and glared as she drove past.

"Looks like it's about to get hella awkward all over again," said Ryan.

He wasn't joking this time.

Kathryn's friends and neighbors might not know the specifics, but they'd seen enough to have an idea of what had happened. They were mad and scared and wanted information. She didn't blame them. But without Mooky around, they'd be looking to her for answers.

How could she tell them that Decker Newcombe had returned?

Chapter 5

The dark room smelled of death. The stench was so bad that Decker was certain something was rotting in the walls. The floor was covered with dust and rodent droppings. He'd spread out a blanket before sitting down. Using the wall as a back rest, he got as comfortable as possible. Then, he opened the lid of his laptop.

The screen glowed. It was the only light in the room.

Hell, it was the only light for miles.

He entered a complicated set of keystrokes. It was the address to a private server buried deep in the dark web. A bar with cycling lines filled the middle of his screen. It took only a moment for a face to appear. The hacker wore gloves and a birdlike plague-doctor mask and a black velvet drape behind them. Their voice was also electronically disguised.

Honestly, he found the theatrics annoying.

But Seraphim, as the hacker called themself, was a true genius.

Decker's own face filled a smaller square on the bottom right corner of his monitor. His hair was long and hung loose around his shoulders. He'd changed clothes after his latest killing. But still, the victim's blood was smeared across his chin. Using the hem of his shirt, he wiped it away.

As had been his habit for years, Decker used free computers to check what was being reported about him on the internet. Two months earlier, he'd been in a small coffee shop near Texarkana. Seraphim had taken over his computer and made Decker an offer he couldn't refuse.

"Work with me," they'd said, "and you'll be the most famous killer of all time."

He'd scoffed, but in that moment, he knew it was possible.

"You did what we discussed." Seraphim's voice was like fingernails on a chalkboard and drew him back to the dingy room.

He held up the phone. "I recorded everything."

"Connect the phone to the computer. Then you can upload the video. I'll tell you how."

"I got it covered," said Decker. True, he wasn't especially comfortable with computers. But he'd be damned before he let the hacker tell him what to do. Besides, he couldn't listen to the obnoxious voice for long. After several moments, the phone was connected.

Seraphim played the video without sound.

In a way, the silence was more terrifying than if it had been filled with screams.

Decker smiled.

"That was…" Seraphim said as the screen went black "…intense."

"Now's not the time to get squeamish," said Decker. "You and me made a deal."

"I'm not squeamish." In the mask, Seraphim's eyes gleamed. "And I'm not backing out of our deal." The hacker spent a few minutes rehashing what would happen next. Decker knew the plan but suspected that Seraphim liked the sound of their irritating voice and ended by asking, "Are you all set?"

He nodded slowly. "But first, tell me. What's in this for you?"

It was a question he'd asked more than once. Seraphim never answered. What's more, he knew next to nothing about the hacker. He didn't know their age. He didn't know their race, nationality, or ethnicity. He didn't even know their gender.

"Why do you keep asking the same question?"

"I'm trusting you and your plan. Seems like you can trust me a little, too."

Seraphim said, "Is that what this is? An exercise in trust?"

Decker imagined that the hacker was smiling behind the mask.

"I've been betrayed before," he began. "It makes me cautious."

"I know, by Ryan Steele."

He refused to feel anything other than ice in his veins. "And others." He paused. "I appreciate your help. I like your idea. But what do you get out of all this?"

Seraphim leaned toward the screen. "I get a front-row seat," they said, "to see the world burn."

Ryan looked out the window as Kathryn drove down the street. He'd seen more than one unfriendly crowd in his life. The people who stood on the sidewalk definitely counted as hostile. The body language said it all. Their spines were straight. Their shoulder blades were pinched together. Their gazes narrowed as the vehicle drove past. In short, they were ready for a fight.

Kathryn pulled next to the curb. A house sat at the end of a walkway. It would have been unremarkable, except for the X of crime-scene tape that was draped across the door. A CSI van was parked at the end of the block. After turning off the engine, she looked over her shoulder. He followed her gaze.

She was staring at her own home.

This was her neighborhood, so he imagined her feelings were complicated. Besides wanting to solve the murder, she must be worried about her own kids.

He turned his attention back to Kathryn. Holding onto the steering wheel, her knuckles were white. "It'll be okay." Without thinking, he placed his hand on her wrist. The energy from her skin danced along his palm.

She let go of the steering wheel, and her arm slipped away from his touch. "I'm not sure it'll be okay, but I appreciate you saying so."

After pulling the keys from the ignition, she opened the door. The outside was hot and sticky. A scent clung to the air, like vegetables left to rot in the garden.

He watched as Kathryn slid slowly from her seat. As she closed the door, he exited the car. The black SUV was already parked behind the cruiser. Jason, Isaac, and Michael exited the vehicle. They stood next to the front fender.

A middle-aged man with dark hair approached. "Undersheriff, I need a word."

She held up a hand, halting the man. "Not now, Joe."

"Not now?" he spluttered. "Something's going on, and you owe us all an explanation."

"Until I know exactly what happened, I'm not going to comment," she said.

Someone from the crowd called out, "Where's Tessa?"

"Yeah," said Joe. "She was with us earlier this evening." He glared at Ryan. "Right after you picked up this guy for trespassing."

"My deputies will be around to talk to everyone soon." She gestured to several people who wore the uniform of the sheriff's office. "We can and will get to the bottom of this suspicious incident—together, all of us—as a community."

Honestly, Ryan liked the way she handled the crowd.

"Suspicious, like what?" Joe asked, a challenge in his tone. "Suspicious like the undersheriff chasing a known felon down the street? Or suspicious like deputies showing up at Tessa's house? Then, a few minutes later, crime-scene investigators arrive. Or is it the kind of suspicious where the people who are in charge aren't willing to say exactly what in the hell is going on?"

"I'm not going to comment on a pending investigation," she said, an edge to her voice.

"So you admit that something happened to Tessa," said an elderly woman. "Is she okay, at least?"

Ryan knew this was not going well for the undersheriff. "Just let the lady do her job, okay?"

His comment wouldn't calm down Joe. But he hoped that at least it'd get the attention off Kathryn and onto him.

Joe turned slowly and took a step toward him. It was a bold move. Ryan was over a decade younger than the other man and more than a head taller. If punches were thrown, the fight wouldn't last long. What's more, it would go poorly for Joe. Still, the other man didn't back down. Ryan wasn't sure if he should be impressed by the dude's bravery or troubled by his stupidity.

Joe said, "Why don't you mind your own business? Or better yet, get the hell out of my town." Then he flipped his fingers toward the trio who stood next to the black SUV. "And speaking of people who don't belong, what are they doing in Encantador?"

"We all need to turn this down a notch." Kathryn stood between the two men. She placed a hand on Ryan's chest. Her touch did nothing to slow his racing pulse. "Joe, go home."

"You can't tell me what to do," he challenged.

"Actually, I can. Right now, I'm asking you friendly-like. Next time, it's going to be an order." Joe took a step back. Kathryn raised her voice so that her words carried up and down the street. "I need everyone to go back into their houses. I will make a statement, but only once I have something to say." She let her hand slip from Ryan's chest. He could still feel her touch on his body. "Go on and get home. It'd be a shame for my deputies to have to start writing out citations for folks disobeying a lawful order given to them by police."

Joe took another backward step. "You know this isn't how Mooky would handle things."

She stood taller. "Well, Mooky's not here."

"And it's a crying shame that he ain't," said Joe.

"Go home before you start trouble," said Kathryn.

The crowd grumbled, but they obeyed her order. People began to move slowly down the sidewalk toward their homes. Standing on the pavement, she watched Joe. "I think he's going to cause problems."

"What gives you that idea?" Ryan's words were filled with sarcasm. "He seems like a real easygoing guy."

She rolled her eyes at him. "Let's collect your friends and get a look at the crime scene."

By friends, she meant Jason, Isaac, and Michael. They all remained by their SUV. He assumed that they'd taken Kathryn at her word and were letting her run things her way. It was honorable of them. They were all honorable men. And Ryan, well, he couldn't keep his mouth shut when Joe gave Kathryn a little lip.

Not that she needed any help.

But still, he'd tried.

Who was he kidding? Ryan was nobody's idea of a hero.

As much as his life had been shaped by Decker Newcombe, he'd helped to create the killer as well. If he really wanted to atone—and then be able to start over—it meant that finding his former friend was his responsibility.

Kathryn waved to the men. They approached, forming a loose circle on the sidewalk.

"Looks like you have some upset citizens," said Jason. "Anything we can do to help?"

She said, "Yeah, find out who murdered Tessa Wray and put the bastard in jail." She trudged up the front walk. "Truly, thanks for coming down to help me. Let's go see this crime scene."

Across the street, the elderly lady held up her phone. "Y'all," she announced to the neighbors who were still heading to their houses. "It's okay. I just heard from Tessa. She sent me a text."

The street was filled with one ping after another. All the neighbors stared at their phones. "I heard from her, too," said Joe.

"And me."

"Me, too."

Kathryn's phone pinged. She looked up at Ryan. Her eyes were wide with disbelief. "She sent me a message, too."

"How did a corpse send all those texts?" he asked, his voice low.

She showed him the screen.

I thought you'd like to see this.

The message contained a link.

Jason, Isaac, and Michael stood close.

"Where's the link take you?" Jason asked.

Kathryn inhaled. She exhaled and then tapped her thumb on the link. That's when the first scream ripped through the night.

Kathryn wanted to watch the clip with an analytical eye. But with the video on her phone of Tessa's murder, it was damn near impossible.

Blood covered every surface.

An arc of blood covered the cabinets. There was a smear of blood across the floor. A bloody handprint was next to the back door. A dark pool, where the body lay, spread across the floor.

Decker Newcombe, covered in gore, looked at the camera and smiled.

Then, the screen went blank.

The street was filled with crying, cursing, and screams as all her neighbors watched the video. Her heartbeat thundered in her own ears, making her all but deaf to the chaos around her. At the same moment, Kathryn felt the enormity of the situation crash down. It pinned her in place, making it impossible to move.

Ryan placed his hand on her shoulder. "Your neighbors are scared. They need you. What are you going to do?"

He was right. But what could she do—or say—to make everything better? After all, everyone had been sent the same horrific video.

"Y'all," she yelled. "Calm down."

Nobody heard her. And even if they did, nobody listened. Then, she saw her car and knew what to do. Walking to the street, she unlocked the cruiser's doors. Ryan followed.

Kathryn slipped behind the steering wheel and started the ignition. She turned on the PA system and let out two long blasts from her siren. The street went quiet. Now that she had their attention, she lifted the mic from the console. Standing next to her car, she said, "Everyone, calm down." Her voice was carried by the PA system in her vehicle.

"Calm down?" Joe repeated. He wiped his eyes with the back of his hand. "You got the same message as the rest of us. Tessa was slaughtered." He gestured to Gladys. The older woman sat in a lawn chair and rocked back and forth. Joe's wife, at her side, patted the back of her hand. "She's never going to be the same. None of us will ever be okay. It's all his fault." He took two steps toward Ryan. "If you won't get him out of here, we'll take matters into our own hands."

Kathryn went cold. The last thing she needed was a vengeful mob. "You better back up, Joe. There won't be any vigilante justice in my town. If you get folks all riled up, it's going to be you in a jail cell. You understand?"

"I understand," he grumbled, "that you'd rather protect a criminal than your neighbors. What is it with this guy?"

Kathryn wanted to deny her attraction to Ryan, but she couldn't. "Ryan was with me when Tessa was attacked. He's not the killer." She scanned the crowd to make sure everyone heard what she said. A few heads nodded. She took the gesture as a win. "We've got the FBI here already. They're going to help us find Decker and stop him once and for all." She paused. "I want everyone to get back in their houses. Lock the doors. If you don't feel safe on your own, stay with a neighbor. Be watchful. Be smart." She knew it wasn't enough. These people had questions, and they deserved answers. "Tomorrow, I'll tell you what I can. For now, we know that Decker's close. We can't let the trail get cold this time."

"When tomorrow will you talk to us?" Joe asked. "And where?"

"I can let you into the high school," said another

neighbor, Armando Cruz, the school's assistant principal. "As for the time, well, that's up to the undersheriff."

Kathryn quickly calculated what needed to be done. Early in the morning, Tessa's parents would arrive. It was only right that she talked to them first. "I'll have a briefing ready at noon." She glanced at Special Agent Jones. He gave a quick nod. Thank goodness, he'd be there. "To say that video is upsetting is an understatement, but I need to get back to work. I'll speak to you all tomorrow."

"How's anyone supposed to know about the meeting?" Joe asked.

Honestly, it wasn't an unreasonable question.

"I'll share the information on the school's social-media account," Armando offered. "We can use the auditorium."

"Thanks, that'd be helpful," she said to Armando. Then to Joe, she asked, "Can you watch Gladys?"

He nodded. "Of course. She can stay with us."

Truly, he wasn't all bad. "I appreciate it."

Turning her full attention to the investigation, she stepped closer to Michael, Jason, and Isaac. "I need some cyber help with this case. My guess is that Decker stole Tessa's phone." Bile rose in the back of her throat as she recalled the first cut. It started out as pink flesh. A seam of red appeared before the wound began to weep blood. But that moment was just the beginning of the torture.

Jason saved Kathryn from having to say anything more. "Send me that link and all Tessa's information. We can get our cybersecurity experts to try to track the phone remotely."

Kathryn did what Jason asked.

"Got it." He glanced at the screen. "I can access the internet from my vehicle. I'll make some calls, and we can regroup in a minute."

Isaac and Michael followed the FBI agent, leaving Kathryn and Ryan. They truly were alone. All her neighbors had gone into their own homes. Despite the fact that it was after midnight, she doubted that anyone would get much sleep.

It meant that in twelve hours, she'd face a scared, angry, and exhausted crowd.

At least there was one thing she could do right now. She turned to Ryan. "I hate to kick you out of town in the middle of the night, but you have to go. This is for your own safety. I can drive you back to your truck and then…" She let the silence say the words she couldn't speak.

"Listen," Ryan began. She could tell he was ready with an argument. "I know Decker. I can help."

She nodded slowly. "You're right, but Joe tried to get a mob to attack you."

Ryan folded his arms across his chest. "I'm not afraid of Joe."

"If they're frightened and mad enough, the best people can turn ugly. I don't want that for you. Can you let me help you out?"

His shoulders sagged. He was going to surrender. "I need to get my dog."

Right. Old Blue was still in her office. "We'll get him first."

Standing next to the black SUV, Jason waved. Isaac stood outside as well.

Ryan nodded toward the FBI agent. "Looks like he has news for you."

Together, they walked to the SUV. "What have you got?" she asked.

"Nothing good," said Isaac.

"It looks like Decker not only sent the video to everyone on the victim's contact list, but he also posted it to her social-media accounts," said Jason. "We've got people working with the companies to take down the posts. But, really, a lot of damage has already been done."

"What are our options?"

"For now, there are people trying to find Tessa's phone," said Jason.

Isaac continued. "We're going to set up shop at the Center." Months earlier, Michael had opened the Center for Rural Law Enforcement in the neighboring town of Mercy. The title was a mouthful, and everyone affectionately called the labs *the Center*. "There are forensics labs and supercomputers we can use."

"I'll run the investigation out of my office," she said, happy to finally have a plan of sorts. "But first, I'm going to get Ryan out of town. Right now, everyone is looking for a scapegoat. If he's here, then he's the most likely candidate."

The other two men nodded in agreement.

Now there was nothing more for her to do. She needed to get Ryan away as quickly and quietly as possible. "Come with me," she said to him, while walking toward her car.

Without speaking, they got into her vehicle and drove to her office. Old Blue was collected. While Ryan took the dog for a short walk, she raided the office's snack closet. There were enough assorted chips, crackers, cookies. She got the case of water from her office and put together a bag.

He was waiting next to her car when she left the building. She handed him the food. It was the least she could do. "I hope this helps you get where you're going."

"Thanks." After settling the snacks onto the floorboard between his feet, he snapped his fingers. The dog joined him on the passenger seat.

Kathryn set her phone on the console before settling behind the steering wheel. After starting the engine, she drove. Her eyes were dry, and her muscles ached. She was exhausted, but there'd be no time for her to rest. Driving through the night, she knew she should say something. After seeing the video of Tessa's murder, she couldn't think of anything helpful.

Her phone's screen glowed, and the device shimmied. The caller ID read *Jason Jones, FBI.*

She swiped the call open before turning on the Speaker function. "What've you got for me?"

"We've found the bastard," said Jason, his tone jubilant. "Or at least, we've found Tessa's phone and it's still active." He gave her an address that she recognized at once.

"That's the McCoy place. Nobody's lived there for years." The ranch had sat empty since the family moved.

"Looks like we can be there in twenty minutes," said Jason.

Kathryn was less than ten minutes away from the old ranch. With grim determination, she stepped on the gas.

Chapter 6

Caught in the beams of headlights, a lone farmhouse sat at the end of a long dirt drive. At one time, the worn wooden planks of the structure had been white, but now only flecks of paint clung to the warped boards. The wide lawn was now filled with dead grass and a Realtor's faded For Sale sign that leaned drunkenly to one side.

During the day, Ryan thought the desolate homestead would've been inhospitable. At night it was downright unnerving.

Old Blue pulled back his ears and nervously licked the air. He rubbed the dog's shoulder.

Kathryn parked near the front porch. A cloud of dust billowed behind the car. Lifting the handset to her radio, she pressed down on the Talk button. "This is Undersheriff Glass," she said. "I need an ETA on the backup headed to McCoys' ranch."

"Backup is on the way. ETA, ten minutes."

"Ten minutes," she said with a muttered curse. "Seems like eternity." Pressing the button again, she spoke to dispatch. "Copy that. Ten minutes."

After setting the mic back on its hook, Kathryn turned off the ignition. The engine went still. The night was filled with silence. "What's your gut tell you?" She glanced at him before turning her gaze back to the house. "Is he here?"

Leaning forward in his seat, he peered out the windshield. The windows on the house were dark, like dead eyes staring across the barren landscape. "This is the exact kind of place that Decker would want. Remote. Abandoned. Creepy." But there was more. "He's not a fool, and he knows that the cell phone can be tracked. If he was here when he posted to the internet, my guess is that he left soon after. Right now, he's halfway to San Antonio or Mexico City or God knows where. The device is still here because he wants you to find it. He's using it as a distraction."

"We didn't exactly sneak up on this place. If he's inside now, he saw the car the minute it turned onto the drive." She paused. "I just don't want him to sneak out the back door while we're waiting out here." Rolling back her shoulders, Ryan could see the look of determination harden her features. "I *am* the undersheriff. I'm going to walk the perimeter."

He unfastened his seat belt. "I'll come with you."

She regarded him but said nothing.

Ryan understood the silence to mean one thing. Kathryn was trying to decide if he were trustworthy—or not.

"You don't know me well, but at least you know I've been honest with you all evening."

"You're right, I don't know you at all. I think it's best if you stay in the car."

"Finding Decker isn't just a job to me—all of this is personal." He paused. "Besides, I won't stay."

She glanced at him before looking out the window. With a curse, she said, "If you want to come with me, then you'll need this." Kathryn leaned across the console and opened the glove box. Her shoulder grazed his chest and a current buzzed through his veins. From the glove box, she removed a black handgun.

She sat upright in her seat and held the firearm. "I assume you know how to use one of these things?"

"I do."

She placed the gun in his hand. "It's loaded. Be careful."

"Always," said Ryan. The gun was a SIG Sauer P226. He pulled back on the slide and took a single bullet from the chamber. Next, he removed the magazine. It was filled with fifteen rounds. He replaced the magazine. Then, he chambered a round. Next, he removed the magazine once more and slid the final bullet back into place.

Kathryn gave him a wry smile. "You are careful. I'm impressed." Her compliment wasn't much, but his chest warmed. "Will the dog be okay if I lower the windows a bit?" she asked.

Ryan scratched Old Blue's head. "Let me put him in the back seat. That way he won't get into the food. This guy will eat anything."

Ryan opened the front and back passenger doors. He snapped his fingers and pointed. The dog understood the command and trotted into the back seat. Then, he closed both doors.

Using a switch, Kathryn lowered all four windows enough to allow in fresh air. Afterward, she exited the car. In the distance, a fork of lightning danced along the horizon. A breeze blew, rattling the branches of the nearby tree. The scent of ozone wafted on the air.

"Smells like rain," he said.

She grunted. "I hope so. We can take some rain," she said, while removing her own firearm from the holster she wore at her hip. "Let's check the doors and windows. See if anything's unlocked or open."

The front door was solid wood with a narrow window at the side. A lace curtain hung limply behind the glass. Ryan's shadowy form was caught in a reflection. With the tattered fabric, he looked every bit like a ghost.

A ghost?

When was the last time he'd been worried about an apparition?

Then again, he was still haunted by Decker, the specter of his past.

Kathryn turned the knob. It rattled, metal against wood, but the door didn't budge.

"It's locked," she said, though that much was obvious. "Feels like the dead bolt is engaged, too." She gave a loud exhale. "Check the windows."

There was a set of windows on each side of the door. Ryan moved to the left. With his back pressed into the grime-coated wood, he glanced into the room. Limiting his exposure, he only looked inside for an instant. But an instant was all he needed.

"What'd you see?" she asked, her voice a husky whisper.

He ignored the fact that her words seemed to stroke his neck on the way to his ear. "Looks like it used to be a dining room. There's an old table and a few chairs." He paused and brought the image of the room back to mind. "Everything's dusty, though. No sign that anyone's been in the house."

He exhaled. Tension he hadn't noticed before slipped from his shoulders. He peered into the window on the other side of the door. The room beyond was bare, the wooden planks of the floor covered in dust. "Nobody's been in that room for a while, either."

After slipping the SIG Sauer into the waistband of his jeans, he gripped the windowsill and lifted hard. It didn't budge. "Locked or swollen shut, I can't tell," he said. "But those windows haven't been open for years."

"Let's check around back, just to make sure." Kathryn gestured to the steps that led off the porch. "I think there's a door in the kitchen."

"Let's go." He removed his gun as he descended the stairs.

A clap of thunder rolled across the plains. A single raindrop hit the dusty ground, creating a tiny crater.

So far, there was no sign of Decker, but it'd be irresponsible to let his guard down now. Kathryn paused at the corner of the house. He glanced around the house. There was nothing and nobody.

But he had noticed a window on the second story. In his mind, he saw a person watching them from above. Ryan started to sweat.

He looked up again.

The window was empty, save for the reflection of the moon.

* * *

Decker stood in the dark and held his breath. From the side window, he watched Ryan Steele and a female cop. It had been over a year since he'd last seen his onetime business manager, former friend, constant rival, and current enemy.

A scabbard was looped through Decker's belt. The hunting knife he used to kill the last woman hung inside. It was easy to imagine hot blood washing over his hand as he plunged the knife between Ryan's ribs. There'd be a look of shock and horror as he realized that Decker had won the ultimate battle between them. He'd twist the knife and smile as the other man died in agony.

But even in the dark, he could see the outline of the gun in Ryan's hand. Since reemerging from a year of living off the grid, Decker had been shot twice. Neither wound had healed right, and he loathed the idea of taking another bullet. It left Decker with a question. Was he fast enough to stab Ryan before his nemesis got a chance to fire a round?

Then again, if he was asking the question, he already knew the answer.

Stepping back, he melted into the darkness once more. He had to get out of the house, especially since he wouldn't be able to hide much longer. The computer, his phone, and backpack all lay in the corner on his blanket. He collected his belongings and shoved them into the sack. Moving quietly and quickly, he descended the stairs.

Two days earlier, he'd broken into the house by jimmying the lock on the kitchen door. Since then, he'd been living on the old farmstead while waiting for tonight. On the main floor, freedom was only a few paces away. It was so close he could taste it.

Then again, he wanted Ryan to know that he'd stumbled into Decker's lair. He wanted to stay and fight. He needed to destroy his old friend, the one whose betrayal was a scar on his soul. But he wasn't a fool. He'd never stand a chance against two guns. Especially since he was armed with only a knife.

Besides, he'd heard the conversation and knew that backup was expected. There wasn't much time before the entire property would be crawling with cops.

Decker moved to the edge of the kitchen. The linoleum beneath his feet sagged. He glanced over his shoulder. A door led to a basement. It was filled from floor to ceiling with boxes of unknown junk the family never took when they moved. Could he hide among the debris now and later sneak away unnoticed?

Not damned likely.

Through a dirt-coated window, he watched Ryan and the woman deputy pass. He had only seconds before they discovered the broken lock on the kitchen door. Which meant he had to decide on his next move—and fast.

There was really only one thing he could do.

With a roar, he launched himself out the door. He caught the sheriff around the middle at the same moment she turned and lifted her gun. They tumbled back as the gun's muzzle erupted with a burst of fire. The stink of gunpowder filled the night. The bullet passed his cheek, missing him by an inch. The air around him crackled and burned.

He focused all his effort on the woman's hand, the

one that held the gun. Gripping her wrist with both his hands, he brought her arm down hard. She screamed. The gun tumbled from her grasp, skittering across the ground.

"Stop, Decker, or I'll shoot." He recognized Ryan's voice and felt the crosshairs of a gun aimed at the back of his head. Yet, he wasn't about to give up. If he thought that getting the deputy to drop her weapon would take the fight out of her, he was wrong. She brought up her knee, catching his inner thigh. She'd obviously been aiming for his crotch. She'd missed, but the impact filled his leg with a tight knot of white-hot pain.

He took the agony and turned it into fuel. Grabbing the woman's hair, he pulled back on her scalp. Then, he drove her head into the sunbaked earth. She went limp. Dazed, her eyes rolled into the back of her head.

His old acquaintance didn't fire his weapon.

Why?

Was it because he'd never get off a clean shot? Even if he did hit Decker with a bullet, it could pass through him and still strike the sheriff.

When had Ryan gotten so weak and spineless?

Or maybe there was another reason he hadn't yet fired.

Pulling the knife from his sheath, Decker drove the blade into the cop's side.

Blood dripped from Decker's blade and wept from Kathryn's side. The coppery stench of blood filled the night. Fat raindrops fell, and thunder echoed in the darkness.

Ryan watched both Kathryn's prone form and Decker,

who stood beside her body. His eyes burned with anger—for knowing that he had yet again failed to act. And because of him, Kathryn might die at the hands of his old partner.

His blood heated, the urge to contain this madness overtaking him.

"You bastard." Lifting his gun, he aimed at Decker's chest.

"I'm the bastard?" he echoed. Rain turned killer's hair and clothes sodden. He wiped his hand across his damp face. "I've never sold out my friend. And what'd you get for helping the feds? A clean record? How long do you think it'll be before you go back to being on the wrong side of the law?"

He'd never admit it, but Decker was right. What Ryan feared the most was that at his core, he was a bad person. He worried that his life hadn't been corrupted by Decker and that his former friend had only accelerated his criminal proclivity. What if he stopped Decker now? Would it be enough to compensate for all his misdeeds? He knew what he was supposed to do. He knew what Kathryn would have done. "Drop your knife."

"You want this blade?" Like a mother holding the hand of her beloved child, Decker gazed at his blade. "You'll have to take it from me."

He aimed at Decker's chest. "Stop effing around. Drop the knife. I've got the gun, and backup is on the way."

"I'll never surrender. You of all people should know that."

On the ground, Kathryn moaned.

He looked in her direction. Her back rose and fell

with each breath. She was alive, but how long would she survive without help? He looked back at the killer and ground his teeth together. "What'd you do?"

Decker shrugged. "Looks like she's not as dead as you thought. Now you gotta ask yourself a question. You want to save her or take me down?"

Ryan blinked away the rain. In an instant, he knew that he'd been played. Decker hadn't meant to murder Kathryn. He only wanted to wound her badly enough that Ryan would be boxed into a corner. He could either save a life or let a killer go. Anger flowed like lava through his veins. His body vibrated with loathing for a man he used to love like a brother.

The past didn't matter anymore.

He had to live in the present, and that meant choosing.

For him, there really wasn't a decision to make.

Ryan lunged to the spot where Kathryn lay.

There was so much blood. It covered her clothes and turned the ground to black mud. He needed to get the bleeding stopped and now.

Holding onto her shoulders, he gently flipped Kathryn onto her back. He lifted her shirt. The wound into her abdomen wasn't long, but he guessed it was deep.

Ryan's chest burned as it filled with mixed emotions. But he'd have to parse out his feelings later. Or better yet, he could ignore them altogether. Right now, he had to save Kathryn, and that meant stanching the blood flow.

Without thought, he pulled the flannel shirt from his waist. He pressed the fabric to her injury.

Kathryn's eyelids fluttered. Her lips moved. He could feel her breath.

Those were all good signs, right?

"Don't." His voice was thick with emotions he didn't want to feel. "Don't talk. Don't move. I'll take care of you."

But how?

Slipping his arms under her knees and back, he gently lifted her from the ground. Then, he ran like hell to the front of the house. A fork of lightning turned the night bright as day. It made it easy for Ryan to see the truth. Kathryn's vehicle was gone. The cruiser had been stolen by Decker, obviously. If he'd taken the car, it meant that Old Blue was gone, too. His gut burned with anger and frustration. Thunder rumbled, and he could feel the echo in his chest. Then, the skies opened. Water sluiced down his shoulders as a spray of cold water hit him in the face.

The storm had arrived in full force.

Gripping the steering wheel with both hands, Decker pressed his foot to the accelerator. The wipers swished back and forth, clearing away the rain that now fell in sheets. He'd stolen the cop's car, but he knew it wouldn't get him far. Certainly, the vehicle had GPS tracking. It wouldn't take the other deputies long to find it.

Which meant he had to find another ride quick.

As he sped through the darkness, he had problems beyond finding and stealing another car.

How had the cops found him?

He assumed they'd tracked him via the internet. But how? Seraphim promised that his connection was secure. His backpack sat on the passenger seat. He reached for the bag with one hand and opened the zipper. After fishing out a phone, he opened the top of the flip phone. A single number was programmed into the memory. He placed the call.

"Decker?" Seraphim's voice was still the same raspy wheeze as before. "I assume you made it out alive."

He went cold with shock. Then, it morphed to a fiery fury. "You knew they were coming for me? How?"

"Easy. I never took the victim's phone off the internet."

Disbelief hit him, like a fist to his gut. "You *what*?"

"For rest of our plan to work, the authorities had to find you. Then you had to get away. Otherwise, they wouldn't believe."

Honestly, he saw the sense in what the hacker said. But still. "What if I hadn't escaped?"

"But you did. You're resourceful. You're careful and you plan. But you can also think on your feet." He paused. "You know what to do next."

Decker did, but he had a detour to make first. "I'll be in touch."

"I'll be waiting."

He ended the call and slipped the phone back into the bag. A growl came from the back seat. Decker swerved as he looked over his shoulder. Behind the metal grille sat a dog.

He looked back at the road before glancing into the back seat again.

It wasn't just any dog. "Old Blue? How the hell did you end up in this car?"

The dog barked, baring its teeth.

Decker had to admit, he'd been surprised more than once tonight. He hated not being in control. He hated seeing Ryan again. He hated the only way to end it between them would be with one of them in a body bag.

His old *friend* knew that, too.

Ryan could've shot him. He assumed that the hesitation was to protect the sheriff's deputy. But why?

Was the woman something more to Ryan?

He hoped so, because then he could use those feelings to his advantage.

Chapter 7

Ryan stood in the middle of the muddy driveway. Rain washed over him in a single sheet. He held Kathryn in his arms. Her face had turned milky white—not a good sign. He had no car. No phone. No way to call for or get help.

He cursed and ran up the sagging porch steps. At least, under the overhang, he could keep Kathryn drier. He found a spot to lay her on the wood porch. Her head drooped to the side. Her lips had turned purple.

His throat tightened, until it felt like he was being choked. "Are you still with me?" he croaked.

Kathryn said nothing.

He tapped her cheek. She moaned.

Sagging with relief, he said, "You have to listen to my voice."

He looked out into the night. There was nothing other

than darkness and the endlessly falling rain. Where was the damned backup? It'd been more than ten minutes since they'd called in. Or maybe not. Time no longer meant anything.

"Stay with me," he urged.

Kathryn's eyelids fluttered.

"I want you to pay attention to my voice," he said to her, hoping like hell she was still lucid enough to hear him. Reaching for her hand, he rubbed her palm. "Can you hear me? Squeeze my hand if you know I'm here."

Her fingers twitched.

Flashing red lights shone on the horizon. "It's them," he said. The first vehicle was followed by others. At the back of the line, he saw a large, white ambulance.

He bent close to Kathryn. "That's the backup. They're here. You'll be okay. I promise."

Her lips moved, but she made no sound. Or did she? Leaning closer still, he asked, "What'd you say?"

She swallowed, grimaced, and muttered a single word. "Decker?"

"He got away. He escaped when I saw that you were still alive." He expected the words to taste like ash and soil. They didn't. He didn't regret letting Decker go— not if it meant keeping Kathryn alive.

She gripped his hand. The strength in her fingers startled him. Her eyes were open. He met her gaze.

"Thank you," she whispered.

The emotion that had choked him before got tighter. He couldn't have spoken, even if he'd known what to say. He gave her a single nod and squeezed her hand. Her eyes drifted closed. Ryan stood. He ran into the rain, waving at the oncoming vehicles. The first car to stop was the black SUV. Isaac opened the driver's door. Ryan met him before he put his foot on the sodden ground.

"I need the ambulance," he said. "Kathryn was stabbed by Decker. She's on the porch and hurt bad."

He tried to run. Isaac gripped his shoulder. "Where's Decker now?"

"Hell if I know where he went. But after he stabbed Kathryn, he stole her cruiser." He shouldn't be worried about a mutt when so much was at stake. And yet, he said, "Old Blue was in the car. And now, he's gone, too."

Isaac opened the back door of the SUV. "Michael, the undersheriff's hurt."

The lanky physician stepped into the rain. Michael O'Brien was a forensic pathologist, but he'd also attended med school. With the physician working with a set of the EMTs, Ryan hoped that Kathryn would get the care she needed.

The doctor said to Isaac, "Get the paramedics up here." Then to Ryan, "Take me to the undersheriff."

Sprinting through the deluge, he bounded up the steps of the porch. Michael followed. It was impossible to miss Kathryn's supine form. The doctor knelt next to her. "Tell me what happened."

He gave a quick rundown of the encounter with Decker.

At length, Michael said, "The good news is I don't think any internal organs are damaged. But she shouldn't lose consciousness with an abdominal wound. I suspect she has a concussion, too." Before he could say anything else, a pair of EMTs approached. One carried a folded stretcher and the other a medical kit. Ryan moved to the side to let the medical professionals do their job.

An EMT knelt next to Kathryn. "Undersheriff," he said, "it's me. Chase Martinez. I'm here to take care of you."

It took only minutes for the paramedics to get Kathryn into the back of the ambulance. Once the back doors closed, the vehicle turned on the muddy yard. Ryan stood on the porch, suddenly exhausted, and watched the ambulance drive away. As the taillights were swallowed by the darkness, he didn't know what to do next.

The desire to be with Kathryn was akin to the hunger of a starving man. He wanted to go to her. Did he have the right to make any demands?

He knew the answer. He couldn't ask for anything where she was concerned.

Jason and Isaac jogged through the rain. They climbed the steps. With Ryan and Michael, the four men formed a loose circle on the sagging porch.

Jason wiped a damp sleeve across his wet face. "Tell me what happened."

His story began with the call where Kathryn was told that the murder victim's phone had been found. He ended with Decker exploding like a cannonball from the back door and the attack that had left Kathryn unconscious and bleeding.

"How'd you know it was Decker?" Isaac asked.

Honestly, he didn't like that he was being questioned instead of everyone looking for the killer. Still, he didn't have a reason to lie. "It's been a while since I saw him last, but I still know what he looks like. After he stabbed Kathryn, I mean the undersheriff, we spoke. Honestly, I thought she was dead." He swallowed. "Once I realized that the undersheriff was alive, I started giving her first aid. That's when Decker took off."

"And you didn't think to chase him?" the FBI agent asked, his tone more an accusation than a question.

Working his jaw back and forth, Ryan spit out his next words. "Kathryn was hurt. There was blood everywhere. I couldn't exactly go after Decker because the undersheriff needed help."

Taking a step forward, Jason said, "Let me get this straight. You think that Decker attacked the undersheriff and wounded her just so he could escape. Is that what I'm supposed to believe?"

"I don't care what you believe. And I don't know how Decker thinks," said Ryan, although the last part wasn't true. "You asked me what happened, and I've told you."

"You know," Isaac said and raised his hands, as if surrendering, "Ryan's probably right. Decker threw Clare from a moving car. It wasn't meant to kill her but to hurt her enough that I had to stop chasing him."

Clare Chamberlain had been on the run from her ex-husband when she'd stopped at the bar in Mercy. Ryan had been working undercover with Isaac at the time. Clare had gotten caught up in the Decker Newcombe case. It ended with her being kidnapped and Ryan being stabbed. Well, since Decker was back, he supposed that the story hadn't really ended—not yet.

Jason and Isaac exchanged a glance that was impossible to miss. The look was a punch to Ryan's gut. "Stop throwing side-eyes at each other and just say what you want to say. Or ask what you want to ask."

Isaac shifted from one foot to the next. "I'm only going to ask you once, and I trust you'll be honest with me. Did you know that Decker was going to be in the area tonight? Are you working with him again?"

Ryan had never been a cop, but he knew how they thought. Decker and Ryan returning to Encantador and Mercy on the same night was too much of a coincidence to be an accident. "I'm not working with him—not anymore."

"Can you prove there's not a connection between you and Decker?" the FBI agent asked, a definite edge in his tone.

"Can you prove that there *is* one?" he shot back.

Jason didn't seem to have an answer to the question, which meant he had no proof.

Isaac was the next one to speak. "Why are you in the area anyway?"

Crap. Now what was he supposed to say? He definitely didn't want to tell them the truth, but he'd gain nothing by lying. He remained mute.

After a moment, Jason said, "You got the federal government to clear your background. That left you without a past at all. Life can't be easy."

Ryan really disliked the fed. It was more than his holier-than-thou attitude, though that was bad enough. The guy was too perfect. His wet clothes weren't muddy or wrinkled. His hair, damp still, looked freshly barbered.

"Life is never easy." He paused a beat. "You charging me with a crime? Because if not, then I'm free to go."

"Go where?" Isaac asked. "It's pouring rain and you're miles from nowhere."

At one time, he had thought that Isaac was his friend.

Guess he'd been wrong about that, too. "Anywhere is better than here."

"I'll need your gun," said Jason. Then he added, "For forensic testing."

What the fed really meant is that he wanted to see if there was evidence to corroborate his story. "It's not my gun. The undersheriff gave it to me."

Holding out his hand, Jason said, "I'll make sure she gets it back when we're done."

He removed the gun from his waistband and slapped the weapon into the other man's open palm. "Anything else?"

Jason shook his head.

"Then, I'm outta here." Ryan jogged down the porch steps.

He was going to regret his decision, he knew it. But he'd be damned before he'd spend another minute at the abandoned farmstead. Shoving his hands in his pockets, he strode past the other collected law-enforcement agents. They were preparing to search the house and gather whatever evidence Decker had left behind.

He walked on. Rain pelted his face. Water rolled down the collar of his shirt. His shoes squelched. With each step, he cursed his decision to come back to Encantador and Mercy in the first place.

The year he'd lived here and run the bar was like a fever dream. All the memories were surrounded in a haze. But he knew life could be good. He wanted it to be good again. At the end of the driveway, he turned to the right.

A set of headlights shone on him from behind, turning his stride into the shadow of a giant. A second later, the shadow passed. From the side of his eye, he could see the large SUV. The window was down, and Isaac leaned on the center console as he drove.

"Can I offer you a lift?" Isaac asked.

"Nah. It's a lovely night for a stroll," he said, knowing full well he was being sarcastic.

"Stop being a smartass and get in the car."

Ryan shook his head.

"I'm trying to be a friend."

He snorted. "Thanks for accusing me of being a criminal again, pal."

"I know you aren't involved with Decker, but Jason doesn't. He would've gotten around to asking you. Trust me, it would've taken a lot longer, and probably he'd put you in custody. I just short-circuited his interrogation."

Ryan stopped. "Am I supposed to thank you?"

Isaac stopped his vehicle. "They found the under-sheriff's car. It's about ten miles from here. Looks like Decker parked the cruiser and stole another car."

"What about Old Blue?"

"He was in the back seat and is doing well. In fact, his barking is what woke up the homeowner." Isaac paused. "I can give you a ride to pick up the dog and then take you back to your truck."

"So I'm not going to be forced to stay?"

"Just get in the car and we can talk. You look too wet and miserable for me to answer any more questions."

"I'm not miserable," he lied, opening the door. He slid into the passenger seat. The back seats were empty. "Where's Michael and the FBI agent with the big mouth?"

Isaac chuckled. "Jason Jones is an acquired taste, that's for sure."

"Acquired tastes," he said, echoing Isaac's words, "are for wines. That guy's a bottle full of vinegar."

Isaac laughed. "I've missed you, man."

He pulled on his seat belt, thankful to be out of the rain and to have a soft leather seat. It was nice to be missed. That was one of the many reasons he wanted to come back to Mercy. "It's good to see you again," he said. What would a good friend do next? Ryan wasn't sure. Instead, he said, "Decker's up to something."

Isaac drove, gripping the steering wheel tighter. "How'd you get this intel?"

After all the talk of friendship, the private-security operative still didn't trust him one hundred percent. "*Intel* is a pretty solid word. Let's call it a hunch on my part."

"Like a gut feeling."

Ryan shrugged and turned to look out the window. He saw nothing but his own reflection. "Something like that."

"What's your gut telling you that he's planning?"

"Honestly, I'm not sure why he's fixated on this town." Although in truth, Ryan was drawn to this area, just like iron to a magnet. "But he wants something here. Revenge, for what happened earlier, maybe."

"Maybe," said Isaac.

Ryan sat without a further word. The drive to the small brick house took less than ten minutes. Kathryn's cruiser was parked in the yard. A collapsible shelter had been set up over the car, presumably to protect any evidence from the weather. Several other vehicles sat on the lawn as well. There was another cruiser from the sheriff's office along with a crime-scene unit's van and several cars from the Texas Rangers.

Isaac parked next to the CSI van. He opened the door and stepped into the rain. Ryan had begun to dry and loathed the idea of getting cold and wet again. The sound of barking came from the house. Old Blue stood on his hind legs and looked out the front window. He couldn't help but smile.

He ran through the storm. A blonde woman opened the door as he approached. "This must be your dog," she said, smiling. "He started making a racket as soon as you pulled into the yard."

Old Blue jogged from the adjacent living room. In the foyer, he dropped to his back and exposed his belly for rubs. "Hey, boy." He bent down to scratch the dog's stomach. "You miss me?"

Old Blue whined.

"I'd take that as a *yes*," said Isaac. Then to the woman, "Thanks for taking care of the dog."

She blew out a long breath, ruffling her bangs. "When I think of the bad that could've happened with Decker Newcombe in front of my house..." she shook her head "...well, I'm just glad he only stole the car."

"We're all relieved that he didn't do anything more," said Ryan.

"I don't know if y'all can comment. But is it true that he killed the bank manager and posted the murder to the internet?" She paused. "I know police can't always talk about open investigations." She looked from Ryan to Isaac and back. Did the woman think he was a cop? He wanted to laugh but kept a neutral expression.

"Sorry," said Ryan, "we really can't comment."

"C'mon," said Isaac, "let's go."

It took several minutes of driving to get to where Ryan had parked. It'd only been a matter of hours since Old Blue had taken off into the dark, but it felt like days. Thankfully, the rain had stopped and taken the oppressive heat with it. Isaac parked next to the truck, and that's when he saw the truth.

"Damn," he groaned. "I left the windows open." He opened the door of his vehicle. Water was pooled on the floor mat. He pressed a hand onto the upholstery and his palm was soaked. "Sitting on these seats will be like lying on a leaky waterbed."

"By tomorrow, they'll be dry."

Isaac was probably right, but Ryan was worried about right now. "It's gonna be a special kind of hell to drive for hours with a soggy butt," he said, trying to make a joke. But even he heard the indignation in his voice.

"I can help you out." Isaac opened the lift gate of his SUV and pulled out two tarps. Both had *Texas Law* stenciled on the back. "Use these for now."

"You have merch for your business now? Nice."

Isaac's chest swelled with pride. "It is nice."

"Brother, I am heading out of town and won't be back."

"Then, keep them. They're yours."

Taking the covers, Ryan tucked them under his arm. "Thanks." The thing was, he really was worried about Kathryn. Isaac was in the loop, so to speak. He might know how she was doing. "Have you gotten an update on the undersheriff?"

Isaac shook his head. "I haven't heard a thing."

"But she's going to be okay, right? Michael said that she was unconscious because of a probable concussion. He also said the wound to her side wasn't fatal."

"You know more than me, man."

So much for an update.

Ryan placed a tarp on the passenger seat and snapped his fingers for Old Blue to get into the vehicle. Now, there really was nothing else keeping him here. His chest ached with disappointment. But did he regret having to leave? Or was he sorry that he'd come in the first place? "If you hear anything about Kathryn..." he began.

"I'll let you know," said Isaac, finishing the request. "And do us both a favor. If the feds call with questions, make sure you answer the phone. It'll be easier on you if you cooperate."

Ryan grunted and slammed the passenger door closed.

Isaac said, "Take care of yourself."

"I always do," said Ryan.

He rounded the front of his truck and opened the driver's door. While spreading out the tarp, he watched Isaac. The operative stood next to the bumper of his own SUV and tapped on his phone's screen. "You are one lucky guy," he called out to Ryan.

"Oh yeah?" He'd had all sorts of luck in his life—most of it was the bad kind. "How's that?"

"I just got a text from Michael. It seems the wound to Kathryn's side has been patched up. She's regained consciousness. And she wants to see you."

Chapter 8

Kathryn lay in a hospital bed. Several pillows were propped behind her head. A monitor was attached to her finger. An IV was stuck in the back of her hand and tubing was taped to her skin. The doctor had given her meds for the pain, and right now, everything was surrounded with a golden halo. Yet, she knew one thing. She had to get out of the bed and back to work. What's more, there was only one person she trusted to help her out.

Now she had to hope that Ryan would come to her aid.

Jason Jones was her first visitor at the hospital. He spent several minutes asking about the incident.

Q: Was it really your idea to walk the perimeter and not Ryan's?

A: Yes.

Q: Did Ryan do or say anything suspicious while you were with him?

A: No.

And then, there was the most important question of all.

Q: In your estimation, was Ryan working with Decker?

The thing was, Kathryn had asked herself the same question more than once. Now she had a definitive answer. "He's not working with Decker." A pain gripped her side and left her breathless. "I'm positive."

A black plastic chair sat next to the wall. The FBI agent moved it next to Kathryn's bed and took a seat. "It's been a long night for everyone, so I have to ask you to clarify. How do you know—for a fact—that Ryan and Decker aren't working together?"

"Easy," she said. A cup sat on her bedside table. She reached for the water and took a sip. "After Decker stabbed me, Ryan wouldn't have bothered to save my life."

"You have a concussion and a nonfatal wound to your side, Undersheriff. I hardly think he gets credit for saving you."

Her heart monitor started to beep as her pulse climbed. "Ryan stopped the bleeding—or slowed it, at least. How long would I have lasted without him?"

The FBI agent shook his head. "I can't answer that."

"Trust me, if he and Decker were working together, then Ryan would also be gone. What's more, I'd be in worse shape than I am right now." She paused. "I need to get a hold of my kids and let them know what happened."

"Your deputy, Todd, reached out to them. They're

aware you were injured and are resting." He held out his cell. "If you want to call them, you can."

Kathryn hadn't expected the simple kindness of a loaned phone from the fed. "Thanks."

She took the phone and placed a quick call to both Morgan and Brock. Neither answered—probably because they didn't recognize the number. She left a voicemail for both. "Hey, it's Mom. You heard I got hurt. I'm in the hospital." Would her kids try to visit her? The last thing she wanted was for them to be on the streets with Decker in the area. "Stay at your friend's, I'll call once I'm home." She handed the phone back to Jason. "Thanks."

He nodded. "I have agents watching the homes where your children are staying."

Kathryn knew that pulling agents off the manhunt was a sacrifice. But knowing that her children were safe was like dropping a huge weight. She nodded her thanks. "Where are we with the investigation?"

"We're still looking for the stolen car."

"Yeah, but Decker's MO is to change vehicles frequently," she said, thinking through what she knew of the criminal's history. "He could've ditched two stolen cars by now and be God knows where."

"We have every law-enforcement officer in the area looking for him. Decker won't get far." After a moment, he asked, "How are you feeling, by the way? What's your prognosis?"

"The doctor thinks I need several days bedrest." *Like that would ever happen.* "Everything will eventually heal."

"I'll be in touch." Jason rose from his seat but didn't move toward the door.

"Anything else?" she asked.

"I was wondering if you'd spoken with Sheriff Parsons."

Letting out a long and slow breath, she tried to stave off her irritation. It didn't work. "I was unconscious for a bit. Then I was kinda busy while the doctor sewed up my side." She didn't bother to keep the snark from her tone. "So, sorry, no. I haven't really had time to make a call."

"My question is really twofold. Has Mooky been briefed on what's happening here, and who's the contact person for your office?"

"As far as I know, Mooky hasn't been contacted. Again, I've been otherwise occupied. You can keep in contact with me."

"You?" he echoed. "But you'll be laid up for a week."

"That's what the doctor said." She didn't bother to add that she disagreed with her assessment. "If anything changes, I'll let you know."

"All right, then. We'll be in touch."

He left, and Kathryn eased back into the pillows. She wanted to sleep. She needed to get out of the hospital. Her eyes drifted closed. When she opened them, Ryan was sitting in the chair next to her bed.

She wanted to speak, but her throat was too dry. She whispered his name. "Ryan."

His eyebrows were drawn together. "Hey. How're you feeling? I was worried about you."

"I'm better," she croaked. "What time is it?"

He pulled a cell phone from his pocket. "Three thirty in the morning."

"How long have you been here?"

He shrugged. "I heard you wanted to see me, but I didn't want to wake you."

She could already tell that the nap had been restorative.

"I appreciate you waiting around." She pointed to the plastic cup that sat on a nearby table. "Can you hand me the water?"

"Sure thing."

He held the cup and guided the straw to her lips. She took several long swallows and lay back in her pillows, breathing hard. "Thanks," she said before adding, "for everything."

He waved away her gratitude. "I'm just glad it worked out in the end."

"I have to ask you two questions. First, you said it yourself, you know Decker. Why'd he come back?"

"Isaac was just asking me the same thing. My best guess—he wants revenge. How that'll look, well, I don't know. But everyone in town needs to be vigilant." He paused. "Look, I'm sorry that Decker found out about Encantador and Mercy because he came looking for me all those months ago." His jaw flexed and released. "Well, I didn't know how it'd work out, and I am sorry. I will give you your wish, though. As soon as I leave the hospital, me and Old Blue will get out of here."

"Stay." The intensity with which she spoke was surprising, even to her. She reached for his wrist. His skin was warm under her palm. For a split second, she recalled being cradled in his arms and knowing she was safe. How long had it been since someone had taken care of Kathryn? She let her hand slip away. "I need you," she said. "I need help, and you're the only one I trust."

She looked up and met his gaze. His eyes were wide. "You need me. Why?"

She pushed herself up to sitting. Her side burned, and she gritted her teeth against the pain. "I need to get out of here. I can't lie around while Decker's on the loose."

"And why do you need me for that?"

"Because the doctor recommends that I stay here until noon. Then she said it'd be a week before I'd be back to work. After that, she wants to put me on light duty." Kathryn refused to be sidelined during the investigation. "I need someone to help me get home."

"I understand that you don't want to listen to the doctor, but is that really best? Your health is important."

"Finding Decker before he kills again is more important. Me being sore because of an injury is an inconvenience." She pointed to the table. A slip of paper lay on it. "Besides, the doctor already left a prescription for pain meds. Todd brought me a change of clothes."

Ryan shook his head. "It doesn't sound like a great idea to me. You should follow the doctor's orders."

"You're one to talk. You don't like to play by the rules."

"Yeah," he said. "But I want to be the good guy and do the right thing."

She tried again. "I can't catch Decker from this bed. And I won't rest if he's still at large."

"I really shouldn't," he began.

"But you will, right?"

"You make it hard to be an honorable man, you know

that?" He gave her a wicked smile. Both his smile and his words warmed her from the inside out. She tried to ignore the sensation, but it was impossible.

"Help me get out of this bed." She carefully swung her legs over the edge of the bed and held out her hand. It was dangerous to trust him. To touch him. Had she been honest when she said she had nobody else to help her?

Yes and no.

Certainly, she could have ordered one of the other deputies to get her out of the hospital and take her home. They would have balked and tried to talk her into staying. Who knows, maybe she would have even listened. Or maybe the truth was far more basic. Maybe she asked for Ryan because she wanted to be in his arms again. She wanted to know once more what it was to feel safe and cared for.

He reached for her hand. She'd come to expect the electric current his touch ignited. This time, discomfort short-circuited her reaction. He pulled her to standing. By the time she was on her feet, her legs shook and cold sweat coated her face and back. She should've taken care with her hospital gown. It gaped in the front and was open in the back. She glanced at Ryan. His gaze was glued to the floor. There was no way he'd caught a peek at anything.

Todd had dropped off the gym bag she kept stowed at work. Inside was a fresh change of clothes. "Hand me that duffel."

"Can you stand on your own?"

She pressed the backs of her legs against the bed. The frame held her steady. "I'm good."

He set the bag on the bed beside her. There was also a plastic bag with her other belongings that had been collected by the hospital. It contained her phone, keys, and such. He picked up the second bag. "I'll carry this for you and stand outside. Yell if you need me."

First, she pulled the IV from her hand and taped a bandage to the puncture mark. Then, she shrugged out of her hospital gown. Her side was covered with a large white compress. The emergency room physician, Dr. McDaniel, had gone over the need to keep it dry for the next few days, which meant no shower or bath. After that, the dressing could be changed.

The thing was, she didn't have time to be weak or wounded or sick.

She carefully donned a fresh set of underwear and bra. She put on a T-shirt, and by the time she was pulling up a loose pair of jogger pants, white dots floated in her vision. There was no way she would be able to get on her socks and shoes.

"Ryan." The single word came out as a wheeze. "Can you help?"

He appeared at her doorway. His shoulders seemed to fill the frame. "Yeah?"

"I hate to ask for this." She picked up a pair of sneakers from the bed. "Can you help me with these? It'll hurt too much to bend down."

"I'm still not sure that you leaving the hospital is the best idea. You look worn-out."

The simple act of dressing had left her exhausted. "I'll rest when I get home."

He shook his head but said, "You got socks?"

She picked up a pair. "Here."

He took them from her. The tips of his fingers grazed her palm. A shiver of desire ran through her, and for a moment she forgot how lousy she felt. He knelt at her feet, and a craving for his touch filled her veins once more.

Carefully, Ryan lifted one foot and set it on his bent knee. "Red toenails," he said. "Nice."

Sure, she felt rotten. Still, she smiled. "I get a pedicure once a month. Kind of silly, if you think about it. Nobody ever sees my feet."

"I'm more than a nobody."

Truer words had never been spoken. He gazed at her with his blue eyes. Her fingers itched with the need to stroke his cheek. She balled her hands into fists and pressed her knuckles into the mattress. "I'm sure you've never been accused of being a nobody."

He watched her for a minute before looking away. He slipped a sock and shoe on one foot then took care of the other. Standing, he dusted his hands on the front of his jeans. "Anything else you need?"

"I'm good." She stood. The floor beneath her tilted, but at least, this time, there were no floating dots. The ground leveled, and she drew in a long breath. "I'm good," she repeated; this time it was closer to the truth.

"Can you walk to the truck? If not, I can grab you a wheelchair."

"If I can't walk to the parking lot, then I have no business leaving the hospital."

"Is this a test?" he asked.

It was and it wasn't. "I'm leaving the hospital no matter what."

He stood at her side. "At least hold onto my arm."

Her fingers dug into his bicep. His muscles were taut. She took one step. Pain radiated from her stomach and wrapped around her back. She drew in a long, slow breath. She exhaled and took another step. And another. By the time they made it to the hallway, her back was damp with sweat.

A nurse's station sat at an intersection of two corridors. The physician, Felicia McDaniel, looked up as she approached. She was the last person Kathryn wanted to see.

The doctor scowled. "What are you doing out of bed? I told you that we were keeping you until noon, at least."

"I'm discharging myself."

"I have to advise against it," the doctor began.

"If it weren't important, I'd stay in bed to recuperate. But with Decker at large…" She wanted to shrug but worried that the slight movement would hurt too much. She finished with, "I just can't."

"Can't or won't?" the doctor challenged.

Kathryn knew the difference. But how could she explain to Felicia that Decker was now her personal problem? She couldn't lie in bed and let other people run the investigation. She held tighter to Ryan's arm. He placed his hand on hers. "I'll take it easy," she said, not sure how she'd keep her promise.

"I can't force you to stay," said the doctor. "But if I could, I would." After pulling a pad of paper from her pocket, she silently wrote on the page. "This is for iron. I don't want you to become anemic. Eat something before you take either this or the pain meds. Got it?" She held up the prescription.

"Got it." Kathryn reached for the piece of paper.

"And you," the doctor said, pointing to Ryan, "make sure she rests when she gets home."

"I'll do my best," he said, patting Kathryn's hand.

The walk through the hospital was slow. Yet, with each step she took, she knew she could get through this. The waiting room was empty. A set of sliding glass doors led to the parking lot. The sky was still dark. The rain had stopped, but clouds filled the sky.

"That's my truck," he said, pointing to a blue and white vehicle two rows back. "I can help you get to the bench. I'll drive to you. It won't take a minute."

If Kathryn sat down, she wasn't sure that she'd be able to stand again. "I've got this," she said. Even she could hear the exhaustion in her voice.

She shuffle-stepped across the pavement. At the truck, he let his arm slip from her grip and opened the passenger door.

Tail a wagging blur, Old Blue stood on the passenger seat. Both seats were covered with dark blue tarps. A white Texas Law logo was stenciled on them in white. "What's up with those?" she asked, pointing to the covers.

"I left the windows open and, of course, it rained. Scoot over, boy, and let her get in." The dog climbed over the console and sat in the driver's seat.

"Thanks, Blue." Kathryn backed up to the truck. The seat was higher than she expected.

"I can lift you up," said Ryan. "That way you won't rip open your stitches or anything like that."

"Thanks."

He stood in front of her. "Hold onto my shoulders."

She did as she was told, and Ryan pulled her close.

Her breasts were pressed against the muscles of his chest. Being this close to him left her dizzy and wanting more. The last thing she needed now was to have her judgment clouded by lust. But in the moment, there was no way she could avoid holding him tight.

He lifted her onto the seat and carefully swung her legs into the car. Standing next to her, he held the seatbelt clip. "I'll wait," he said. "You get settled."

Her side throbbed with each beat of her heart. She concentrated only on her breath. The pain didn't go away, but the sharpest edges seemed to smooth. She reached for the seat belt. "I'm okay."

"Don't twist," said Ryan, his hand still holding the metal clip. "You'll make everything worse. I've got you."

He leaned across her, his torso skimming over hers, and buckled the latch. "All better?"

His lips were close to hers. She could kiss him if she wanted. And she did want to kiss him. Yet, she knew better.

Giving a single nod, she said, "I'm okay."

He rounded to the driver's seat and got behind the wheel. It took only a few minutes to get back to her house. Ryan helped her from the truck and let her hold onto his arm while he walked her to her front door. He still had the bag with her belongings. From inside, he fished out her heavy key ring. "Which one is for the front door?"

"The silver one," she said.

He opened the lock and helped her across the threshold. She stood in her living room and glanced at a clock that hung on the wall. It was almost 4:00 a.m. If she lay down now, she could get several hours of sleep before she had to get up again for the meeting.

"What can I do for you next?"

"Help me get to my bed, and then I'll be okay." Who was Kathryn kidding? She was far from okay. Leaving the hospital had been a mistake, but she wasn't going back now. "My room's the last one on the left."

Then again, he knew that already. She'd seen him peeking in through her window.

Had that only been last night?

She stood at her doorway. Her room looked the same as it did before. Her bed was made. The pile of clean clothes still sat on a chair. But everything was different. Her neighbor was dead. A killer was once again loose in her town. And she was injured. She lifted the clock from her nightstand and set the alarm for eleven o'clock. Setting it back down, she said, "It seems like I haven't been here for a million years."

He steered her toward the bed. "Lie down," he said, as she slowly sat on the mattress. "Get some rest, and everything will be okay."

She settled on top of the covers, and sleep came to claim her. But before it did, she had one final thought. Ryan was wrong. Nothing would be okay—not now and maybe not ever.

Chapter 9

Kathryn woke to the sound of her alarm clock beeping. Her side throbbed and her head ached. Before she opened her eyes, every moment of the night before flashed through her mind.

Finding the mutilated body.

A video of the murder coming to her from the victim's phone.

There was undisputed evidence that Decker Newcombe had returned to terrorize her town. Hell, she'd even been attacked by him personally.

And yet the memory that truly sent her heart racing was when she recalled Ryan holding her in the rain.

Sitting up slowly, she rubbed her gritty eyes.

Where was he now? Certainly, he had left Encantador as soon as she fell into bed. It was all for the best, really. He was a distraction that neither she nor the town needed right now. Carefully, she placed her feet on the floor and stood. The pain wasn't as bad as she expected. And what's more, she could smell the nutty aroma of coffee coming from the kitchen.

She listened for the telltale sounds that one of her kids had come home early. Loud music. Banging dishes. Or the voices of them chatting with a friend on a video call. There was nothing. She walked slowly down the hall that ended at her living room.

The room hadn't changed much in the dozen years she'd lived in the house. A large window looked out onto her front yard and the street beyond. A set of sheer curtains was pulled over the pane, providing privacy while still allowing for light to seep into the room. An *L*-shaped sofa sat beneath the window. There was a coffee table in the middle of the floor. Two chairs stood on the opposite side of the table.

A TV sat on a stand. Pictures of her Morgan and Brock, from round babies to gangly teenagers, hung on the walls.

Old Blue sat on the floor. Tail thumping, he looked up as she approached. Ryan sat on the sofa. His eyes were closed. His head was back, and he snored softly. A half-full cup of coffee sat on the coffee table.

The dog rose. Nose down, he walked toward her. She bent to scratch his head.

"Looks like we all had an eventful night."

Ryan opened his eyes, his gaze darting from one corner of the room to the other. "Sorry," he said, raising his arms over his head. His shirt crept up, exposing his hard abs and a sprinkling of dark hair. It had been years since she'd seen such a fit and virile man. Her throat went dry, and she swallowed. "I dozed off."

"I'm surprised that you're here at all. I thought you were leaving town."

"I was," he said. "I mean, I will. It just didn't seem right to leave you alone in case there was an emergency."

Her cheeks warmed. "That was kind of you."

He rose from the sofa. "I made coffee, I hope you don't mind. Also, Dr. McDaniel called. She got the pharmacy to deliver your prescriptions. I also figured you'd need something for the pain as soon as you woke up. I hope you don't mind."

In a lot of ways, his actions were too personal for someone she barely knew. But in other ways, it was just right. "It seems like I keep thanking you for being so kind."

Taking two steps toward her, he closed the distance between them. "That's not something I hear every day. Or ever, really." He shook his head. "But I am trying. You know, I ask myself, *What would a good person do?*" He gestured to the sofa. "Sit. I'll get you coffee, your pills, a piece of toast."

Before she had a chance to think better of it, she reached for his arm. "Good people help, no matter what. Seems to me like you're a decent guy."

"No," he said with a sad smile. "I'm not."

He took a step back, and her hand slid from his wrist. "Well, it smells like you can make a decent cup of coffee. And in my book, that's enough," she said jokingly.

"And how d'you take your coffee?"

"Black. The way mother nature intended."

He gave her his wicked smile. "Black coffee. You

are definitely a woman after my own heart. Sit. I'll be right back."

She sank into the sofa. Old Blue leaned his head into her thigh, and she scratched him behind the ear. For years, her kids had begged for a dog. She'd never allowed it. She couldn't take care of an animal considering the hours her job required. Any time that was left to her, she dedicated to her kids. Yet, as she petted the dog now, she wondered if she'd made the right decision.

Ryan returned a few minutes later. In one hand, he held a cup of coffee. In the other was a plate with two slices of buttered toast and two pills. He set both on the coffee table in front of her. "The white pill is for the pain. The other is for your iron."

After picking up the two pills, she placed them on her tongue. She swallowed them both with a drink of coffee. The hot liquid burned her throat as the caffeine began to buzz through her system. Maybe she would be able to make it through the day.

The plastic bag from the hospital sat on the coffee table. She picked up a piece of toast and took a bite. While chewing, she reached for the bag and found her phone. She glanced at the screen. "Forty-five missed calls?"

She scrolled through the log. Brock had called and texted dozens of times. Morgan had called and texted as well. Her chest ached with guilt and appreciation. Her kids really did care. But what would have happened to them if things had gone differently last night?

She sent a quick message to the family group chat.

Not sure what you heard, but I'm okay. Home now. We'll talk later.

She also sent another text to Todd.

Can you be at the office to meet with Tessa Wray's family?

He replied: I figured you'd need me, so I'm here already.

Truly, she was lucky to have good coworkers.

She sent him another message.

Thanks. I owe you.

She continued to look through the messages and calls. More folks than just her kids had reached out.

Alicia, from the newspaper, had both called and texted. Caller ID showed several cable-news channels had called as well. Between all the messages from the media, she'd missed an important call. The phone log read, Sheriff Parsons. Certainly, Mooky had heard all about last night. He was probably wondering why she hadn't briefed him already. True, she had her reasons. But right now, they didn't seem so solid. She tried to swallow, but the toast stuck in her throat. "Damn."

"Bad news?" Ryan asked. He picked up his cup from the table and took a sip.

"It's nothing about Decker. It's just I have to make a call." Kathryn pushed up from the sofa. The stitches at her side pulled and she gasped.

Ryan held her elbow, keeping her on her feet. "What is it?"

She gritted her teeth. "I stood up too fast, I guess."

She drew in air through her nose and blew it out of

her mouth. The pain didn't vanish, but it became bearable. "Thanks," she said.

"I've been stabbed by Decker before, too." He let go of her elbow and lifted his shirt. A scar ran across his abdomen. "See?"

Without thinking, she brushed her fingertips over the raised, red line. "Does it hurt?"

"Right now, I can only feel your touch." His words danced on her skin.

She looked up at him. He was watching her. A smile tugged at his lips. "Oh, really?"

"Yeah." The single word came out as a sigh.

Then, his mouth was on hers. She ran her fingers through the hair that covered his abs. That electric charge she'd come to expect sparked to life again. Her side still ached, but pleasure mingled with pain.

In the back of her mind, she knew that kissing him was wrong on so many different levels. Yet, it had been years since she'd been kissed. But in all honesty, she'd never been kissed like this.

What the hell are you doing?

She didn't have an answer and she pushed him away. It was the same instant the door hit the wall with a crack.

Heartbeat thundering, she turned to the sound.

"Mom? What the heck?" Morgan stood on the threshold. She wore flannel shorts and an Encantador High School hoodie. Her dark hair was piled on top of her head in a messy bun. But her eyes were wide. Twin spots of red, like the burn from a coal, colored her cheeks. "I heard you got hurt. I got your message from a strange number. I called your phone, like, a million times. Then, I saw your text, so I rushed home. Now I find you…you…" she spluttered, unable to finish. Her eyes filled with tears.

Damn. She'd messed up. Her chest tightened with guilt and regret. Stepping toward Morgan, she opened her arms. "Oh, honey, I'm so sorry."

Morgan held up her palm. "Don't apologize to me. Don't try to hug me, either."

"Can we at least talk?"

From the floor, Old Blue whined.

Morgan spied the canine. Then, she glared at Kathryn. "A dog?" Her tone dripped with incredulity. "When did we get a dog?"

"He's not our dog, honey. He belongs to Ryan."

"Oh, he's your *friend's* dog. Stellar. Well, since you are obviously fine, I'm going to bed. I was up all night, worried about you."

"Young lady, you cannot talk to me like that." Really, she didn't have the energy for a power struggle. "Why is it always an argument with you?"

Morgan sighed. "I'm not fighting. I'm just stating facts. So unless you need something, good night."

This time, Kathryn let her leave. She sank to the sofa, exhausted once more. She was never able to find a balance with Morgan. Either Kathryn was too strict or too lenient—and neither option suited. Her gaze shifted to where Ryan stood. "Do you have kids?"

He shook his head. "I figured one of me was all the world could handle."

"She was sixteen years old when her dad died. It's a hard age to lose a parent. We wiped out our savings with his cancer treatments, so the life insurance went into a college fund. Maybe if I'd quit working to spend time with them..." She sighed. "Who knows?"

"I might not have kids, but that doesn't mean I can't recognize a loving parent. You're a good mom, Kathryn. That's why your daughter rushed home as soon as she knew you were here. Trust me."

"I don't feel like a good mom, but it's nice to hear you say so." She paused. "I mean, what parent gets caught making out at..." She glanced at her phone for the time. Her stomach dropped. "Oh, crap. Is it really almost eleven thirty? I have to get ready for the town hall." She stood and shoved her phone into her pocket. "I have to change. Then call one of my deputies to give me a ride. I hate pulling an officer off the manhunt." She sighed. She really didn't have any other choice.

Her cruiser had been recovered from the home where Decker had dumped it. The vehicle still had to be processed for evidence. Morgan had certainly driven the family car home. But Kathryn knew she shouldn't be driving with pain meds in her system.

Ryan said, "Take your toast and coffee with you. Then, I can take you to the meeting. After that, Old Blue and I will get out of town."

"I'd appreciate a ride," she said, picking up a slice of toast. While taking a bite, she walked down the hallway. The pain in her side had eased from fiery to a dull ache. Maybe the pain meds really were working. Maybe she really could get through today. And tomorrow. And every day after, until Decker was captured or killed.

Kathryn pushed open the door to her room as her phone began to ring. She didn't have time for a call.

Grinding her teeth together, she pulled the device from her pocket. The caller ID read *Sheriff Parsons*.

Well, this was one call she had to take.

She answered with a swipe. "Sheriff?"

"I'm glad to hear your voice," said Mooky. "Todd called last night. He said you'd been stabbed and were getting stitched up."

She should've known that one of the deputies would reach out to their boss. "Let's just say that it was a long night." She paused a beat. "Today's going to be a long day."

"Long day?" he repeated. "You need to rest, Kathryn. You were injured."

She turned on the Speaker function and set the phone on her dresser. "That makes it sound a lot more serious than it was. The doctor just stitched me up where I was stabbed."

"How many did you get?" he asked.

"Umm, I'm not sure," she lied. It had taken seven stitches for Dr. McDaniel to sew up the wound on her side. "But I'm on meds. I've gotten some rest. I'm ready to answer questions and then get back to work. You can count on me." At least now she was being honest.

"Of course I can count on you," Mooky said. "But you need to reconsider speaking at a town hall. Folks are scared and mad. They're going to take it out on someone, and that someone's going to be you."

"I know." She wanted to sigh but refused to give in to the anguish. "I have a job to do."

"You're dedicated to the department. I respect that. But think on what I said. Jason with the FBI can handle the town hall. You don't need to make things worse for yourself."

"I'm not hiding at home and pretending to be sick."

"It's more than pretending. You were stabbed."

"My mind's made up. Unless you have anything else, I need to get off the phone." She had to make herself look presentable.

"Hold on a second. I'm trying to get a flight back home. So far, looks like Saturday is the best I can do."

Kathryn wasn't sure how she felt about Mooky's return. Was she annoyed that he was cutting his vacation short? Or was she thankful to turn all the responsibilities over to her boss? "I can handle things till you get back."

"I know you can. Take care, and keep me informed."

"Will do," she said before ending the call.

Using the en suite bathroom, Kathryn washed her face and brushed her teeth. She combed all the tangles from her hair and pulled it back into a ponytail. She dressed in a fresh uniform. As she stood in front of the dresser, she checked her reflection. Dark circles ringed her eyes. Her complexion was pale. The shadow of a bruise colored both her cheek and chin, and there was a cut beneath her eye.

Her gaze drifted from her reflection to her hands. All her knuckles were scraped and swollen. For the first time, her wedding band looked out of place. She could feel Ryan's lips on hers. It was crazy to think that anything would ever come from that single kiss.

Still, it was time to leave the past and move into the present. Did she dare look to the future? She pulled the band up her finger. It caught on the knuckle. A zing of pain shot through her hand. She cursed and shook her palm. Well, her wedding band wasn't coming off today.

Without a backward glance, she left her room.

* * *

Encantador High School had been built in the 1970s. The parking lot separated the campus from the frontage road. The two-story structure sat behind a wide lawn. It was the same school Kathryn had attended, where she'd been on both the soccer and track teams at the adjacent sports complex. On a typical Sunday, both the frontage road and parking lot would be empty.

But not today. Cars filled the lot and were lined up on either side of the street. Sunlight winked off windshields, until it looked like a field of diamonds. Media vans had pulled up on the grass. Satellites sat atop the vehicles, like weeds that had grown overnight.

"You can drop me off here," she said, as Ryan pulled into the parking lot. "I can walk."

"What you mean is that with all these people, you don't want to explain why I was your chauffeur." After pulling to the side, he stopped his car.

He was right, but she didn't want to admit as much. Instead, she gave him a weak smile. "Thanks for the ride."

"If you need moral support, I can sneak into the back of the room."

She gave him an exaggerated eye roll. "I doubt you've ever snuck in anywhere."

"You'd be surprised." He paused a beat. "You better get going, unless you want to be late."

The last thing she wanted to be was late to her own town hall. Her fingers grazed the door handle. "You take care of yourself, okay?"

"I'll do my best. And how are you?"

"I'm okay." It was the second time she'd lied that morning.

"I know you'll be fine."

This time, when she reached for the handle, she opened the door. She turned to face Ryan again. She pressed her hand onto his cheek and brushed her lips against his. The kiss was over before it began and still, it stole her breath.

She inhaled and cast a quick glance around the parking lot. What if someone had been watching? It was that moment, Kathryn realized something important. She was entitled to live her own life. The notion left her lightheaded. Or maybe that was from the pain meds.

"I need to get going," she said, her voice a hoarse whisper.

He gave her a wan smile. "I know."

There was nothing else to do or say. Easing out of the seat, she stepped to the pavement. After closing the door, she gave him a small wave. In that moment, she caught her reflection on the side window and stood taller. She didn't know what would happen next, but she was ready.

Chapter 10

A perfect Texas sun, a bright yellow ball, hung in a sky of cornflower blue. Last night's storm had chased away the oppressive heat, but Ryan knew that the break wouldn't last more than a day or two. He'd pulled the tarps off the damp seats and opened both doors of his truck. Soon, the interior would be dry. Until then, he had time to waste.

Leaning against the bumper, he threw a tennis ball across an open field next to the high school. Old Blue gave a happy bark. As the dog chased the ball, he couldn't help but wonder how Kathryn was doing. Certainly, the meeting was standing room only. What's more, he imagined that she was being grilled about last night's murder.

Still, the moment that was top of mind for Ryan was the kiss. Holding Kathryn just felt, well, right. She was the perfect combination of soft and strong. The sound of her sigh might be the sexiest thing he'd ever heard.

Get a grip, Ryan. You've kissed other women before.

In fact, in his life, he'd kissed a lot of other women.

But none of them were Kathryn.

Old Blue dropped the ball at Ryan's feet. He picked up the toy and threw it again. The dog raced across the field. In the distance, he could see the baseball diamond. Sun glinted off the top of the dugout. In high school, he'd been the team's pitcher. He wasn't like a lot of the guys—hoping for a chance to play professional baseball. Still, he was the star of the bunch.

Where would he be today if he'd had a different dream?

Hell, he still didn't know what he wanted to do— or become.

Being a criminal was behind him. But legitimacy was a goal he might never reach.

Old Blue brought back the ball again. As he bent to pick it up, his phone pinged with an incoming text. After throwing the ball, he pulled the device from his pocket. Ryan didn't recognize the number. It didn't matter. As soon as he read the message, he knew who'd sent the text. His mouth went dry.

You're going to want to see this. A link was attached.

Ryan tapped the link with his thumb. Old Blue dropped his ball and whined. For once, he ignored his canine companion. The link led to a video.

Decker held a camera at arm's length. A brick wall was at his back. "I'm not sure if anyone in Encantador noticed or not, but y'all need to check the dates. August 31 was the same day Jack the Ripper killed his first victim. That's important because now you know when my next murder will take place. Since I can't stay in Encantador and Mercy anymore, I've gone somewhere else. I'll give you a clue."

The camera aspect changed to show a street lined with brick storefronts. The aspect changed quickly, but he'd seen enough to notice a restaurant on the corner.

Decker's face once more filled the screen. "But I'm not like Jack. I won't hide in the shadows. In fact, the next murder is going to happen live on the internet." He gave a wide smile. "I know that everyone will want to watch. And as far as Ryan Steele… I'll see you in hell."

The screen went black.

For a moment, Ryan stood there, as if frozen in place.

Then, his pulse started to race. He coaxed Old Blue into the truck and left the windows down to allow for fresh air. Without another thought, he ran toward the front doors of the high school. It didn't matter what was happening in that auditorium. Kathryn needed to see this video—and now.

Kathryn had made a serious mistake. She should never have come to the town hall. There was no way she could appear that weak in front of the whole community.

And yet, a headache pounded in her skull. The pain in her side was hard to ignore. The meds she'd taken earlier now churned in her stomach. She prayed that she wouldn't get sick. She should've eaten more than a slice of toast and two sips of coffee, but it was too late to correct her mistake now.

At the back of the room, news crews were filming the meeting. All the seats were full. People stood along the walls. Everyone stared at her. The expressions on their faces said everything. They were mad. They were scared. They blamed her for the predicament. At the same time, they expected her to apprehend the elusive killer.

She'd given a briefing of last night's events. Nobody was satisfied with her explanation.

Her neighbor Joe stood and spoke into a microphone on a stand. "Decker Newcombe is one man. How is it that everyone up there..." He swept his arm, taking in all the law-enforcement officials on the stage. Beyond Kathryn, there was Jason Jones representing the FBI. There were also two members of the Texas Rangers. Lou and Georgiana covered this part of the state. "Can't seem to find one man? You had him cornered in a house last night. How'd he get away?"

How was she supposed to answer that question?

She was the reason he had escaped. She drew in a long breath and exhaled. Leaning toward the microphone, she tried to find the right words.

The back door opened, and Ryan entered the room. His T-shirt was damp with sweat. His breath was ragged as he jogged down the center aisle. "You gotta see this."

She tensed, and her headache throbbed. "Ryan, what're you doing here?"

"No questions." He approached the foot of the stage and held his phone out. "Just watch."

Jason and the Texas Rangers moved in close enough to see the screen. After reading the message, she looked up from the device. "Who sent you this text?"

"Just click on the link."

She pressed the underlined code. A video began to play.

As she watched, a chill ran down her spine. The sweat on her skin turned clammy. She had about a million questions. The first one was "Any idea where he shot the video?"

Ryan shook his head. "No clue."

Georgiana, one of the Rangers, said, "I think that's London. Show the street again."

Kathryn restarted the video an instant before Decker showed the roadside view. She stopped the recording.

"See that?" Georgiana pointed to the screen. "That building on the corner with the green sign. It's the Ten Bells. It's in London—Whitechapel to be precise."

"How do you know that?" Jason asked.

The Ranger shrugged. "I took my wife there for her fortieth birthday a few years back."

"London?" Jason echoed. "What in the hell is Decker doing in London?"

Ryan cursed. "It makes sense, though. He murdered the woman here on the same day as the first Ripper killing. Looks like he's trying to recreate all the Ripper murders. Since Kathryn and I found him outside of town, he split."

"London, as in England?" she asked, trying to connect all the dots. "How would he even get there?"

"Maybe he has cash we don't know about," Ryan suggested. "Or connections."

"I'm going to need your phone for analysis." Jason held out his hand. Ryan gave him the device. "And you're going to need to stay in town for a bit."

Kathryn didn't know what the FBI would find on Ryan's phone. But she did know that she was beyond relieved that the killer was gone.

And Ryan? Well, where he was concerned, her feelings were far more complicated.

Decker brought the bottle of beer to his lips and took a long drink. He smothered a burp with the back of his hand and looked around his temporary home.

From the outside, the warehouse looked like any dilapidated old building. And honestly, it was. But a twenty-foot square had been cleaned. What's more, walls had been erected, separating Decker's temporary home from the rest of the warehouse.

Seraphim had provided everything he needed. There was electricity. Internet access.

His open laptop sat on a card table. Several boxes filled with video equipment had been left for him as well. Aside from the table, there was a chair, a cot, and a small refrigerator/microwave combo. The fridge was well-stocked with water, beer, and microwavable entrées. In short, he'd be fine hiding here for a few days. In fact, the only reason he'd ever need to leave would be to find his next victim.

The computer pinged with an incoming message. Holding the bottle by the neck, he walked to the table and checked the screen. Seraphim had sent him a link to their dark-web chatroom. After dropping into the seat, he typed in the preset combination of letters and numbers. Then, he hit Enter.

The hacker, complete with the plague-doctor mask, appeared on the screen. "You made it to the warehouse."

"I did. This place is nice." It was the closest he'd come to giving a compliment in a long time. "What's on the other side of the wall?"

"Junk," said Seraphim. "You can check it out if you want."

True, he could. A door led to the rest of the warehouse. "I might."

Changing the subject, they continued. "Any video you want to post, you can send to me. Just call to let me know that you have something to upload."

Calling Seraphim would be a problem. "Before leaving, I stashed the phone someplace safe."

As if slapped, the hacker reeled. "You left your phone? Why would you do something stupid like that?"

Stupid. The word pecked on his nerves. For now, he'd ignore the insult. "I have two ways to contact you—this computer and the phone. If both are together and they get lost, I can't reach out."

"But I can find you. I've done it before. I can do it again."

He shook his head. "Not good enough."

"I hope you uploaded the video to the computer first. If not, you'll have to go back and get the phone."

"That's not happening. I left the phone in Mexico before coming here." He found the file with the video and sent it to the hacker. He didn't mention that he'd already sent it to Ryan. There was nothing Ryan could do to stop him anyway. "Now what?"

"Once the video's been shared, I'll create a link to your next..." the hacker searched for the right word "...performance."

Performance. He smiled. "Makes me sound like an artist."

"Oh, but you are an artist. Your medium is death. And the world is your canvas."

Sure, the hacker could be a pain. But the thing was, Seraphim saw into his soul. The hacker understood all the dark needs that controlled his actions. It was why he wanted to be remembered for centuries—just like Jack the Ripper. The first Ripper killing took place on August 31, the same day he'd killed Tessa Wray. Now, he had to find another victim and be ready to livestream the murder by September 8. Already he had an idea for who would be next. "I'll be in touch."

"Before you go, I need to ask you about Anastasia Pierce."

Anastasia "Ana" Pierce. Now there was a name he'd like to forget, and yet, he never had. Picking up his bottle of beer, he took another swallow. "She's none of your concern."

"She's the other person who betrayed you."

Decker stared at the black eyes in the plague mask and said nothing.

"I'm right," squawked Seraphim. "I can tell."

Sweat dampened his back. He took another swig of beer. The alcohol hit his gut like a bomb. "Why do you care who betrayed me?"

"I want to know what makes you tick."

"Makes me *tick*?" he scoffed. "I have to go." He ended the video call before the hacker said anything else.

He drained the last of his beer. He didn't like Seraphim nosing around in his past, especially into something as personal as his relationship with Ana. Damn. He hadn't thought about her in years. Yet, the pain in his chest was the same as it had been on the day he came home to find that she was gone.

Rising from the seat, he pulled another bottle of beer

from the fridge. After twisting off the cap, he took a long swallow. There wasn't enough booze to numb his hurt or blunt his memories. Seraphim had opened a wound that Decker thought was healed.

Ana Pierce. He wondered where she'd ended up— and why she had left him in the first place.

Ryan drove on a road he knew well. It was the route that connected Encantador with the smaller town of Mercy. Kathryn's police cruiser still hadn't been returned to her, so she rode shotgun. Sure, she could've gotten a ride in any of the three vehicles that made up the convoy, but after the town hall broke up, she'd come with Ryan. No questions. No conversation. Honestly, he liked having her with him. And maybe that was a problem. He needed to remind himself that he was little more than a chauffeur for the undersheriff. Once his phone had been analyzed, he'd be told to leave town. This time, he'd have no choice but to go.

Old Blue sat in the passenger seat as well. The dog leaned in to Kathryn as she scratched his side. Tongue lolling, the dog absolutely seemed to be smiling.

Lucky dog.

Ahead, he could see a blinking light hanging across the road.

Finally, he was home. Unbidden, the thought came to him.

The blinker of the first car flashed for a moment before it turned into a parking lot. Ryan followed. For over a year, he'd run a bar, a tattoo parlor, and a motel that occupied the newly renovated space. Sure, the businesses had been a front for an undercover sting operation. But the work he'd put into managing the property and the people had been real.

He'd actually made it as a legitimate businessman. He took care of the people who worked for him. The businesses turned a profit. The clientele was rough, but he'd made friends. Too bad it had been a ruse. The neon signs were gone. The building was now cream with blue trim. There was blue lettering on the door.

Center for Rural Law Enforcement.

By appointment only.

The Center was the best—and closest—place for Ryan's phone to be analyzed.

He noted that the parking lot was freshly paved. The once pitted asphalt was now smooth as ice. Muscle memory took over. He parked, as he had for a year, next to the front door. Yet it was all different. His throat was raw. "It's hard to remember what this place used to look like."

"Is it difficult to be back?"

How had she guessed? Putting the gearshift into Park, he said, "Let's get this over with so me and Old Blue can get on the road."

Michael came out of the front door. He shaded his eyes with a hand. Ryan turned off the ignition and hopped to the ground. The other two vehicles parked as well. One was a sedan, driven by the two Texas Rangers. Isaac drove his SUV and Jason was with the Texas Law operative.

"I can't believe all the changes," he said.

Kathryn and the dog exited from the passenger side of the truck. "Having this facility in the area has really helped the local economy," she said. "Aside from having seven well-paid techs on the payroll, law-enforcement officers come in from all over the state." She nodded toward the gas station across the street. "Stu hired a cook. They now serve breakfast and lunch. Only two different options are on the menu, but the food's pretty good."

Michael picked up where Kathryn left off. "Right now, we only use what was once the bar and tattoo parlor. I'm hoping to partner with more law-enforcement agencies to have offices in the old motel. Kathryn will have a space there soon." He opened the door. "C'mon in. Let me show you around."

"Is it okay if the dog comes in?"

"Sure, but we'll leave him in the forensics lab."

Ryan snapped his fingers, and Old Blue loped across the threshold. Kathryn followed. Next came Jason and Isaac. Lou and Georgiana were the last in line.

What used to be a dark room with a mahogany bar, dance floor, and pool tables was now filled with light. Long lights hung from the ceiling and reflected off the white floors and walls. The lab was filled with tables, microscopes, and a variety of equipment that Ryan couldn't name.

The bar was gone. In its place was a wall of glass, with a pressurized door. On the other side of the wall, in what used to be the tattoo parlor, was a computer lab. It had its own server and three wall-mounted monitors.

The change was remarkable. He hated it. What had happened to his old dive bar? "I like what you've done with the place," he said wryly.

"Let's go into the computer lab," said Michael. "One of the cybersecurity techs has been looking at the video. He's found some things that you'll want to see."

Old Blue settled into a corner, and Ryan knew he'd be fine for a bit. "Lead the way," he said.

A young man with bright red hair and a beard sat in front of a keyboard. "This is Hal," said Michael. "He's my resident computer genius. Since the video of Decker surfaced, he's been looking for evidence that it's real. Hal, you want to show them what you've found?"

"Sure," he said, typing on the keyboard. "The timeline from when Decker attacked the undersheriff to when he shows up in London is tight. But it's not an impossible feat—assuming he got to the Dallas–Fort Worth Airport in time to catch a red-eye to Heathrow. I didn't think he'd travel under his real name, so I didn't worry about looking through the passenger manifest, but I was able to access security video from the DFW Airport. Using facial recognition, I found this." He hit a key, and an image appeared on the middle screen. It was of a solitary man walking through the terminal.

"No question about it," said Ryan. "That's Decker."

"We know he was at the airport," said Jason. "That tells us some things, but not enough."

Hal typed again. "Because of international laws, I can't access the British airport's security cameras. But I was able to pick this up in London." The first screen filled with a social-media post. The caption read *Made it to London!* Two smiling young women posed for a selfie. Yet, he was there, in the background of the picture. "I checked. The two students in the picture were on the flight from Dallas. I'd say that's proof positive. Decker's in merry old England."

"If he left the country," Jason asked, "what does that mean?"

Ryan knew the case was complex. There was still evidence to be collected and witnesses to interview. But if the killer was on a different continent, it meant one thing for certain. Decker was no longer an immediate threat. He might not have stopped the killer, but at least he'd chased him out of town.

Chapter 11

Ryan was supposed to stay in town while his phone was being analyzed. Jason had called it a request, but it was really an order by the FBI. Thankfully, the motel in Encantador had a vacant room. Isaac, from Texas Law, made the arrangements. By 4:15 p.m., he and Old Blue had their key. In the room, the curtains were drawn, and the air conditioner was running. Cool and dark, crossing the threshold was like stepping into a cave.

The motel had a Western theme. It started with the name: the Saddle-Up Inn. There was also a whiskey-barrel fountain near the door to the office. The theme stayed consistent with Western-themed prints on the wall and a sign that hung on the bathroom door, which read *Outhouse*.

Once in the room, he kicked off his shoes. He lay down on the bed and stretched out. Old Blue got onto the bed near his feet and curled into a tight ball. Ryan couldn't remember the last time he'd been so tired. Reaching for the remote control, he turned on the TV and flipped through a few channels. His eyes grew heavy, and he teetered on the edge of oblivion.

A knocking pulled him back to consciousness.

At the foot of the bed, Old Blue lifted his ears.

Ryan stood. Every part of him ached. Walking slowly, he peered through the peephole. Kathryn stood outside. She no longer wore her uniform. Instead, she was dressed in a pair of black yoga pants and gray tank top. The tank top hugged her curves in an alluring way.

True, she looked good—great, really. But why had she come at all?

After unfastening the lock, he pulled the door open. "Hi. I wasn't expecting to see you. How's your side?"

She touched the wound. Beneath the fabric of her shirt, he could see the outline of a large bandage. "It's actually not too bad, which is why I stopped by." She shifted from one foot to the other. "I never thanked you for saving my life."

"Actually, you did." He could still feel the caress of her fingers on his cheek. "And you're welcome."

"Just saying *thank you* doesn't seem like enough. I'd like to invite you over for dinner. It'd give me a chance to fire up the grill and make a few steaks."

Old Blue's tail thumped on the bed.

"Sounds like he'd like to join us," she said, pointing to the dog. "What about it? You want to stop by around six?"

"Blue and I have a policy. We always accept invitations for a steak dinner."

She laughed. "I'll look forward to seeing you both."

He recalled how her daughter had reacted to Old Blue. He didn't want to cause any more problems in the family. "I might leave him here, but I'll accept your invitation."

"How's your room?" she asked. "Got everything you need?"

"The room's great. I even have one of those fancy indoor outhouses," he said, making a joke about the sign on the bathroom door.

She laughed.

He understood that she was just making conversation. The thing was, he was also keenly aware of the bed just a few feet away. Erotic images—his mouth on hers, his hands on her breasts, his hips between her thighs—came to him without warning. His pulse thundered in his ears. Turns out, he wasn't as exhausted as he'd imagined.

"I better get going," said Kathryn. It was like she'd read his mind. Had his expression given away his carnal thoughts? "I was on the way to the grocery store to pick up all the fixin's for tonight."

He rested his hand on the doorknob. "Thanks for the invite."

After closing the door, he walked back to the bed. Just like before, he stretched out on the comforter. But now, it was all different. He couldn't get the images of him and Kathryn, naked and tangled in the sheets, out of his mind.

And what was up with her invitation?

Was she just being friendly? Or was there something else?

Kathryn was undeniably attractive. She was smart. Dedicated to her job, and a good mom. He knew that long-term she'd never want a guy like him. Yet, there was a physical connection between them that was impossible to ignore.

Maybe she wanted to use Ryan for sex.

Honestly, he'd been tempted into bed by lesser women for worse reasons.

Still, the thought of a single night with Kathryn and nothing more left a bad taste in his mouth.

Sitting up, he scrubbed his face. He wasn't sure what he needed next, but he sure as hell wasn't going to find it by lying in bed. Wandering to the bathroom, he turned on the shower to cold. After stripping down, he stepped under the spray. The water revived him, and hopefully, it would wash away his thoughts about Kathryn. But it was going to take more than a cold shower to do that.

Between her children's busy schedules and all her responsibilities at work, Kathryn rarely invited company over for dinner. The clock on the microwave glowed with the time: 5:42. Since the town hall, she'd taken another nap and her second round of pain meds. True, she wasn't feeling perfect, but she was happy to have Ryan coming to dinner.

Standing in the kitchen, she chopped romaine lettuce for the Caesar salad.

"Hey, Mom." Her son, Brock, wandered into the kitchen. Brock had inherited his father's height. At fifteen years old, he was already over six feet tall. He had Kathryn's brown hair and blue eyes but her late husband's features. "What's up with all the food?" Aside from the salad she was preparing, there was corn ready to be roasted on the grill, potato salad, and steaks in marinade. "Are we having a party or something? What's the occasion?"

"It's not a party," she said. "Just one guest. And I suppose that we're celebrating Decker Newcombe finally leaving us alone."

"Plus the fact that he didn't kill you." The account of Decker's escape to England was a top news story. Details of her fight were mentioned, but most of the attention was focused on the promised live murder.

"You're right, he didn't kill me." She scraped the chopped lettuce into a bowl. "So we should probably celebrate that, too."

"I'm glad that you're okay. Can I help with anything?"

His offer surprised and pleased her. "Sure. You want to make some lemonade?"

"Who's our guest? Is Aunt Quinn in town?"

Quinn was her late husband's sister. She called Encantador home but worked all over the country with the Department of the Interior. "I think she's still in DC but should be back next week."

Brock pulled a pitcher out of a cabinet. From another, he found a container of powdered drink mix. "Why're you being so secretive about a dinner guest?" Brock put the pitcher in the sink and started filling it with water. "I'm going to find out who it is once they show up, anyway."

He had a point. "It's the man who helped me last night. Honestly, I'm not sure how things would've turned out if he hadn't been with me."

"You mean that gangster guy is coming over for dinner? What's his name? Something Steele, because his bar was called House of Steele."

"His name is Ryan, and he's not a gangster." Because of the pain meds, the stab wound was more of a dull ache she could ignore. She opened the refrigerator door and took out a bottle of salad dressing. As she pushed the door shut, a zing of pain caught her side. She breathed deeply and the discomfort passed. She said, "How do you know about the bar?"

"I'm not an infant. I can understand when people talk. There were a couple of guys on the football team last year who drove all the way out to Mercy to go to the club. They figured since Ryan was a criminal, he wouldn't care that they were underage."

Maybe she'd underestimated Ryan. "What'd he do?"

"Don't worry, Undersheriff." Brock winked at her to show he was teasing by using her official title. "He threw them out. Said he wouldn't serve booze to kids."

"That's a relief." She paused a beat. "Besides, he's not a criminal. His record was cleared."

"But he did a lot of bad stuff in the past." Brock measured out scoops of lemonade mix and dumped them into the water.

"He did," she agreed. "But he had an arrangement with the government. They forgave all his crimes since he helped them out. He put himself in jeopardy to try to stop Decker. That counts for something."

Silently, Brock stirred the lemonade with a long-handled wooden spoon. After a moment, he said, "To be honest, I'm kinda surprised that you're defending him."

In fact, she was kind of surprised that she was defending him as well. "You've done bad things in your life. What if you wanted to make amends but nobody would give you the chance? See my point?"

"I guess," he grumbled. "I just don't see why he's coming over for dinner."

"Because Mom kissed him." Morgan stood at the back of the kitchen. Her arms were folded across her chest.

"I didn't hear you come in," said Kathryn.

Morgan glared. "Obviously."

Brock had gone pale. "You kissed him?"

Great. Now what was she supposed to say? "It's not like that."

"Yes, it is," Morgan interrupted. "Gawd, they were full on swapping spit. It was so gross that I'll never be able to unsee it."

"You kissed him?" Brock repeated.

Anger flared in her chest. Kathryn could feel a flush climbing from her neck to her face. "Both of you, listen to me. I am an adult and your mother. If I want to kiss someone—which I almost never do—I can. I don't need your editorial, Morgan. Or your permission, Brock."

"But what about Dad?" Brock's face turned from pale to bright red. "I never thought you'd want to re-place him."

"Oh, honey. I loved your dad. I still love him. But he's gone, and well, I'd like to start living my life again." True, she was ready to move forward, just not neces-sarily with Ryan.

She waited for Brock to say something. He didn't.

She reached for his shoulder. He shrugged off her touch.

This was not what she'd planned for the evening. She

should call Ryan and reschedule. Or better yet, the dinner could be canceled altogether.

From the street came the sound of a car door slamming. Ryan had arrived. It was too late to cancel now.

"I have a guest at the house for dinner. Neither of you need to eat with us—but you do have to be polite. Do you understand?"

"Understood," said Morgan. "I'll be in my room."

She left without another word. Kathryn knew that this time next year, her daughter would be in college, and she'd miss her terribly. It made the harsh words sting more than ever.

"What about you, Brock?"

"I'm eating the steak," he said, his tone glum. "I'm starving."

The doorbell chimed. Kathryn wiped her hands on a towel and went to answer it, but Brock blocked her path.

"Hold up, Mom. I'll answer the door. I want to speak to this guy first."

Kathryn was touched that her son wanted to also be her protector—even though she was the undersheriff. "Okay kiddo. I'll finish putting together the salad."

While adding croutons and cheese to the salad, she listened intently to the door being answered.

"Hey," said Brock. "C'mon in. My mom's in the kitchen."

"I forgot to ask if I could bring anything, so I picked up a pie." The sound of Ryan's voice brought a smile to her lips.

"What kind of pie?"

"Apple," said Ryan.

"Nice. Come with me."

Brock's tone was still gloomy, but at least Ryan had passed the first test. Then again, her son liked anyone with food. She poured dressing on the salad and tossed it with tongs.

"Mom, Ryan's here," said Brock, as if she hadn't been eavesdropping the whole time. "He brought pie."

Looking up, she smiled. Yet, she hadn't prepared herself for how nice Ryan looked. He was freshly showered. His hair was still damp and curled at the ends. He wore jeans along with a white button-up shirt. He'd left the shirt untucked, and the top three buttons were undone. A sliver of skin was exposed at his neck. Her throat went dry, and her heart raced. Her side throbbed, but she didn't mind the discomfort. It reminded her that she was alive. "Thanks for coming—and bringing pie. I have ice cream for dessert, so they'll be perfect together." She bumped Brock with her shoulder. "Right?"

He shrugged. "Sure."

"You set the table outside, and I'll get the steaks on the grill," she said to her son. He slunk out the back door with a stack of plates and a handful of silverware. Then to Ryan she said, "You want anything to drink? Beer? Wine? Water? Lemonade?"

"I'll take a lemonade."

Four glasses, already filled with ice, sat on the counter. She poured lemonade into one of them and handed it to Ryan. Then, she picked up the casserole dish with steaks and marinade in one hand and the plate of corn in the other. "You can come with me, if you want."

"Sure thing, but let me take those for you." He reached for the dishes. "You had a rough night and should rest as much as possible."

She wanted to argue—it was instinct alone. Over the years, she'd learned not to ask for favors because of her gender. But Ryan's offer was too nice to ignore. She let him take the dishes. "Thanks."

Brock held the back door open as she approached. "Thanks, honey."

He nodded as she passed. Once she and Ryan were outside, her son went back in. The sun was setting. The awning provided them with shade. Ryan set the corn and steaks on a side table. "Where's Old Blue?" she asked, while igniting the grill.

"I left him in the motel with food, water, and a nature channel on TV. He'll be okay for a while." He took a sip of lemonade. "How're you feeling?"

"Considering everything, it all worked out." She placed the steaks on the grill. They started to sizzle, and the scent of cooking meat filled the air. "Since Decker's out of the country, he's not really my problem anymore, although I won't be happy until he's been caught. I decided to follow the doctor's orders and took next week off from work." It was the closest thing she'd had to a vacation in years.

"I'm surprised you're taking time off at all."

She put corn on the upper rack of the grill and closed the lid. The local law-enforcement community worked well together. Other officials were able to cover the tasks that Kathryn would have taken on personally. But there was more. Even with Decker out of the country, patrols would be increased. Yet, she knew that everyone in town would be more vigilant. "My job's important, sure, but so is my family. I wanted to spend some time at home with my kids. Surviving a serial killer's attack gives you some perspective, you know?"

"Actually, I do."

He was right. He'd survived a run-in with Decker, too. Did that make them kindred spirits? "Have a seat. I'll grab the salads and be right back." Her limbs were heavy. Maybe having Ryan come over for dinner wasn't the best idea. All the same, she wasn't going to send him away.

"You sit. I'll get the salads." She opened her mouth, ready to argue. He held up his hand. "You were nice enough to invite me over and like I said, you've been through a lot in the past 24 hours. At least let me help you out."

"How 'bout we bring everything out together?"

"You bet." He held the door open as Kathryn slipped inside.

"You get those," she said, pointing to the salads on the counter, and he picked up both bowls. "I'll get the lemonade." In the living room, Brock sat on the sofa. She looked at him through the doorway. "Can you grab two glasses and come outside?" she asked. "Dinner's almost ready."

Brock looked up from the couch. "I'm not really hungry anymore."

Was he still upset about Ryan being over?

"Not hungry?" she teased. "I thought you were starved a few minutes ago."

"I was, but I got a text from my coach."

"That doesn't sound good." She paused. Ryan was still standing in the middle of her kitchen with potato salad in one hand and the Caesar in the other. "Grab the glasses from the counter and join us. You can tell me all about the text while you eat. Trust me, you'll feel better with food."

With a sigh, her son rose from the sofa and slumped into the kitchen.

They all returned to the patio. Brock had set the table. Without being asked, he walked over to the grill and flipped the steaks. "Not much longer now," he said, his tone still disconsolate

"I can take care of the food, you know," she teased.

"You sit." He pointed with a set of meat tongs. "And rest."

"I agree with your son," said Ryan. "You have to be tired. Sore."

"You're right." Her side had started to ache and it wasn't time for her next dose of pain meds. Dropping into a chair, she sighed, "Thanks."

Brock grunted and poked at the steaks.

She glanced at her son. "Why don't you tell me about that text you got?"

Brock raised one shoulder before letting it drop. "Coach said he likes me playing tight end. He said I did really good."

"That's great, honey." At the game last week, her son had excelled in the position.

"It's not great if I want to play quarterback again."

Until this year, her son had always been the team's quarterback. It was not just his athletic abilities but his leadership talents as well. As a freshman, his junior varsity team had been undefeated. She knew when he got put on the varsity team, he'd hoped for the QB spot. It broke her heart that he wouldn't be able to play the position he loved. Then again, life didn't always give people what they wanted, and sometimes, important lessons could be found in adversity. She'd save the pep talk for later. Still, she said, "Every player on the field is important."

"Yeah, but I love being QB." He sighed. "Coach says my throw needs work."

She said, "You can work on your throw."

He gave her a side-eye. "Not like it'll help. The guy he has playing is also the pitcher for his church's baseball team. Because of that, he's got terrific aim."

"I wish I could help you, bud. But I played soccer, not softball." She glanced at Ryan. Using his thumb, he wiped condensation from the side of his glass. "Sorry for all this talk about football. Let's find something we can all talk about. You and I can chat about your throw later. Okay, Brock?"

He shrugged. "Whatever."

Ryan shifted in his seat. "I was the pitcher for my high school's baseball team. It's been a while, but I still remember some of my old tricks for accuracy. If you have a spare ball, I'd be happy to show you."

Brock eyes were bright with excitement. "You'd do that?"

"Sure."

Her son closed the lid to the grill. "Hold on a minute. I'll be right back." Brock went inside the house.

Kathryn glanced at Ryan. "Thanks for helping out my son."

"Don't thank me yet. Honestly, I haven't thrown in years." He stood and rolled his shoulders around several times.

Brock came through the back door. "Here you go," he said, tossing a ball to Ryan. "What do I do first?"

"The first thing—let's warm up." Ryan and her son walked to a spot in the middle of the yard. As they stretched, Kathryn returned to the grill. The steaks were done. The corn was perfect. Using a set of tongs, she set the food on a clean platter.

Still, she watched Ryan and Brock. They were too far away for her to hear their voices, but Ryan was explaining something. Brock nodded and then smiled.

Funny, she'd been worried that the dinner was going to be a disaster.

Tonight was turning out better than she ever could have imagined.

Chapter 12

The sun had set an hour earlier. Kathryn stood in her kitchen and marveled at the clean counters. Brock and Ryan had worked together. The dinner dishes were loaded into the dishwasher, and the leftovers had been placed in the fridge.

After the cleaning was done, Brock went to study in his room. Morgan had yet to emerge. She should really check on her daughter but knew enough to wait until after Ryan left.

"Well, I better get going," Ryan said. "Old Blue's gonna start missing me."

"Speaking of your dog." She held up a plastic container filled with scraps from the steaks. "Does he eat table food?"

"I've had to pull him away from roadkill more than once. That dog'll eat practically anything." He took the offered container. "He'll appreciate you thinking of him. I do, too."

"It's the least I can do since you spent so much time with Brock. Even after one lesson with you, his aim is better."

Leaning against the counter, he stood right beside her. She could reach out and touch him if she wanted. Her side twinged, reminding her of everything she'd been through. "Your son's a good kid," he said. "I was happy to help."

Kathryn didn't hold much stock in gender roles. After all, she did quite well in a field traditionally dominated by men—thank you very much. But she knew that Brock missed having a man around the house. Morgan probably did, too. Though she doubted that her daughter would admit as much.

While looping a dish towel through the handle of the fridge, she said. "I know he enjoyed your company. I did, too. I'm glad I invited you over."

Damn. Why'd she have to be so honest?

"I haven't had such a nice evening for a long while." He gave her that smile and shook his head. "Hell, I can't remember a better night."

"Your life must be pretty boring," she said, kidding.

"Actually, my life's been the opposite of boring. It's the chaos that's worn me down. I don't necessarily want things to be monotonous. But I'd take stable any day."

She looked over her shoulder and regarded Ryan. For the first time, she saw him as a man who lived behind a brick wall. Sure, he'd constructed the wall to hide a lot of his misdeeds. Now, he was more of a prisoner. At the same time, he'd been honest about wanting a place to call home. Was the wall starting to crumble?

She wiped her hands on the towel one last time. "Let me walk you out."

Without comment, they moved through the kitchen and to the front door. Since both kids were in their rooms, nobody had bothered to turn on the lights. The foyer was shrouded in shadows, but she knew the way. Stopping at the door, she rested her hand on the handle. "You got Old Blue's snacks?"

Ryan lifted the container. "Right here."

"Do you have any idea how long it's going to be before you get your phone back?"

"I don't have a clue. It could be as early as tomorrow."

"Looks like this really is goodbye."

"Guess so," he whispered.

The room was quiet and dark. It was like they were the only two people around for miles. For a moment, neither one spoke. Ryan took a step toward her. And then another. She could feel his breath wash over her shoulder.

A bomb of nervous energy exploded in her stomach. Good Lord, Kathryn was a grown woman, not a teenager. Who was she to get anxious over standing next to a man? But he wasn't just any man. It was Ryan who stood next to her. What's more, she wanted him to kiss her. The question was—what did *he* want?

She shifted toward him and reached out in the dark. Her fingertips brushed the back of his hand. He set the container of leftovers on a nearby table. Then, he laced his fingers through hers.

"Kathryn." His voice was a husky whisper. It pierced her heart and her pulse started to race.

"Yes?"

"The last time I kissed you, things didn't go well."

That was an understatement. "They didn't."

"The thing is," he said and pulled her closer, "I'd like to kiss you again."

Her breasts were pressed against his chest. Even in the dark, she could see his pulse thrumming at the base of his neck. "I'd like to kiss you again, too."

He smiled, and her toes began to tingle. "That's all the invitation I need," he said.

He pressed his mouth to hers. She closed her eyes and surrendered to the sensations. In that moment, Kathryn was no longer the undersheriff but only a woman. The kiss with Ryan became her world. Parting her lips, she sighed. He slipped his tongue into her mouth. She was ready to be explored and conquered.

Kathryn reached for his shoulders and pulled him to her. She wound her arms around his neck. And still, he wasn't close enough. He rested his hands on her hips. Using the tips of his fingers, he traced the waistband of her shorts. Her stomach tightened with anticipation. A zing of pain radiated from her side. Breathless, she broke away from the embrace.

"What's wrong?" Even in the dark, she could hear the concern in Ryan's voice. "Oh hell. I tried to be careful. Did I touch your wound?"

He hadn't. His hand was well away from the bandage on her side. "Must be time for my meds." Where she stood, she could see the clock on the microwave. Actually, she should've taken them thirty minutes earlier.

"Let me get you the pills and some water," he offered.

"No." The single word came out with more force than she intended. Kathryn drew in a shaking breath. She could still feel his lips on hers, but her side throbbed with each beat of her heart. She exhaled and tried again. "No, thank you. I'm just going to take my prescription and call it a night."

He lifted the container of leftovers from the table. Then, he opened the door. "You're a hell of a woman, Kathryn Glass." He pressed his lips to her cheek. "Take care."

From the front porch, she watched as he walked to his truck. He opened the driver's door and slipped behind the wheel. He looked at her and waved. After starting the engine, he turned in the middle of the quiet street and drove away.

She closed the door and engaged the lock. Decker might be on the other side of the world, but until he was in custody, she wouldn't feel safe.

Leaning against the door, she pressed her fingertips to her lips, as if her touch could trap the kiss. It really was silly to be so smitten with a man she barely knew. But being around Ryan reminded her of something she'd forgotten. Kathryn was more than a mom and a cop. She was also a woman who had needs of her own.

Her steps were slow as she walked down the hallway to her bedroom. Had it just been just twenty-four hours since she noticed Ryan in her backyard?

It seemed like it all happened weeks ago.

Her meds were stowed in the en suite bathroom. Kathryn took the pills as directed and washed them down with a glass of water. She changed into a large T-shirt for sleeping and returned to her bedroom.

A figure stood at the door.

She started. "Morgan, you scared me. Everything okay?"

"Can I come in?"

"Of course." She pulled back the blankets and slid onto the mattress. "So long as you don't mind me lying down. It's been a long day."

Morgan moved to the bed and lifted the covers. "I'll tuck you in."

Of course she could arrange her own blankets, but the act was kind. She dutifully lay back on the pillow. Morgan took a minute to gather the comforter around her mother. "Just like you did for me and Brock when we were little."

She assumed that Morgan coming in was a bit of a peace offering. "You can lie down with me for a minute—just like I used to do when you were little."

Morgan said, "So long as you don't ask me to read the same picture book over and over."

"Promise." Kathryn placed her hand over her heart.

Then, her daughter stretched out atop the covers. She rested her head on the pillow. "I'm glad you're okay. It really was scary to think that I might lose you, too." Tears swam in her eyes, and she bit her bottom lip. Blinking hard, Morgan continued. "Besides Brock, you're all I have."

"I'm here, honey, and I'm okay."

"You might not always be here. I mean, your job is dangerous."

"Safety is always my top priority. That, and coming

home to you and your brother." She inhaled. Exhaled. "Do you want me to quit my job?"

Morgan shook her head. "You wouldn't be happy."

Her daughter was right. Being undersheriff wasn't just something Kathryn did. It was part of her being. Still, she said nothing.

"I want you to be happy, Mom."

"You're with me. How could I be anything but content?"

Morgan giggled. For an instant, she was a little girl again. "You're slurring your words. I think the pain meds are making you giddy."

"Well," she said and sighed, "they don't hurt."

"You like him, don't you?" Morgan asked.

Kathryn didn't need to ask who her daughter meant by *him*. "Ryan? He's nice."

"Now I know it's the meds." Morgan flopped to her back. "He's not nice. He's too unfriendly to be nice."

"Maybe he's a little serious, but he's been through a lot. It'd make anyone somber. Or maybe it's cautious." Good Lord, Morgan was right. The meds were making her loopy.

"Did you mean what you said to Brock?"

Kathryn pried her eyes open. The thing was, she didn't recall letting her eyelids close to begin with. "It depends. What'd I say?"

"Something about loving Dad but wanting your own future and your own life?"

"Of course I loved you father. I still do."

"No. The other part," said Morgan. Her daughter watched her from the other pillow. She felt the bed undulate, as if she were being carried away on a wave to the edge of oblivion. "Are you ready to start a new chapter in your life?"

Her eyes were so heavy, yet she refused to let them close. "Yes. Maybe. Not tonight, that's for sure."

"I think that's where you're wrong," said Morgan. "I think you did start a new chapter tonight. You've kissed that Ryan guy twice."

Now Kathryn was fully awake. "Twice? I only kissed him once."

"Liar."

She was lying, but she wasn't going to admit anything to Morgan. Unless… "Were you spying on me from the hall?"

"No, Mom." She rolled her eyes. "I have ears. I can hear. You two were talking. Then whispering. Then nothing. Obviously, I can figure out how you were filling the silence."

"Okay, I think we're done."

"Mom, I do want you to be happy. I do know that you like Ryan. Brock likes him—especially since he helped with his throw." She paused. "Maybe he is nice."

"It really doesn't matter." Her eyes burned. She tried to tell herself that it was all fatigue, but she knew that was a lie. Ryan was the first man to spark her interest in years. "He's only in town for another day. Two at the most."

"Then, I'm sorry for you."

"You don't have to worry about me. It's my job to worry about you." She looked at her bedside clock: 9:15 p.m. "You need to finish your homework. You have school in the morning."

"I got all my homework done earlier. If you don't mind, I'll stay here with you until you fall asleep."

"Just like I did when you were little?" She let her eyelids close.

Morgan softly kissed her forehead. "G'night, Mom."

As she fell down, down, down into deep sleep, she had one final thought. Tonight had been something special. Too bad it couldn't last. Out there—somewhere—was Decker Newcombe.

Ryan woke with a start. As his eyes opened, he wasn't sure what was real and what had been a dream Old Blue stood at the end of his bed. Ears up, the dog gave a low growl.

The feds believed that Decker was in England. But what if he was back?

Someone knocked on the door. Then again, Decker wouldn't knock on the door. Besides, it must've been the knocking that had woken him up. "Just a minute," he called out.

He rose from the bed. His legs were heavy. His knees popped, and his shoulder was stiff. He'd thrown the ball with Brock for less than an hour and that was Sunday night. It was Tuesday morning, and he felt like he'd been hit by a truck.

As was his habit, Ryan slept only in his boxer shorts. Yesterday's jeans were draped across a chair. By one of the chair legs sat the container Kathryn had used for the leftover steak. Ryan had used the plastic dish as a food bowl for Old Blue. The dog had licked the container clean.

After stepping into his jeans, Ryan looked through

the peephole. Isaac stood on the sidewalk. He raised his hand, ready to knock again.

Unlatching the locks, he pulled the door open. "You're here early," he said by way of a greeting. "And eager to see me. What's up?"

Isaac pulled a phone from his back pocket. He held up the device. "They're done looking through your cell. I wanted to give it back to you on my way back to San Antonio."

Taking his device, he tapped it against his palm. "And? Did they find anything?"

Isaac said, "As suspected, the text from Decker originated from a cell tower in London. The area's being searched now. So far, nothing's been found."

"Decker's just like a rat. If there's a hole he can sneak out of, he'll find it." He paused. "At least he's not your problem anymore."

"I hate that he got away," Isaac said with an exhale. "The FBI's catching hell that a serial killer hopped on a plane from Dallas to Heathrow."

"Maybe Decker will stick out in England," he said, thinking out loud. "After all, he's an American and not able to blend as easily as he does here."

"Well, I hope you're right."

Old Blue jumped off the bed. He nosed the empty container. The dog needed breakfast first and a walk second. Still, he could wait a minute for both. "What's next for you and the investigation?"

"Last I heard, Jason is heading to London to assist with the investigation. And I'm going back to San Antonio. It's nice of Michael to let me use the Center, but I need my own space to work." He sighed. "What about you?"

"Me and Old Blue are gonna hit the road."

"Where're you headed?"

"To be honest, I don't know. But once I find it, I'll let you know."

Isaac shifted from one foot to the other. "Jason left me with directions for you. If Decker reaches out again."

"I'll let you know that, as well," he said, finishing the anticipated directive.

Isaac extended his palm. "Good to see you again."

Ryan shook the other man's hand. "Good to have been seen," he said, recycling his old joke.

Isaac waved once before walking away.

"Looks like it's just me and you," Ryan said, after closing the door. "How'd you like some food?"

The dog raised his ears and licked his chops.

The bag of kibble he'd purchased the day before sat on a small dresser. He filled up Old Blue's dish. While the dog ate, Ryan donned a clean T-shirt, socks, and shoes. By the time his canine companion had finished his breakfast, he was ready to take the dog for a walk.

The motel was close to Encantador's downtown area. They walked several blocks to the only restaurant that was open. Over Easy served breakfast and lunch. On this Tuesday morning, the crowd was thin. A bicycle rack was pushed up against the wall of the restaurant, and a metal bowl of water had been placed nearby. Ryan wrapped Old Blue's lead around a rung. "I'll be back in a minute." He scratched the top of the dog's head as he passed.

Mae, the owner of Over Easy, stood behind the counter.

She smiled as he entered the restaurant. "Well, look what the cat dragged in. Ryan Steele. I heard you were back in town. What brings you here?"

He liked the warm welcome. "This morning, I'll take a cup of coffee, along with a bacon egg and cheese sandwich. All of it to go."

"Lots of excitement around here," said Mae. "We're famous on the news again."

He wasn't going to comment on the investigation. "So I heard."

"You know anything about it?"

"You know I'm not going to say anything, even if I did."

"Well, I've heard some rumors." She poured coffee into a cup and handed it to Ryan.

Of course, Mae wanted the latest gossip. She served up town news with the same exuberance as her pancakes. Sipping his coffee, he said nothing.

She slipped a piece of paper with his order into the kitchen through a pass-through. "Your sandwich will be ready in a minute."

"Thanks, Mae."

"How long are you planning on staying in town?" she asked.

"Not long. In fact, I'm leaving right after breakfast."

After a few minutes, one of the cooks passed a white paper bag back through the window.

"Looks like your order is ready." Mae retrieved the bag and set it in front of Ryan.

Reaching for his wallet, he asked, "How much do I owe you?"

She shook her head. "It's on the house."

He gave her a wave of thanks and walked out the door. Old Blue stood as he stepped outside. "You ready?"

The dog wagged his tail. They walked back to the motel.

Ryan ate his breakfast while sitting at the small table. As he ate, he knew that Kathryn had been right. There were lots of small towns in the world. He just had to find the right one and make it his home. Popping the last bite into his mouth, he chewed and swallowed. "Well, boy," he said, "once we get packed, we'll find a new place to call home. What d'you say?"

Old Blue nosed the empty, plastic dish and looked up at Ryan.

"You're right." Bending over, he picked up the container from the floor. "We should return this before we leave."

Ryan doubted that Kathryn cared about a cheap tub. But really, that didn't matter. He'd use any excuse just to see her one last time.

Chapter 13

Kathryn rarely had the house all to herself and never at 9:00 a.m. on a weekday. Her kids had left for school ninety minutes earlier. She'd taken the week off from work to recuperate from her run-in with Decker Newcombe. On Monday, she'd slept most of the day. Morgan had made dinner. Brock had cleaned the kitchen. It was Tuesday morning, and she was definitely starting to heal. Now, the day stretched out before her with endless possibilities.

A steaming cup of coffee sat on the coffee table. Since she still couldn't shower, she'd washed off with a damp cloth in the sink. Her hair was pulled back into a ponytail. She wore a pair of sweatpants and a tank top. They were the most comfortable items in her closet.

Yet, Kathryn was determined to do more than rest this week. She was truly ready to move forward in her life.

Sitting on her sofa, she twisted her wedding band around her finger. She gave it a hard tug. The ring slipped from her finger. The skin beneath the band was smooth and white. Eventually the mark would fade. For now, it was a reminder of where she'd been and where she was going.

She set the gold band on the coffee table and picked up the remote. She turned on both the TV and a streaming service. There was a show everyone at work talked about, but she had yet to watch. Shoot, she hadn't picked out a TV program for years. Well, today was the day of new beginnings.

On the street, a car door slammed. The noise was followed by a dog's bark.

She glanced out the window.

Ryan strode up the walkway. The container she'd given him on Sunday night was in his hand. Rising from the sofa, she crossed the room. She opened the door as he approached her stoop.

"Morning." He held up the container. "I wanted to get this back to you."

She stepped outside. The morning air was already sultry and sweat dotted her upper lip. She imagined that the oppressive heat was about to return. But there was more besides the weather that left her warm. Ryan wore jeans and a dark blue T-shirt. Both garments fit him like a second skin and accentuated his muscular chest, flat stomach, and long legs.

"You didn't have to stop by so early. I hope you didn't go out of your way."

"Actually, me and Old Blue are about to leave town."

Disappointment struck her chest. "You must've gotten your phone back."

He nodded. "I did."

"And?"

"I talked to Isaac. The IT people could tell that Decker's text came from England. So they really didn't learn anything new."

"Did Isaac know anything about the investigation?" Kathryn had taken a week off work, but she was still a cop. Decker was still wanted for several murders in her jurisdiction. Bringing him to justice was more than her job—it was her mission.

"He didn't say much of anything." Ryan held up the container. "This is yours, and Old Blue says thanks."

She took the dish from his hand. Without thinking through her actions, she said, "I just sat down with a cup of coffee. You want to join me?"

Ryan turned his face to the sun. "I'd love to, but it's starting to get hot. I can't leave the dog in the car."

"Bring him in," she suggested. "He'll be fine for a few minutes."

"Yeah, but the other day your daughter seemed pretty upset to see him in the house. I don't want to cause an issue."

"Old Blue's not a problem," she said. "Besides, my kids are at school. They won't be home until after football practice ends."

A look flashed across his face.

She'd invited him into her empty home. What's more, they wouldn't be interrupted for hours. Suddenly, there was much more that she wanted to do with her day than binge watch a show on TV.

It brought up two important questions. What did Ryan expect? And what did she want?

She knew the answer to the second question. She wanted Ryan. He'd ignited feelings that she thought had died years ago. It turns out that her libido wasn't dead after all, only buried so deep that she forgotten she had needs at all.

She knew there was something to the timing as well. It was more than simply thinking she was ready to start over. But she'd survived an attack by a serial killer. Somehow, that made life even more precious.

Besides, Ryan was leaving soon. After, she'd never have to see him again…

"Only if you're sure," he said.

She took a moment to consider his words. "Absolutely."

While he got Old Blue out of the truck, she held open the door. As master and dog crossed the threshold, she asked, "How d'you take your coffee?"

"Black is fine."

Old Blue sniffed the edge of the sofa before settling on the floor.

Kathryn let the door close and engaged the lock. "I'll grab you a cup."

He pointed to her television set. The streaming service menu filled the screen. "What're you watching?"

"Nothing, yet." Using the remote, she turned off the power. "Hold on a sec. I'll be right back."

Ryan followed her into the kitchen. She didn't mind. She could feel his eyes on her as she pulled a clean mug from the cabinet and lifted the pot from the coffee maker. "I made this a few minutes ago," she said, while pouring the coffee. "It's fresh."

She handed him the cup. His fingers grazed hers, and he gripped the handle. Their gazes met, and he lifted the coffee to his lips. He watched her over the rim as he took a sip. "It's hot, just like I like it."

Her skin tingled. Was he trying to seduce her over coffee? God, she hoped so. "So, you like things that are hot?" Okay, maybe that wasn't the best line. Seems like flirting was a skill that she'd forgotten.

He didn't mind her cheesy line. Closing the space between them, he reached for her waist. His fingertips grazed her side. "What do I like that's hot?" he repeated the question, never taking his eyes from hers. "I like hot summers, hot pizza, hot coffee, and you."

She laughed. "Are you calling me hot?"

"Of course."

"Nobody's said that to me in years." *Correction, make that decades.*

"That's too bad because you're a beautiful woman. You should have someone tell you every day that you're gorgeous."

"So you say," she said, her tone flirtatious.

"It's not just words. It's true."

"You know what?" She moved closer to Ryan and wrapped her arms around his neck. "We're talking too much."

"We are?" His mouth was next to hers. His words mixed with her breath. "What should I do instead?"

"You should kiss me."

He smiled and placed his lips on hers. His tongue was in her mouth. His hands were on her hips. Then, he gripped her rear. She ran her fingers through his hair and let the strands slip through her fingers. But she wanted more of him, and she wanted it now.

She pressed her hips into him. It didn't matter that they were both fully dressed, she could tell that he was hard. That was fine with her because she was already wet. Her hands traveled from his shoulders to his chest to his abs to the fly of his jeans. She cupped him with her hand, and he moaned. "Oh, Kathryn."

He moved his mouth to her ear and kissed her lobe.

"I like to hear you say my name." She rubbed him through his jeans.

"Kathryn," he growled, "you're driving me wild."

"That's kind of the whole point, isn't it?"

He kissed her harder and slid his hand inside her tank top. His fingers blazed a trail across her skin. His lips were still on hers as he stroked her breast. She hadn't bothered with a bra today, and her nipple hardened under his touch. He moved his fingers to her other breast and rolled her nipple. It was pleasure mixed with pain. She hissed with ecstasy.

"Oh, Kathryn. What do you want now?"

Even in the middle of a lust-fueled fog, she understood the irony. For years, she'd simply avoided sex. But since she'd decided to take Ryan as a lover, any delay was torture. Once more, she asked the question *What did she want?*

The answer was simple. "I want all of you."

He kissed her harder. Lifting her into his arms, he carried her into the living room. Ryan set Kathryn on the sofa. She opened her thighs, and he settled between her legs. The need to have him inside her was powerful and primal. She undid the top button of his jeans. He untied the laces at her waistband, and suddenly her pants were loose. She refused to think too much. Shimmying hips, she worked her pants down until they fell to the floor. She also slipped out of her panties. She spread her legs open further. He finished opening his fly and freed himself.

There was one word in the back of her mind—a word she couldn't ignore. "Condom?"

"Yeah," he said, breathless. "I have one. It's here." He pulled his wallet from his back pocket. He opened a foil packet from it and rolled the condom down his length.

Kathryn watched as he entered her slowly. Then, at the last moment, he drove in hard.

She threw back her head and moaned.

"You like it like that," he said, his breath hot in her ear.

"Yes," she cried out. "Oh God, yes."

He adopted a rhythm. Slow. Slow. Hard.

She wrapped her legs around his waist. He reached between them and found the top of her sex, stroking her. She knew it wouldn't be long before she came.

She pulled him in closer with her legs. "Faster," she panted. God, she was so close to her release. "Faster and harder."

He obliged, driving into her hard and quick, while still rubbing the top of her sex. She cried out with an orgasm. Ryan placed his palm on the cushions behind her. His hips pumped. With a guttural moan, he threw back his head and came.

His breath was ragged. He kissed her shoulder first,

then said, "I was wrong about you being hot. You're a damned inferno."

"That's quite the compliment, considering." She bit her lip, worried that she almost shared too much.

"Considering what?"

She shook her head. "It's nothing." But that wasn't true. "It's personal."

"I can tell that it's a whole lot more than nothing." He lifted her chin, so she had to look him in the eye. "We've gotten to know each other pretty well over the past two days. I hope you know that you can trust me."

He was right. She did trust him. "It's been a while since I've had sex." Longer even than the two years since her husband's death. He'd been so ill at the end that she'd been his caretaker only—not his lover. "I was worried I'd forgotten how."

He placed a noisy kiss on her cheek. "Trust me, you haven't forgotten a thing." He backed up, sliding out of her. "I need to take care of the condom before it gets messy."

"There's a bathroom down the hall. First door on the left."

Her pants and panties lay in a pile on the floor. She bent over to pick them up. The movement left her dizzy. She sat on the sofa and waited for the faintness to pass.

As the sensation abated, she surveyed the living room. The room was just as it had always been. The TV still sat on the stand. Pictures still hung on the wall. As far as she could tell, there were only two differences to her normal living room. First, she was naked from the waist down. And second, her pants and underwear were bunched up in her hand.

Oh, wait. She found a third difference. There was a butt print on the fabric. Even if she cleaned the spot a million times, how was she supposed to just watch TV in here now?

Her side definitely hurt. She dressed slowly. Ryan appeared in the doorway as she was tying the drawstring at her waist.

"How're you doing?"

"Good. Tired." But she was more than weary. She was drained and sated at the same time. "Actually, I think the right word is *spent*."

"C'mon. I'll get you settled on the sofa."

Lying on his side, Old Blue slept on the floor. He opened one eye and regarded them. "He's a good dog," she noted. "It was kind of you to rescue him."

"I know it sounds like a saying that belongs on a bumper sticker or a T-shirt or something, but he's the one who rescued me." He bent over to scratch the dog's belly. "Before I adopted him, I was alone. Sure, I knew people. There were a few I even liked." He gave her a quick smile and stood. "But I never had anyone who counted on me. I never had anyone I needed to care for—not until him, at least."

"After my husband died, I was angry. I felt alone. But I had my kids, and they needed me." Having to take care of her children was the one thing that had helped her get through the days when the grief was a weight that could crush her soul.

"You think that's the key to life? Having someone who needs you, even if they are a dog?"

She thought he might be right. Leaning back into the sofa, she said, "Maybe."

Ryan sat next to her, before reaching for her hand. She slipped her fingers between his. In that moment, she realized there was another key to life as well. It was to find another person who completed you. But the fatigue was starting to take over, and she couldn't find the right words. She closed her eyes and drifted to sleep.

Ryan hadn't meant to doze. Kathryn had fallen asleep holding his hand. He hadn't wanted to risk waking her by getting up. Eventually, he'd faded as well. In their sleep, they'd stretched out on the sofa. Kathryn lay in his arms. From the floor, Old Blue regarded him. The dog thumped his tail on the floor and whined.

Ryan understood what the look meant. Old Blue needed to go outside. But how was he supposed to get off the sofa without waking Kathryn?

The dog whined again, louder this time.

Kathryn's eyelids fluttered open. "Looks like we drifted off."

"I guess so." He sat up. "I need to take Old Blue for a walk."

"What time is it? I'm starving."

Ryan pulled the phone from his pocket. There were no missed calls. No texts, either. He really was a man alone in the world. "It's already two thirty."

"No wonder I'm hungry." She sat up. "You want something for lunch? I have leftover steak and potato salad."

Her offer of a late lunch sounded perfect. Too bad that afterward, he really would have to leave. After leading Old Blue through the kitchen, Ryan let the dog walk around the backyard. When he came back into the house, Kathryn was wiping off the counter.

While putting salad and slices of steak onto two plates, she said, "Let me get some forks." She opened a drawer and grabbed the utensils. "We can sit outside."

He picked up both plates. "Lead the way."

She opened the back door as the front door opened. Brock bounded through the front door. "Mom! Mom! Where are you?"

"I'm in the kitchen." Did he hear a tinge of alarm in her words? Even with Decker half a world away, Ryan imagined that Kathryn was still on high-alert. To be honest, he was, too. "What're you doing home? I thought you had practice."

"I do but I had one of the guys bring me home for a minute. I have huge news." He came into the room and saw Ryan. He smiled. "Oh, hey. I'm glad you're here, too."

The kid's reaction surprised him. "You are?"

"Yeah. After you and I practiced with the baseball on Sunday, I knew my throw was better. I stopped by Coach's classroom during my free period and told him I wanted him to reconsider letting me play QB." Brock drew in a deep breath and continued. "He let me throw for him today at lunch. He liked that I spoke to him and that my accuracy had improved."

"And he made you the quarterback?" she asked.

"Not exactly," Brock admitted. "But he said he'd keep an open mind for Friday night's game."

"Honey." She pulled her son in for a hug. "I'm so proud of you. And you came home between school and practice to tell me. I love it."

The kid let his mother embrace him and then stepped away. "I wanted to tell you. But I also wanted to ask about Ryan." The kid turned to face him. "How long are you staying in town? Because I'd love to work with you more. I mean, if you're available."

Sure, Ryan was planning on leaving soon. But he couldn't say *no* to Brock. "I can stay a couple of days longer." He hoped that there was still a vacancy at the motel.

"Thanks, man." Brock smiled wide again. "I appreciate it." He kissed his mother's cheek. "I'll see you both after practice."

The door slammed, and he knew that Brock was gone.

"You don't have to stay and help him," said Kathryn.

A thought came to him, and it filled his chest with acid. Yet he had to know if he was right. "Are you kicking me out of town again?"

"I just don't want you to feel obligated."

"There's nothing else I'd rather do than help your son," he said, even though his words were a lie. Sure, he liked the fact that the kid wanted his help. But really, he was looking forward to spending more time with Kathryn.

Yet, he knew for every minute he spent with her, leaving once and for all would be that much harder.

Chapter 14

It was Friday at 5:30 p.m. Ryan stood in the kitchen of Kathryn's house. The last week had been one of the best in his life. As had become his habit, he slept at the Saddle-Up Inn. In the morning, he walked Old Blue. They always stopped at Over Easy for breakfast. Then, he and the dog would go to Kathryn's house.

In the morning, he put his construction skills to work. So far, he'd installed a new toilet, fixed a leaking sink, and rewired the garage-door opener. He'd even repaired the back fence where several boards were missing.

But he'd done more than odd jobs around her home. When it got too hot, he came inside. Over the week, he and Kathryn had streamed an entire seven-season TV series set in a postapocalyptic world, complete with zombies and an evil dictator. In the afternoon, they made love in her bedroom and slept in each other's arms.

They prepared dinner together, and he ate with the family. After supper, he coached Brock on his throw. Old Blue always brought the balls back. The kid had secured the QB spot for this week's game, and Ryan had promised to attend.

There were two hours left until kickoff. Honestly, he was a little excited and a lot proud.

It was the exact life that he wanted. Too bad it would be over in the morning. He still wanted to move to Encantador. But what he needed was for Kathryn's invitation to stay. She hadn't said anything, and he wasn't about to beg.

"There you are." Brock came into the kitchen. He wore a red and gold football jersey and shorts. "I have to get to the school for warm-ups, but I figured you could use this." He tossed Ryan a red T-shirt. He opened the garment. In gold lettering were the words *Encantador High School Football*. Brock continued, "It's mine, but I don't wear it much. You can keep it if you want."

To Ryan, it was a treasure. "Thanks, man. I will keep it."

"I figured that you deserved your own shirt. If it weren't for you, I wouldn't be starting as quarterback."

"It's all your hard work," said Ryan. He wasn't the kind to give pep talks, but it seemed like the right thing to say. "I just gave you a few things to think about."

"Well, thanks for all that, anyway."

"There's my two favorite men," said Kathryn. She stood in the doorway of the kitchen, next to her son. She wore a similar T-shirt to the one he'd been given, but the gold lettering said *Encantador High School Football Mom*. Her dark hair fell loose over her shoulder.

She looped her arm through Brock's. "How are you? Excited? Nervous?"

"Both," said her son with a quick laugh. A car horn blared from somewhere on the street. "That's my ride. I'll see you at the game."

Kathryn rose to her tiptoes to place a kiss on her son's cheek. "Go get 'em."

Brock ran from the room. The front door opened and slammed shut, then he was gone.

"What's that?" She pointed to the shirt in his hand.

Holding up the garment so she could see, he said, "Brock gave it to me." He paused. There was so much he wanted to say, but what was the point? By this time tomorrow, he'd be long gone. Instead, he said, "If he keeps working on his throw, he might have a career as a pitcher, too."

"He likes you a lot."

"What about Morgan?" Brock had warmed up to Ryan. But Kathryn's daughter had not.

"Morgan doesn't really like anybody. It's part of being a teenage girl, I think."

"She glares at me whenever I walk into the room. I tried to talk to her the other day, and she actually rolled her eyes and groaned." He shook his head. "I've known some brutal people before in my life. But teenage girls might be the worst."

Kathryn laughed. "Go and change into your shirt. We'll have dinner at the game. The senior class is running the concession stand as a fundraiser for an after-prom party. Morgan is the APP chairperson. So we definitely need to get there early and eat a lot."

Ryan went into Kathryn's bedroom and stripped out of his old shirt.

He pulled on the new one before checking his reflection in a mirror.

"Looks good on you." She stood in the doorway. He hadn't realized that she'd followed him to her room.

"Yeah, it fits pretty well," he said, smoothing his hand down his torso.

She came into the room and stood behind him. Wrapping her arms around his stomach, she leaned her head into his back. "It's hard to believe that the week's already over. I hope you know how much I've appreciated having you around."

Placing his hand on hers, he said, "I've liked being here."

Please, ask me to stay.

She pressed her lips into his back. "It's going to suck saying goodbye."

His chest ached. For the first time in his life, he understood how heartbreak felt. "I guess this really is the end."

She held him tighter. "It sounds so permanent."

Turning to face her, he lifted her chin and gazed into her eyes. "Don't worry. I'm not the kind of guy who gets a fairy-tale ending." He wanted to be with her but knew a cop and ex-con couldn't be together—not permanently anyway.

"Don't say that. You deserve to be happy. You'll find someone."

What about her? Would Kathryn find another man? A shock wave of possessiveness rolled through him. Cupping his hand behind her head, he brought his mouth to hers. The kiss was hard, fierce, and made to be remembered.

Winding her arms around his neck, she sighed. "Oh, Ryan."

"I want you, Kathryn," he said, slipping his hand down the front of her shorts. He worked his fingers into her panties. She was already wet. His dick hardened knowing that she wanted him as much as he wanted her.

"Yes," she said into the kiss. "Take me."

If this was all they had left, then he intended to make it something she'd never forget. Holding onto her hips, he turned her around. They both faced the dresser, and he pushed her shoulders down so she bent at the waist. He worked her shorts over her hips and pulled them down her thighs. They pooled at her feet, and she kicked them away. She took off her panties.

Pulling down his pants, he slipped on one of the condoms he'd kept in his wallet. Using his tip, he traced Kathryn's opening. She gave a sexy little mew. He entered her slowly, watching as he disappeared inside of her.

Over the course of the week, he had learned what she liked and knew how to make her orgasm. While he was deep inside of her, she lifted her hips, taking him in deeper.

"Oh, God, Ryan. Yes."

She tightened around him. He knew that she was close. He moved his hips, driving into her hard. The dresser started rocking, the back corners hitting the wall.

"Ryan," she cried out. "Don't stop."

He could see her reflection in the mirror. A flush crept up her neck and left her cheeks red. Her eyes were closed. His lips were moist. She gripped the dresser's edge. Then, she came. Panting, she relaxed.

He didn't hold back. Focusing only on the sight of him inside of her, he let go. He lay on top of her for a moment, breathing hard, not wanting to let her go. Pulling out, he held onto the edge of the rubber. "I'll be right back."

Hustling to the en suite bath, he closed the door.

Kathryn had to see that they were perfect for each other. More even than the amazing sex, they got along well. Brock and Ryan had bonded over sports. It seemed that Morgan didn't really like most people. So her feelings for him weren't worse than for anyone else.

He had to wonder if there was anything he could do to change Kathryn's mind, especially since she was so determined to say goodbye.

There was no doubt about it, England was in an uproar. A serial killer had been imported from across the pond, specifically the United States. And Yankee Jack, as the press was calling Decker Newcombe, meant to murder someone live on the internet.

Jason Jones had come to the United Kingdom to find the killer.

Sure, the FBI already had an office in London. As far as he could tell, it was being run by capable agents. But Jason was going to personally take care of Decker.

If Newcombe was following the calendar laid out by Jack the Ripper, another murder would take place on Sunday. It was 11:30 p.m. on Friday night. That meant he didn't have much time to find and stop the killer.

The Bureau's London office was in the US Embassy complex at 33 Nine Elms Lane. He sat in an interview room on the fifth floor. The windowless room held a table with four chairs and had room for little more. His palms were wrapped around a paper cup of cold coffee. Across the table sat Tiffany Hoffman and Isabella Kang.

Both girls were students at a large university near Dallas, Texas. They were in England for a semester abroad. What made them interesting—at least to Jason— is that they'd inadvertently captured a photo of New-combe after disembarking from the flight.

It was the same one they'd posted online and part of what proved that Decker was in the UK.

Even though both girls had been interviewed before, he had them brought down to the embassy. He wanted to speak to them personally. Neither were happy.

"You know," said Isabella, tossing her long black hair over her shoulder, "my father's an attorney. He says that you people asking us all these questions is harassment."

He was neither impressed nor intimidated. "Yeah? Well, I went to law school, too. And I have the right to ask my questions."

"If I refuse to say anything?" she challenged.

"Well, then, I'd stop talking to you."

The girl smirked. "That's what I thought."

"But I'd take you back to Texas with me and let you answer my questions there."

The smile slipped from her face. "Oh."

"Just cool it," Tiffany said to her friend, her voice a stage whisper. Then, to Jason, she said, "This has all been wild. I mean, that murderer was on the plane with us. I don't remember seeing him at all."

"Me, either," chimed Isabella. "I mean, the flight was totally packed, but still, he seems kinda hard to miss."

"Yeah, and you want to know something else that's weird?" Tiffany said and didn't wait for an answer. "I don't even remember him standing behind us when we took the selfie. I checked our background and everything because, obviously, I hate having some random person in my pic. Plus, posting some rando on social media is bad manners."

He paused and mulled over what the coed had said. There was something important…something he'd missed. "Say that again."

"It's bad manners on social media…"

"No, not that part. You said you checked your background," he said, clarifying her statement.

"Yeah. Nobody was behind me."

"And you didn't recall seeing him on the flight, either."

The girls looked at each other. Isabella shook her head. "Neither of us did."

"Can I see your phone?" Jason held out his hand.

"Do you have a warrant or something?" asked Isabella.

"Do you want me to get one?" Jason was done playing games with the college students. "Because I can. But it also means you'll be spending all night in this conference room."

Tiffany glared at her friend. "Just chill. We don't have anything to hide. Besides, I want to help." She pulled her phone from the tote bag that was slung over the back of her chair. "Here you go."

"Can you open the photo app for me? And can you find the original picture you took at the airport?"

"I can," said Tiffany. "But I can't."

Jason was getting fed up with the coeds and their attitudes. "What's that supposed to mean?" he snapped.

"It means she can open the photo app," said Isabella, "but she can't show you the original. She took the picture on social media. The photo isn't stored on her phone."

Because of the nature of his job, Jason didn't have any social-media accounts. But he did understand how they worked. What's more, he knew the original photo was in the phone somewhere. He just needed the right person to find it.

At this time of night, most everyone on the FBI's staff was gone. They were either home or out looking for the serial killer. "I'd like to find someone to look at your phone, if that's okay with you."

Tiffany wrote a six-digit number on a slip of paper and handed it to Jason. "That's my passcode."

He took the piece of paper and nodded his thanks. "You two need to hold tight here for a little longer. Can I have something brought to you? Water? A coffee?" Hell, they were in England. "Do you want some tea? I heard the stuff they serve in the embassy is pretty good."

"A tea is fine," said Tiffany.

At the same time, Isabella asked, "How long is *a little longer*?"

"I'll get back to you as soon as I can." He rose to his feet. With his fingers resting on the door handle, he added, "I'll have someone come in and take your order for food or drink."

He walked out of the interview room. At the end of the hall, the duty agent sat at a shared desk. Sherise, a Black woman from Boston, wore an FBI polo shirt along with black slacks. She looked up as Jason approached.

"How's it going?" she asked.

"That depends on if you can help me out or not."

Sherise straightened in her seat. "What do you need?"

"First, can you check on the college girls? Get them food if they're hungry or something to drink. One of them wants a cup of tea. Keep an eye on them, too. I doubt they'll leave the building, but I'd like them to stay."

"Sure, I can. But are they being detained?" Sherise asked, her Boston accent heavy. *Sure* sounded like *Shoer*.

"No, but I have one of their phones. That brings up the next favor. I need someone who knows a thing or two about tech, especially phones and social media."

"All of our IT people have gone home. But…" She drummed her fingers on the desk. A phone sat on the corner of the worktop. Picking up the handset, she said, "Let me check with someone."

Jason listened to one half of the call.

"Hey," said Sherise. "It's me…Yeah, I'm the duty agent this weekend…Are you still here?…Listen, I've got someone in from Texas. They need help with a phone and social media. Can you take a look?" She smiled. "Great, I'll send him down." She hung up the phone and looked back at Jason. "You're in luck. Theo Fowler works with the NSA and is a tech genius. He's on the third floor." She pointed down the hallway. "Take the elevator and he'll meet you when you get off."

Jason followed the directions. On the third floor, a tall man with brown hair and eyes stood next to the bank of elevators.

"You the Texan?" the man asked.

Jason wasn't sure what to expect from a cybersecurity genius. But this guy wasn't it. Aside from being tall—taller than Jason's six feet—the guy had broad shoulders and muscular arms. He wore a polo shirt and ID on a lanyard around his neck.

"You must be Theo Fowler." The two men shook hands. "I'm Jason Jones, from the FBI's San Antonio Field Office."

"Nice to meet you. You got the phone?"

He handed Theo the device, along with the passcode.

"Follow me and tell me what you need." Theo led him down a long, dark hallway. Motion lights clicked on overhead as they passed.

"On Sunday morning, two coeds from the Dallas area took a photograph on an app at an airport in London. They then posted that image to social media. I want to see the original picture."

Theo stopped in front of a door. An electronic lock was attached to the wall. Bending slightly, he tapped the ID on the keypad. A light switched from red to green. He then entered a seven-digit code, and the door clicked as the lock disengaged. "I'm not going to ask about the case," he said, opening the door, "but I might be able to guess."

Of course he'd be able to figure out this was related to the Decker Newcombe investigation. The photo of Decker at the London airport had been blasted by the media all over the world. Besides, why else would a federal agent from Texas be in England? He followed Theo into a computer lab. A single desk lamp at a workstation illuminated the large room. "If you guessed, you'd probably be right."

"Do you have a warrant to search the phone?"

"The owner gave consent."

Theo wove his way to the lit desk. He pulled a chair from another terminal. "Have a seat, and I'll take a look."

Theo unlocked the phone. Using a USB cord, he attached the device to a computer. "Here's the trick. How much of the phone's memory is used will determine whether or not we can access the picture."

"How long will that take?"

Theo shook his head. "Not long." He typed on the computer's keyboard. A line of letters and numbers began to fill the monitor. A moment later, a grid of pictures filled the screen. "Let's see what we have," said Theo, while scrolling through the images.

There were pictures of Isabella and Tiffany in front of Parliament. There were photos with the two coeds in the foreground and Buckingham Palace and a Beefeater in the background. There were several pictures of food and even more of drinks. Finally, they came to a series of four pictures. All of them had been taken in the airport's Terminal Five. "Is this what you're looking for?"

Jason sat up taller. "It is."

"Looks like those girls took four pictures in the app before settling on this one to post." Using the mouse, he circled one picture with the cursor.

Jason had seen the picture so many times that it was burned into his brain. But this time, the image was slightly different. His pulse pounded, making him deaf to every sound but the thud of his heartbeat. Decker Newcombe wasn't in the background. "Where are you, you bastard?" he asked the screen. "And how'd you get into the picture to begin with?" He turned to look at Theo. "Is that possible—to insert someone into a social-media post?"

"Possible? Yes. Easy? No."

"Could an image be inserted into a video taken from a public camera? Like one at an airport?" After all, Decker had been seen in security footage at the Dallas–Fort Worth Airport. Those two pictures were the whole reason everyone was looking for the killer in England. But what if both images had been altered?

Energy surged through his veins. Jason rose from his seat and began to pace.

Theo said, "Hacking into a securities video system isn't impossible, but there aren't many people who could do it."

"Could you?"

Theo paused, seeming to consider the question. "I could."

"So it's possible that video might not be legit, either?"

"Yeah, it's possible." Theo paused. "What're you thinking?"

"I'm thinking that Decker Newcombe might not be in England after all."

"If he's not in England, where is he?"

He stopped walking and looked at the NSA agent. "That's really the only question that matters—and honestly, I don't have a clue."

Chapter 15

It was late in the second quarter of the football game at Encantador High School. Only two minutes remained until halftime. EHS was up 13 to 10. So far, Brock had played well as quarterback. He'd run in one touchdown and gotten the team close enough to kick a pair of field goals. Morgan had kept the line moving at the concession stand. For the first time in a long while, Kathryn was content.

Yet, there was more to her happiness than her children's successes.

She and Ryan sat side by side in the stands. She dared not hold his hand—small-town gossip being what it was. But occasionally, his thigh grazed hers, and her skin tingled with the touch.

It seemed like everyone in town had come out for the game. Her neighbor, Joe, sat behind Kathryn. With him were his wife and Gladys, the elderly woman who lived across the road from Kathryn. Another neighbor, Stan Vargasky, and his wife sat nearby. They attended every game since all three of their daughters were on the cheer team. Armando Cruz, the assistant principal, divided his time between patrolling the students' section and sitting with his wife and their twin toddlers.

As the buzzer blared, ending the first half of the game, Joe leaned forward and clapped Ryan on the shoulder. "I've seen you working with Brock this week. His throw has improved a lot. Who knows, with an arm like his, we might be in contention for a state championship."

"The kid works hard, that's for sure," said Ryan.

Joe exhaled. "I didn't get a chance to thank you for everything you've done for the town. Chasing Decker out of hiding. Helping the QB get his pass accurate." He paused. "I might've said some harsh things before, but you're all right in my book."

Kathryn assumed that was the closest thing Ryan would get to an apology. He seemed to know it, too. "I appreciate you saying that."

"If you ever need anything from me, either of you," said Joe, "let me know."

"Go to the concession stand and get your wife and Gladys something to eat. The senior class is raising money for after prom," said Kathryn. The least she could do was send some business to Morgan and her cause.

"I could use something to eat," Ryan said as he stood. She stood as well. "Shall we?"

Kathryn had been coming to games in this stadium for decades. She could probably find her way to the concession stand with her eyes closed. It was tucked into a small building on the outside of the track that surrounded the football field.

A long line of people waiting for concessions snaked around the side of the track. She and Ryan took up their place at the back of the line. "Looks like everyone's hungry," said Ryan.

"It'll be good for the APP committee," she said, hopeful that Morgan would be pleased to have such a successful fundraiser.

"It's not just that there's a lot of people," grumbled a young woman standing in front of them. "The line is moving so slow."

"That's odd." She peered into the concession stand. From where she stood, she could see seven kids behind the counter. Morgan wasn't one of them. Correction. It was more than odd. Where was her daughter? "I'm going to check and see what's going on."

"I'll come with you," Ryan offered. She didn't need his help. But there was no reason to turn him away, either.

As they walked toward the front of the line, it was impossible to miss all the complaining.

"What's taking them so long?"

"This is too much of a wait for popcorn."

"If the school can't run the concession stand right, then they should let spectators bring in their own food."

She shouldered her way to the counter. The vice president of the APP committee stood behind the cash register. "Hi, Courtney," said Kathryn. "You guys look a little understaffed. Where's Morgan?"

Courtney rolled her eyes. "Like I would know. Twenty

minutes ago, she and Elliot took a break." She hooked air quotes around the last word. Then, she checked her watch. "Oh, wait. She's been gone for twenty-four minutes."

Okay, it was time for Kathryn to step in. Morgan might be trying to find her way in the world. But disappearing with a boy when she was supposed to be working was definitely the wrong path. "Any idea where she went?"

Pointing toward the parking lot, Courtney said, "They were going to get something from Elliot's car."

"I'll find her and send them back."

The other girl slumped with relief. "Thanks."

She'd pulled over Elliot more than once and knew he drove a blue sedan. But it might take some time to find his car in the sea of vehicles that filled the parking lot. She started walking toward the lot. Ryan was at her side.

"You don't have to come with me," she said, before warning him. "It might get messy for a few minutes."

"That's okay. I'm good with messy."

As it turns out, Elliot's car was easier to find than she feared. He was parked at the back of the lot. The headlights on his blue sedan were on—as were the high beams. Even with the lights shining in her eyes, she could see the outline of Elliot in the driver's seat.

For a moment, she was angry with her daughter—and herself. She should've used more discipline than understanding. But as she walked closer to the car, she realized an important fact. Elliot was in the driver's seat, but the passenger seat was empty.

"What the heck?"

"What the what?" Ryan asked.

"Where's my daughter?" Her anger morphed to concern, twisting in her gut.

She increased her walk to a trot. Then her trot became a jog. By the time she reached the blue sedan, she was covered in sweat. After looking in the window, she went cold. Elliot was unconscious. Had he not been wearing his seat belt, he would have fallen over. His hair was wet and matted with blood. One eye was swollen and ringed with a bruise. There was a cut to his cheek.

The interior of the car was red with gore.

Morgan wasn't there.

Kathryn swallowed down her rising panic. She opened the driver's door and reached for Elliot's arm. His skin was warm. The pulse at his wrist was surprisingly strong.

"He's alive," she said with relief. To Ryan, she said, "Call 9-1-1."

He stepped away from the vehicle and pulled his phone from his pocket. "I need emergency medical services," he began.

Certainly, dispatch would send EMTs who were already at the game. They'd be here within minutes. She looked inside the car. Morgan's purse lay on the passenger floorboard. Her jacket was in the seat. "What in the hell happened?" Certainly, there were clues in the car as to who'd committed this crime and why. She tried to think like the undersheriff. It was impossible since she was also a mother. Then she asked the question that made this nightmare all too real. "Where's my daughter?"

Elliot groaned. "Morgan. Revenge."

Kathryn knelt next to the open car door. "It's me,

Morgan's mom." She reached for his hand. "You're safe now. We're going to get you to the hospital. They'll patch you up. What happened?"

He held onto her fingers. It was like being trapped in a vise. "I'm so sorry. I tried to protect her. But he was everywhere. Hitting. Kicking. Cutting. He slammed my head into the hood of the car, and I blacked out. The last thing I saw was Morgan being thrown into the trunk of his car."

"Who?" Her pulse raced. "Who attacked you? Who took my daughter?"

"It was him."

"Him who?"

"I can't remember his name."

"Think, damn it," she said, as a wave of grief and fury pushed her under.

Elliot's head drooped to the side. Once again, he slipped from consciousness.

There was nothing more he could give her—not now, at least. No, that wasn't true. He'd said plenty already. The attacker was male. Elliot recognized him. It means that he knew the kidnapper.

A thousand faces flashed through her mind. Of course, she'd arrested rough men over the years. Even now, some might want revenge. But to kidnap her daughter and beat her boyfriend to a pulp?

Nobody made sense.

Did Elliot—or even Morgan—have enemies at school?

Then again, kidnapping someone was difficult. More than getting the victim to go with the perpetrator, they had to control them afterward. How could a lone student hope to pull off such a crime?

Yet, someone had. Her stomach cramped, and she thought she might retch.

Two EMTs sprinted through the parking lot. She waved her arms. "Over here. We have one victim, male, aged eighteen. He's been beaten pretty badly." She stepped away from the car, giving the paramedics room to work.

Ryan stood nearby. He opened his arms, and she stepped into his embrace.

"What's going on?"

Her eyes burned, and her throat was raw. "Honestly," she croaked, "I don't know. Someone attacked Elliot, and they took Morgan." She knew there were video cameras in the high-school parking lot. Several nearby businesses had cameras, too. They could get the footage. And then what? She was having a hard time thinking. Her mind was a tire stuck in the mud. It turned but got her nowhere.

"It'll be okay," Ryan whispered the words into her hair.

Far from being soothing, his sentiment left her pissed. "You don't know that," she snapped. She pushed on his chest, but he held her tighter.

"Undersheriff," one of the EMTs called out, "the patient's awake, and he wants to talk to you."

Elliot had been removed from his vehicle. He was strapped onto a gurney and a blanket covered him to the chest. A white bandage had been placed over the cut to his cheek. He regarded Kathryn with a single eye. "I know who took Morgan."

Her pulse raced, as if she'd just run a marathon. She gasped for air and information. "Who was it?"

"It was him. The guy everyone keeps talking about."

Elliot touched his forehead and screwed his eyes shut. "I can't remember his name, but I'll always remember his eyes. They were ice cold. More than just being blue, there was nothing behind them. Like his soul was empty. You know?"

She did know because she'd seen those eyes before. Until now, she'd tried not to think too much about the attack at the abandoned ranch. But it all came back to her in a frigid rush of memories. As she'd fought with Decker, he'd regarded her with eyes so cold that his gaze burned.

"Was it Decker?" she asked, knowing full well that she shouldn't give any information to the victim of a crime. It tainted their recollections of the event. Yet, she had to know. "Did Decker Newcombe attack you and take my daughter?"

Elliot nodded slowly. "Yeah," he said. "That's him."

"Excuse me, Undersheriff," said one of the EMTs. "We have to get the patient to the hospital."

She stepped away from the stretcher. An ambulance had been driven to the scene. Elliot was wheeled into the back. The doors were closed. With lights strobing, they drove away.

She looked at Ryan. "Decker's taken my daughter."

"That's impossible," he said. "He's in England."

She didn't know how he'd done it. As bad as things were now, they were about to get worse. "If he is back, then it means my daughter is his next victim." How could any of this be happening? Good Lord, this was worse than any nightmare. "He's going to murder her on the internet."

Ryan drew his eyebrows together. "Why would he want Morgan?"

At least she knew the answer to that question. "Elliot said he wants revenge. He must want to get even with me for finding him at the old McCoy ranch."

She'd never felt more lost before in her life. But she refused to give in to the hopelessness. Her daughter was missing but she was the undersheriff. It was her job to find Morgan and bring her home.

She stared at the brightly lit stadium. There was a clawing in her throat. It was ultimate need—she had to find her child and bring her home. "I'm coming for you, Decker. But this time, you won't get away."

Ryan knew that Kathryn's daughter being kidnapped was serious. But he had a hard time believing that Decker had actually taken the girl. There was evidence that Decker was on the other side of an ocean. He might've been able to sneak out of the country once. But he doubted that the killer would be able to get back in.

He was determined to help Kathryn find her daughter. Right now, she wasn't thinking like a cop—only a mom.

It left him with a simple explanation for what happened. Morgan's friend, Elliot, was mistaken.

"I'll call Jason," he said. The FBI needed to know about the kidnapping. But, he also hoped that the special agent would have more proof that Decker was in London. That way, Kathryn wouldn't waste her time looking for someone she'd never find.

Kathryn nodded. "I'll call my deputies and the duo from the Texas Rangers. We also have to see if any of these cameras caught the kidnapping. Get a description of the car. Start looking for witnesses."

He gave her wrist a squeeze and took a few steps away from where she stood. After pulling up the contact information, he placed a call to SA Jones. He answered after the third ring. "Ryan, did you hear from him again?"

Of course the FBI agent was hoping that he'd received another message from Decker. "Sorry," he said. "No."

"Then, I have to call you back. I'm tied up right now."

"You have to give me a minute." Before Jason could refuse, he added, "Kathryn's daughter was kidnapped from a high-school football game."

He cursed. "I'll call my people in San Antonio and have them send a team. But right now, I'm in London."

Ryan wasn't dissuaded. "There was one witness to the kidnapping. He's a friend of the victim's and was beaten. He can't recall everything, but he identified the kidnapper."

"That's good news. It'll help find the undersheriff's daughter and bring her home."

"The kid thinks it was Decker," he said, interrupting. He took another step away from Kathryn and lowered his voice enough that he wouldn't be overheard. "The undersheriff's convinced it's Decker, too. My fear is that after her attack, she's got some posttraumatic stress. She's convinced herself—and the witness—that Decker took her daughter. Since she's the undersheriff, people will listen to her. A lot of time is going to be spent looking for the wrong guy."

He waited for a reply. A moment passed. And a moment more. Had Jason hung up?

Ryan glanced at the screen. A timer continued to count the seconds of their open call. Pressing the phone to his ear, he asked, "You there?"

"I'm here."

"I know that you're busy and all, but if you could talk to Kathryn? Tell her there's no way that Decker took her kid. She'll listen to you." He wasn't sure the last bit was entirely true, but he had no other options.

"I can't do that."

"Damn it, you aren't that much of a coldhearted bastard." Then again, maybe he was. "A young woman is missing. Her mother needs to hear someone talk sense. Otherwise, she's going to go off on some damned wildgoose chase." He looked over his shoulder to make sure Kathryn hadn't overheard his outburst. She hadn't. "Even if this isn't your case, protecting and serving is still part of your credo. All's I'm asking is for you to do your damn job."

"Are you done?" the FBI agent asked.

Ryan grunted. "I guess."

"I can't tell Kathryn that Decker didn't kidnap her daughter because he may not be in England. We have proof that his image was added to a social-media post after it was taken. Same for the video from the Dallas Airport."

Like the first plunge of a roller-coaster, his stomach dropped to his shoes. "Is that even possible?"

"I've been working with a cybersecurity expert from the NSA who happens to be stationed in London. He says it's possible, but not easy. Seems like you were right when you suggested that someone was helping Decker. Any idea who?"

Decker never had friends, other than Ryan. "Not a clue."

"All this time, I've been wondering how the killer got out of the country. Or where he was hidden now. It seems like I have my answer. He never left Texas." Jason paused. Ryan's ears filled with buzzing. The agent continued, "Did the victim say anything else, other than it was Decker who took the girl?"

"He said she was being kidnapped for revenge."

"Revenge?" Jason echoed. "Because Kathryn was first on the scene at his last hiding place?"

His chest felt as if it were being torn in two. He rubbed his breastbone. "That's what she thinks."

"I'll get a flight back to San Antonio as soon as it can be arranged. In the meantime, my people will come to Encantador. I'll contact Isaac, too." He paused. "If Decker did take Kathryn's daughter, he'll post about it soon. And we only have until Sunday to save her life."

Ryan knew that everything Jason said was true. But there were other things he knew to be true as well. Decker was out for revenge. But so was Ryan. He'd do anything to help the woman he…

No. Now wasn't the time to name his feelings. He had to find Morgan and get her back. Then, he needed to face Decker—and finish him.

Chapter 16

The time on Kathryn's phone read 4:17 a.m.

Her daughter had been kidnapped at approximately eight o'clock the previous evening. The game had been suspended, and Brock was staying with friends with a sheriff's deputy guarding the house 24/7. She'd gone home briefly to change into her uniform and get her car.

A statewide manhunt had been launched to find Decker and Morgan. So far, neither had been found. Everyone knew what Decker planned to do next. He was going to livestream Morgan's murder. If she didn't save her daughter in the next twenty hours, it'd be too late.

She sat in the computer lab at the Center. With their supercomputers, the Center was able to set up a secure video call between Kathryn and four others. Isaac Patton was in San Antonio. Jason Jones was on a private jet that had been furnished by the FBI. He was somewhere over the Atlantic Ocean as they spoke. In London was the cybersecurity expert from the NSA, Theo Fowler. It was Theo who confirmed that the images of Decker had been added to photos and videos. Mooky Parsons, the sheriff, was still in Mexico, but he was also on the call. His flight home was in the afternoon, and he was expected back in Encantador around midnight.

Aside from Kathryn, there were three other people in the room. Michael O'Brien, Hal the computer expert, and Ryan. To be honest, there wasn't a reason—official or otherwise—for Ryan to be part of the briefing. But she liked having him with her, so maybe his support was reason enough.

"It looks like Decker used a stolen car to transport Morgan. As per his modus operandi, he took an older-model car without GPS tracking. This is where the car was found." A large screen was filled with a map of the county. A red star marked a section of road that was rarely traveled. Everyone on the call could see the map. She finished her briefing with "From there, the trail goes cold."

Her throat was tight as she tried to swallow down her rage, sorrow, and worry. At her very core, she was terrified of what might happen to her daughter. On the surface, she had to be calm and in control. Otherwise, she'd be pushed out of the investigation, judged to be the emotional mother.

"Do we have anything else?" Jason asked.

Everyone on the video call shook their heads.

"How in the hell does this guy simply disappear?" Isaac asked.

Ryan raised his hand. "Back when we worked together, we figured out how to get away before we ever agreed to committing a crime." He paused. "Decker always had a car that wasn't connected to anyone—especially him—so nobody was looking for it. But it was legally purchased and registered. It'd be parked out of the way. Then, he'd drive to that spot and take off."

The plan was brilliant in its simplicity. And yet... "How does this help us?" she asked.

"Well, there are two things. First, he'd have to have a car near where he left the stolen vehicle. There's no way for him to transport Morgan without another ride," Ryan said.

Hearing her daughter's name was an arrow to her heart.

"Which means what?" she asked, her voice hoarse.

"My guess is that he's always had another car hidden for transport—even after he left the abandoned farmhouse with your cruiser." Ryan paused. "Where was the final car found last week?"

After stealing her cruiser, he'd taken four other vehicles.

"I can show you right now." Hal tapped on the keyboard. He created another star, this one blue, and placed it where the final stolen car was found.

"I'll be damned," said Isaac. "The cars were left close to one another."

He was right. Each car had been abandoned on a county route. The roads ran parallel to each other for three or four miles before veering off in different directions. The spots were separated by two miles of hill country and nothing else.

"Any idea what's in between those roads?" Jason asked. "Perhaps he's hiding somewhere between those two spots."

Kathryn knew the whole county better than anyone other than Mooky. "I can't think of an old house in that area. And there's definitely not someplace where he'd be able to set up internet access."

"There's no dwelling around for miles," Mooky confirmed. "Although there's a trail from one county route to the other. Sometimes people go out there to hike and ride mountain bikes and such."

"It'd be easy for Decker to leave a car on one road and walk to the other," said Ryan.

"Yes, it would," Mooky confirmed. "Folks do it all the time."

Folding his hands together, Ryan leaned his elbows on the table. Narrowing his eyes, he stared at the map. "I know he's close. But where?"

Nobody had an answer to that question.

After a moment, he spoke again. "Decker's somewhere on the southern road."

"That's decisive. What makes you say that?" Isaac asked.

"Decker and I used to meticulously plan his jobs. Like I said, we also knew how he planned to escape. If it were me, I'd tell him not to be on the road for long with a victim. I bet he drove straight from the kidnapping to where he left his getaway car. Then, he drove to wherever he's keeping Morgan."

"You're assuming a lot," said Isaac. "Decker's been known to steal three or even four cars while getting away."

"That's true. But he's not trying to get away. He's trying to transport Morgan. Getting her out of one car and into another is the hardest part of a kidnapping. An unexpected motorist could drive by and see the exchange. Morgan might land a lucky punch in a fight. Basically, one simple thing could go wrong and the victim could escape. He wouldn't expose himself to that same risk time and again."

As Kathryn listened to Ryan's explanation, she had two opposite thoughts. First, it was no wonder that Decker had gotten away with so much and for so long. But she was a sworn law-enforcement officer. It didn't matter what Ryan's rap sheet said after helping the feds. He was still a criminal.

Second, she really did care about him. How had she let herself fall so hard and so fast?

Good Lord, now was not the time to worry about her feelings.

Isaac said, "I assume that CSI looked for tire prints."

"They found only one set of tracks. Those belonged to the stolen vehicle we recovered," she said. But she was willing to try anything if it meant finding a clue to her daughter's whereabouts. "But we can widen the search and look again in the daylight."

"I think that'd be best," said Mooky. "What else do we know?"

"Morgan wasn't taken at random," said Ryan. "He chose her."

"You mean he took my daughter to get even with me."

A look flashed in his eyes. It was gone as soon as it appeared. But what had it been? Sadness? Misery? Regret? It was all of that and more. Well, Kathryn didn't want his sympathies. She pinned him with a razor-sharp glare, daring him to say more.

"At the moment, motive doesn't concern us," said Jason. "We all know what Decker plans to do. What we need is a plan to find and stop him."

"I want to know how he is getting around so easily. And who's adding his image to pictures and videos? It seems like the killer has made some talented and well-moneyed friends," said Isaac.

"Theo has some theories as to who might be helping Decker," said Jason.

The cybersecurity expert had been silent through the exchange. He now sat taller in the seat and leaned forward. "Being able to add images after something's been posted—or to hack into a security system and add video—takes a special kind of talent. It's a skill set even the best cyber people don't usually have. I made a list of everyone who might have those capabilities. Then, I looked at the images for an electronic fingerprint of sorts."

Her head swam. "Did you find anything?"

"I did," said Theo. "But it's not good news. Years ago, the NSA hired a young hacker, who went by the name of Seraphim, to try to get past our latest firewalls. They were more than competent and found several ways to breach our security. That job led to another and then another. After a few years, Seraphim had gained our trust." He paused. "It was all misplaced. In the end, they stole government secrets and sold them to our enemies."

Isaac asked, "You think Seraphim is helping Decker?"

Theo nodded.

"Can that help us find my daughter before...?" She

knew what Decker planned to do to Morgan. It's just that she refused to say the words.

Theo shook his head.

"Why not? You said they'd left an electronic fingerprint."

"Just like a physical fingerprint, you can only find it after it's been left—not before. And nobody knows Seraphim's real identity, or where they are now."

"I have a question," asked Michael. "What does a hacker who sells state secrets have in common with a guy like Decker?"

"Seraphim wanted to cause a global incident. According to them, there should be a new world order. I imagine that Decker is a part of the plan to sow chaos," Theo said.

"Where does that leave us?" Frustration burned a hole from the inside of her chest. "We've got nothing and no way to find Decker—or save my daughter." Even she heard the anguish in her voice.

"We've got clues to follow," said Ryan.

Sure, he was trying to make her feel better. But she wasn't in the mood to be soothed.

"It's my daughter who's stuck with that monster," she snapped.

Her mind was a jumble of thoughts. It was impossible to even think straight.

Theo said, "I might not be able to find Seraphim. I can use info from the NSA's satellites. I'll upload all images for the past two weeks. I can't guarantee that we'll find anything, but we might get lucky."

Is that what it had come to? She was now relying

on luck. Well, she supposed that she'd take anything. "Yeah," she said, suddenly exhausted. "Thanks."

She checked the time. It was almost 5:00 a.m. She rose from her seat. Her whole body ached. Exhaustion pulled her toward a deep, dark void. But if she allowed herself to slip into the blackness, she'd never find her way back to the light. "The sun will be up in an hour. I'll head over to where we found the car. Maybe we'll find something if we increase the search parameters."

Ryan stood as well. "I'll go with you."

"Hey, guys," said Hal. "Wait up. Something just got posted that you'll want to see."

One of the large monitors on the wall winked to life. Morgan's tear-stained face filled the screen. She was gagged, and her arms were bound behind her with rope. The same rope was tied to her feet, and a noose was looped around her neck. If Morgan moved at all, the ropes tightened, and she'd get choked.

Staring at the face of her child, a wave of shock rolled over Kathryn. Balling her hands into fists, she focused on her breath, on the sound of her own pulse, on Morgan's face.

With her daughter's image still filling the screen, Decker's voice came from off-camera. "This is what you've all been waiting for. You know what surprised me—although maybe it shouldn't—is how many of you people have already accessed the link. There are almost a million of you sick bastards out there. That's why I decided to go live a little early. Just so you could see what terrified really looks like."

The screen went black.

"He's not logged into the internet anymore," said Hal. Then to Theo, he said, "Were you able to track him?"

Theo shook his head. "I didn't get a lock on the location, but I'll see what was left behind in the broadcast."

As the IT specialists talked, speaking a language that was all but foreign to her, Morgan's face was burned into her brain, her heart, her soul. Kathryn's hands started to tremble. The walls in the small room closed in on her from all sides. "I need some air."

Without looking back, she marched from the room. The computer lab led to the forensics lab. From there, she pushed open the front door and stepped outside. The sky was black, and the air sizzled with heat. She walked to the edge of the sidewalk. Her legs refused to hold her any longer, and she sank onto the curb.

"Hey."

She looked over her shoulder. Ryan stood behind her.

"Hey," she said, her voice a whisper.

"I wasn't sure what you wanted. I decided to come out in case you need some company."

The last thing she wanted was to be alone. "I just couldn't think with everyone around." She pressed her palms into the concrete curb. The rough surface bit into her flesh. "I should get back inside."

Ryan sat beside her. "You can take a minute, if you need one." He paused. "There's no playbook for how a parent should handle something like this."

"Do you think I should step away from the investigation?" It was a question she'd asked herself more than once. "Can I really be the acting sheriff and the victim's parent?"

Ryan exhaled. "What do you think is best?"

"If Mooky were here, I'd let him be in charge." Admitting that she'd turn the case over to the sheriff left her hollow. At the same time, she'd gain nothing with bravado or false confidence. "I can't be an impartial law-enforcement officer when my child's life is at stake." Then again, she could use the agony to make her stronger. Or would she be crushed by the weight of hopelessness? She raked her fingers through her hair. "I don't know what to do."

"Back when I lived here before, there were a lot of late nights at the bar. It was part of the job. I didn't mind because it meant I got to see this." He pointed across the desert. In the distance, a thin line of gold ran across the horizon.

"Is this where you tell me that if the sun can rise every morning, I can rise from this adversity, too?"

He raised his brow. "I'd never say something like that. Just watch."

She stared across the desert. The sky brightened, turning orange and pink.

It was hard to appreciate the glory of a sunrise. Still, she said, "Beautiful."

"I hope it made you feel better."

"It did, a little, at least."

"Glad I could help." His phone trilled with an incoming call. He pulled the cell from his pocket. "It's Isaac. Mind if I take it?"

A flicker of hope came to life in her chest. He might have news about Morgan. "Go ahead."

After swiping the call open, he pressed the device to his ear. "Any news?"

Ryan hadn't turned on his Speaker function. It didn't

matter as she could hear Isaac's voice. "No news on my end." He paused. "I liked the way you thought in the meeting."

"Liked the way I thought?" Ryan echoed. "I just outlined how Decker and I used to commit crimes."

"You know how the NSA hired the hacker to find the weaknesses in their security system? It got me thinking. You have a unique perspective that'd be invaluable to Texas Law."

"Because I'm good at committing crimes, I'd be good at solving them?" Ryan asked.

"You'd be even better at preventing them, but yeah." Isaac cleared his throat. "Back when we were undercover, we didn't like each other much. Still, we worked well together. Basically, I'm offering you a job."

Ryan glanced at Kathryn. "Can we talk about this later?"

"Let me tell you one final thing," said Isaac. "It wouldn't be in San Antonio. I'm going to open a satellite office in Mercy. Texas Law will take one of the office spaces that Michael's trying to fill. Promise me that you'll consider it, at least."

"Yeah. Sure. I promise."

"Call me if you hear anything new."

"Will do," said Ryan, before ending the call.

Filling her lungs with air, she held her breath until she found the fine line of pain. She exhaled. "That worked out well for you."

"You heard that Isaac offered me a job," he said, slipping the phone into the pocket of his jeans.

"It sounds exactly like what you wanted." She didn't

have the bandwidth for any more emotions. "Congratulations."

"I thought you wanted me to leave town." He waved away his words, as if erasing writing from a whiteboard. "I have one priority. To find Morgan before anything bad happens to her."

"Bad things have already happened," she said. And then, "I think you should take the job."

He reached for her hand. She laced her fingers through his. On the eastern horizon, crimson and vermilion filled the sky. It was a new day. Right now, she couldn't think about anything other than saving her daughter. And yet she'd heard everything that Ryan said during the meeting. It was more than knowing how Decker thought—he had the mind of a criminal as well. She couldn't keep the acid from her veins. The only reason Decker knew about her community was because of Ryan.

She rose quickly, wobbling as she stood. "It's you."

"What about me?"

"You know what I mean," she said. "You helped Decker become the monster he is today."

Guilt was etched into each line of his face. "You're right."

How had she been so naive? So stupid? From the beginning, she'd known that Ryan was no good. But she'd been blinded by lust and hope and the tingling in her stomach every time he looked in her direction. Walking backward, she said, "You stay away from me, you hear? I don't ever want to see you again. I don't ever want to speak to you again."

Turning her back on Ryan, she strode toward her cruiser. Sure, she'd given him a ride to the Center. But she sure as hell wasn't giving him a ride back to town. Wrenching the door open, she slid into the driver's seat. Every cell of her body vibrated with hate and rage as she started the engine and backed out of the parking space.

She hated Decker for all the pain he had caused. She also hated Ryan for making her community a target of the killer. But mostly, she hated herself. It was more than the fact that she should've sent Ryan away but hadn't.

She hated herself because after everything, she still wanted him at her side.

Chapter 17

Sitting on the curb, Ryan watched the taillights of Kathryn's car as she drove away. He knew that Kathryn was right. He had created Decker.

Yet, he hated that his past caused a split between them. It left him with an interesting question.

What should he do next?

He could go back to the motel, get his dog and his gear, then leave. He imagined that few people would be sorry to see him go.

If he left now, he'd never be able to look in the mirror without loathing his reflection. He couldn't abandon Kathryn and her daughter now.

But she'd been clear. She hated him. She never wanted to see him again. It made helping her difficult. No, it made it impossible.

Rising from the curb, he knew what he needed to do.

His legs were stiff as he walked to the Center and opened the door. Standing next to one of the lab tables, Michael looked up as he entered the building.

"Hey," he said. "Any chance you can give me a ride back to the motel in Encantador?"

"Sure." He paused. "I thought you rode with the undersheriff."

"I did," he said simply. He didn't owe the doctor an explanation. "She had to leave."

"Uh, okay. Give me a minute to shut everything down. Then we can go."

He nodded. "I'll wait outside." Pushing open the door, he stepped into the parking lot and drew in a deep breath. He'd stood in this exact place countless times. The last of the stars were disappearing from the night sky and the horizon had started to brighten. The landscape was as familiar to him as his own face.

He knew what he had to do. Pulling the phone from his pocket, he placed a call.

Isaac answered after the second ring. "Hey, is there an update?"

"I was thinking about that job offer." Straightening his shoulders, Ryan was certain of his decision. "I've made up my mind."

Kathryn drove without seeing anything other than the endless line of asphalt. Sure, she was furious. The question was: What should she do now?

She pulled onto the shoulder of the road. A cloud of dust surrounded her car. Holding tight to the steering wheel, she wiped her face with her shoulder. Only then did she realize that she'd been crying. She had to get her emotions under control. Sobbing wouldn't bring her closer to finding Morgan.

Then again, there was someone who might be able to help.

She'd left him sitting in the parking lot of the Center. What's worse, she'd told Ryan that she never wanted to speak to him again. Or see him. She wouldn't blame him if he never wanted to talk to her, either.

Yet, for Morgan, she had to call a truce and ask for his help.

She inhaled a deep breath and counted to ten. After exhaling, she turned the car around in the middle of the road. Within minutes, she was back at the Center. She'd hoped to find Ryan still sitting on the curb. All the same, she wasn't surprised that he wasn't there.

A single car was parked in the lot. Lights from inside shone through the front door. She let herself into the building. The forensics lab was spacious and filled with light. One look around the room told her all she needed to know.

Ryan was gone.

She tried to draw a deep breath. This time, her chest was too tight.

Hal was still in the IT lab. He looked up as she approached the glass wall that separated the two labs.

Rising to his feet, he met her at the door. "Can I help you with something?"

"I was looking for Ryan," she said.

"He left with Dr. O'Brien. They haven't been gone long—only a few minutes."

"Any idea where they were going?"

Hal shook his head. "The doctor said something about dropping Ryan off at the motel."

Kathryn tried to smile but the expression hurt her face. "If you hear from Ryan or Michael, ask them to give me a call."

"Will do." After letting the door between them shut, Hal gave her a small wave.

She hurried out to the parking lot. After slipping behind the steering wheel and starting the engine, she turned on the emergency lights atop her cruiser. She drove toward Encantador and watched the speedometer climb to seventy miles per hour, eighty. She settled in at ninety miles per hour. Scanning the road, she hoped that she'd catch sight of Michael O'Brien's sleek blue car.

There was nothing.

A sign on the side of the road read *Welcome to Encantador. A Nice Place to Live.*

After letting her foot off the accelerator, she turned off the strobing light. She drove down the quiet and deserted street. It took her a few minutes to get to the motel. Letting her car idle, she stopped in front of the building. A dozen rooms stretched out in a row. Several cars filled the parking lot. Ryan's truck was gone.

So, he had finally listened to her and left town.

Well, after everything, she didn't blame him.

Yet, a hard ball of regret stuck in her throat.

The car used to kidnap Morgan had been found twenty miles outside of town. She headed straight to the location. By the time she arrived, the sun had fully crested the horizon. Pulling onto the shoulder, she parked on the opposite side of the pavement. Last night, a team of forensic investigators had scoured the area, looking for clues. Was there something they'd missed?

Ryan thought so.

She hoped he was right.

Turning off the ignition, she opened her door. Heat rolled over her in a wave. The desert spread out in all directions, and the silence was complete. There was no breeze to stir the hair on her neck. No call of a bird, circling its prey. It was like Kathryn was completely alone in the world.

In some ways, she was.

She refused to feel anything. It was the only way she'd survive.

Slipping on a pair of sunglasses, she crossed the road. A small marker still sat next to where a set of tire tracks had been found. Using an electronic database, investigators were able to prove they belonged to the stolen car. Kneeling, she picked up the slip of paper.

She heard a deep bark and looked toward the noise. That's when she saw him. Tail a wagging blur, Old Blue ran toward Kathryn.

"Hey, boy." She ruffled the fur on his back. "What're you doing here? Where's Ryan?"

The dog looked over his shoulder. Clad in the same Encantador High School Football T-shirt from the night before, Ryan sprinted up the side of a gully. "Old Blue," he called. His gaze landed on hers, and he skidded to a halt.

Her mouth went dry. Despite the circumstances, she wanted to smile.

The dog dropped to his haunches.

"You know, I can give you a ticket for not keeping your dog on a leash," she said, standing up.

He glared. "Is that supposed to be a joke or something?"

"Well, I guess it's not a very funny joke."

He shrugged. "It's kinda funny. There's something I want to show you." Without another word, he turned and walked down the hill.

The dog barked and ran after his master.

She jogged, trying to keep pace with Ryan. "Where are we going?"

"I found something," he said, without looking over his shoulder.

His truck was parked at the bottom of the ridge. No wonder she'd thought she was all alone. He'd walked fifty yards beyond his bumper and knelt. "I found these. They're tire tracks."

She stood next to him. A set of ridges had been formed from the ground.

True, he'd found a set of tracks. But were they from Decker's vehicle?

She didn't dare to hope these tracks were a link in the chain of clues. "I can take a picture of this and get it to SICAR." SICAR stood for *Shoeprint Image Capture and Retrieval*. It was a database where thousands of tread imprints—for tires and shoes both—were stored. "If they can do an analysis from a photo, we might get a brand or type of tire."

Otherwise, it was back to old-fashioned policing. The CSI team would come out to the location. A cast would be made of the tire print and then submitted physically.

Really, it'd be a waste of time. Morgan would be dead before the plaster was done drying.

The ground seemed to tilt. Kathryn focused only on her breath. Once the vertigo passed, she pulled her phone from her pocket. After opening the camera app, she focused on the ridges again and snapped several pictures. "Hopefully, these are good enough to find a manufacturer's match."

Ryan stood. "That's it? I thought you'd be happy."

"Right now, I can't feel anything." She didn't want to discuss her emotional state anymore. "What're you doing out here anyway? Aside from looking for tire tracks, I mean."

Standing, he dusted his hands together. "Me? I'm working."

That was news. "Oh?"

"I decided to take the position with Texas Law," he said.

Her heart skipped a beat. "I guess you'll be staying in town."

He shook his head. "Not necessarily. You were right when you said that I created Decker. He's my mess and I intend to clean up. After that…" He shrugged, using the gesture as some sort of answer.

She shouldn't care. Yet the sour taste of disappointment coated her tongue. "Listen, about what I said earlier—"

He held up his palms. "Don't apologize."

That's exactly what she'd planned to do. Now she was left with nothing to say.

He continued. "You should be furious with me. I'm furious with myself."

"I'm not angry with you—not anymore, at least." She took a step toward him. God, she wanted to lean in to his chest. To feel his arms around her. To listen to the soothing sound of his heart.

"I promise you," he said, closing the distance between them. "I will find Morgan."

She nodded. "Can we just move forward from here?"

"I'd like that," he said.

She blew out a long breath. "Well, I need to text the tire tracks to Hal. Come with me if you want."

"I'm with you," he said, "all the way."

She wondered about his choice of words. Were they meant to buoy her sprits or was there more? She couldn't let herself think about that now. Finding her daughter was the only thing that mattered.

Decker had installed a countdown app on his computer. He sat in the dark warehouse and stared at the screen.

Twelve hours and twenty-three minutes remained until midnight.

Then he'd livestream the murder and secure his place in history. For all eternity, Decker would be the world's most famous killer. The girl he'd kidnapped, Morgan Glass, lay nearby and cried quietly. He hadn't thought about what it was like to spend hours with a victim. But her constant weeping was getting under his skin.

He needed to do something and soon, or else he was going to explode. If he killed her now, all his work and planning would come to nothing.

His computer pinged. It was a message from Seraphim. After clicking the link, he entered the preset password. The hacker's plague-doctor mask filled the screen. "Everything's going as planned. The authorities are trying to find the origin of your latest post, but I've added so many layers to the encryption it will take an army of IT specialists a year of working to find you."

Decker didn't believe in luck. But the day that Seraphim reached out had certainly been fortunate. "How many people are signed up to see my...performance?"

"Right now, over two million people have gotten access," the hacker squawked. "I've implanted tracking on all their devices. I'm not surprised that there are so many people willing to watch a live murder. After all, society is a cesspool. What shocks me is how easily they gave me access to their computers."

Like he'd been sucker punched, Decker's stomach clenched. He finally understood. "This murder has nothing to do with making me famous or causing the world to burn. It's all about you gaining access to people's computers."

"It's not just their computers I want, but everyone keeps their life on their devices. It gives me a window into their soul. I'm sure there are a quiet a few people who would pay to keep their secrets hidden."

For the most part, he had a low opinion of humanity. It kept him from being disillusioned. Yet, he was disappointed. "Money," he spat. "This is all about money."

Seraphim waved away his concern. "You are about to make history. Soon, you'll be immortal."

He knew the hacker was playing to his vanity. But he didn't mind. Still, he said, "I don't like being lied to."

"I don't blame you. Which is why I have a gift for you."

A gift? "Yeah? What?"

"I did a little digging into Ana Pierce."

"I told you that she doesn't matter." He leaned toward the screen and glared into the dead eyes in the mask. "I also told you to leave my past alone."

Seraphim held up their hands in surrender. "Then, I won't tell you what I found. Forget I ever mentioned anything."

Their words were bait. He refused to walk into the trap. Yet, he sighed. "What'd you find out about Ana?"

"She has a son. His name is Seth."

He didn't want to care. He shrugged. "I figured she'd get married eventually and have a kid. Back when we were together, she wanted children."

"She's not married," said Seraphim. "She's never been married."

Who was he to judge? "So?"

"Do you know her son's age?"

He really didn't want to play games with the hacker. Then again, anything was better than listening to the girl cry. "How could I? Until a minute ago, I didn't even know that she had a kid."

"The child turned eleven years old on his last birthday. It was in May."

The hacker had his attention now. That was eleven years and eight months after Ana ended the relationship. The math would be right for the child to be Decker's son. "So?"

"You don't fool me," said Seraphim. "I can tell that you're wondering the same thing I did. You want to know if Seth Pierce is your child."

Decker's throat was suddenly dry. Without a word,

he rose from the seat and walked to the small refrigerator. From it, he pulled out a bottle of beer. He returned to the computer desk and twisted off the cap. After taking a long drink, he let the alcohol buzz through his blood. "Congratulations, you can add *mind reader* to your résumé. There's no way to know for sure if that kid is mine—or not."

The hacker tapped their keyboard. The ridiculous mask disappeared. In its place was an electronic copy of a birth certificate for Seth James Pierce. Scanning the document, he found what he wanted.

Name of father: Newcombe, Decker.

He didn't trust anyone completely, Seraphim included. Sure, there was a birth certificate. But the document might not even be real.

But what if it was?

Crap. It meant he was a dad.

With all the other women, he'd taken extra precautions. But Ana had been different. At the time, he wouldn't have minded if they'd made a baby together.

"You know," said Seraphim, their squeaking voice pulling Decker from his thoughts. "She was difficult to find—even for me."

He stared at the screen and said nothing.

"Don't you want to know all about your ex-girlfriend's life? Don't you want to know about your son?"

Taking a drink of beer, he exhaled. "Not really. What Ana did with her life is her own business—not mine."

It was then that he realized the crying had stopped. He looked at the girl. Even in the dimly lit warehouse, he could tell she was watching him. Looking back at the screen, he ended the video call without a word.

The girl's eyes were on him, tickling his skin. He rubbed the back of his neck. "What?"

She said nothing.

He looked back at her.

Oh yeah, he'd left her gagged.

"I know you heard everything the hacker said. I don't care what you see or hear. You know what's going to happen to you next. You'll have no choice but to take my secrets to the grave with you." He glanced back at her. Despite the fact that she was hog-tied, she shrugged. He mimicked her gesture. "What's that supposed to mean?"

She wasn't going to answer him. She couldn't. But if she could, what would she say? He was intrigued. Rising from his seat, he crossed the floor. Kneeling in front of the girl, he said, "I'm going to take this gag from your mouth. If you scream, there's nobody around to hear you except for me. You'll annoy me. Then I'll give everyone a preview of what's going to happen next." He pointed to the camera. "I'll tie you to a chair and cut out your tongue. Got it?"

Wide-eyed, she nodded.

After loosening the knot just enough, he pulled the gag from her mouth.

She gasped for air. "Thanks."

"Thanks?" he scoffed. "What're you thanking me for?"

She worked pressed her lips together and then opened her mouth wide, probably to ease some of her soreness. "I don't know. Only it's more comfortable without that rag in my mouth."

"Well, don't get used to it." He paused. "You heard that freak on the computer."

"About you having a son?"

"Yeah."

"First of all, what's up with their voice? That screeching is obnoxious." She drew in a long breath. "Talk about annoying."

"Agreed," said Decker. "But what d'you think? Are they lying about the kid?"

"Honestly, I'm not sure. It's hard to guess because you can hear their words but not their actual voice. Ya know." She shifted her hands and feet, trying to find a comfortable position.

Decker loosened the knot that kept her arms and legs tied together. It gave the girl another inch of room.

She relaxed a bit. "I do know one thing. You're lying. You care about having a kid. And you care a lot."

Decker's jaw tightened. "What makes you say that?"

"I saw the way you got tense when you heard the news. Your shoulders pinched together. You sat up taller. Your voice held an edge."

Had he reacted that much?

"You're pretty good at reading people."

"Not really." She made a face. "I'm just really good at lying."

Her answer surprised him. He gave a bark of a laugh. "The undersheriff's daughter is a liar. Who knew?"

"Everyone but my mom." A single tear leaked from the corner of her eye. It snaked down the side of her face until it was lost in her hair.

"Why you gotta lie to your mom?"

"I don't have to lie to her." She exhaled. The sound was filled with a lot of sorrow for a teenager. "I just do."

Now Decker was truly curious. "About what?"

"My friend Elliot and I smoke weed. Not all the time, but enough. She's smelled it on us before, and I told her skunks live under his deck."

He laughed again. "And she believed that bull?"

"I guess. Or she's too busy with her work or my brother, Brock the Perfect, to care."

Decker sat on the floor next to the girl. "What makes your brother so perfect?"

"First of all, he's athletic. All the girls think he's cute. He works hard in school, and he's always happy. It's like having a damn golden retriever for a brother. Everyone wants to say *hi* and pet him."

He laughed again. "Kid, you're funny."

"My name is Morgan," she said. "Not *kid.*"

"Seems like you're funny and brave. Not many people have the courage to correct me."

"I guess in some ways, I'm my mom's daughter. She's brave, too." She paused. "You wonder what your kid's like? Do you think he's like you?"

"You mean a killer?"

"That wasn't what I meant, but it's a good question. I was more wondering if he looked like you. Or sounded like you." A lock of hair slipped into her mouth. She spit it out. "Everybody says I sound just like my mom. It's weird."

"Until just a few minutes ago, I didn't even know I was a father. Not that I entirely believe Seraphim's story. I really haven't had any time to think about Seth at all," said Decker.

"What're you going to do?" she said.

It was a question he'd eventually have to answer. But for now, he said, "I don't know."

Morgan exhaled. "You don't have to do this. You don't have to kill me." The last two words came out as a squeak. "You're a father now. You know how precious life can be. You can drop me off somewhere and I won't tell anyone where you took me." Her eyes darted around the small room "Besides, I don't even know where we are."

Did Decker regret kidnapping Morgan? Maybe a little. But now, the world was waiting for her death. He couldn't walk away from this murder. "I get what you're trying to do," he said. Other victims had done it before. "You're trying to appeal to my sense of humanity. It's not going to work." With a shake of his head, he shoved the gag back into her mouth. "I'm not a decent man. In fact, I don't even have a soul."

Chapter 18

Kathryn pulled into a parking place in front of the Center. It was already 1:12 p.m., which meant that Morgan had ten hours and forty-eight minutes to live.

Ryan parked his truck next to her police vehicle. When he opened his door, Old Blue scrambled over his master and bounded into the parking lot. Ryan followed.

She watched it all yet remained frozen in her seat. Ryan knocked on the passenger window. She lowered the window, and a cloud of hot air rolled over her.

"You okay?" he asked.

She wasn't sure that she'd ever be okay again. "I'm just giving myself a moment."

"This is a lot to deal with. Take all the time you need."

The word *time* stuck a chord. With each second that passed, with each beat of her heart, time was being wasted. If she wanted to save Morgan—and for her, there was nothing else—she had to act.

She turned off her engine. Without a word, she walked from her car to the front door of the Center. She entered the facility. The air inside was cool and dry. It was only as perspiration dried on her skin that Kathryn realized she'd been sweating.

Ryan and Old Blue followed. The dog found a corner and lay down.

Hal sat at a keyboard in the computer lab. All three wall-mounted monitors were divided into six screens each. Each screen was filled with different aerial images. Some were of streets in downtown Encantador. Some were of deserted roads around the county. There was even an image of Kathryn's home.

They entered the lab, and Hal looked up.

He gestured to the monitors. "The guy from the NSA was able to get these images. I've been going through them, looking for something out of place. So far, nothing."

"We have pictures of tire tracks taken not far from where the car used to kidnap Morgan was found," said Ryan.

"We can do a manufacturers' search," said Hal. He tapped on his keyboard, and a desktop monitor winked to life. "You got those pictures?"

"I'll send them to you in an email." She found the photos in her camera roll and attached them to a message. She hit Send, the email leaving her phone with a whoosh.

In the other room, Old Blue started to bark.

What had gotten the dog so riled? Gooseflesh covered her arms. Fingers trembling, she unfastened the snap on her holster.

Ryan shot her a worried expression. "I'll see what's going on."

He opened the door between the two labs. At the same time, Stu, the gas-station owner, opened the outside door. The old man held a pizza box in both hands. "Whoa, boy," he said as the dog's barking continued.

"Come," Ryan commanded. Old Blue trotted to his owner's side and sat.

Stu held the box higher. "I saw all the cars and thought y'all might want something to eat."

The scent of pizza sauce and melted cheese wafted into the computer lab. Kathryn's mouth started to water, and her stomach rumbled. When had she eaten last? Was it the hot dog she'd had before the football game? It must've been.

"That's kind of you." Ryan reached for his wallet.

"No charge," said Stu, pushing the box forward. "I just want to help. And Ryan, it's good to see you again. Stop by and say hello now that you're back in town."

Ryan took the pizza box. "I'm not sure how long I'll be staying. But it's good to see you. Thanks again for the pizza."

Stu let himself out.

She hurried to the door between the labs. After pushing the door open, she stepped back to let Ryan pass.

"Man, I'm starved." Hal rose from his seat. He moved a stack of papers from the end of a conference table. "You can set the box there. Doc O'Brien keeps plates in his office."

Ryan lifted the lid of the box and fragrant steam filled the room. "I don't need a plate."

"Neither do I." She grabbed a piece from the pie and took a bite. The cheese burned the inside of her mouth, but she didn't care. Everyone ate silently and with relish. It was then she realized that a whole team of people—many of whom she didn't even know—were looking for Morgan. People, like Stu with his pizza, were willing to help the cause.

They all felt as worried and helpless as Kathryn.

Gratitude and guilt swept over her like a gale. She swallowed the final bite. "How long will it take to run a search of the tire imprints?"

Hal lifted another slice of pizza from the box. "Let me check." While chewing on a bite, he returned to the workstation. Using the mouse, he rewoke a monitor. "We're in luck. They were able to identify the tires." He read off the name of a manufacturer. "It looks like they're from an eighteen-inch wheel and haven't been made in the last six years. It also looks like the vehicle is probably a minivan."

Kathryn had driven a minivan when her kids were small. Most of her parent friends had as well. Their popularity had waned, replaced now by small SUVs. But that didn't mean that an older minivan was a rarity. In fact, it was the kind of car that people would look at once and forget they ever saw.

"I can send out an APB on a late model minivan." It wasn't much. What's more, it was going to end up with a lot of inconvenienced drivers and busy law-enforcement officers. Right now, she didn't care. "Any way we can narrow down which types of vehicles, to only look for the one that uses these tires?"

Hal typed in a search. "Looks like they're aftermarket, so they never went on anything new."

"Well, I'll send out the APB anyway." The slice of pizza sat in her gut like a rock. Perhaps eating wasn't such a great idea after all.

"Then again, if that van belongs to Decker, I doubt he's driving it around," said Ryan. "My guess, or what I'd counsel him to do, is to park somewhere that it wouldn't be seen."

He was right. If Decker didn't have the minivan on the street, there'd be no way to identify him by the car. Almost certainly, he was holed up somewhere with Morgan. She choked down a sob. "As a police officer, hearing those insights is invaluable. As a mom," she said and shook her head, "not so much."

"I don't mean to upset you," said Ryan. "But there is some good news."

Unlikely. "What's that?"

"Decker's driven the minivan before. We have images to look through. All we have to do is match the two."

Hal rose from his seat and returned to the table to grab another slice of pizza, "I can add search parameters to the images. The computer can look for us."

"How long will that take?" she pressed.

Hal took a bite and seemed to consider while he chewed. "Not long," he said, speaking around his food. "An hour."

To her, it seemed like an eternity. "Let's assume that we find a possible vehicle for Decker. What then?"

"Then, we figure out what comes next," said Ryan.

His tone was soothing, but his words didn't help her feel any better. Because with each second that passed, her daughter came closer to losing the ultimate game.

During the hour that the computer searched through satellite images, Ryan had taken Old Blue for a walk and purchased a bag of dog food at the gas station across the road. He spent a few minutes visiting with Stu. By the time he returned to the Center, it was after 2:00 p.m.

Less than ten hours remained, and they were no closer to finding Morgan.

For her part, Kathryn had called in the APB. An Amber Alert had also been issued. In less than sixty minutes, over two hundred and seventy-five minivans had been pulled over and searched. So far, none were associated with Morgan's kidnapping.

In the cyber lab, there was a running tally on the computer screen.

Report 96% complete.

Report 97% complete.

Report 100% complete.

Click here to view your report.

"Guys," said Hal, "it's in."

"What does it say?" Kathryn sat in a chair and rolled across the floor to sit next to Hal.

The computer generated a convenient spreadsheet

with a description of the vehicle. The date, time, and place it was picked up by a satellite were listed. There was also a link to the image.

In the week before the kidnapping, a minivan had been picked up by an NSA satellite ninety-five times.

Ryan dropped into a chair. "How do we organize all of this?"

"Hal, you're going to set Ryan and me up with monitors," said Kathryn. "Then, it's just old-fashioned police work. We're all going to look at each of the entries."

"I can do that," said the cyber tech. "What are we looking for?"

"First," said Kathryn, "we find out if the vehicle uses the same size tire. If the tire isn't right, we can dismiss the entry. Then, we look for discrepancies."

"Like what?" Hal asked.

"Like if a car and the license plate don't match. Or if the car is reported as stolen," said Ryan.

Kathryn leaned in to him, knocking her shoulder against his. "You'd be a pretty good cop."

Sure, he had skills. It's just that he'd gained them through dubious means. He gave a quick smile. "I just spent a lot of years avoiding cops is all."

"Kathryn, you take that computer. And Ryan, you go over there." Hal pointed to different workstations as he spoke. "I'm sending everyone the report and the ability to access the DMV's website. When you've checked out an entry, click it. That way, it'll get highlighted as finished."

Ryan rose from his seat and moved to his assigned station. Going through the list of cars was tedious work. After looking at ten entries, he'd found nothing. His neck was sore. His head hurt. And his back was tight. He stood, stretched, and checked the time: 3:17 p.m.

Less than nine hours left.

A sour taste filled his mouth.

"How's everyone doing?"

Kathryn leaned back in her chair and rubbed her eyes. "I've got nothing but…"

"But what?"

"But I can't stop because there's nothing else to do. We know Decker has my daughter. We know what he plans to do to her and when. What we don't know is where she's being held. If we could find his car, then we'd come closer to finding him. Finding them." She cursed. "I've been at this for over an hour, and only cleared nine entries. How 'bout you two?"

"I've gone through nine entries as well," said Hal.

"Ten," said Ryan.

She sighed, "That's not even a third of the list. There's got to be a more efficient way."

He considered her words for a minute. "We all agree that Morgan isn't a random victim. Decker chose her. It means that he was waiting for her at the game. But more than that, he knew she'd be there. How? Easy, he'd been following her all week." His pulse raced, leaving him jittery. "Hal, can you find all of the times that a minivan is near Kathryn's home?"

"Sure can." He typed and the spreadsheet appeared on one of the wall monitors. Seventeen entries were highlighted with a new color.

"Let's go through these together," he suggested. "That way Kathryn can let us know if the vehicle is legit or suspicious."

Kathryn rose from her seat. "Good plan. What have you got for us, Hal?"

The computer tech said, "The first minivan on the list is a blue 2012 van—"

"That belongs to Gladys, my neighbor," said Kathryn, interrupting.

"Are you sure?" Hal asked.

"I'm positive. She rarely drives and leaves her car behind my driveway all the time. I almost hit her side panel twice a week, at least."

Hal marked the entry as checked. "Next one," he said. "On Tuesday, this car that was parked down the street from your house, Undersheriff. The paint is dark gray or faded black."

The image of a darker van appeared on another screen.

Kathryn drew her eyebrows together. "I've never seen that car before. What's the license plate?"

Hal tapped on the computer. "The tags aren't visible in this picture."

"Does that car use the same tires as the tracks we found?" Ryan drew in a deep breath, trying not to get too excited.

Hal's chairs sat on rollers. He wheeled himself to another workstation. He brought up the list of cars that used the same sized tires. "It's a match."

He wanted to smile, but he kept his expression neutral. "You can alter your APB and Amber Alert," he said to Kathryn.

She flicked her fingers toward the screen. "Assuming this is Decker's car, we aren't any closer to finding him or my daughter. If he's hidden the car, no cop will run across him on the road." She paused. "In the end, it won't matter."

Her pain and anguish squeezed his chest, making it hard to breathe. "We'll find her. I swear." Even as he spoke, he knew full well it was a promise he might not be able to keep.

But he knew the killer. He'd personally helped plan dozens of crimes. If he were working with Decker, what would he do? "His comfort zone is the middle of nowhere. Is there any way we can expand the satellite search, say, twenty miles outside of town? But we need to search with purpose. Where else could he hide?"

"You mean another place like the abandoned farmhouse where he was hiding last time," Kathryn suggested.

"Exactly," said Ryan.

"There are a handful of abandoned houses in the county," said Kathryn. "The railroad used to have a line that ran through the northern part of the county. There are some buildings near the depot. But nobody has used those since the railway left the area in the fifties."

"Do you want to get a real-time image? Because if you do, then that's going to require a call to the FBI or the NSA or some other federal agency," said Hal.

Decker wouldn't just leave his car parked outside. "Let's see what we have from Tuesday. That's the same day the minivan was seen parked down the block from Kathryn's house. If it was Decker, he drove to and from somewhere."

"There's a farm off the interstate," said Kathryn. "The family moved out about five years ago." She gave Hal an address.

After a moment, he found the correct coordinates for the images. A dilapidated home, surrounded by crumbling outbuildings, filled the screen.

Kathryn sighed. "The property was flooded about three years ago." She bit her bottom lip. "There's another farm near that one." She pointed to the screen. "But there was a fire. The family took the insurance money and left. I'm not sure what's there beyond the foundation."

"We won't worry about looking at that property right now." Ryan was intrigued by what she'd said about an old railroad. He bet that Decker would be interested, too. "Can you bring up an image for the depot?"

The cyber tech typed on the keyboard, and after a few clicks, the image changed to an aerial view of three buildings in the middle of the desert. Weeds grew around the train tracks. Surprisingly, the metal structures still stood. Yet, there was no evidence that anyone was using the property now—nor that anyone had been there in years.

Disappointment burned in his chest. He'd been so sure. "Is this the only satellite image the NSA sent?"

"Let me see." Hal typed some more. "I have two more. The first one was taken on Friday morning, and the other is from a week ago, Sunday at four in the morning."

The two images replaced the first, splitting the screen down the middle.

To Ryan, there was no difference between the images, save for the direction of the sun. But the one taken in the early hours of Sunday was different. The area was dark, the buildings nothing more than outlines in the night.

He tried to recall where he was at 4:00 a.m. on Sunday. It didn't take long for the memories to surface. He'd just brought Kathryn home from the hospital. She was sleeping. He and Old Blue were on guard.

On the other hand, Decker had stolen several cars throughout the night. The last stolen car had been found by four. But if Decker was staying at the old depot, would he have made it back?

He looked back at the screen. Was there a clue in the photo?

"Just show us the night image," he said.

The large screen was filled with the murky picture.

"What're you looking for?" Kathryn asked.

"I'm not sure." He scanned the picture, inch by inch. "There." He pointed. His pulse jumped. "A light's coming from the largest building."

"Where?" Rising from her seat, Kathryn stood at his side. "I don't see anything."

"Look at the left side of the building, on the ground."

Everyone went quiet as they looked for what he saw.

"I guess." Hal's tone made it clear. The computer tech was unconvinced. "But all these buildings are made of metal. It could be a reflection from the moon."

Kathryn shook her head. "There was no moon that night. Saturday night we had the big storm. The clouds didn't clear until after sunrise." She swallowed and looked at Ryan. "I have to go and check out the old depot. Are you coming?"

He was going with her. Turning to Hal, he asked, "Can Old Blue hang out with you?"

"Your dog can stay here as long as you need." Hal's voice quavered. "But are you sure this is a good idea?"

She said, "I'm not sitting around and waiting." Her eyes were moist. She shook her head. "I'm not waiting when I could be doing something to save my daughter."

Ryan had to remember that Kathryn wasn't just the undersheriff but also a scared mom. The way she'd held it together was admirable.

"Are you coming?" She pinned him with her stare.

"You know I'd follow you anywhere," he said, his tone light-hearted even though his words were deadly serious. "Even to the gates of hell."

She nodded once and walked to the door. Following her, he realized how apt his sentiment had been. Decker was as close as anyone was to being the devil. That meant his lair could be nothing other than a fiery pit of damnation.

Chapter 19

The adage *You can't get there from here* was true of the old depot. During the Second World War, the railroad had built a spur near Encantador for transporting cattle to the Fort Worth stockyard and then on to feed the troops. After the war, the depot and tracks were abandoned. As was the infrastructure that served the site.

Yet, Kathryn knew where the road leading to the depot was. Correction. She *basically* knew where the road had been laid. Gripping the steering wheel, she stared out the side window. "It's around here somewhere," she said, half speaking to Ryan, half talking to herself.

"We might have an easier time getting out of the car to look," Ryan suggested.

He had a point. She pulled onto the shoulder, parked, and slipped the keys into the breast pocket of her uniform. Ryan had already stepped from the car. He stared out across the horizon.

Low clouds filled the sky and promised another storm. So far, the fat gray rain clouds had only trapped the heat closer to the ground.

"See anything?" she asked, coming to stand at his side.

"Maybe." He pointed into the scrub. "What's that?"

It took her a minute to find the spot. There was a path where the weeds didn't grow as high. "It might be a road. Let's check it out."

Together, they trudged over the rocky ground. Kneeling, Ryan picked up a flat rock. To her, it was unremarkable—just a stone covered in red dust.

"Asphalt," he said, breaking a piece from the edge. The inside was black tar and smaller stones.

How had she missed that clue? "We should get the car," she said.

Ryan didn't move. "How far out is the depot?"

Kathryn shrugged. "Less than two miles."

"We should go on foot." He turned to her. "Decker won't hear us coming. Then, what happened before won't happen again."

She touched the wound in her side. After Morgan was kidnapped, she'd forgotten all about being stabbed. "I've got water and binoculars in my trunk. Plus a little extra."

Turning, she walked back to her cruiser. The pull to find her daughter was strong. But she was going to be prepared this time. The first thing she did was place a call to Hal. He'd been coordinating all the other arms of law enforcement. "We've found the road," she told him. "We're going to walk. I'll be in touch *if* we find anything."

"And remind him to feed Old Blue," Ryan *called* out.

"Tell Ryan that he has already been fed, *walked,* and is perfectly happy," said Hal before she could *relay* the message.

"Will do." She ended the call.

"What'd he say?" Ryan asked.

"Old Blue is fine," she reassured him. Using *the* key fob, she unlatched all the locks. She opened the *trunk* and pulled out a prepacked bag. She unzipped the *main* compartment and checked the contents. Binocu*lars.* Matches. A first-aid kit. Four quarts of water. A bo*x of* extra ammo for her gun. After rezipping the backpa*ck,* she slipped her arms into shoulder straps and tighten*ed* the sternum strap across her chest.

"I can carry that, you know." He added quickl*y,* "And it's not a sexist thing. I'm trying to be consider—ate. You're still healing from a stab wound."

"I've got the bag because there's something else that I want you to carry." She took the key ring from her pocket and found the correct key. Lying in the bottom of the trunk was a long metal box. She unlocked it and lifted the lid.

"Whoa," said Ryan as he caught a glimpse of the Benelli M4 Super 90. It was the same weapon used by Navy SEALs. "That's quite a gun."

"Have you ever fired one before?"

"Not that exact type."

"Do you think you can?"

He shrugged.

"Then, it's yours."

Ryan lifted the gun from the case. Also tucked into the foam were four shells. He slid them into the stock, before pulling back on the slide to rack them all. "If we run into Decker, I'll be ready."

"Good. Let's go."

The broken road was easy to follow. A breeze began to blow, making the trek into the desert less oppressive. The sun stayed behind the clouds, but in the distance, she could see a wink of glass. "I think the depot's just ahead."

"You got those binoculars?" Ryan asked.

"Sure do." After dropping the backpack to the ground, she opened the main compartment. First thing, she handed Ryan a bottle of water. She also took one for herself and opened the cap. Neither one would be able to save Morgan if they suffered from heatstroke. "Stay hydrated."

He finished half in one swallow. "Thanks. I needed that."

She drank all the water in her bottle and stowed the empty in her bag. Then, she found the binoculars. Looking through the eye cups, she found the old depot. The buildings came into focus. The larger building of the three stood in the middle. It was surrounded by broken pavement, and a tree had the temerity to break through the blacktop and grow.

Certainly, there were no signs of life. She handed Ryan the binoculars. "I don't see anything, but you can take a look."

He raised the ocular lenses to his eyes and studied the scene. "I say we keep going. It's less than a quarter mile away."

After tucking the lighter into his pocket, he rolled off the cot. As he crossed the room, he could feel Morgan's eyes on him. He sat at the desk and jiggled the mouse to wake the monitor. As he expected, Seraphim had sent an encrypted link. After clicking on it, he entered the password.

The plague-doctor beak appeared. But the eyes behind the mask were wild. "You've been found," the hacker squawked.

He sat up straight. "By who?"

"The undersheriff and your former friend."

A million thoughts swarmed his mind. He wanted to know how they'd found him. And if he was surrounded. He'd never give up. But what was he supposed to do with Morgan? "Are you sure?"

"I just got an alert from one of the perimeter cameras. This is what it recorded."

The image on his monitor changed. The plague doctor was gone. In its place was a grainy recording of two people. Ryan lifted the camera from the ground. He stared into the lens. There was no sound, but his lips moved. Then, the video became a jumble of images. Sky. Rocks. Dirt.

Ryan had obviously thrown the camera. It crashed into the ground, and the screen went black.

Seraphim reappeared on the monitor. "I've been able to do an aerial search. There's only two of them. They're on foot. Backup hasn't been called."

In the corner, Morgan started to struggle against her bonds. Certainly, she'd heard that her mom was close. She screamed into the gag. Decker looked back at the computer. A new plan was already forming. "Start the live feed."

"It's not midnight yet," said Seraphim. "If you kill the girl now, you won't be following the dates of the Autumn of Terror."

"Who cares about that?" After tonight, nobody would remember Jack the Ripper: Decker Newcombe alone would be the most famous killer in the world. He didn't have long before Ryan and the undersheriff would be at his door. Morgan had to be dead before they arrived. Then, the real performance would begin. "Give me two minutes to set up the camera and the light."

Seraphim said nothing.

"You know I'm right. This is the only way."

They exhaled. "You'll be live in two minutes."

Decker moved quickly, collecting everything he needed. The chair. His knife. He unplugged the camera from the charger. Then, he grabbed the ring light on a stand. But even as he created his set, he still saw Ryan's face as he looked into the camera. True, the video hadn't come with sound. But it'd been easy to read the other man's lips.

"I'm coming for you, you bastard. This time, you won't get away."

From fifty yards out, the setup was obvious to Ryan. The generator was stored in one of the two smaller buildings. A long brown cord ran to the building that had once been the cattle warehouse and stockyard. A large bay door had rusted in spots, and light shone through the chinks in the metal. A satellite dish was hung under one of the eaves.

Ryan knelt behind a large rock. Kathryn was at his side. He could feel the pull of a mother to save her child. "I want to rush in there and grab Morgan and hold her to me," she said, her voice a whisper. "But I won't. Please tell me you have a plan."

"Decker plans to kill Morgan on the internet."

Kathryn squeezed her eyes shut, as if trying to block out the horrible truth. "I know."

"What if we stopped him from broadcasting?" It'd be only a temporary distraction, but it might be enough to save Morgan. "You turn off that generator, and his power supply is gone. I'll go in through the bay door and introduce him to this." He lifted his M4. "Then you'll come around from the back."

"Will it work?" She looked at him. There was so much hope and trust in her gaze that his chest ached.

Her question echoed in his soul.

Would his plan work? There was a lot that could go wrong. Hell, he didn't even know if Morgan was still alive. Or if Decker was still in the warehouse.

Holding the gun with one hand, he stroked her cheek. "It will work." He paused a beat. "You ready?"

She nodded once. "I am."

He started to stand.

Gripping his arm, she pulled him down at her side. "I—" Kathryn placed her lips on his, the kiss frantic, then broke from the embrace "—I'll see you on the other side." She sprinted toward the outbuilding and disappeared inside.

Moving as quickly and quietly as possible, he ran to the side of the warehouse. Pressing his back into the wall, he sidestepped to the large bay door. After years of weather and neglect, the door and wall no longer met. Peering through the seam, he could see only a sliver of the room. Yet, he'd witnessed enough for his blood to turn cold.

Sweat dripped down Decker's back, and his breathing came in short gasps. It had been a struggle to place Morgan in the chair. Despite the fact that she was tied up, she'd fought him at every step.

The light shone on her red and tear-stained face. The camera was on. Everything was being streamed online.

Turning, he faced the camera. "I know y'all were expecting to see this later tonight. But sometimes plans change. This is one of those times." He held his hunting knife. Using the blade to point to Morgan, he continued. "I'd also planned on giving you more of a show with her. But she got lucky and gets to die quick. Don't you turn off your computer when I'm done with her. After is when the real fun will start."

One quick flick of the blade across her throat and Morgan would be no more. He stood behind the chair and gripped her chin in one hand. She thrashed in the seat, sending the chair toppling to the side.

"Damn it," he growled.

After righting the chair, he pulled Morgan's hair until her head was pinned to the back of the seat. Holding the knife in front of her eye, he asked, "How much pain do you want?"

Then there was a pop. The overhead lights went dark. The ring light was no longer on. *What the hell?*

The bay door rolled upward. A wedge of light spilled across the floor. A man's shadow stretched into the warehouse, and Decker didn't need to see a face to know who it was. "Ryan."

"Let her go," said Ryan.

"You know I'm not going to do that." He pressed the knife into the soft flesh under her chin. The skin opened and wept blood. There was a boom and a flash of light. The scent of gunpowder filled the room. The gunshot had punched a hole through the ceiling. A circle of daylight shone on the floor. With the stock tucked into his shoulder, Ryan stared down the barrel of a shotgun. "Take that as a warning. Don't move or the next round goes through you."

He didn't doubt Ryan's sincerity. It's just that the old Ryan would've blown a hole through Decker's middle already. His old compatriot really had changed. Lifting his hands, he feigned surrender.

Holding the shotgun with one hand, Ryan kept the weapon pointed in Decker's direction. With the other hand, he worked on the knots that bound Morgan to the chair.

Decker knew this was the best chance. He lunged forward and reached for the gun, making it impossible for Ryan to aim. Sure, he was strong—but Ryan was stronger. He wrenched the gun away. Then, Ryan brought barrel down on his skull, holding the gun with both hands. The pain was blinding and the blow knocked Decker off his feet.

Before he could pull the trigger, Decker scrambled to his hands and knees. It was all about survival. Pushing past the roaring pain in his head, he ran for the door that led to the dark corners of the warehouse.

* * *

Once Kathryn turned off the generator, she ran from the outbuilding to the warehouse. The report of gunfire exploded in the silence. All at once, she thought of every bad thing that might've happened. Her eyes stung. She blinked hard, refusing to cry. Drawing her own weapon, she sprinted the rest of the way. The bay door was open, and she looked inside.

A bloodstain covered the floor. Morgan was tied to a chair. Ryan stood behind her daughter and worked at the knots.

Blood ran down her daughter's neck.

"Oh my God, what happened? Is she all right?" Morgan met her mother's eyes.

She holstered her gun and ran to Morgan's side.

"Decker cut her, but the wound's not deep," said Ryan.

Pulling the gag from her mouth, she kissed her daughter's cheek. "I can't believe we found you." Until that moment, she hadn't admitted the truth to herself: she hadn't believed the story would have a happy ending.

"Mom, I'm so happy to see you! I thought…" she swallowed as tears gathered in her lashes "…I thought I'd never see you again."

"We're here now, and you're safe. That's all that matters," she said to Morgan. Then to Ryan, she asked, "Where is he?"

Raising his chin toward the back of the warehouse, he said, "There, somewhere."

Through the open door, she could make out stalls and pens that at one time had been used to hold cattle. Machinery—a tractor missing a wheel, a sharp-edged tiller, and who knew what else—had also been stored in the warehouse and forgotten.

"I'm going after him," he said.

"No way." Her heart slammed into her chest. "Come with me. We found Morgan. We can get out of here, the three of us, together."

"How long do you think it'll take for Decker to disappear? But he won't be gone forever. He'll come back." He shook his head. "I have to stop him."

She couldn't imagine leaving without Ryan at her side. "No."

"Once she's free, you both get out of here," he said. "Head back to the car, and call for backup."

"I'm not leaving you."

Placing a fierce kiss on her lips, he stopped whatever else she had to say. "Just go."

Standing taller, he walked into the shadows. For a moment, she could make out his outline in the darkness, and then even that was gone. Working on the knot that held Morgan to the chair, she feared she had just seen Ryan for the last time.

Chapter 20

Decker stumbled through the darkness. His head throbbed with each beat of his heart. Somehow, he'd made it into a narrow corridor. On his right, oil drums had been stacked into a wall. On his left was a long line of enclosures, meant to hold a cow or two. His vision was blurry. He tried to focus on something. But what? He heard footsteps coming up from behind. Ducking into a stall, he crouched in the corner.

In the dim light, he watched Ryan as he passed. His gait was slow. He held the gun with both hands across his body. Then, he stopped and took a step back.

Touching a wooden beam, Ryan examined his fingers. Brows drawn, he searched the darkness. His gaze never landed on Decker. After wiping his fingers on his jeans, he walked on.

His best guess was that Ryan had found his blood.

Must've been that he brushed against the post, while staggering into the pen. It also meant he was leaving a blood trail—one that was easy for Ryan to follow.

If Decker wanted to get away, he had to staunch his wound. He sat for a moment and then scanned his surroundings. An old blanket lay in the corner. He picked it up. Rodent droppings and dust scattered into the stale air. The fabric was filthy and threadbare. But he didn't have any other choices. He pressed the cloth onto his scalp. A bolt of pain shot all the way from his skull to his toes.

The taste of rot coated his tongue. He swallowed down the urge to vomit and instead quietly spit onto the ground. He focused on his breath and after a moment, the pain lessened enough that he could think.

Ryan's arrival had ruined everything.

Had he really been smacked down during a livestream? Well, he hadn't done himself any favors by running away. He could only imagine the memes.

Grinding his teeth, Decker knew there was only one path to redemption. And that it ended with Ryan in a grave.

Kathryn dropped her backpack to the floor. The only light in the warehouse came in through the open bay door and the hole in the ceiling. It wasn't much, but a little was all she needed. After unzipping the top, she searched for her emergency knife. She cut the rope holding Morgan onto the chair. Without the bonds, her daughter slumped to the floor.

"Crap. That hurt," Morgan said.

"I'm so sorry."

"Just get me out of here." She could hear the panic rising in her daughter's voice.

Morgan's anxiety left her own pulse racing.

She didn't know where Decker had gone or if he'd come back. She had to get her daughter out of the warehouse and to safety. Nothing else mattered. Yet, she realized that Ryan mattered to her as well.

Slipping her shoulder under her daughter's arm, she pulled Morgan to her feet.

"Mom," she cried, "I can't walk."

"Are you hurt?" A protective fury filled her veins. "What did he do to you?"

Morgan was heavy in her arms. "He didn't do anything to me, but my legs won't work."

"You've lost feeling from being tied up for so long. But I've got you."

Blood still seeped from the wound under her daughter's chin. "Let me see that cut."

Morgan lifted her chin and grimaced.

Ryan had been right—the wound wasn't deep. But still she needed care. Setting Morgan on the ground, Kathryn looked in her backpack. She found a large bandage. After placing the sterile pad over the cut, she pressed the adhesive into place.

"Better?" She slid her shoulder under Morgan's arm. After lifting both her child and the backpack, they hobbled to the door.

Outside, the sky was dark as dusk. Dirt and bits of gravel skittered along the ground, blown by the wind. They were far from safe, but at least Kathryn could breathe. She reached into her backpack and found some water. "Here," she said handing the bottle to her daughter. "Drink this."

Morgan took the drink and clumsily opened the lid. Lifting it to her lips, she swallowed half the water. The rest washed over her shirt. "Thanks," she said, gasping.

Kathryn wanted to hold her daughter forever and ever. But she knew that if Morgan could stand on her own, it'd be best. Not only could they move faster but she'd be able to keep her weapon out and at the ready.

With one hand on her daughter's side, she stepped away. Morgan swayed and started to fall. Diving forward, she caught her daughter before she hit the ground. There was no way they could make it back to the road on foot.

Kathryn turned and looked at the warehouse. The bay door was open in a silent scream. Ryan was in there, somewhere. He could carry Morgan. But waiting left them both exposed.

Right now, she needed to think like a cop.

"What do you remember of your kidnapping?" she asked her daughter. "Do you recall the car Decker used to bring you here?"

"I was pretty terrified so everything's a blur." Morgan's eyes filled with tears. "But it was a dark-colored minivan."

So the search had turned up the correct vehicle. "Where is it now?"

Morgan shook her head. "I don't know."

The car hadn't been parked in the outbuilding with the generator. She hadn't seen it in the warehouse, either. That left them with one building to search. "Come with me," she said.

Even with Kathryn's arm under her shoulder, Morgan stumbled as she tried to walk. Finally, they made their way to the last building. The door was off its hinges, but inside was what she'd hoped to find. The car. The driver's-side door was unlocked. She pulled it open. "Get inside." She ushered Morgan into the vehicle. "Do you see any keys?"

Morgan flipped both visors open. Nothing. The cup holders and console were both empty. There was nothing in the glove box.

It was too much to hope that Decker would have left the keys in the vehicle. "Did you ever see a set of keys?"

Morgan shook her head. "Never."

Decker might have the keys with him. But if he didn't, they must be back in the warehouse. She knew what she had to do next, and her mouth went dry.

"I want you to stay in this car," she ordered. "Keep the doors locked. Even if Decker shows up and he has the key, you don't let him in. If you see him at all, use the horn. I'll come running."

"I can't be by myself again." Morgan gulped down a sob. "I don't want you to go."

Her chest ached. Pulling her daughter in for a tight hug, she whispered into her hair, "I know I'm asking a lot of you. But I need you to keep being brave. Can you do that?"

She blew out a breath. "I can."

After shoving the backpack into Morgan's chest, she said, "Keep this with you. There's more water. Drink it."

"Mom." Morgan's tone stopped her. "I love you. Be safe."

"I love you, too." Kathryn slammed the car door shut. "Lock these doors."

Morgan obeyed. With a click, she engaged the automatic lock.

Kathryn drew her firearm. With a final glance at her daughter, she ran toward the warehouse. Each footfall brought her closer to the unknown and her heartbeat thundered. She wondered about Ryan. She also wondered about Decker. If the killer was still alive, she'd be walking into an ambush. It didn't matter—she had to go back.

Walking through the warehouse, Ryan searched for the blood trail he'd been following. Somehow, somewhere, in the darkness, he'd lost the path.

The last time he'd seen a trace of blood had been near the pens. Turning, he retraced his steps. He found the stall. A smear of blood still stained the wood. He stepped inside. With his eyes adjusted to the darkness, he could clearly see drops of blood on the floor.

So Decker had been here. But where had he gone?

He had to find Newcombe before he escaped again. Or, worse yet, caught up with Kathryn and her daughter. Backing out of the pen, he inhaled deeply. The stench of old motor grease hung in the air.

From above came a metallic screech. Ryan only had a moment to look up. An oil drum somersaulted down. The metal rim hit his back, knocking him over. He only had a second to curl into a ball before the next container landed on top of him.

A thick liquid oozed over his shoulders. The stench burned his eyes and his lungs with each breath. The oil drums rolled to the side, clanging against each other as they came to rest. Eyes watering, he looked up.

Decker stood just a few feet away. "I may be destined for hell. But I'm sending you there first."

He held a metal lighter. Using his thumb, he rolled the spark wheel. Ryan didn't have time to think—only to react. Using the butt-end of his shotgun, he swung out with his weapon. The comb caught Decker's ankles. The momentum swept him off his feet.

The killer landed on his back at the same moment a flame caught on the lighter. The fire spread along the ground. Scrambling to stand, Ryan jumped back before the flames could ignite his clothes or hair. Aiming his gun, Ryan pulled the trigger. Then, everything happened in slow motion.

There was a boom. A flash of fire erupted from the muzzle. The stock slammed into his chest as the stench of gunpowder rolled toward the ceiling.

But Decker had been ready. The killer charged forward. He reached for the barrel, pulling it to the side. He screamed as the hot muzzle burned his palm. The shot scattered, punching holes into a stack of old oil drums. Sludge began to slide down the sides and pool onto the ground.

Decker still held onto the gun. Ryan kicked out, aiming for his chin. He missed, but his boot connected with the killer's shoulder. It knocked him down. Scrambling to his knees, Ryan rose to his feet.

Decker lay on his back. Flames danced along the ground.

Before the killer could lift his palms in surrender, Ryan pulled the trigger.

Click.

Damnit. The gun had jammed. Decker smiled and dove forward, reaching for Ryan's leg. Flipping the gun around, Ryan shoved the firearm down, hitting Decker in the head with the butt-end of the gun. The blow left the killer dazed. Ryan would have reveled in his success. But that's when the first flames caught the leg of his pants and started to climb.

Kathryn found the car keys on the desk. She gripped the ring tight in her palm, the metal teeth of the keys biting her flesh. She sprinted for the door. A single blast of gunfire erupted from the darkness.

She froze as her breath caught in her chest.

She didn't know who'd fired the gun. Or who'd been the target.

Could she really leave without Ryan?

Her stomach twisted into a knot. But she shoved the keys deep into her pocket. At least now Decker wouldn't be able to unlock the minivan doors. Weapon in hand, she rushed toward the sound of the gunfire.

Smoke hung in the air. It burned her eyes and her lungs. What had caught on fire?

"Ryan?" While yelling out made her an easy target, she had to find him. "Ryan! Can you hear me?"

He didn't answer. Using her sleeve to shield her nose and mouth, she ventured farther into the warehouse. Flames danced along the floor. The railing of an old indoor corral was alight. Sparks rose in the air. She took a step. Then another. And another. A wave of heat crashed down on her. She looked up: flames raced along the ceiling.

She couldn't stay in the building much longer. But she couldn't leave without him, either.

"Ryan!" she called out. "Where are you?"

An oil drum rolled along the floor.

She turned and that's when she saw them. In the middle of the inferno were Decker and Ryan. Both men were on their feet. Ryan's pants smoldered, and blisters covered his arms. Swinging out, the killer struck Ryan on the cheek. She felt his pain as her own. Despite the waves of heat that obscured her vision, she could see the determination in each man's eyes. And she knew this was going to be a fight to the death.

Ryan refused to lose. Gripping the butt-end, he lifted his weapon high. He brought down the firearm at the same moment that Decker charged.

The killer grabbed him around the middle and the two tumbled back. The gun skittered from his grip. Decker slammed his fist into Ryan's face. He shook off the blow and reached for the other man's wrist. He squeezed hard.

Decker screamed and reeled back.

Flames were everywhere. If Ryan wanted to escape, he had to go now. Otherwise, he'd be trapped in the inferno. But what kind of life would he lead if he let Decker get away again? He couldn't let the killer go free and hurt someone else that he loved. Kathryn's face flashed in his mind.

Then he saw her. For a split second, he thought she was a mirage in the blaze.

Kathryn stood only yards away. What the hell was

she doing? He wanted her to be safe. Not in this burning building with him.

He'd turned his attention to her for only a moment, but a moment was all it took. Decker scrambled to the gun. He brought the barrel up. It caught Ryan under the chin, and the blow knocked him off his feet.

Shaking his head, Ryan tried to stand. Decker slammed the butt into his back. It knocked him to the ground. Decker hit him again. And again. His side filled with a searing pain, and one of his ribs snapped. Rolling to his back, Ryan looked up.

Standing over him, Decker held the gun above his head. The hems of his pants had caught fire. He didn't seem to notice the flames. He sneered, "Looks like I was right. We are going to die, but you're going to hell first."

Tensing, he braced for the blow.

Kathryn couldn't let Decker shoot Ryan. But she couldn't risk causing an explosion by firing her own gun, either. Rushing through the flames, she brought her firearm down on the back of the killer's head. He dropped to his knees, then fell, face first to the ground.

Later, she'd wrestle with any emotions that might arise for attacking a man from the back. For now, she had to get Ryan and then get out.

Dodging the flames, she ran to Ryan. "Come with me." She slipped her arm behind his back. The stab wound to her side pulled and she sucked in a quick breath. Ignoring all pain aside, she said, "We have to get out of here while we can."

He sat up and cursed. "I think my ribs are broken."

She'd heard the crack. He might be right. "Let's get you out of here."

He stood slowly and took a step. Then, he stopped. "We can't leave him."

Oh yes, they could. For all his sins, Decker deserved to burn. "He kidnapped my daughter. I can't even count the number of people he's killed."

"Somewhere I heard that good people help—no matter what," he said, giving her a wan smile.

At least he had his sense of humor. Then again, she knew he was right. "I hate to have my words quoted back at me."

The path between the flames was narrower than before. But Decker was easy to reach. He lay on the floor, unconscious and surrounded by a pool of blood. She tried to find some sympathy for the man. It was impossible. "Help me get him to his feet."

Ryan grimaced as he bent down to lift Decker's head and neck. They hefted him to his feet. Yet, there was one more thing for her to do. She jammed her gun into Decker's side. "If he so much as twitches," she said, "I'm going to blow a hole in his side."

Decker's head hung forward. She wasn't sure if he'd heard her or not.

They made their way toward the door. Once outside, she exhaled sharply. "Drop him here."

She let Decker slip from her arms. Ryan dropped him as well. He landed on the ground in a heap. She held out her gun to Ryan. He took the firearm. His fingers grazed the back of her hand. An electric charge danced along her skin. She wondered if she'd always be excited by his touch. Lord, she hoped so.

She said, "You watch him. I'm going to get Morgan and the car."

"What's that?" He pointed toward the broken road.

A cloud of dust rose on the horizon. She stared for a moment. Then, she could see red and blue lights in the haze. Her knees went weak with relief. "That's backup. I wonder how they knew."

"Must be that Hal saw the livestream and told them where we were."

He was probably right, but really, it didn't matter. She placed a kiss on Ryan's cheek. "I need to get my girl."

After running to the outbuilding, she got her daughter from her hiding place in the minivan. An explosion came from the warehouse. The ground shook and flames shot out of the open door. Oily smoke wafted into the air. It mixed with the dust until the air was filled with noxious fog. Breathing hurt. Her eyes watered. But at least it was over.

Decker wouldn't get away this time.

Her daughter would get the care—both physical and emotional—she would need to heal.

That left Kathryn with one important question. What was next for her and Ryan?

Three state police officers led the caravan of law enforcement. They parked their cars around Decker's prone form.

One of the troopers placed the killer in handcuffs. "There's an ambulance on the way," he said. "Does anyone else need care?"

They should all be seen by a medical professional. "Ryan has burns, and my daughter's having trouble walking. There's a cut under her chin, too," she added, although the trooper could see the bandage.

Ryan said to Kathryn, "Make sure Morgan gets seen first. I'll be okay."

The ambulance stopped. One of the troopers helped Morgan to the waiting EMTs.

"You should go with your daughter," he said.

"I will. But first I want to make sure you're okay." She took his hand in hers. Turning his palm up, she gently traced his raw skin. "Does it hurt?"

"Not when you touch me."

She smiled. "What happens now?"

"I thought you'd be the expert in that. I assume Decker will be charged with a ton of crimes. Then, there will be a trial. But he'll go to jail for the rest of his life." He paused. "Right?"

His assessment was correct. "That's not what I'm asking. What's next with you?"

After pulling her to him, Ryan wrapped his arms around her waist. "That depends, Undersheriff. Are you telling me again to leave town?" He gave her a grin, and she knew he was teasing.

"I'd like you to stay." He was now employed by Texas Law. More than once, Ryan had proved he was a man who had changed. And wasn't it change she was looking for as well? Who knew what the future might hold for them? "We can start with right now and see what the next chapter holds."

Ryan placed his lips on hers. Despite the chaos, they were the only two people in the world. "I'll start with having you for now. But don't be surprised if we find our own happily ever after."

Epilogue

Two weeks later

It was Sunday evening, and the shadows were starting to lengthen as Ryan parked his truck next to the curb. He turned off the ignition. Old Blue sat in the passenger seat and looked out the window, his tail thumping like a bass drum. He knew how the dog felt, just seeing Kathryn's house surrounded him in a halo of warmth. He supposed it was happiness.

Yet, the latest report buzzed through his system like a caffeine high. He'd thought about texting Kathryn with the news but had decided to tell her in person.

In the two weeks since Morgan was kidnapped and Decker was arrested, a lot had happened in his life. First, he'd spent several days recuperating from a bro-

ken rib and a concussion. Kathryn had invited him to
stay with her—an invitation he'd accepted. His presence in the home meant that Brock had to give up his
room and sleep on the sofa, so Ryan had stayed only
as long as necessary.

He'd used the recovery time to find a place to live.
Turned out that Mae owned the whole building where
her restaurant was located. The floors above Over Easy
had been renovated to apartments and Ryan was able
to rent one that was fully furnished. For now, it suited
his needs. And in the morning, he'd start his new job
as an operative for Texas Law.

Opening the door, he got out slowly from the truck
and stepped to the pavement. Old Blue followed.

Across the street, Gladys sat on her porch. "Nice
night," she called out.

He waved to the woman. "It definitely is."

"Enjoy your evening. Smells like there's chicken on
the grill."

She was right—the scent of spices and smoke hung in
the air. "How's the light above your sink? Is it still working?" He'd done more than just rest and find an apartment over the last two weeks. He'd also helped Gladys
with some work around her house. Brock had helped.
The kid enjoyed learning about home maintenance.

"The light's perfect, as is the sink in the bathroom,
and the pictures you hung. Thank you."

He waved as he started up the walk. "Happy to help.
You have my number if you need anything else."

"That's a dangerous offer to make. My driveway
needs to be resealed."

He laughed, hoping she was joking. Although, in

truth, he'd reseal her driveway if that was what she needed. He might have a job now, but he'd discovered that he liked being useful. He liked being of help to people.

It helped make up for the past. For the unforgivable things he'd done.

The front door opened as he approached. Morgan stood on the threshold. "I heard you yelling down the street."

"Hello to you, too," he said. "How was your weekend?"

Morgan had gone to San Antonio to see Elliot, who was getting PT after the Decker Newcombe attack. She leaned over and scratched Old Blue behind the ears. "Elliot's ready to come home. His doctor says he should be released by next weekend."

He nodded. "Sounds like good news."

"It is. We're both lucky to be alive." She paused. "All of us are lucky, really."

"How're you?"

She snorted. "I wasn't even hurt." The cut to her chin had turned into a red line. She touched the scar. "Not unless you count this."

"Not all injuries can be seen, you know."

"Yeah, that's what my therapist says. But they don't really know what it's like to survive Decker, do they?"

She was right. "Still, talking will help." He paused. "You know, your mom has some experience with Decker. Me, too. You can talk with me anytime."

Folding her arms tight across her chest, Morgan pressed her lips together. Damn. He'd said the wrong thing. Talking to Morgan was the equivalent of walking through a minefield. He'd gotten too confident and had accidentally stumbled onto a land mine.

Sighing, she let her arms drop to her sides. "Maybe."

Maybe? He'd take that as a win.

"Mom and Brock are outside. You can hang out with them. I'm making my world-famous brownies."

"World-famous? That sounds pretty good."

"It is." Morgan slapped her thigh, trying to call Old Blue to her. "Who's a good boy? You want to come into the kitchen with me?"

Old Blue trotted over to Morgan.

Ryan grinned. "It's nice of you to notice that I'm a good boy, but I should really go and see your mom first."

"Not funny," she said. "I was talking to the dog."

"Be honest, it was a little funny."

Without turning around, she held up her thumb and forefinger, measuring a small space.

Yeah, he'd definitely take that as a win.

On the back patio, Brock was at the grill. Kathryn was sitting at the table, sipping a glass of lemonade. She looked up and smiled as he stepped out of the house. "There you are." She held out her hand to him. "I was starting to wonder when you'd get here."

He laced his fingers through hers. They fit together perfectly. "I had to take a call." He'd wait until they were alone to discuss what was said. To Brock, he said, "The chicken smells good."

"Thanks. I need lots of protein to keep playing QB." He looked past Ryan. "Where's your dog?"

"Old Blue is learning how to make the best brownies in the world."

"Morgan really likes having the dog around," Kathryn said. She filled a glass with lemonade and handed it to Ryan. "She might even be warming up to you, too."

"That'd be nice." He took the glass before sitting down.

"So, you start your job tomorrow..." Kathryn began.

"I do. Me and Old Blue will open the Mercy branch of Texas Law."

"I'm glad you'll be around. You'll get to see the whole football season," Brock said while turning off the grill. "The chicken's done. I need to get a clean platter. Be right back."

Ryan waited until the kid was inside before speaking. "About that call. Isaac told me Decker's going to be transported." Since being arrested, Decker had been at the San Antonio Medical Center, treated for a severe concussion and burns to his legs. He'd been guarded around the clock. During the same time, a complaint had been issued by Mooky for all five murders that occurred in Encantador and Mercy over the past year. The complaint had gone to a grand jury, who'd heard the case. They found there to be enough evidence to charge Decker with multiple counts of first-degree murder, and likely several second-degree as well. He'd been deemed healthy enough to come back to Encantador and be charged for his crimes. A trial would happen sometime in the future. And until then, he'd be kept in a regional jail. Kathryn knew all the ins and outs of law enforcement, so he didn't need to explain anything to her. Yet, she needed the particulars. "He's coming back for a hearing early next week."

She cursed. "He's just going to stand in front of a judge and hear the charges against him. The judge will ask how he pleads. Then he'll plead not guilty. Why in the hell does he need to be here? He can have a virtual hearing."

"Yeah, but since he won't get bail, he's going to be housed in the jail in Laredo until his case goes to court. He has a right to be close to his attorney to get a fair trial."

"You don't have to tell me all about the criminal justice system," she snapped. Kathryn held up her palms. "Sorry, I just hate to tell Morgan that he'll be in town again. Right now, she seems strong. Who knows what this news will do to her?"

He didn't blame her for worrying. She was a mom. Wanting what was best for her kids was her job. Kneeling next to Kathryn, he took both of her hands in his. Looking up at her, he said, "Decker's finally been caught. He won't get away this time."

She pinned him in place with her gaze. "You promise me?"

He knew to never make assurances with Decker. Still, he said, "I promise."

The door leading from the house opened. The evening was filled with a shrill scream. "Ohmigod! Brock, come quick. He's proposing."

"What? Wait. No." Ryan rose quickly. He understood how Morgan would get the wrong idea. "I'm not proposing. We were just having a serious chat."

"False alarm," she called to her brother, before going back into the kitchen and letting the door slam in her wake.

Kathryn held her hand in front of her face, hiding a smile. As soon as they were alone, she laughed. "It's not funny," she said, "but it is."

He chuckled, too. Placing a hand on his chest, he said, "That got my pulse racing. Who'd think that we'd ever, you know, get married."

She stood and walked to him. "It's not the worst idea in the world. I mean, not today or anything. But maybe. Sometime."

Ryan was always quick with a comeback or a joke, but she'd left him speechless. Actually, he did know what to say. Reaching for her hand, he pulled her to him. "I never thought you wanted us to be a permanent thing. You are a cop. I'm an ex-con. The two don't usually mix."

Wrapping her arms around his neck, she pulled him closer. "You and I are good together," she said. "The past doesn't matter."

"At all?"

"Here's what I know. You're a good man. You've proved that time and again. And besides…" She sighed and shook her head.

His interest was piqued. "Besides, what?" he coaxed.

He could look into her blue eyes forever. "I love you," she said.

Ryan's pulse started to race again. "I love you, too."

"It's settled, then." She placed her lips on his. "We are both starting over."

"To starting over," he echoed. But with Kathryn, there was more. "You are my second chance. Every time I hold you, I know where I am."

"Oh yeah? Where's that?" she asked.

"With you, I'm finally home."

* * * * *

Romantic Suspense

Danger. Passion. Drama.

Available Next Month

Colton's Dangerous Cover Lisa Childs
Peril In The Shallows Addison Fox

....

Operation Rafe's Redemption Justine Davis
The Suspect Next Door Rachel Astor

....

LOVE INSPIRED
Alaskan Wilderness Rescue Sarah Varland
Targeted For Elimination Jill Elizabeth Nelson
Larger Print

....

LOVE INSPIRED
Dangerous Texas Hideout Virgina Vaughan
Wyoming Abduction Threat Elisabeth Rees
Larger Print

....

LOVE INSPIRED
Deadly Mountain Escape Mary Alford
Silencing The Witness Laura Conaway
Larger Print

10 brand new stories each month

Romantic Suspense

Danger. Passion. Drama.

MILLS & BOON

Keep reading for an excerpt of a new title
from the Intrigue series,
POINT OF DISAPPEARANCE by Carol Ericson

Chapter One

The smoke unfurled like a suffocating blanket, obscuring Tate's view of the green pines in the distance. Despite the damp weather, sweat ran down his back beneath his fire shirt, which clung to him like a second skin. He hoisted his ax and buried it into a smoldering log.

The fire had already rushed through this area, but his hand crew wanted to make sure nothing reignited as the helicopters dumped flame retardant on the blaze, shifting to the right with the wind. He kicked at some blackened logs with the toe of his boot, and a flurry of sparks scattered in the air.

Turning around, he pulled the N95 mask away from his face. "I think we're almost finished with this area. The rain should be helping us out soon."

As if on cue, the skies opened, and a torrent of water pummeled the December forest fire, sending plumes of dark gray smoke billowing upward to meet the clouds. The sudden onslaught of rain turned the ashy ground beneath Tate's feet to mush.

His teammates whooped and hollered behind him,

the wait for the storm break finally over, making their job easier.

Tate yelled over his shoulder. "We're not done yet, boys. Let's break up a few more of these fallen logs. Plenty are still live."

To emphasize his point, Tate hoisted his pick ax over his head and brought it down on a smoldering stump. It hissed at him, as the rain soaked the wood, dampening the embers.

As Tate kicked at a few more logs with the toe of his heavy boot, the ground gave way beneath his other foot. He slid down an incline to the amusement of his crew.

Rivulets of water rushed past him, pooling into a muddy dip in the land. He grunted and propped himself up on his elbows, surveying the scorched trees before him.

As he scrambled to his knees they sunk in the soft earth, and he pitched forward. He thrust out a hand. It landed on a smooth rock, and he pushed against the solid object to gain some purchase.

The rock moved beneath his palm, shifting to the side. The eye sockets of a skull stared back at him. Choking, he snatched his hand back.

Like a faint echo, his teammates' voices swirled through the roaring in his ears. He licked his lips, his tongue sweeping through the wet ash clinging to his mouth.

"How long are you gonna stay down there wallowing in the mud, Tate? C'mon, man. It's almost quittin' time."

A twig cracked behind him, and Tate twisted around. "Stay where you are. We have a crime scene here."

James Clugston, his second-in-command, snorted. "What the hell are you talking about? The crime scene is where this firebug lit this blaze. We'll find it, but this ain't it."

Tate struggled to his feet, his legs rubbery. One arm windmilled for balance, as he planted his boots in the muck. "I found a skeleton down here, so I guess we have two crime scenes."

The whooping and hollering stopped, and James coughed and spit. "Are you kidding me? How old is it?"

Turning his back on the bones, Tate faced his teammates and took a deep breath, tasting the smoke from the fire on the back of his tongue. "What the hell do I look like, a medical examiner?"

"You look like a tired, overworked US Forest Service agent. Like I'm looking in the mirror." Aaron Huang stepped aside as Tate slogged up the incline.

James stood on a fallen, blackened log and peered down the gully. "Who are we calling for this? Dead Falls Sheriff's Department? I'm sure they'll be able to crack the case in about fifty years."

Despite Tate's agreement that the Dead Falls Sheriff's Department was useless, his crew's laughter rubbed him the wrong way. He snapped. "Have some respect. That's someone's kid."

Aaron choked. "Kid? That's a kid's skeleton down there? I thought you didn't know crap about forensics."

Tate gulped. Was it a kid's skeleton? Did the skull seem small? "I—I just mean, that's someone's family member. I don't know the age or the sex or anything else, but we'd better call someone who can figure that out before we trample all over everything."

Cocking his head, James said, "Haven't we already done that? We just put out a major fire on top of this crime scene."

"As incompetent as he is, we need to start with Sheriff Hopkins." Tate unzipped his vest and dug in his pocket for his cell phone.

His thumb quivered as it hovered over the numbers on the display. Was Hopkins too inept to handle the discovery of these bones? One part of Tate hoped so. He wasn't sure he wanted to know the identity of the person in that shallow grave.

BLANCA LOPEZ STEPPED off the ferry from Seattle to Dead Falls Island, rolling her suitcase beside her and clamping her laptop bag between her arm and her body. Her heels clicked authoritatively on the concrete dock, even though she hadn't a clue where she was going.

The words of her mentor, Manny Rodriguez, pinged in her brain. *Always act like you know what you're doing and where you're going.* Even though she now despised Manny, he had gotten a few things right.

She mumbled, "Got it, Manny."

"Ah, miss, er, ma'am?"

She spun around so quickly her heel caught in a crack in the concrete and she stumbled. The young deputy caught her arm, a sea of red suffusing his baby face. "Yeah, sorry."

She flicked her ponytail over her shoulder and straightened her shoulders. "No need to apologize, Deputy. You saved me from an embarrassing start to my assignment."

Dropping her arm, he said, "I'm Deputy Fletcher."

Blanca thrust out her hand. "Good to meet you, Deputy Fletcher. I'm FBI Special Agent Blanca Lopez."

When he took her hand, she squeezed hard to make up for her earlier klutziness. Had Manny ever fallen on his face when meeting the local law?

When she ended the handshake, Fletcher flexed his fingers and said, "Do you want me to take you to your hotel or straight to the station? We have a car for you at the station."

"I think station." She jiggled the handle of her suit-case. "I can dump my stuff in the car, maybe have a quick meeting with Sheriff Hopkins and pick up any files he has for me."

"Sounds good, ma'am. Can I take your bags for you?"

Blanca wrinkled her nose. "You can call me Agent Lopez, Deputy, and I can handle my own bags."

"Sure, ma— Agent Lopez." He strode ahead of her, his back stiff. "This way to the car."

Blanca bit her lip. Manny always told her to command respect, but she didn't want to get off on the wrong foot with the locals. Manny never seemed to care about local law enforcement, but Blanca had come to realize it helped the investigation if they didn't hate you. Manny wasn't always right.

She cleared her throat. "The island looked beautiful coming in on the ferry. So green. Are the falls dead? Is that the reason for the name?"

"Dead?" Fletcher cranked his gaze over his shoulder and raised his eyebrows. "Not sure what a dead waterfall would look like, but no. It's called Dead Falls because the angle on that water is a dead drop. Get it?"

"Makes sense." A lot more sense than a dead waterfall. What was a dead waterfall?

Her high heels wobbled on a pebble in the parking lot, and she took a little hopping step to avoid further embarrassment.

She eyed the suitcase trundling beside her over the rough asphalt. She'd filled it with similar work clothes—skirts, slacks, jackets, blouses and heels. She just hoped her new hiking boots would work out here and that she'd packed enough jeans and sweaters to last for the duration of her stay, and that depended on how much information the Dead Falls Sheriff's Department had on her cold case.

Maybe that fire a few days ago had already done her work for her. Case closed if the bones exposed by that blaze belonged to Jeremy Ruesler…or at least that part of the case solved. They could put Jeremy down as a murder instead of a missing child, but most law enforcement agencies and probably the poor boy's family already knew that.

If that skeleton did belong to Jeremy, they still

needed to figure out who killed him—and she had a perfect starting point for that.

Fletcher pointed out a few landmarks on their drive from the dock to the station. The rugged terrain of the island that she'd spied from the ferry spread inland, covered by dense forest and rushing bodies of water, including those falls. She'd never been much of an outdoorsy girl, but the sight of that deep green and the smell of pine mingling with the salt of the ocean had caused prickles to rush across her skin. The atmosphere of the island charged her with a sense of awakening, a new start, and she sat on the edge of the passenger seat, drinking in Fletcher's impromptu guided tour. God knew she needed a new start.

By the time the deputy pulled into the parking lot of the Dead Falls Sheriff's Station, Blanca's newfound appreciation of the world hit reality. The beige, one-story stucco building looked like police stations all across the country. She had a hard time believing the course of her future resided within those prosaic walls, but she *had* turned a corner this past year, and this assignment was going to be the culmination of her reset.

She could almost hear Manny's low laugh in her ear. *Follow me, kid, and I'll steer you right.*

She curled her fingers around the strap of her purse. Manny had steered her straight to hell. Maybe the fresh air of Dead Falls Island could blow his memory right out of her mind.

"Agent Lopez?" Fletcher sat beside her, his door

open, one foot already planted on the parking lot. "This is it."

"That didn't take long. Thanks for the guided tour." She flashed him a quick smile before releasing her seat belt and pulling the handle of the door.

The deputy waited for her at the entrance of the station and held open the door for her. "Would you like me to transfer your suitcase to the trunk of your car, Agent Lopez?"

"Whatever's most convenient for you, Deputy Fletcher."

"That way, when you're done talking to Sheriff Hopkins, I can just hand you the keys to the car and you can be on your way. There's a GPS in the car, so you can follow that to your hotel."

"That works for me. Thanks." She walked through the swinging door he held open for her and followed him down a short hallway. Her heel taps echoed in the mostly empty station. All patrol cars must be out on duty. These small stations definitely didn't have the same buzz as their big-city counterparts. The fact that they couldn't handle homicide investigations didn't surprise her. It had been a PI and a forensic psychologist who had solved the latest murder in Dead Falls. No wonder they'd had this cold case on the books for the past nineteen years.

The clicking of fingers on a keyboard intensified as they drew closer to the end of the hallway. Deputy Fletcher tapped on an open door, and the clicking stopped.

"Sheriff Hopkins, I have FBI Special Agent Blanca Lopez with me."

Blanca peeked around the corner of the office door, and a balding man with crumbs on the chest of his uniform stood up behind the desk. "Thanks, Fletch. Agent Lopez, welcome to Dead Falls Island. C'mon in. Car ready, Fletch?"

"Yes, sir. I'm just going to move Agent Lopez's suitcase from the squad car to the sedan…and the other stuff." Fletcher backed out of the sheriff's office awkwardly, his long legs almost not up to the intricate maneuver.

Blanca thanked the deputy again and stepped into Hopkins's office. Family pictures populated the bookshelf behind his desk, and plaques and awards dotted the wall. Her gaze tracked across his messy workspace, noting the absence of anything that looked like cold-case files.

Clearing her throat, she reached over the desk to shake hands. She didn't give this one the death squeeze, as his hand lay limp and damp in her own. When they broke apart, she resisted the urge to wipe her palm on her slacks.

She shuffled back, and when the back of her knees touched the edge of the chair, she sat. "Thanks for having me here, Sheriff Hopkins."

Smiling, he folded hands. "When the FBI calls and tells you they want to look into one of your cold cases, you jump."

"We appreciate the response." She settled her laptop case on the floor. "I'm assuming you haven't gotten any DNA results back from the bones, yet?"

"Nope." He transferred a batch of papers from one side of his desk to the other. "We don't have the familial DNA yet for comparison."

She widened her eyes. Were the locals just waiting for the FBI to do all the work? "Is the Ruesler family still on the island?"

"The mother is. She's not being particularly cooperative. Never was, after the initial investigation failed to locate her boy." Hopkins finally folded his hands as if to keep them from fidgeting among the mess on his desk.

"I would think…" Blanca rubbed her chin. "No, I take that back. Maybe she doesn't want to know. Some people would prefer to have that closure, and some would rather keep believing."

Hopkins lifted his rounded shoulders, spreading his hands, as if he'd never even considered the matter. "Maybe as an outsider, you can get her DNA."

"I'll try." She bent forward to retrieve a notebook and pen from the side of her bag, her ponytail slipping over her shoulder. "Is there anything you can tell me about the site where the skeleton was found? Any items there beside the bones?"

His rather dull eyes, a muddy gray, stared at her. He blinked once. "I wasn't there. US Forest Service Agent Tate Mitchell found the remains while wrapping up a forest fire."

Blanca gripped the arms of her chair, as a zing

shot up her spine. Tate Mitchell found the remains? How had she missed that all-important detail?

"Tate Mitchell? You mean the one…?"

Hopkins nodded. "Yep. Strange, isn't it?"

Strange and fortuitous at the same time. Anxious to end her pointless interview with Hopkins and start the real investigation, she shoved the notebook back in her bag, her hand hovering over the strap. "The files. Do you have the cold-case files?"

Hopkins sat back in his chair, his hands folded over his paunch, a satisfied smile on his lips. "I asked Fletcher earlier to put them in the trunk of the car we're loaning you for your stay. You'll find them next to your luggage, most likely."

"Perfect." She sprang up from the chair, hauling her bag with her. "Thanks for your time."

Hopkins nodded, a look of relief spreading across his face as he eyed the half-eaten sandwich on his desk. "Anything we can do for you, just ask."

Blanca hoisted her bag over her shoulder and stopped at the door. "One more thing."

Hopkins's hand paused, halfway to his sandwich. "Yes?"

"Do you know where I can find Tate Mitchell?"

After Hopkins scribbled down directions to Mitchell's cabin, Blanca clutched the piece of paper in her hand and strode from the station. As she pushed through the glass door, a fat drop of rain plonked on the back of her hand.

She glanced at the darkening skies. Something had to keep this island green.

Deputy Fletcher emerged from a dark sedan and waved. "I got your car, Agent Lopez. Suitcase in the trunk."

Taking a zigzag path as if she could avoid the scattered rain, she navigated to the open driver's-side door. "Thanks, Deputy. Ruesler case files?"

"In the trunk with your suitcase." He dropped the key fob in her hand. "Ma'am, you can call me Fletch. Everyone does."

"Okay, Fletch, and you can call me Blanca. Just anything besides *ma'am*." She curled her fist around the fob and ducked into the car. To hell with Manny's rules of conduct. Where had they ever got her?

She tucked the key fob into her purse on the passenger seat and punched the ignition button with her knuckle. The sedan's engine purred to life. At least they hadn't saddled her with a junker.

She smoothed the crumpled piece of paper with Mitchell's address on the console and tapped in the name of the road on the GPS. The cabin didn't have an actual house number to enter, but the GPS should get her to the general location, and then she could rely on Hopkins's directions.

Hunching over the steering wheel, she peered at the sky through the windshield. As far as she could tell, no forest fires were currently consuming the island, so Mitchell should be around and available. What were the odds that Tate Mitchell had been the one to find those bones? He must have something buried in his memory—and she was going to find out what it was.

The journey from the station took her on a windy road that ended in the town, but she took the bypass. After a few miles, the coastline and Discovery Bay disappeared as she wound her way inland, getting sucked into the emerald landscape. She'd figured it would be gray and dull out here at this time of year, but the vibrant blue of the bay and lush green of the forest dazzled her vision.

The rain had stopped by the time she made her way to Mitchell's cabin. She rolled up behind a Jeep, the tires of the sedan crunching over dirt and gravel. The *cabin* label hardly gave this abode justice.

The log exterior and Alpine roof screamed cabin, but the deck running the length of the house and the massive windows that had to afford views of the forest and bay beyond gave off luxury-resort vibes. Once again, she got the feeling of her chest expanding and her pores opening.

As she cut the engine, a tall blonde woman exited the structure, dragging a suitcase, a boy trailing behind her, a backpack slung over one shoulder. Uh-oh, had she stumbled on the Mitchell family leaving for a vacation? Maybe a Christmas vacation?

Blanca shoved open the car door, her high heel landing on the uneven ground. She should've changed before coming out here, but then maybe she would've missed the Mitchells completely.

The woman parked the suitcase on the driveway and called over her shoulder. "It's okay. The car's already here."

Blanca opened her mouth to protest when the

woman's head whipped around, her long, blond hair cascading over one shoulder. Tate Mitchell's luck must've changed somewhere along the line: he had a beautiful wife, cute son, gorgeous home and exciting job. Jeremy Ruesler was just dead.

"Go on, Olly. You can put our bags in the trunk yourself. Don't make the driver do it." The woman nudged the boy while flashing her pearly whites at Blanca.

A man clumped down the steps of the house behind the woman and child. "I told you I'd drive you, Astrid."

Blanca kept her jaw firmly in place as she eyed the tall Nordic-looking man dressed like a lumberjack in jeans, boots and a blue-plaid flannel shirt. Tate Mitchell had lucked out in the looks department, too. He resembled a modern-day Thor. All he needed was a giant square hammer over his shoulder.

So, Thor wasn't going with his wife and child. She'd lucked out, too.

The boy, Olly, grabbed his mother's suitcase and dragged it behind him as he trundled toward Blanca. "C-can I put this in the back, please?"

Blanca waved her hands. "I'm so sorry for the confusion. I'm not your driver."

"I didn't think so." Mitchell drew up beside his statuesque wife and hung his arm around her shoulders, but his gaze flicked from Blanca's ponytail, which was now frizzing in the moisture, to the tips of her high heels. Her toes curled in the very shoes under his scrutiny, and a little ball of fury formed in her gut at his assessing stare. Men shouldn't eye other women like that in the presence of their families.

The rattle of an engine behind her took away Mitchell's focus as he leveled a finger at the small car. "That must be your ride. Is the car even big enough for your bag?"

"Stop worrying." Astrid placed two hands on his broad chest and shoved. Then she gave Blanca another smile that made her skin glow even more. "My apologies for the mistake."

"No worries." Blanca held up her hands. "I'm actually here to see Tate Mitchell."

"That would be him." Astrid jerked her thumb toward her husband. "Olly, put the bags in the car."

Both she and her husband followed the boy to the car. A young man jumped out and took the suitcase from him. "I got this, my man."

With Olly settled in the back seat, Astrid turned to Tate and gave him a kiss on the cheek. "Don't forget to join us for the holiday. I'll text you from Mom's."

If her husband seemed disappointed in the chaste farewell, he didn't show it. Hunching his shoulder, Tate shoved his hands in his pockets and watched the car turn in the driveway.

Then he faced her and raised his eyebrows over a pair of eyes so blue they could've been drops from Discovery Bay. "I suppose you're here about the bones. Hopkins call you in from Seattle?"

Blanca squared her shoulders. "I'm FBI Special Agent Blanca Lopez, Mr. Mitchell. I'm here to investigate the cold case of Jeremy Ruesler. And I want to start my investigation by asking you what you remember about the day you two were playing in the forest and authorities found you tied to a tree with blood in your shoes...and no sign of Jeremy."